CHILDREN OF THE BAND

BEN MARNEY

Ben's first novel, SING ROSES FOR ME has been downloaded to over 30,000 readers and has received great reviews. It was an Amazon's top 100 bestseller and received the category ranking of #1 in THRILLER - SUSPENSE - MYSTERY and ROMANCE. If you haven't read it yet, get your free copy at: www.benmarneybooks.com

For Dana, Pat, John, Larry and Gordon
My real life family band. What a fun and crazy way to grow up.

Dedicated to my wife Dana
*I know you spent too many lonely hours
again while I wrote this book, even though
I promised not to disappear again into my strange
writing world... I did it anyway*

*I just can't help myself. Please forgive me.
I love you*

AUTHOR'S NOTE

I spent my twenties traveling from one end of the United States to the other, singing and playing my guitar in a rock band. In those days, the 1970's, in every town and in every city there was at least one bar that featured live entertainment.

It was a great time to be in a band. If you could play and sing and were willing to travel you could find work. Because there was so much work, there were literally thousands of bands just like mine traveling up and down the highways in vans, pulling trailers full of equipment, performing in one gig after another.

Since it was my band and my gigs, I got to set the rules. And two of those rules were no drugs and no children traveling with us. My wife, Dana, and I didn't have any kids, but some of my musicians did. Of course, we didn't mind an occasional visit for a few days, but it was our opinion that the road was not an appropriate environment for children. It was after all the 1970's; the era that the term sex, drugs, and rock 'n' roll was invented.

Unfortunately, that was not the rule in all bands. It was not uncommon. In fact, it was more the norm to run across bands that had their kids of all ages, from infants to teenagers, traveling with them.

Knowing that fact has haunted me for years and is the inspiration for this book. I have often wondered...

What happened to those kids?

EPIGRAPH

"Hey Joe. Where you going with that gun in your hand?"
Jimi Hendricks
Woodstock -1969

BUMMER

I don't write so good, but Joe wanted me to tell you my story, so here goes. I will do my best.

My name is Billy Driscoll, but everybody calls me Bummer. They call me that, 'cause I guess I say that word too much, but I think it's a pretty good word to use, cause you know, in life when shit happens, like it always does, it's a bummer.

I guess if I was smarter with book learning and stuff I could probably think of something else to say, but it's always what I say. I don't mind people calling me Bummer; it's not a bad name I guess. It's better than, Retard, or Special Ed... I don't like those names.

I didn't do good in school, so I quit going when I was 15. I don't really know what I did wrong, but all the kids used to make fun of me there; they called me bad names and stole my books, and stuff like that.

My daddy didn't like me quitting school and told me that if I was going to live in his house I had to go back to school or leave, so I left. That was in 1968. All I took from my room was my guitar and some of my clothes. I didn't have any money and didn't really know what I was going to do, but this really nice man let me ride with him in one of those big trucks and he took me all the way to San Francisco, California. He even let me drive it and bought me food on the trip along the way. When he let me out by a big bridge, he gave me $20 and told me he thought I'd be OK there, because there were a lot of other kids there like me. That's where I met Hannah. Her last name wasn't Jensen then, but I don't really remember what it was. I just called her Hannah.

It was pretty cool there, because there was a whole lot of us living on the streets together. Hannah would give me flowers and tell me to give them to strangers and when I did they would give me money. That's how we bought food and drugs and stuff. I had never done any drugs before, but Hannah showed me what to do.

One night Hannah took me to a party. There were a lot of people there, and they were all eating little square cubes of sugar, so I ate one too. I can't really explain what happened next because it was sort of weird, but the best part was when Hannah taught me about sex. It was my very first time and I really liked it. After that night, Hannah let me do sex with her almost every day. It was great!

We were together for a long time, but then she met Luke. After that, she told me that we couldn't do sex. Something about true love, but I *did* love her! I didn't really understand, but anyway we didn't do it anymore. It was a real bummer. The first time I saw her do sex with Luke it made me cry, but pretty soon I got used to it.

I really liked Luke; he was always nice to me. We all hung out together and did what Luke called panhandling to make money. For some reason, I was a lot better at it than Luke or Hannah. People would always smile at me and give me their change or a few dollars when I walked up and talked to them, but most of the time when Luke did it people just yelled at him to go away. I thought it was pretty funny that people liked me better, and so did Hannah.

One day, Luke told us about a place he'd heard about called a commune. It sounded really nice, so a bunch of us got into his van and we drove there. There were a lot of people there all living together. It was kind of like a big family. Everybody treated me really nice and didn't seem to care that I wasn't very smart. Nobody made fun of me or called me bad names. They taught me how to grow vegetables and catch fish. It was great!

At night, we would all sit around this big fire and play guitars and sing together. I wasn't really a very good guitar player, like Luke; he was really good. So he showed me how to play the bass guitar. It took me a while to learn how to play, but pretty soon Luke started telling me that I was playing good. That made me feel great, so I started practicing every day and I got really good.

We had lived at the commune almost a year when Hannah got pregnant and started to get real fat. Luke didn't seem to like it and sometimes even made fun of the way she looked, making jokes about her big belly. It didn't bother me, I thought she looked pretty, but she did get really fat.

I was with Hannah the night she had little Joe. I don't know where Luke was, but he wasn't there. I was right beside her holding her hand. I didn't like it watching her hurt so much. It made me cry. It took a long time and she was really yelling, but when little Joe came out and she heard him cry, she started laughing and crying at the same time. Everybody was. I couldn't believe what I'd just seen. It was really amazing. And when I saw little Joe for the first time and he grabbed my finger with his little tiny hand, I guess that's what Hannah meant by true love.

Hannah taught me how to hold him right and how to change his diaper and stuff. They let me watch him a lot and I loved to do it. Pretty soon little Joe was walking and talking and we would play games together all the time. It didn't take Hannah long to lose all that fat and pretty soon everything was back like it used to be. Luke and Hannah seemed really happy and everything was going good.

Right after that, about once a week, Luke, Hannah, little Joe, and me would drive to a bar about an hour away from the commune to play music for the people there. Everyone seemed to love the way Hannah could sing. When Luke played a lead on his guitar people would yell and clap real loud. It was so much fun. On the ride back, we would all smoke weed together and listen to Luke talk about all the applause and cheers we had gotten that night. He was always really excited after we played.

We played at that bar for almost a year and with the money Luke gave me from the gig, I was able to buy a new bass amp and it filled out our sound. I was really happy then.

Then one day the police came to the commune and told us that we couldn't live there anymore and had to leave. They made us pack up everything right then! They were pretty mean to us. It was sad saying goodbye to all my friends. I didn't know what I was going to do because I had no other place to go and I was really scared.

Then Luke and Hannah drove over to my camp and started loading my clothes and stuff into their van and said, "You're coming with us. We're starting a band."

We drove to Los Angeles and met with this booking agent guy who told us that if we could find a piano player and a drummer, he could get us lots of jobs playing in bars all across the country. Then he gave Luke some phone numbers of some musicians to call, and that's where we found Mooch. I liked him right away. He had this big Hammond organ that he could really play good.

This booking agent guy got us this room where we could set up and practice. They told us that we couldn't sleep there, but we did anyway. We had 4 or 5 drummers come there and play with us, but Luke didn't think they were very good, so he didn't hire them. Then one day this real tall, handsome guy came to play. He had long blond hair that flew everywhere when he played. He was real good, so Luke hired him. He always wore those shirts that didn't have any sleeves that showed off the big muscles in his arms. I liked him right away too, but for some reason Luke got real mad at him one night and fired him on our second job. The next drummer I didn't like very much. He wasn't nice to me and I was glad when Luke fired him. After that, Smooth joined the band and he's been our drummer ever since.

I love Smooth; he's my best friend. He taught me how to drive and helped me buy my first van. He even lent me the money to buy it, but I paid him back every cent.

Smooth always got real mad at me if I said anything about not being very smart. "Stop saying that. You're smarter than you think you are!" he'd say. That made me feel good.

He's so funny. He was always making me go talk to girls after we got through playing. He told me I should be doing lots of sex with them and sometimes I did, but most of the time the girls I talked to just wanted to do sex with Luke.

I didn't know why, but Hannah didn't like me to do sex with other girls and when I did she got real mad at me. Smooth told me not to worry about what she thought, but I couldn't do that. I didn't like it when Hannah got mad at me.

I got real good at driving, because we drove a lot. Sometimes we would finish playing on a Saturday night at 2 o'clock in the morning and then pack up our equipment and start driving. We would drive all the next day on Sunday and then all day Monday and get to the gig just in time to set up and play. It was pretty hard sometimes to stay awake, but I really liked it.

We had these CB radios in our vans, so we could talk to each other as we were driving. Everybody had real funny names they called themselves on the radio; Luke was the Cadillac Cowboy; Mooch was Sex Maniac; I was Bass Boy, but the funniest one was Smooth, he called himself the Teeny-Weeny. It made me laugh real hard every time he came on the radio.

We traveled like this for years and years. I called my daddy a couple of times to tell him what I was doing, but he didn't seem to want to talk to me, so I stopped calling. I didn't really care because I had the band, and they were my family now.

I watched Little Joe grow up, and boy he grew like crazy. By the time he was 8 he was taller than me, but we still played together all the time. Luke taught him how to play guitar real good, and sometimes he would get on stage with us and play with the band, but he didn't like to.

It was about that time that Mooch met this girl in Abilene and got married and had a little baby. Not long after that, Smooth met this really nice lady that had two kids and he married her too.

They all went on the road with us and it was like a real family then.

One time, when we finished playing a gig in Florida, Luke told us that we were going to take a couple weeks off for vacation. Luke and Hannah were going to California, and Mooch and his wife were going to Houston to see his family, but I wasn't sure what I was going to do. Then Smooth and his wife invited me to go with them to the Florida Keys, to a special place there called Big Pine Key. They said it was kind of like the hippie commune where we lived in California. When we got there, I really liked it. There were a lot of cool people there and it was a lot of fun.

For some reason, Smooth's wife didn't like it there so they didn't stay, but I met this really nice girl who let me do sex with her, so I wanted to stay longer. Her name was Lisa. She was real pretty and real nice. Since Luke and Hannah and Smooth and Mooch were married, I thought that I should be too. So, I asked her if she wanted to get married and be part of our band family and she said sure! There was this guy who lived there who said he could do it, so we got married standing in the water on the beach. It was cool!

I was so happy, but when I showed up at our next gig with her and her son, everyone got mad at me and told me that I shouldn't have done it. Even Smooth was mad at me. They said it was a bad idea to marry somebody I didn't really know. I guess they were right, because one day Lisa just took off and left her boy, Austin, behind with me.

Austin was only thirteen when she left. He was Ok, but sometimes he wasn't very nice to me and wouldn't listen much. One time I caught him smoking weed and I didn't think that was right, but he called me stupid and a lot of other bad names and said he was going to run away. I didn't want him to do that, so I didn't say anything about it anymore. Austin got into a lot of trouble after that–shoplifting and fighting and stuff. He was a pretty bad boy, but I did my best to raise him as good as I could.

Then one day, when he was fifteen, some police officers came to our van and woke us up. I'm not sure why, but they took him and little Joe and the other kids away. I tried to get Austin back, but this judge guy wouldn't let me. He said that Austin wasn't really my son, so he had to go to a foster home. I was real sad after that.

Then about six months later, he ran away from that foster home and found me again. I didn't tell nobody he was there and I was real happy.

THE FIRST ONE

He stood over the bed staring down at the tanned, naked, lifeless body. "Wake up! Please wake up!" He screamed. "Oh my God, what have I done? She's dead!"

He climbed off the girl and stood at the foot of the bed in the silence, staring down at her. She was tied to the bed with her arms above her head and her legs spread wide, tied to the footboard. The slight sweet vanilla smell of the young girl's cheap perfume lingered in the air.

"Oh God! She was so nice and so beautiful. What do I do now?" He felt nauseous and weak. "Why didn't you stop?"

JOE JENSEN

To the disdain of my parents, as long as I can remember I'd always wanted to be a cop. I'd searched my memory banks and for the life of me couldn't come up with any specific reason why. There was no memory of the friendly old cop who found me lost and alone and then took me to the local precinct, bought me a coke and tussled my hair while waiting for my parents to come get me. No favorite aunt or uncle that was on the force. No next-door neighbors, no friends of my parents. Ha, now that's a good one. No, there was no specific moment or epiphany that I could recall that gave me this never-ending desire.

What I *could* recall, was never wanting or asking for the toy drum set, guitar, BB gun, or cowboy outfit that came with boots, six shooter and holster for Christmas. That's what I got, but all I really wanted was the police outfit that came with the cool hat and badge. I really wanted that badge. But of course, that could never happen at our house, because my parents were, for lack of a better word, hippies, flower children, space cadets.

My name is Joe, Joe Jensen. Well, at least that's part of it and it's the name I go by. The name on my birth certificate, believe it or not is "Hey" Joe Jensen. That's right. *Hey Joe* like the Hendrix song. For those of you too young to remember, Hey Joe was the song Jimmy Hendrix opened his set with at Woodstock in 1969. It's a tender ballad about a man who shoots his girlfriend and runs away to Mexico. Apparently, it was my mother's favorite song and fortunately won out over my father's first choice, which was "Mr. Tambourine Man," a song written by Bob Dylan, my dad's favorite musician at the time. On my FBI credentials, it said, H. Joe Jensen. My parents laughed about the fact that they were both pretty stoned when it came time to name me. So, H. Joe Jensen wasn't too bad considering that it could have been... Orange, Sky, Muddy (as in Muddy Waters) or Purple Haze... those were also on their list.

My parents would gladly tell you about the time they got stoned out of their minds and danced naked for a week in the mud pits at Woodstock, or when they walked barefoot through the streets of San Francisco in the Summer of Love, handing out flowers to anyone walking by. My parents were not ashamed of those years of sex, drugs, and rock and roll, and waved like a flag of pride the fact that they were arrested more times than they could remember while protesting the Viet Nam war.

My parents made their living as rock musicians and singers for their entire lives, but the years hadn't really changed them much. Dad still had a full beard and shoulder length hair. It was just a bit thinner and a lot grayer. Actually, it was almost white. He was somewhere between Santa Clause and Leon Russell. He was a little thicker around the middle and the hard years he'd lived had carved deep lines around his steel blue eyes and across his forehead.

My mom had aged more gracefully. Her face was still amazingly wrinkle free. Her long blonde hair showed only a few strands of gray and I'd bet she could still wear the clothes she wore in her 20's. In fact, sometimes when I looked at her in certain angles of light, I'd have sworn she wasn't a day over 30. Even as they grew older, they remained hippies at heart... just "old" hippies.

Their outspoken politics hadn't changed; they supported our soldiers, but hated war of any kind; they didn't trust big government; they would rant and rave for hours about the necessity of term limits for senators and congressmen; they despised the IRS; they were cautious of the police, and they were big supporters of the legalization of marijuana because they still loved to get stoned and they did it often. Your typical senior citizens they were not. They'd always been a bit crazy and irresponsible I guess, but they were *my* crazies and no matter what they'd done or who they were, I loved them.

I also knew that they would never, ever understand my career choice. After I graduated from law school, after I passed the bar, I became a prosecutor and then worked as an assistant district attorney for two years. I filled out and handed in my application to the FBI on my 27th birthday. Three months later, I was sent to the FBI training Center in Quantico, Virginia.

As you can imagine, my chosen profession was not a pleasant topic of discussion at our Thanksgiving dinners. It's something we tried to avoid. I knew it would have helped if I could have explained it to them better, but I didn't even know why myself. All I knew was... I'd always wanted to be a cop. That is what I was, and I loved it.

THE DEATH OF SHERRI MARTIN

He jumped back when the naked, lifeless body moaned and turned her head to look at him.

"Please... untie me," she whispered.

"Now, why would I do that? Looks like you enjoy being all bound up. Is that what gets you off, slut?"

"I'll scream and my neighbors will call the police!" she growled with a husky voice.

"If you scream, you die. Do you understand me?"

Her frightened beautiful green eyes opened wide and she nodded.

"I wish you hadn't said anything about the cops, that changes everything." He walked to the kitchen and began opening the cabinets and pulling out the drawers. In the last one, he found a roll of silver tape.

Tearing off a long piece, he covered her mouth and whispered in her ear, "Not one sound!" Then he quietly cracked open the front door and walked slowly to the van.

Opening the back doors, he rummaged around, eventually locating a black duffle bag. Looking inside the bag, he saw a Polaroid camera and a pack of film. He jerked open the passenger door and stuffed a macramé guitar strap and a pair of black leather gloves in the bag.

"This just might work." He walked slowly back to the girl's apartment, attracting no attention.

The sight of the naked girl tied to the bed was arousing. Her panicked eyes followed him.

Unable to resist, he slipped off the gloves and lightly ran a hand over her thighs and up to her breasts. She jerked her body away and thrashed against the bindings, trying to scream, but the tape muffled her sound.

"I warned you," he said, slipping on the gloves. Then he removed the scarf from her neck and replaced it with a macramé guitar strap.

"I've always wanted to do this," he whispered, pulling the strap tight.

It only took a few minutes before she stopped thrashing and grew still, but to make sure, he continued pulling, staring into her eyes, watching her die.

He stood by the bed, quietly admiring her tanned naked body. "What a rush!"

Reaching into the bag for the Polaroid camera and pack of film, he tore open the pack, loaded the camera, and took two pictures.

Suddenly the air filled with a horrible, foul aroma. The young girl had lost her bowels and the sheets under her were brown with her urine and excrement. Instantly nauseated, he ran into the bathroom.

After cleaning up the mess and flushing the commode several times, he ran back into the bedroom and untied the beautiful dead girl's hands and feet from the bed, pulled the macramé guitar strap from around her neck, and stuffed everything into the bag. After one last check to make sure nothing was left behind, he wiped down every area that was touched to remove any possible fingerprints and then as quietly as possible, opened the front door and slipped away into the night.

THE REUNION

My first FBI field assignment was in Denver, Colorado. Because of my background as a lawyer and the years I spent working as an assistant district attorney, a lot of my time there was spent working in partnership with local law enforcement, the district attorneys' offices and all the way up to the states attorney. I was directly involved in the capture and prosecution of several major cases and soon developed a respected reputation as an FBI special agent, which helped move me up the ranks.

Three days after my 38th birthday, I was selected to head up the Denver Behavioral Analysis Unit or BAU. It was a special division of the National Center for the Analysis of Violent Crime.

My appointment to this position did not happen by accident. I had been pushing for years to be assigned to the BAU–Specifically to unit 4.

There were four units in the BAU; Unit 1 concentrated on counter terrorism, arson, and bombing; unit 2 dealt with threats, white-collar crime, and public corruption; unit 3 investigated crimes against children.

Unit 4, my unit, investigated crimes against adults. My team's assignment was very specific. We investigated repeat killers, better known as serial killers. It was our job to create a suggested identity of the killers. We did this by gathering anecdotal evidence to create a psychological profile.

The BAU was founded in 1987 and since its origin has been the sole division of the FBI that its purpose and effectiveness had been questioned due to the psychological profiling techniques used in the unit. Because psychological profiling had not been empirically proven to actually work, we were under constant scrutiny from the other divisions of the FBI, local law enforcement officials, and the courts. Unlike forensic science that is based on hard physical evidence, psychological profiling is based on observations gleaned at the crime scenes and the volumes of research done on repeat killers' actions and thought processes. Although every repeat killer or serial murderer had their own unique MO, their choice of victims, their childhood, economic and social status, among other things showed striking similarities. Using these similarities and our careful observations at the crime scenes, allowed us to create an overall profile or identity of the perp.

When I first joined the BAU, our suggested profiles were ignored and given about as much weight as a tarot card reader or a psychic. But after 8 successful captures in a row where our profiles were dead on, things began to change. Although our skeptics and critics remained, our profiles continued to be accurate and as a result, we began to be assigned to more and more cases.

Because of that success in building profiles of repeat killers, I was assigned to go back to Quantico, Virginia. It was a major promotion with a nice raise, but the trade-off was that I was no longer a field agent. My assignment was to supervise the training for the new special agents assigned to the Behavioral Analysis Units. As it turned out, instructing other agents was something I was really good at, but I had to admit, I missed my team and the fieldwork.

In my third year in Quantico, Virginia, I finally broke down and moved out of my cramped, tiny apartment and bought a house, garage, flowerbeds and all. I was 42 and for the first time in my entire life, I had a backyard. And what a backyard it was—fire pit, a patio, and a pool with sparkling blue water.

Unfortunately, through all those years, my relationship with my parents had grown distant. To be honest, things had been strained between us since my thirteenth birthday. I *did* called them every couple of months, usually only talking to my mother, and I flew a few times to visit them, but we were certainly not close.

In my second year in the bureau in 1989, my parents became partners in a nightclub in Jackson, Mississippi. Two years later, they shocked me and actually bought a house, mortgage and all. This was something my father claimed he would never do.

He never wanted to have a permanent address, sign up for public utilities, or have a home phone number, because once you did that the government would secretly invade your privacy; put you into their secret files and track your every move. And of course, he never, ever planned to open a bank account.

To quote my father, "the FDIC was a dark secret society of evil men, whose sole purpose was to control the world's economy, so a handful of very rich people could get even richer." He actually believed that crap, but there he was, a new house, and a new bank account. I almost laughed out loud when my mother told me.

Surprisingly, their nightclub lasted almost 8 years and for a while my parents seemed to be almost normal and doing very well. But once it closed down in 1996 my parents were broke, and found themselves once again searching for gigs.

The problem was that they were older; in their late 40's and the music business had taken a dramatic turn in the last decade. Finding a bar that still hired live bands was a rare find. The appeal of live bands with real musicians had been replaced with either Karaoke or a DJ spinning records. They began to struggle to make ends meet.

Things really started to fall apart for my parents when the band began to break up. Since there was no work, the band members had to move on to other things to earn a living. Smooth was the first to leave, moving to Orlando.

He had been offered a job as a drum rep for Pearl Drums and

jumped at the chance. Mooch and Bummer soon followed. Mooch moved back to Houston, his hometown, and set up a teaching studio and soon built a good business, teaching piano to kids.

Bummer moved to Oklahoma City and went to work for a company based there, driving a truck; an 18-wheeler delivering furniture cross-country.

My father was devastated. When I suggested that perhaps it wasn't the end of the world that the band had gone their separate ways and threw out the idea of he and Mom working as a duo, he went nuts and slammed the phone down. My mom called me back immediately apologizing, making excuses for him as usual, but I could hear him cursing my name in the background.

When I hung up the phone after talking to my mom, I felt sick to my stomach. I had never worried about my parents before. They were extremely talented; my father was an incredible guitar player with such stage charisma you could not take your eyes off him when he was performing. My mother had the same stage magic, and even in her 40s she was as beautiful as ever and could sing anything from Bonnie Raitt, to Barbara Streisand.

I had always assumed, even as they got older, that their talent would take care of them; that there would always be a gig for them out there somewhere. Never in my wildest dreams would I have thought that listening to a live band with incredibly talented musicians would be replaced by, of all things... karaoke. As sad and ridiculous as that sounds, it was the unfortunate truth and as a result, my parents were in serious trouble.

I had hoped that during the 8 years they had performed in their own club they might have been able to save a little money to help them get through this unforeseen rainy day, but my parents were your typical musicians living from paycheck to paycheck, gig to gig, week to week. My mom told me that they were flat broke and in danger of losing their house. Their only income was from the few guitar students my father had reluctantly taken on, and from the sales of her macramé.

My mom was a master at macramé. She'd been doing it as long as I could remember. She started out making beautiful guitar straps for my guitar, my father's guitar, and Bummer's bass, then moved on to making key chains, belts, and purses for the rest of the band. Eventually she began making amazing wall hangings, which were her best work. Everything she made, even the guitar straps and belts were one of a kind, unique with her own original designs and patterns. She was great at it, and I had been trying for years to get her to sell some of them. They were truly beautiful works of art.

But even with Dad teaching and Mom selling her macramé, they couldn't pay their bills. I wanted to help them, but there was nothing I could do. I was barely surviving myself. I wasn't sure what they were going to do, but fortunately my stubborn old man took my advice and landed a few bookings around Jackson as a duo.

According to my mother on their third duo gig, a woman came up to them and asked if they would like to work on a cruise ship. It turned out, that she was an entertainment buyer for the Norwegian Cruise Line in town visiting friends. It was a life-saving, lucky break for my parents. For the next 17 years, my parents traveled the world performing on cruise ships.

It was a great run for them but unfortunately the ship gigs began to dwindle. They were in their 60s and most of the major cruise ships were marketing for younger passengers, and therefore younger entertainers. But, believe it or not, they had actually been able to put back a little money over the last 17 years and had opened up a small store in a refurbished historic area of Jackson called the Fondren District, where my mom displayed her macramé artwork in the front, and my dad had a small studio in the back where he could teach his guitar students.

They were still doing a cruise ship once in a while, and picked up a few duo gigs in country clubs and hotels in Jackson. They were doing pretty good and seemed to be happy, but when I talked to them, I could tell that they really missed those good old days, traveling and playing with the band.

"Working as a duo is ok," my mother told me, "but there is just nothing like singing with a band. The synergy that comes from the other musicians... well, it's hard to explain."

"Do you keep in touch with Mooch and Smooth and Bummer?" I asked her.

"Not really, we haven't heard from them in a long time."

"Why don't you call 'em up and maybe put together a reunion concert or something. You guys were pretty popular here, I bet a lot of your old fans would come see you."

My father, who I thought was ignoring our conversation, looked up from his magazine. "I'd love to do that and I think the guys would too, but finding a place to do it would be the problem." He was actually smiling and had a spark in his eyes, something I hadn't seen in a long time.

Dad put down his magazine. "Do you really think people around here would remember us? It's been over twenty years since we closed the club."

I had watched that spark in his eyes slowly fade over the years. Although he never complained about performing on the ships, I knew he didn't really like it. The music they had to play on the ships was unchallenging and boring, but the money was great and with it came free medical, free food, and a free place to live. They rented out their house when they were out there, so when they were on the ships they had no real expenses. That's how they were able to open up the store and had a surprising amount of cash in the bank. But with just the mention of the possibility of getting the band back together, there was that spark again shining bright in his eyes.

I wasn't sure exactly how I was going to do it, but I knew then, I had to do something to help make that reunion concert come to fruition.

In my seventh year, at an FBI convention, I had the opportunity to meet and hang out with the newly appointed Special Agent in Charge of the State of Mississippi, John Kelly. He was a few years older, but we hit it off instantly, so after the daily meetings, we would jump in a cab and do some bar hopping together. Over the years, he had become one of my few close friends within the Bureau. He had married his high school sweetheart, but although she'd never smoked a cigarette in her life, she somehow developed stage-four lung cancer. He was an only child like me and had no siblings to help him through it, so the last few weeks before she died, I was with him every day and that bonded us together like brothers.

Trying to find some way to help my parents pull off the reunion concert, I decided to give John a call.

"This is special agent John Kelly, what can I do for you?" he barked into the phone.

Disguising my voice, I said, "I'm trying to figure out how to cut eye holes in my sheet and I understand you were involved in arresting a few members of the KKK. Could you tell me if they are vertical eye slits or horizontal?"

"Joe Jensen! How the hell are you?" he yelled.

"I'm doing pretty good, John. Just doing my best to teach these rookies how to profile."

"You still teaching that BAU voodoo crap?"

"Absolutely!"

He laughed. "Well you know what they say, those who can, do, and those who cannot, teach."

"Up yours!" I said with a chuckle.

"So, what can I do you for Mr. Hendrix?"

I had mistakenly, after a few too many Chivas Regas told John about the origin of my name, and he had called me Mr. Hendrix or Jimmy ever since.

"Biggest mistake I've ever made, letting you know my real name. You're never going to let me live that down, are you?"

"Well, I could call you Mr. Tambourine Man if you prefer," he said laughing.

"Actually, my crazy ass parents are the reason for my call. On that regretful drunken night, when I told you about my name, did I mention that my parents were musicians?"

"Jesus, Joe, how drunk *were* you that night? Yeah, you told me they had a band and traveled a lot. So, what's up with them?"

"Did I mention that they lived in Jackson?"

"Ahh, no. I don't think you did. When did they move to Jackson?"

"Actually, they've owned a house there for over twenty years," I said, "Back in 1988, they bought into a little bar there. It was open about eight years. When it closed down they started working on cruise ships and did that for years. Now they have a little store in the Fondron district where Dad teaches guitar and my mother sells her art."

"Really?" he said. "That was a little before my time here. So, what's up with them?"

"I know it's a long shot, but when they had their night club, they had quite a following. I'm trying to help them get the old band back together to put on a reunion show. I thought that you being such a Mr. Big Shot in Mississippi, you might know someone in the bar business that might be willing to host the reunion. I think they'd pack the place.

"What was the name of the night club they owned?" he asked.

"It was sort of a dive out by the reservoir called 'The Shrunken Head.'"

"Are you serious? That was the name of your parent's club; The Shrunken Head?"

"Yeah, weird I know."

He laughed. "What was the name of the band?"

"Blackfish," I said.

"Wait!" He yelled into the phone. "Are your mother and father Luke and Hannah Jensen?"

"Yes," I said shocked. "How do you know them?

"They put out a few albums, right?"

"Yes, they recorded three when they had their club. Sold them out of the bar. Why do you ask?"

I heard him chuckling.

"What's so funny?"

"You're not gonna believe this, but I have their albums!" He was cracking up having trouble talking. "And they're worth a fortune! Your father is a friggin' genius on guitar and your mother sings her ass off!"

"Wait, back up! Where did you get their albums? They weren't on a big record label, they just sold them in their night club. How the hell..."

"On ebay," he said. "I collect old rock and roll albums and anything by Blackfish is a collector's dream. Did you say they recorded three albums?"

"I think so, but hold on. You're telling me that my parent's old albums are being sold on eBay... for a lot of money? How much money?"

"About 175 bucks."

"Each?" I was standing, but had to sit down to wrap my head around what he'd just said.

"Go on ebay and see for yourself," he said. "I want that third album! Tell you what, you get me a copy of that third album and I'll see what I can do about this reunion concert. Deal?"

After I spent almost an hour on my computer, I clicked off eBay, shut my laptop, and stared out my window. John was right. The last three Blackfish albums listed sold for over $200 a piece. I picked up the phone and dialed my parents' number.

"Dad, do you still have any of your old albums somewhere?"

"Yeah," he said, "I still have a ton of them in my hall closet. They're just taking up space, collecting dust. I've been meaning to throw them out for years, but just couldn't make myself do it."

"How many do you have?"

"I don't know, fifteen or twenty boxes full; I think there's a hundred in each box. Why do you ask?"

THE REUNION CONCERT was a huge success; it sold out quickly, so they added another night. John Kelly had really come through; he had talked the Holiday Inn into giving my parents the ballroom for free in return for the liquor sales. The band sold over a hundred of their old albums and also split the revenue from the ticket sales, the Holiday Inn cleaned up on selling whiskey, and John Kelly got an autographed copy of the third Blackfish album.

I hadn't seen my parents that happy in 20 years. It was like a real family reunion, and I actually enjoyed performing with them. Even Mooch and Smooth's kids were there. Bummer had one of his rough looking, tattooed trucker friends there to help him with his equipment, but I saw no sign of his stepson, Austin.

After the show on the first night, we all went to a restaurant together and caught up. It was a great night. Unfortunately, the second night, we didn't get a chance to visit with everybody packing up and trying to get on the road back to their homes. Truthfully, it was a little shocking to me, because the guys looked so much older than I expected, but they all seemed to be pretty healthy and doing well.

Over the next few weeks, my father and I had several long phone conversations about the best way to sell his old Blackfish albums and we even talked a little about the old days when we were all together traveling around the country in that beat up old van. It appeared that we had finally made it across that bridge that had separated us for so many years. It was nice to have my father back in my life again. The feeling I had inside was euphoric, but that feeling only lasted for a blink of an eye.

THE DEATH OF TINA WALTERS

I t had taken longer to convince this one. Aging had a way of making one less appealing to young girls, but the promise of strong weed and Ecstasy won her over. With her 4-inch heels, she towered above him as they walked.

Once they got to her apartment, the young, beautiful girl blushed and began adjusting her skirt, "I've never done this sort of thing before."

"Really?"

"I never bring home strangers, there's a lot of crazies out there. You promise you're not a serial killer?" she said laughing.

"I wouldn't be much of a serial killer if I told you, but don't worry, I promise."

"Good, I didn't think so." Her green eyes sparkled as she smiled. "I've always wanted to try Ecstasy. Does it really make you lose control and... enhance sex?"

"Oh yes, all that and much more."

The tall beauty was slow to respond to his touch, but after the Ecstasy kicked in and she took a few deep hits of weed, she relaxed and was ready to play nasty.

When the black duffel bag was opened and she saw the macramé straps and sex toys, she moaned and purred, and didn't resist as the straps secured her beautiful long legs and slender wrists to the bed. Firmly bound with her legs and arms spread wide, she squirmed and moaned loudly with sexual anticipation.

"I love that," she whispered, as the macramé noose slipped over her head and around her neck.

Looking down at her, he smiled, "Oh, you like that, do you? You're into choking?"

"Oh, yes... I love it."

He gradually increased the pressure on the macramé loop around her slender neck, until she opened her beautiful green eyes and began to climax, jerking and spasming with her intense orgasm.

This one didn't have to die, no doubt she wouldn't scream rape or call the cops, she loved it, but it was too erotic looking into her beautiful eyes to stop.

After removing the macramé straps from the hands, feet, and neck of the beautiful, lifeless body, he stood at the foot of the bed and breathed in deeply. The musk of the patchouli oil, the slight hint of her perfume, and the smell of death... was intoxicating.

JUDGE DAILY

I was sound asleep when the phone rang. It was not good news. Judge Daily had suffered a massive heart attack and wasn't expected to live. I caught the next plane to Little Rock. On my flight there, my mind filled with memories of the judge. I had met him when I was only thirteen years old at a hearing...

IN 1983, my parent's band was booked in a small beer joint in Jacksonville, Arkansas that didn't supply hotel rooms, so we were camped out behind the bar in our vans. I had left my parents sleeping and was walking to the public library a few miles away, when I was stopped by the local truant officer, accompanied by two uniformed police officers. When I told them I didn't go to school in that city and why I was there, they asked me to take them to my parents. I was too young to understand the consequences, so when I did, they busted my parents for possession of marijuana, child abuse and neglect. I met Judge Daily at that hearing and I can still remember that day vividly, because that hearing changed my life forever.

My father was wringing his hands. My mother was stoic, still as a stone, clutching her purse. Her only movement was to put her hand on my knee to stop my unconscious knee bouncing that was shaking the table. My hands were clammy and my shirt was sticking to my back from perspiration. It was my first time to be inside a courtroom and I was frightened.

My court appointed Attorney Ad Litem, Martha Brookshire and my parent's lawyer, Jack O'Keefe had been arguing back-and-forth for over an hour when Judge Daily held up his hands and glared at them over the top of his glasses. "I've heard enough from you two. I want to talk to the child alone in my chambers in ten minutes." Judge Daily stood and walked out of the courtroom.

Ten minutes later, I was sitting in a big leather chair next to the judge, scared to death.

"Want a coke?" he asked, handing me a can. "You hungry? I've got some M&M's in my desk. Want some? But you've got to promise not to tell my wife I'm hiding candy in my desk. Promise?"

"Sure," I said. "I promise."

The judge walked to his desk and pulled two bags of candy out of his top drawer.

"Here you go." He handed me a bag, tore his open, and popped some candy into his mouth. "Joe, do you know what my job is?"

"Sure," I said. "You're a judge."

He smiled at me, still chewing on the M&M's in his mouth. "Do you know what a judge does?"

"I think so."

"Really? What's that?"

"You, ahhh... judge people. Send people to jail and stuff."

His face lit up and his round stomach shook as he laughed. "Yes, that's right. I do judge people and I have sent some of them to jail, but in your case that's not what I'm here for. My job today is kind of like a referee in a boxing match."

Shifting in my chair and wrinkling my forehead, I looked up at him. "Huh?"

"Let me put it this way." He popped more candy in his mouth. "My job is a little different today. I'm not here to judge you or your parents. My job is to listen to what Ms. Brookshire and Mr. O'Keefe have to say, and then try my best to figure out what is the best thing to do for you. What's best for you is all that really matters. Do you understand?"

"I think so," I said. I was just a kid, but I liked the way he looked me in the eyes when he talked and seemed sincerely interested in what I had to say.

"Good," he grinned. "See that big file on my desk? That big fat green one? Ms. Brookshire gave me that file and in it is everything I'd ever want to know about your parents. I know every detail about them; where they've lived, how they met, all the places they've played... stuff like that. And after reading all about your parents, I've got to tell you... I like them. They sound like fun people. I like them a lot. But do you know the one thing that's missing in that file?" He looked down at me.

"No, sir."

"There is nothing in that file that tells me who you really are. Not one thing. Oh, there's reports in there, like mental health assessments and psychological profiles and so on, but they don't really tell me what I need to know. So how in the world am I supposed to decide what's best for you when I don't know you?"

I shrugged my shoulders. "I don't know."

"Well, I think a good way would be for us to just hang out here a while and talk about stuff. Maybe get to know each other a little better. Does that make sense to you? Are you ok with that?"

"Sure," I said. "I guess that'd be all right."

"Great!" he said. "So... I understand for the first time in your life you've been going to a real school–in foster care the last few months. What'd you think about school—hanging out with kids your own age? Did you like it?"

I wasn't scared anymore. I tore open my bag, poured some candy into my hand, and popped them in my mouth. "It was ok." I said, crunching on the candy.

"Just ok?" he asked. "Didn't you make some new friends?"

I swallowed my candy and popped in a few more. "Not really. They didn't like me much. They called me names like geek and brainy-ack, stuff like that. I guess they thought I was weird or something because I knew the answers to the teacher's questions."

"Humm. You must be pretty smart to know all the answers."

"I don't know, they were easy questions. The other kids were just stupid, I guess."

His belly shook again. "That's too bad, sounds to me like they were just jealous. Kids can be mean sometimes. Well then, what about your teachers? Did you like them?"

"They were ok, I guess."

"Did you learn a lot?"

"Not really. I sorta already knew what they were talking about. I learned that stuff a long time ago."

The judge looked at me, scrunching his gray brows together. "If you've never been to a school, where did you learn all that?"

"From my mom and from library books and stuff," I said.

The judge shook his head and smiled. "So, when the truant officer found you walking down the street that day, you were walking to the library, and you were going there to learn stuff?"

"Sure. What else do you go to the library for?"

He laughed out loud. "You're right, Joe. That's what a library is for, to learn stuff. How often did you go to the library?"

"That depended on what town we were in. Some libraries aren't open every day, but I went every day they were, except my music lesson days with my dad."

The judge stood and began to pace the room. "So, let me make sure I understand you. Are you saying that when you and your family are traveling around, you spend your days at the public library?

"Yes, sir," I said.

"What do you do there all day?"

"Read."

"What do you read?" he asked. "What's your favorite kind of books?"

I thought about his question a moment. "Not sure I have a favorite kind of book. I like 'em all."

We drank our cokes, ate M&M's and talked for a long time about the different books I had read and about some books he'd read. He seemed impressed.

Then the judge walked to a closet and pulled out a guitar. "I understand you play. Can you play this one?"

"Sure," I said.

He handed me some sheet music. "Ever heard of this song?"

I looked at it. "No, sir. Never heard of that one."

"Can you play it?"

"Sure, but this is piano music. It would sound better on the piano." I played the song.

After I finished, I looked up to see his smiling face and eyes twinkling down at me. "That was very good, young man. I'm impressed." He laid some papers down in front of me. "Would you mind answering a few questions for me?"

I looked down at the papers and frowned. "Is this a test? I don't like tests."

He chuckled again. "I don't either, but it would really help me if you could try to answer some of these questions for me."

After I finished, he called for the bailiff to take me across the street to the cafe to buy me a hamburger and fries. That was it. He never asked me if my parents had ever smoked dope in front of me, or if they ever had wild parties in our hotel rooms after the gigs. Those were the kind of questions Ms. Brookshire told me he would ask, but he never asked about that.

WHEN I LANDED in Little Rock, I rented a car and drove the 16 miles north to Jacksonville. It was a small hospital and before I reached the information desk in the lobby, John Simon, Judge Daily's friend and bailiff for 33 years, walked up with tears in his eyes and gave me a hug.

"It's not good, Joe," he said. "I don't think he's gonna make it through this."

I had met John Simon on the same day I'd met the judge. He had been my direct contact with Judge Daily through all these years.

When Judge Daily decided that it was time for him to retire from the bench, John decided to stop working the very same day. That was 10 years ago, and although we had talked on the phone many times, I hadn't seen him in years. He was looking great for a guy in his 80s. His white hair and white beard contrasting against his dark brown, almost black face, disguised his age.

John wiped his sad eyes with his handkerchief, then followed me into the hospital lobby. "What happened?" I asked as we walked.

"I don't really know, his next-door neighbor found him and called for the ambulance yesterday. We don't know how long he'd been lying there. The doc said it was a pretty bad one."

"Can I see him?"

"I don't think so, he's in intensive care and they won't even let *me* see him. They tell me it's immediate family only. Maybe when his daughter gets here she can get us in."

"Is she on her way?"

"Yeah, she should be here in a few hours. She actually lives over in Little Rock, but as luck would have it, she was on a cruise with her daughter and her daughter's new fiancé in the Caribbean, so they all had to get off the ship and fly back. I think their plane lands around two thirty."

"What's their names?" I asked.

John narrowed his eyes. "You've never met Judge Daily's daughter?"

"No, I never have."

"Ain't that something, after all these years. What about his grand-daughter, you never met her either?"

"No," I said. "I only knew his wife, but I've never met any of his children or grandchildren."

"The judge only has one daughter, her name is Ruth Weller and one granddaughter and her name is Elizabeth. I guess she's about your age. That girl is the judge's pride and joy. She turned out to be a big-time defense attorney down in Little Rock. Of course, you know the judge, he'd rather her be a judge like him, but she went the other way. Real pretty too, just got engaged!"

Since I couldn't see the judge, I decided to go get checked into my hotel and grab something to eat. I wanted to make sure I was back when the judge's daughter and granddaughter arrived, but I was a few minutes late and they had already gone into the ICU to see the judge when I got there. I saw John sitting on a couch in the waiting room and settled in beside him.

"Did you talk to his daughter about getting us in?" I asked.

John nodded. "She said she'd see what she could do."

We waited there almost 30 minutes before Judge Daily's daughter came out and walked over to us. "So, you're the Joe that Daddy has been talking about all these years." She extended her hand. "I'm Ruth."

I shook her hand, smiling up at her.

"He is so proud of you, Joe. Thank you so much for coming,"

Still holding on to her hand, I stood so I could look her in the eyes. "I had to come. Your father changed my life."

She wiped her eyes with her hand and forced a smile. "If you'd like to see him, I can take you in now."

She walked toward the ICU and we fell in behind her, but before we got to the entrance, one of the double doors opened and Elizabeth walked out. I froze, staring at her. I knew that face immediately, I'd dreamed about that face. It was Elizabeth... My Elizabeth.

She gasped when she saw me. "What are you doing here?"

I opened my mouth, but no words came out. I just stood there motionless, staring at her face.

"Ms. Elizabeth, this is Joe," John said. "The one the judge is always talking about."

She glared at me, her brown eyes piercing. Then the ICU door behind her opened again, and a tall, thin man walked out and put his arm around Elizabeth's shoulders. His eyes lit up. "You must be Joe. You're with the FBI, right?"

My brain was so fogged I was having trouble thinking. "Ahhh, yes, yes I am."

"I've heard a lot about you. I'm an assistant district attorney in

Little Rock. We work with the FBI field office all the time," he said. "How do you like being in the Bureau?"

"Could we go? "Elizabeth interrupted. "I'm tired and I want to go home!"

Rob's eyes widened, darted between me and Ruth, then he looked down at Elizabeth. "Sure honey, we can go." He looked at me and shrugged. "Hey Joe, it was really nice to meet you. I'm Rob by the way. See you tomorrow?"

"Yeah, sure Rob. I'll be here, we'll talk more tomorrow. Nice to meet you too."

Elizabeth walked away in a rush, leaving Rob behind hurrying to catch up to her.

Ruth and John looked at me. "I thought you said you'd never met Elizabeth. Sure looked like you two had met before to me. What was that all about?" John asked.

"It's a long story. I'll tell you later. Let's go see the judge."

8

ELIZABETH

Although Judge Daily was supposedly conscious, he gave us no signs of recognition. The cardiologist told us that he had apparently suffered a major myocardial infarction and possibly a minor stroke. He had no signs of movement, recognition, or communication. The only good news was his CT scans showed definite signs of brain activity.

"All we can do now is wait," the doctor said. "The next forty-eight hours are critical."

"Can he hear us?" I asked.

The doctor shook his head. "I don't know. He is showing good brain activity, so it's possible."

I took Judge Daily's right hand and gave it a firm squeeze. With my other hand, I stroked his soft, white hair. "Judge, this is Joe. I'm here and I'm not going anywhere until you get better. I really need to talk to you about something important, so could you hurry this up a little bit?"

I wasn't whispering, in fact I was using my full voice, kind of loud. Ruth and John were both smiling at what I'd said.

"Yeah," John added. "I don't have time for this, judge. I'm a busy man and you know I don't like hospitals. Will you hurry this up, so we can go fishing?"

After my brief visit with the judge, I left the hospital and drove to my hotel. It was a Hampton Inn, I like their beds and usually I slept like a log there, but after tossing and turning for several hours, I knew that wasn't going to happen, so I gave up and just laid there in the darkness thinking about Elizabeth. Meeting Elizabeth, as well as almost everything else in my life, was a direct result of that hearing with Judge Daily when I was thirteen back in 1983.

THE BAILIFF ANNOUNCED, "The 6th Division of the Lincoln County Circuit Court is now in session. Honorable Judge Royce Daily presiding."

Judge Daily walked in and sat behind his desk. "Be seated." He leaned forward and adjusted the microphone. "My case load is extremely backed up and this case has been on my docket for over six months! That is very unusual and normally I wouldn't have allowed it to go on this long. However, from my first review of this case, I've known there's something special about this boy and decided to spend extra time on it, and I'm glad I made that decision.

I've just spent an hour with a very impressive and enlightened young man, and I learned a lot about Joe. He, in fact, can read music and plays guitar very well. And because Joe scored so high on the standard tests, I wanted to find out more.

"I'm holding in my hand thirty-six questions prepared by my staff. Which answers he got correct and how many, was supposed to give me a much better idea of his true IQ and let me know if he actually was equal to or behind his age in his education. However, the results of this test have me very confused, and I'm not exactly sure what to do next." He rubbed his temples and took a deep breath. "Mr. and Mrs. Jensen, would you give me your permission to ask Joe a few more questions?"

My parents glanced at our lawyer and then said, "Yes, your honor, of course."

My knee was bouncing again under the table.

The judge smiled at me. "How you doing, Joe, are you scared? You look scared."

"A little," I said.

He laughed. "No reason to be scared. I'm just going to ask you about some of the answers you wrote on my test. Ok?"

"Ok," I whispered.

"You're gonna have to speak up a little more, Joe. I want everyone to be able to hear what you're saying." I sat up in my chair and took a deep breath.

"Joe, on question number thirty-six, remember that was the one I wrote out myself, the last one, do you remember that question?"

I squirmed in my seat. "Yes, sir." I thought I must have gotten it wrong.

"Good. I'm going to read your answer so everyone will know what you said. Are you ok with that?"

"I guess so," I said.

"Ok, before I read what you wrote, I'd like to give the esteemed state's attorney a chance to answer the same question. How about it counselor? You up for a question?" Judge Daily smiled and looked down at Ms. Brookshire.

"Sure, your honor, fire away." She rose to her feet.

"Ok, here is the question I asked young Joe. Recite the first sentence of any book you have read, fiction or non-fiction." He looked down at the attorney.

"Ahhh. Let me think about that. Ahhh. Ok, ok... It was the best of times, it was the worst of times." Ms. Brookshire smiled and looked up at the judge.

Judge Daily raised his hands and grinned. "Go on councilor, there's more."

She just shook her head and held up her hands. "Sorry sir, that's all I can remember."

The judge's smile broadened. He looked over at my parents' lawyer, "Care to take a shot, Jack?"

Mr. O'Keefe said, "Sorry sir, nothing comes to mind."

"Ok, one last question before I read you young Joe's answer. Ms. Brookshire, can you tell me who wrote those lines you just recited and from what book they came?" He leaned back in his chair, still smiling.

"Was it James Joyce?" she asked.

Judge Daily roared with a huge belly laugh. "Not even close." The entire courtroom broke into laughter.

When the laughter died down, Judge Daily said, "Ok, now let me read you what young Joe here had to say about it. Joe started by saying, and I'm quoting him exactly, 'I know several, but these are my two favorites. Call me Ishmael.' Then he wrote 'Moby Dick by Herman Melville.'" The judge raised his eyebrows and looked around the courtroom.

Then he wrote, and you should appreciate this councilor, 'It was the best of times, it was the worst of times, it was the age of wisdom, it was the age of foolishness, it was the epoch of belief, it was the epoch of incredulity, it was the season of light, it was the season of darkness, it was the spring of hope, it was the winter of despair.' Then he wrote, 'A Tale of Two Cities by Charles Dickens.'"

A hush came over the courtroom. No one spoke a word. My mother's mouth was open and she was about to cry. My father sat there motionless, staring up at the judge who was grinning ear-to-ear.

"Is that what you wrote on this test?" he asked me.

I shifted in my chair. "Yes, sir."

The judge looked around the courtroom and smiled. "Ok, Joe, just a few more questions. You wrote, 'it was the epoch of incredulity,' right?"

"Yes."

"Can you tell me and the rest of us what the word 'epoch' means?"

I thought about it a moment. "It has a real long definition, but it sort of means the start or the beginning of something."

The judge's smile grew even wider. "Ok, now can you tell me what the word 'incredulity' means?"

"It means not believing something," I said, still not sure what was going on.

"Are epoch or incredulity words your parents use often?"

"No, sir. I don't think they've ever used them."

"Then how do you know what they mean?" he asked, still smiling.

"I didn't at first, but this real nice librarian showed me how to look words up in the dictionary. So, when I come across a word I don't know or understand, I look them up and learn what they mean. I do it all the time. I don't know what a lot of words mean."

With a chuckle, Judge Daily said, "Ha, neither do I, Joe. You did great, son. You can relax, we're all through now." The judge adjusted some papers on his desk and started to speak, but stopped several times. He seemed to be searching for the right words. "It should be obvious to everyone in this room the dilemma I'm facing. The question before me is, has Joe been neglected? In my opinion, Mr. and Mrs. Jensen love Joe and have not and would not intentionally neglect him. However, I'm also charged with what is in his best interest from here on. And it's also my opinion that it's not in his best interest to just let him go back to traveling around the country like a Gypsy not getting the education he so obviously deserves. This is a very intelligent boy you have here Mr. and Mrs. Jensen. My question to you is... were you aware of his intellect?"

My father slowly stood up, his hands shaking as he spoke. "Sir, your honor, Sir... ahh... Joe has always been a good boy. He's never given us a lick of trouble. I think we both knew he was a quick learner and pretty smart, but to be honest with you, we didn't know he was *this* kind of smart."

The judge shook his head, apparently understanding how my father might not have noticed this before. "Well, Mr. Jensen, now that you *do* understand, what do you think we should do about it?"

My father shrugged his shoulders. "Sir, I'm a musician. That's really the only thing I'm good at and it's the only way I know how to make a living. To do that, we have to travel. But I'm here to fight for my boy and if you think it's bad for him, I guess I could quit playing music and see if I can find some other job somewhere so we can stick in one spot and then he can go to school like a regular kid. If that's what you want, sir, then that's what we'll do."

I'd never seen my father cry before. My mother was crying, our lawyer was crying and I'm pretty sure I saw some tears well up in Judge Daily's eyes too. It would be difficult to describe the feelings that were welling up inside of me. My father was not a man to show his emotions. He wasn't the kind of father that said, I love you or would give you a hug or a kiss. Up to that point, our relationship had always been standoffish and distant. But there he was, crying like a baby, begging the judge not to take me away. It was the first time I'd ever heard him say anything like that about me, and my heart over-flowed with love for my father.

The judge actually wiped his eyes. "Mr. Jensen, I'm convinced we want the exact same thing for Joe. I have a few more questions to ask you and the way you answer will have a lot to do with my final ruling. Do you understand?"

My father was still standing, but his entire body shook. "Yes sir, I understand."

Judge Daily gave my father a gentle smile. "Why don't you sit down and relax a little. There is no need for you to stand to answer my questions."

My father slowly sat down next to me, apparently very weak and unsteady, and that's when I saw it... and I was crushed. My father covered his face with his hands, so no one could see him and then gave my mother a wink under his hands and rolled his eyes. He was lying. It was all just an act. He was putting on a big show for the courtroom and the judge. All those emotions and love I thought he had toward me weren't real. I wanted to cry, but I didn't. I just sat there hurting inside.

My father stopped crying, but kept the poor, pitiful, uncontrollable shaking going a while. It was very effective.

Judge Daily smiled again. "Mr. Jensen, why do you make your living as a traveling musician? You appear to be an intelligent man;

can you give me a reason why you would choose such a difficult way to earn a living? Do you do this because someday you hope to hit it big and become a big star?"

My father thought a long time before he answered. "I'm too old to hit it big, your honor. I know I'm never gonna be a star. That's not why I do it. I do it because... I love it. Is that a reason?"

Judge Daily seemed to believe his story, but I had to fight back the urge to roll my eyes and laugh. Becoming a big star was all my father ever talked about. "One day I'll get discovered and everything will change," he'd preach to us. "Someday the entire world will know my name!" I'd heard that almost every day for as long as I could remember.

"Oh yes, Mr. Jensen," Judge Daily said. "That's a very good reason. It's the same reason I decided to be a lawyer and now a judge. The law stirs my soul. Is that what your music does for you?"

My father put on his gleaming smile for the first time that day. "Yes sir, that's exactly what it does. When I'm on stage performing, it's... it's like the only time I really feel alive. I can't explain it, but I do love it."

"And you're telling me that you are willing to give that up and get a job selling shoes or maybe working construction? You'd do that for your son?" he asked.

"Yes sir, if that's what it takes to keep my boy, that's what I'll do. Wouldn't you do the same for your boy?"

Judge Daily raised his eyebrows in surprise. "Yes sir, that's exactly what I'd do. Good answer, Mr. Jensen. A very good answer." He leaned back and fiddled with some papers on his desk, then looked my father directly in the eyes. "Now for the hard questions. This is for both of you. Have you ever smoked marijuana in front of Joe?"

Without hesitation, my parents both said, "No."

"Has there ever been an after-hours party in your hotel room or wherever that may not have been appropriate for young Joe to have witnessed?"

Again, without hesitation they both answered, "No."

Judge Daily frowned, shifted in his chair, and leaned forward. "Ok, one last question. "If you don't smoke it in front of Joe, can you explain why there was marijuana found in your van?"

My father put his arm around my mother and they both stood up. "Sir, we're not going to tell you that we don't smoke marijuana, we're just saying that we don't smoke it around Joe."

I wanted to jump up and scream, "He's lying, judge, don't believe him!" but I didn't.

"Ok. I'm going to take a thirty-minute recess and I'll be back to render my final ruling." He slammed down his gavel, stood, and walked out of the courtroom.

We spent the next thirty minutes outside on the courthouse steps talking with Jack O'Keefe. He was convinced we had won. He predicted that the judge would dismiss the case and give them back custody of me, just like he did for Mooch and Smooth and their kids.

"I hope you're right," my father said. "I just want this shit over with and to get the fuck out of this hick town!"

Judge Daily's face was blank when he returned to the bench. My stomach churned around inside of me. I didn't want my parents to be in trouble anymore and wanted the judge to rule in their favor—even if they were lying. But at the same time, deep down I think I knew that wasn't the best thing for me. Tears rolled down my mother's cheeks and my father went back to his shaking routine.

"Mr. and Mrs. Jensen, I promised to rule on the issue of truancy earlier, so I will begin there. The question is whether or not I have jurisdiction to enforce the state of Arkansas's truancy laws, due to the fact that you are not residents of the state. My clerks have searched for several weeks trying to come up with some similar case that would help me with this decision. Unfortunately, there appears to be no case precedent in the state of Arkansas for me to turn to other than my previous rulings a few months earlier of your other band members, Mr. Driscoll, Mr. Martin, and Mr. Williams. It was my opinion at that time and still is now, that I did have jurisdiction, simply because the truancy offense took place in this state and landed in my court. I assume you understand the reasons behind my ruling for Mr. Driscoll. It was unfortunate, but I had no real choice because of Mr. Driscoll's mental capacity and the fact that he wasn't the child's actual parent.

"The situation was much different for Mr. Martin and Mr. Williams, and as I'm sure you know, I ruled in their favor. I ruled that way because I believe they were sincere and wanted to be good parents, but were sort of trapped by their occupation."

The judge sifted through some papers on his desk for a few minutes. When he found what he was looking for he held up the page. "I have come across something you and your band members need to know about. There is a movement spreading across the United States as we speak. Due to the fact that most of our public schools are over-crowded, underfunded, and understaffed, there are many people that believe in something called homeschooling. Although it is not legal at this point, it's my opinion that it will be soon. Mr. and Mrs. Jensen, you are a perfect example of why I believe in and support this move-ment. You've done a wonderful job with Joe's education so far. He is incredibly bright and well above most formally educated children his age, so again you've done well with his homeschooling. However, at this point in time it is still against the law in all fifty states not to have a child registered in school. If you continue traveling and not regis-tering Joe in a school, I recommend you get in touch with an organi-zation called the *Home School Legal Defense Association.* It's an organization founded this year by two attorneys, Michael Farris and Michael Smith, to help people just like you and your band members. I honestly believe there is a very good chance that this might happen to some of you again and next time the judge may not be as lenient. And just so you know, the maximum penalty for truancy in the state is jail for the parents, but I think I've already showed my hand, so let's make this formal.

"Although you did break the truancy laws of the state of Arkansas, it's my ruling to overlook that offense and dismiss that part of this case." Judge Daily took a drink of water and wiped his brow with a cloth. "Now, to the neglect charges. In this area, there are case prece-dents and going by those rulings, which I must use to render my deci-sion, I find no substantial convincing evidence of child abuse or neglect in this case. Therefore, it is my ruling that all neglect charges against Mr. and Mrs. Jensen be dropped and the child, Joe Jensen, be returned to their custody. Case dismissed!" He banged the gavel and it was over.

But instead of walking out of the courtroom, Judge Daily did something very unusual and unexpected. He stood up, walked down from his bench, moved up to our table, pulled up a chair, and sat down directly across from my parents. He looked over at Ms. Brookshire. "Pull up a chair, I'd like you to hear this as well." Without a word, she pulled her chair over and sat at the table next to the judge.

"Mr. and Mrs. Jensen, if you ask Mrs. Berkshire or my bailiff, John over there, they will tell you that what I'm doing now, sitting here talking to you like this, is something I rarely do. To be honest with you, I'm not even sure it's ethical. As a judge, I am not supposed to get personally involved in my cases. Lady Justice is supposed to be blind, but once in a while when I meet someone like Joe, I just can't help myself. I'm only human.

"I meant what I said, you've done a great job with Joe's education so far, but in the future I personally don't believe it's going to be enough for Joe to achieve the success he deserves in this life. I hope you realize how special he really is. I'm not going to tell you that I think young Joe here is some kind of a boy genius. He might be, but I don't think he is. I will tell you that he is extremely bright and has an enormous desire to learn and deserves to have the best education he can get. I can tell you that he's smarter than me. I took the same test and I missed two of the answers... Joe got them all right... every single one." He smiled with a wide grin.

"You heard my ruling. And as far as I am concerned, that's all I can do within the law; from here on I'm out of the equation. However, I want you to know, you didn't fool me. I didn't believe you about the wild parties in your room and smoking dope in front of young Joe. I'm sure that's happened and you've done it many times before. However, because there is no proof, I have no choice but to take your word on that. Honestly, even if I had proof, I more than likely would have ruled the same way because taking a child away from loving parents is something I'm not prepared to do.

"I honestly believe you are good people who just made a few stupid mistakes in the past and didn't realize what you were doing was wrong. I'm hoping that now that you know it was, you will never expose Joe to that sort of thing again. I'm sure Ms. Brookshire disagrees with me and thinks Joe would be better off in foster care. That's her job. My job is to use my judgment and make the final decision and that's what I've done. There are no more charges against you. You are free to gather up young Joe, hop in your van, and drive away."

My father remained silent.

"Mr. Jensen, it's not in my power as a judge to force you to change your job, and settle down in one place so Joe can go to school and get a proper education. I can't do that. If I could I would, but the law won't let me. So, my ruling has taken away any power I had over Joe and his future. It's all up to you now."

My father nodded, never taking his eyes off of the judge.

"All I can do now," Judge Daily continued, "is offer you an idea; a possible solution that would allow you to continue doing what you love, touring and playing your music and at the same time allow Joe a way to receive the education he deserves. Is this something you'd be willing to consider?"

My parents looked at each other and began nodding their heads. "Yes, of course," my father said. "What is it? How can we do that?"

Judge Daily reached for the pitcher, poured some water into a glass, and took a sip. "Don't misunderstand me, this is not a perfect solution, but I think it just might be the right one for Joe. Have you ever heard of a boarding school?"

My father's expression dropped. "Sure, but aren't they really expensive? We can't afford that."

"Yes, they can be expensive, but let's not worry about what it costs right now, let's talk about what it can do for Joe."

The judge sipped his water and thought about his words. "In a top rated boarding school, Joe would live in a nice room, and eat healthy food. He would be taught by the best teachers in the country, work with state of the art equipment and have his mind opened up to a world of education he can only imagine living on the road with you. His future would be unlimited. Also, he could travel with you in the summers and come for visits during all the school holidays, like Spring break and Christmas. You would still be able to spend a lot of time together. What do you think?"

"Judge Daily, that sounds great, but again, we can't afford to send Joe to some fancy boarding school. I don't make that kind of money."

"I understand your concerns," the judge said, "just answer this question. If this could be arranged, is it something you, your wife, and Joe would want to do? Don't answer now. I want the three of you to think about it carefully tonight. It's a big decision. Call me at this number tomorrow and let me know what you decide."

He handed my father a card and stood up. "The decision of what is in Joe's best interest is now up to you. I'll be waiting for your call."

I wish I could say that after the hearing my parents took me back to the hotel and the three of us had a long, serious, and intense discussion about Judge Daily's suggestion of me attending a boarding school, but I can't. The truth is, my father pitched Judge Daily's card out the window and fired up a joint the second we pulled out of the courtroom parking lot. He and my mom shared it all the way back to the hotel. Bummer, Mooch, Smooth, their wives, kids, and three other women I'd never seen before were waiting for us in the hotel room and the celebration began.

It was fun at first. I was actually getting along with the other kids. Bummer had bought me a welcome home cake and Mooch bought some ice cream. I had two big pieces of cake and three giant scoops of vanilla bean before I was through. We were all having fun!

Then Smooth handed my dad a bag full of white stuff that looked like sugar, and Mom, Dad, and Smooth went into the bathroom together. I wasn't sure what they were doing in there, but I knew it wasn't anything good. When they came out they were all smiling and acting silly. Smooth turned up the volume on the stereo and pretty soon everybody was dancing around, laughing, and yelling really loud. Two of the girls took off their clothes, and danced around the room naked.

I curled up in the corner, trying my best to ignore what was going on around me. Of course, it wasn't the first time something like this had happened, but it was the first time that I knew it was wrong. I was so disappointed in my parents for doing this again. I was angry and sad at the same time—angry at my parents, and sad for myself because there wasn't one thing I could do about it.

Around midnight, the hotel security guard banged on the door. He told my father that they were disturbing the other hotel guests and asked him to turn down the music. My father cursed at the guard and slammed the door in his face.

It seemed like just a few minutes later when someone started banging on the door again. My father jerked the door open to find two uniformed police officers standing in the doorway. When Smooth and Mooch saw the cops, they both jumped up and ran into the bathroom.

I didn't understand it at the time, but apparently Mooch and Smooth successfully flushed the cocaine and pot before the cops got the door open. So there were no drug possession charges filed that night, but they were all handcuffed and hauled off to jail anyway. All of their kids were once again taken away by Child Protective Services, but for some reason they didn't take me. Instead, they left me behind in the hotel room in the care of a really nice lady police officer.

I wasn't sure why or what we were waiting for in the hotel room, but about thirty minutes later Judge Daily walked into the room. He smiled at me. "How are you doing, Joe?"

The second I saw him I burst into tears. He took me home with him that night and that's where I stayed for the next three weeks.

To this day, I'm not exactly sure what happened next, because I wasn't allowed to see my parents. All I do know is that my parents had a long private meeting with Judge Daily and agreed that a boarding school was in my best interest and going back on the road was in theirs.

Although everyone failed a drug test, Judge Daily used his influence and somehow got the charges against my parents, Bummer, Mooch, Smooth, and their wives dropped.

I was left behind in the care of Judge Daily and over the next few weeks, the judge had me take a battery of tests. He said it was the best way to determine my aptitude and what grade I should be in.

A week later he told me that I had been accepted into the Lowell Whiteman School in Colorado, a small, private, co-ed boarding school located in Steamboat Springs. He said it was ranked in the top 10 of the best college prep schools in the country. He also thought it was important for me to understand that the yearly cost for my room and board and tuition was over twenty thousand dollars. That number may not sound too bad in today's world, but to a 13-year old kid it sounded like a king's ransom, especially considering that I was going to need that much every year I was there.

The judge explained that somehow he had arranged for three anonymous benefactors to pay for everything as long as I maintained a B average. I made a vow to myself that someday I'd find out who those people were and pay them back every cent.

I'd only seen my parents one time since the night of the big celebration. That was the day they drove back to Jacksonville and came to Judge Daily's chambers to sign the custody papers and my enrollment documents for the Colorado boarding school. My father's face was flushed bright red, matching his squinted, bloodshot steely eyes he used to glare at me. He never said a word, he just signed the papers and walked out of the room.

My mother never stopped weeping and just kept repeating, "I'm so sorry, Joe. Please forgive me. I love you so much." She said that over and over and over. After she signed the papers, she hugged me for a long time and promised to write me every week. It was a promise she kept.

I didn't cry that day. I know that may sound strange, but not one tear. I just felt sort of numb all over. When they were gone, Judge Daily sat down next to me.

"That must have been very hard for you," he said. "and I know you are mad at your parents and pretty upset, but they are not bad people. They are who they are and will probably never change, but they love you and I want you to try to forgive them. Will you try?"

I nodded.

"Good boy," he said. "Trust me, everything is going to work out." He handed me a package of M&M's. "I know it may not seem like it now, but I promise this is a great opportunity for you. It's not going to be easy, and I know you're scared, but if you work hard, everything is going to work out for you. You just wait and see."

The next day, Judge Daily put me on a plane to Colorado. He was waving as the plane pulled away from the terminal. I waved back, but I was pretty sure he couldn't see me through the small window. When I felt the first motion of the plane pulling back, my heart jumped. I hadn't told the judge, but this was my first time to fly and I didn't really know if I was going to be afraid or if I was going to like it.

I loved it. I don't think my face left the window the entire flight.

When we landed in Denver my heart started pounding hard. My mind whirled with the reality of what was actually happening to me. My life had changed so quickly, and I was having trouble processing it all. I was torn between emotions—afraid and sad about being alone and away from my parents for the first time in my life, but excited about attending a real school. With my knees shaking, I took a deep breath, stepped off that plane, and walked into the scary unknown.

The flight to Denver seemed short compared to the almost 4-hour drive over the winding mountain roads from Denver to Steam Boat Springs. All the twists and turns only seemed to increase the anxiety building inside of me, but the moment we turned onto the tree-lined drive of the Lowell Whiteman campus, all my fears and anxiety disappeared. Somehow, I knew I was where I belonged.

The school was located in the middle of 170 acres. I'd never seen anything like it before. It was like looking at a postcard—absolutely beautiful. My emotions bounced off the walls as we walked into the building and up the stairs to find my room. Some might describe the room as small, but compared to living in a van with my parents, it was like living in a mansion.

It had everything I needed—a good bed, a desk, a closet, a bathroom and an amazing view out my window. I lived in that room at Lowell Whiteman for four years.

Although I was only 13 years old at the time, I was enrolled in the ninth grade. That made me younger than the other students in my grade, but I was tall for my age and no one seemed to notice. Lowell Whiteman was a very small private school—only 77 students total, ranging from elementary through high school, so there were only 16 kids in my grade. In a school that small it didn't take me long to get to know all of the students and teachers. Although I got along with the other students, I didn't really make any close friends... even my roommates. Each year I got a different one and each year we just didn't seem to click. I was only interested in one thing, studying and making good grades.

My roommates and the other kids in my grade seemed to hate going to school and spent most of their time avoiding studying, or hanging out on the slopes skiing or snowboarding. The other, non-skier students only seemed to want to get high, stoned, or drunk on beer. I didn't know how to ski or snowboard and getting high or drunk held no interest for me. So, I wasn't what you'd call the cool, popular kid on campus.

I did make one friend at Whiteman, sort of—Elizabeth. She was the first girl my age I'd ever kissed. I was sitting at my usual spot in the library, (yes, even at Whiteman I spent most of my days in the library) when she tapped me on the shoulder, bent down, and kissed me right on the lips—a big, wet, sloppy one.

She told me later that she'd been trying to get my attention for six months and just got tired of waiting for me to make a move. The truth is, I had noticed her looking at me, but was just too shy to do anything about it. But after that day we were inseparable, spending every spare minute of every day together. I didn't want her to know about my parents, so I never talked about them, and she never really told me about hers. We would talk for hours and hours about the things we liked and the things we didn't like, what we wanted to do with our lives...

Elizabeth was my first love, and I'm pretty sure I was hers. We didn't have sex, we were a little too young, but it did get hot and heavy a few times. Our relationship progressed from first, to second, and even to third base once, but that was as far as we went.

Then, inexplicably, after the summer break, Elizabeth didn't return to Whiteman. I never saw her again. I was completely devastated. It was my first heartbreak. Well actually, my only heartbreak; I've never let anyone get that close to me again. It made no sense and I just couldn't understand it. There wasn't even a letter explaining why... she was just gone...

As I TOSSED and turned in that Hampton Inn bed, twenty plus years later, I tried to come up with some reason for Elizabeth's hostility toward me. I searched my memory banks trying to recall every moment we had spent together at Lowell Whiteman. She seemed so happy back then. Had I gone too far with her? Could that explain it? Did she think I had taken advantage of her or something? Was it something I said? Was that why she had just disappeared?

I got out of bed, sat down at the desk, and flipped on my laptop. I spent the next few hours trying not to think about Elizabeth. At 7:30, I jumped in the shower and started getting ready so I could head back to the hospital and hopefully see the judge again. A familiar chime rang on my laptop. This one was business, something from the Bureau, so I went to the FBI secure site and opened it. It was not from my boss at Quantico, it was from the director... in Washington. He wanted to see me immediately. I was instructed to drive back to the Little Rock Airport at 2 p.m., where an FBI jet would be waiting for me.

"What the hell?" I said out loud.

I quickly finished dressing and ran to my car. When I got to the hospital, around 8, they told me that visiting hours started at 9 and that they couldn't let me in anyway, unless I was with a member of the immediate family. As a last resort, I flashed my FBI credentials, but that didn't work either.

At 9 o'clock sharp, Elizabeth walked in the door. When she saw me she frowned and glared at me.

I ignored it. "They told me I couldn't go in unless I was with a family member. I have to leave soon and head to Washington, so could you please take me in to see him before I go?"

She nodded her head, still frowning. "Follow me."

For the next 45 minutes, we stood on opposite sides of Judge Daily's bed, holding his hands, not saying a word to each other.

When Ruth and John showed up at 11, they chased Elizabeth and me out, claiming too many people in the room.

I told the judge that I would be back as soon as I could, and walked out. Elizabeth was waiting for me in the lobby.

I held up my hands. "What the hell did I do?"

Her eyes flew open, shooting daggers at me. "What did you do? Are you kidding? What did you do?"

I'd had enough of her hostility. "You were the one that disappeared, not me! You knew where I was!"

"What?" she shrieked. "You never answered one of my letters, Joe. Not one!"

That rocked me back on my heels. "What letters? There were no letters!"

"What are you talking about? I wrote you about a hundred letters! You didn't get them?"

"Not one," I said. "I wrote you about a hundred too, but..."

Her jaw dropped and her eyes widened. "Oh my God, Joe, how could that have happened? I thought that... that you..." Her eyes filled with tears. "I was so devastated."

"I know... you broke my heart too."

"How's Judge Daily this morning?" A voice said behind us.

We both turned around to see Rob, Elizabeth's fiancé, standing there. We had no idea how long he'd been there, or what he'd overheard.

Elizabeth spoke first. "He's about the same."

"Unfortunately," I said, "there's been no change."

"That's a shame," Rob said. "I was hoping he'd be better this morning."

"Yeah, we were too," I said frowning.

The three of us stood there silent for a moment, lost in our thoughts about the judge.

"Hey Joe," Rob said, "are we going to be able to do some shop talk later, maybe over lunch? I'd love to hear about some of the cases you've worked on."

I looked at Elizabeth, trying not to smile about the 'Hey Joe' comment, but she lost it and burst out laughing.

"What's so funny?" Rob asked.

"How much did the judge tell you about me?"

"Not that much. He told me that he'd helped you get through school and now you were a big shot profiler at the FBI. That's about it."

"He didn't mention anything about my parents?"

"No, why?"

Elizabeth was still laughing, I was grinning, and poor Rob was totally confused.

"Actually Rob, we're not going to be able to talk today. Something's come up and I've got to catch a plane to Washington. Elizabeth can tell you what we're laughing about. Sorry, but I'm late."

When I turned to leave, Elizabeth yelled, "Wait! When will you be back?"

"I'm not sure," I said.

She ran up to me, put her arms around me and hugged me, a little too long. She looked up into my eyes and whispered, "Please come back."

With Rob there, it was an awkward moment, but I loved it.

9

THE WORST CASE

W hen I boarded the plane, I quickly realized that this wasn't just any plane. It was the director's plane. The frigging director of the FBI's personal aircraft and other than the two pilots, I was the only one on board. What in the hell was going on? I couldn't imagine.

When we landed in Dulles, two field agents were waiting for me and whisked me away to the J. Edgar Hoover Building, in the back of a black Escalade.

I found the one remaining seat available at the conference table, sat down and began flipping through a large stack of files that were placed on the table in front of my seat. Besides the director, I counted 7 agents at the table, all special agents in charge of various states of the U.S., including my good friend John Kelly, the special agent in charge of the state of Mississippi.

The director started the meeting by asking me how Judge Daily was doing.

I cleared my throat. "Sir, he suffered a pretty serious heart attack and a minor stroke. At the present time, he's stable, but non-responsive."

"I understand how important he is to you," the director said, "and we're all praying that he pulls through."

"Thank you, sir, so am I."

I was a little surprised that the director of the FBI actually knew Judge Daily, or at least his name. Apparently, the director knew a lot more about me and my background than I thought.

"I'm sorry we had to rush you back from there, Joe," the director said, "but this is a little time sensitive."

I shook my head. "I understand, sir. So, why am I here?"

"Well, everyone at this table tells me that you're the best profiler we have in the Bureau. I realize that it's been a few years since you've been in the field, but we've got a special case here that I need your help on."

I wasn't sure what a proper response would be to that statement, so I didn't say a word. I just sat there silently listening.

"It's all in the files in front of you, but to summarize: a young girl named Tina Walters was murdered two weeks ago in Jackson, Mississippi. She was Congressman John Frank's granddaughter. I assume you know that he is the Chairman of the House Appropriations Committee who oversees our funding.

"Yes, sir, I know who he is," I said.

"Normally this would be handled by the local law enforcement," the director continued, "but when Tina's file was put into the record management system, six other unsolved murders stretching over twenty-six years were linked to her case with three very specific matching identifiers.

"Like Tina, all six were young, beautiful girls that had been bound to their beds and strangled with some type of a strap that created a unique imprint pattern on their necks, wrists, and ankles. The second identifier..." He flipped the page of his report. "Except for the first one, all of the victim's lower extremities, specifically their genital areas, were drenched in a scented oil we've identified as patchouli. The third identifier and this was at all of the cases including Tina's, was the remains of a tear away portion of a Polaroid picture. They stopped making that tear away film twenty years ago. These six, now seven murders were committed in seven different states. That's when it became an FBI problem." He took off his reading glasses, laid them on the file, and looked at me. "I'm sure you can appreciate the amount of pressure I'm getting from the congressman to get to the bottom of this."

It was finally clear why I was there. The director was going to personally head up this investigation and he needed a profile of this killer, and fast. "I don't suppose there are any matching fingerprints or DNA evidence?" I asked.

"If we had that, we wouldn't need you, Joe. Unfortunately, except for Tina, these cases pre-date DNA. We didn't start collecting DNA evidence until about 1989. Apparently, this perp wiped down all the surfaces, so there were no fingerprints left behind. And how he still has film and a working Polaroid camera manufactured thirty years ago, is even a bigger mystery. The negative he leaves behind is a picture of his work—probably his calling card."

John Kelly spoke next, "Joe, I know I've kidded you for years about your profiling voodoo, but this last one happened on my turf and we've hit a wall. We need you to do whatever it takes to work that magic of yours and give us some kind of a profile, so we'll have a starting point to work this case."

"Joe, I'm told that you have a unique talent for seeing things in a case that may have been overlooked," the director said. "I don't know your process, and I know I'm asking a lot, but I want a report by morning with anything you've got. We've got to find this bastard and fast."

I loaded the files into my briefcase and caught a cab to my hotel, but before I could get started, my cell phone rang; it was John Kelly.

"Joe, there's something I think you need to know that's not in those files. I wanted you on this case, so I purposely left it out. I was afraid the director might see it as a conflict of interest and not bring you in.

"Ok," I ran my hands through my hair and narrowed my eyes. "What did you leave out?

"Tina was at your parent's reunion concert. That was the last time anybody saw her alive." He paused and cleared his throat, "and the last person she was seen with was your father."

"What do you mean? Where were they seen together?"

"She went to the reunion concert with her mother, who was a big fan of Blackfish. She told her mother that she was going to go backstage and see if she could get your father to autograph one of her mother's old albums. The last time anyone can remember seeing her was when your father was signing that album."

"Are you telling me my father is a suspect in this?"

"No!" he said firmly, "of course not. I just wanted you to have all the facts. I do think it's possible that the killer was at that concert though."

"You're probably right," I said. "But my gut reaction is that this is not the same guy."

"Why do you think that?" John asked.

"It's the break, 17 years between murders... that doesn't make any sense. I know these cases are linked with the garrote, the patchouli oil and the pictures, but it's just too much time to be the same guy."

"Are you thinking a copycat killer?"

"I don't know, maybe," I said. "Let me study these files and see what I can come up with. I'll let you know what I think in the morning."

I was hungry, so I ordered room service and then took the files out of my briefcase and spread them across the bed. I started with the oldest murder and worked my way up.

As I munched on my club sandwich, on a yellow legal pad I wrote down the date and location of each murder. The first one, in 1983, happened in Cape Girardeau, Missouri; the second one, in 1984, was in Sikeston, Missouri... only a few miles away. I bracketed those two with a note about the close locations. I continued through the files, running down each date and location with notations of any similarities, but no real geographical pattern emerged. In fact, there was just no connection at all between the locations of each murder. The only connection I could make was that they were all small towns, no big cities, with the exception of the last one. Although Jackson wasn't what you might call a big city, it was considerably larger than the others.

I couldn't put my finger on it, but I knew there was something in those files I wasn't seeing. Still, I seemed to recognize the names of most of these small towns. I racked my brain for how I knew them, but nothing came clear.

I put down the yellow pad and started studying the crime scene photographs. First were the pictures of the tear away Polaroid negatives. They were obviously negatives of the women tied and bound to beds. Then I went to the official crime scene photographs. My first observation was in the difference in the quality between the photography of the old cases and the new one. The old ones were not as sharp and made it more difficult to make out the fine details, like the pattern on the skin left behind by the murder weapon. Although the photographs were not as sharp as I would like, it was obvious that the impression marks on the necks of each victim were identical.

I had been concentrating on the old murder files, so I picked up the new one, Tina Walters, and pulled out the photo of the ligature marks left on her neck. As I studied the photograph an uneasy feeling grew once again in my gut.

"What is it?" I said to myself out loud, "what are you missing here?"

Suddenly John Kelly's words repeated in my head, "The last person she was seen with... was your father." That's when I saw it and felt a chill race through my body.

I could see it as clear as day. The unique impression left on this poor girl's neck—the circle with a double x pattern... I'd seen it many times before. Suddenly my vision blurred, I was light headed and I couldn't breathe. I gasped for breath, my entire body breaking into a cold sweat.

That circle and double x was the exact pattern on my father's macramé guitar strap—the strap my mother had made for him 30 years earlier. It was one of a kind, one of her unique, original designs. My mind filled with a childhood memory of my father's amazed expression as he peeled apart the film of a picture he'd just taken with his new Polaroid.

Suddenly, my stomach heaved with waves of nausea. I rushed to the bathroom and threw up. When I finished, I collapsed next to the commode with the cold tile floor pressing against my face. I tried to get up, but I couldn't, my arms twitching, my legs not obeying my brain's commands to move. My mind whirled, putting all the pieces together. I thought about running to the airport to fly home so I could find the box with my mother's postcards she'd sent me every week they were traveling and compare the dates with the killings, but my body still wouldn't move. It didn't matter anyway, I knew they would match... The nausea came back... I wanted to die.

When I finally recovered and pulled myself up to my feet, I paced the room for the rest of the night, reading and re-reading the files, studying the photographs, trying to come up with some other possibility... anything except what was running through my mind. But no matter how hard I tried, there was just no other explanation. Everything in those files pointed directly at my father; the strap, the film, it all fit; everything except the patchouli oil.

My father hated the smell of burning patchouli incense and he especially hated the smell of patchouli oil. Bummer, Smooth, Mooch, even my mother sometimes reeked of it, but my father couldn't stand it. I didn't like the smell of it either, but it literally made him gag.

I flipped through the pages of the files once again, hoping something I'd missed would jump out, but there was nothing there. On my yellow legal pad, I listed the evidence; the names of the small towns, the time lines, the patterns on the victim's neck, my father's guitar strap, the film and finally the patchouli oil.

I could see it now; it was obvious. If I told the director what I knew, my father was going to be arrested soon, but my guts were telling me... because of that patchouli oil... it just didn't fit. It was more than my guts, it was my years of experience investigating hundreds of serial murders that convinced me. In all those cases, all the pieces fit, every single one.

In my heart, no matter what the evidence showed, I knew my father was not the murderer... but without a doubt... someone in the band was.

THE ARREST

I spent what was left of the night staring at the evidence, almost in a trance as I argued with myself about what to do next. I had to meet with the director and the rest of the special agents at 9:00 a.m. and I had to tell them something. I could just ignore the evidence of that strap and tell them I came up with nothing and needed more time, but that strap was one of a kind and eventually someone else would discover it. And when that happened, and they realized I'd withheld that evidence, although understandable because it was my own father, it would no doubt be the end of my career with the FBI, but if I disclosed what I'd discovered...

I continued to argue with myself in the cab to the director's office and all the way up the long elevator ride. Until I actually opened my mouth and began talking, I had no idea what I was going to say.

Once everyone arrived and were seated around the table, the director looked at me and smiled. "Joe, you don't look so good. Did you stay up all night working on this?"

"Yes sir, I've been up all night."

The director raised his eyebrows. "That's admirable, Joe, but it's a little above and beyond don't you think?"

I could feel beads of perspiration rolling down my temples, my hands were clammy and stuck to the files as I spread them out in front of me. "Normally I would agree with you, but when I tell you what I've discovered, I think you'll understand why I couldn't sleep."

The director sat up erect in his chair and glanced around the table making eye contact with the other agents. "You have something? Already?"

Forcing myself to remain calm, breathing slowly trying not to hyperventilate, I shook my head. "Yes sir, I'm afraid I have."

"I don't understand Joe. Afraid you have? Please explain."

I took a deep breath and for the next thirty minutes slowly laid out the evidence, incriminating my father further and further with each word I spoke.

At the end, I reiterated my belief in my father's innocence, but as I heard my words, I knew they were not convincing. When I finally stopped talking, the room was eerily silent. After several quiet, awkward moments passed, with a grim look the director said, "I'm not sure how to respond, Joe. I'm... I'm sorry, but..

"I know sir." I interrupted. He didn't have to finish his sentence. I knew what his next move would be.

After the meeting, as I was walking down the hall to the elevator, I heard a voice behind me. "Let's go get a drink." It was John Kelly. And although it was only 11:00 a.m., I knew it was exactly what I needed.

We found a small bar a few blocks down from the FBI building and ordered a double scotch, neat. We sat in silence for a while, sipping our drinks.

John finally broke the ice. "That had to have been tough. I'm not sure I could have done that."

I set my drink on the small table between us. "I wasn't sure I could either, but I had no choice. You or someone else would have made the connection sooner or later. If I'd withheld it... well, you know."

The conversation lulled again. Finally, John said, "If it's not your father, even though all the evidence points directly at him... then who do you think it is? Any ideas?

I shook my head. "That's the problem, it could be any of them and I haven't a clue which one, but I'm convinced it has to be someone in that band. Murder in a small town is a rare occurrence, but seven murders in seven small towns that the band just happened to be playing..." I took another sip of my scotch and looked John in the eyes. "Someone in the band, is a killer."

"I agree, but your patchouli oil theory isn't gonna cut it. Just because your father didn't like the smell... well, that's just not enough to..." John paused, trying to find a gentle way to say it.

"I figure the director has already contacted the Jackson D. A. My father will be arrested within the week and there will be a grand jury indictment soon after."

John didn't react, only shrugged in silent agreement.

"I guess I need to fly to Jackson soon." I drank the last swallow of my scotch and ordered another one. "My father is not gonna take this well; it's going to be ugly. My mother is going to go nuts! Of course, they'll blame me."

Because it was the murder of a United States Congressman's granddaughter, the wheels of justice moved in high gear. I'd immediately flown from Washington to Jackson and was there, trying my best to explain to my parents what was about to happen, when they knocked on the door with the search warrant.

I was sitting with my parents with the officer in charge when we heard a yell from the bedroom. "We found something." The officer walked into the room holding the blue macramé strap. "Mr. Jensen, is this your strap?"

My fathers eyes widened, shot a quick glance to my mother and then back to the officer. "Yes, that's mine."

He turned back to my mother, locking eyes. She raised her brows, lifted her hands exposing her palms and shrugged, answering his unasked question—I didn't put it there.

I might as well have been the officer that read my father his rights, snapped on the handcuffs and stuffed him into the patrol car from the look he gave me. When they drove away, I turned to see my mother standing in the doorway. She was frozen, standing very still, glaring at me.

Still staring into her eyes, I walked up to the front door. "Mom, I'm so sorry but I had no choice. I had to tell them."

She didn't' respond. She was trembling and I wanted to hug her, but before I could, she dropped her brow and with hard narrowing eyes staring directly into mine, she slammed the door in my face.

<hr />

THEY CHARGED my father with capital murder. Then he was informed that he was also a person of interest in six other murders. Capital murder with special circumstances allowed the district attorney to ask for the death penalty. During his arraignment, with his hands and feet shackled, dressed in an orange jumpsuit, he just stood shifting from one foot to the other as the judge read the charges. His court appointed lawyer entered a plea of Not Guilty. My father never said a word and never made eye contact with anyone other than the judge. I tried to get his attention as they led him out of the courtroom, but he turned away and ignored me. When the door closed behind him, I finally made eye contact with my mother, but she looked away and raced out of the courtroom.

I ran after her, but she quickened her pace. "Mother!" I yelled. "We have to talk about this."

She actually ran to the parking lot. I jumped behind the van as she cranked the engine, blocking her in. "We have to talk about this. Please don't do this. I want to help dad."

"GET OUT OF MY WAY, JOE! She screamed. "I DON'T WANT TO TALK TO YOU! I THINK YOU'VE HELPED YOUR DAD ENOUGH FOR ONE DAY! MOVE!"

I stepped back and let her leave. I had no idea what to do next, but I knew I couldn't just go home to Virginia with my father in jail. I went to the Jackson FBI field office to talk to John Kelly, but he wasn't there so I drove to the Holiday Inn downtown and rented a room for the night.

When I drove to the jail the next morning and tried to talk to my father, I was told that he didn't want to see me. So I drove to my parent's house, but again no luck. My mom wouldn't open the door. In fact, she didn't even acknowledge my knock at all, like I wasn't even there standing on her front porch ringing her doorbell. I knew she was inside, but there were no sounds of movement, nothing. After standing there ringing the doorbell for ten minutes, I gave up and drove to the Jackson FBI field office again.

John was on the phone, but waved me into his office when he saw me standing in the doorway. I sat in one of the oxblood leather chairs facing his desk. He was on the phone a few more minutes. When he finished, he said, "How's your father taking all of this?"

I shrugged. "I don't have any idea. He refused to see me this morning. The guard told me that he called me a few unrepeatable names along with 'HELL NO!' Same with my mom; she won't even answer the door."

"Want some coffee?"

"Yeah, I could use some."

John punched a few buttons on his phone and ordered us two cups then leaned back in his chair. "You up for some advice?"

"Fire away," I said.

"You need to find a new lawyer. I've had dealings with Jeffery Jacobs in the past and he's a complete bonehead—probably the most inept public defender in Mississippi. Run his ass off and quick!"

"That was my first impression when I met him, but the problem is, I'm not sure my parents have any money. I've got a little, but a good criminal attorney is gonna cost at least a hundred grand! I don't have that and I'm pretty sure my parents are close to broke."

John sipped his coffee and leaned forward in his chair. "Why don't *you* do it?"

I almost spilled my coffee. "John, I was an ADA, a prosecutor, not a criminal defense attorney. I was on the other side and that was a long time ago. I haven't tried a case in twenty years."

He put down his coffee and leaned back in his chair. "Joe, you're my friend, to be honest with you probably one of my best friends, and I don't want us to get sideways over this. You know you can't work your own father's case, not officially, not as an FBI special agent. But I know you, and I also know you can't just sit by and do nothing. As his attorney of record, you can work this. There's no conflict of interest there. I understand you were a damn good ADA. How hard would it really be to change to the defense side? Seems to me being an ex-ADA just might give you an advantage. I know you can do it, and honestly, you may be your father's only hope..."

He was right. I was the only lawyer my father could afford, and maybe his only hope from getting the needle. I didn't respond. I just sat there staring out the window at the Jackson skyline sipping my coffee.

When I finished my coffee, and stood up to leave, John picked up a green file off his desk and handed it to me. "Don't forget this," he said with a grin.

I took the folder. "What's this?"

He leaned back on his desk, and shook his head. "I have a no idea what you're talking about, Agent Jensen. Didn't you have that file with you when you walked in?"

When I made it back to my car, I cranked the engine, turned the AC on high, and opened the green file. It was a complete work up on Jeffery Jacobs, my father's court appointed attorney. It wasn't an official FBI work up, not a typical criminal investigation file. It was more like something a private investigator would come up with. I wondered how John got it, but after all he was the special agent in charge of the state of Mississippi for the FBI and had a long reach. After reading it there was no question in my mind what I had to do next.

To gain access to my father, I had to do a little bluffing with Jeffery Jacobs. When I told him what I wanted, he got a little indignant with me and told me if my father didn't want to see me, there was nothing he could do about it.

I let him rant for a few more minutes, then smiled, reached into my briefcase, and pulled out a file, making sure the FBI logo was in plain sight.

"Mr. Jacobs, do you know anything about me? What I do for a living?" I asked coyly. I had his full attention, but he didn't respond. "Mr. Jacobs, this is the first report of an investigation I had my team do on you." His face turned ash white. "Would you like for me to read what my team has dug up in only a few days?"

Of course, the file I was holding was empty, and I had no " team," but he didn't know that. The one thing I'd learned about people, especially during my time spent as an assistant district attorney was... everyone has something to hide.

He actually began to tremble and I knew I had him. "Look, Jeffery, I really don't care about you or what you've done. All I want is to see my father and talk to him. You can do that for me, and if you help me I can stop this investigation."

His eyes filled with tears and he whimpered like a guilty child. "I'm not a bad person... I just... I... I needed the money... I met this girl and..."

"Jeff," I interrupted, "I know you're not a bad guy. I already told you I don't give a shit about what you've done, just get me in to see my father and this will all go away."

He wiped his eyes. "All right I'll help you, but how can I get you in the jail if he doesn't want to see you?"

His reaction to my bluff made me wonder what the hell he'd actually done, but I didn't have time for that now. "Just make me your co-counsel, and before you ask, yes, I am an attorney."

At the jail, Jeffery signed me in, naming me as his co-counsel and I followed him into the inmate interview room. It was a dreary place the size of a one-car garage with a stainless-steel table in the middle, and three very uncomfortable metal chairs. The concrete block walls, ceiling, and floor were painted with an oppressive greenish gray.

Metal clinked as the guard brought my father into the room. He shuffled forward, eyes fixed on the ground, the bright orange jumpsuit making his skin seem pasty. His long gray hair hung in oily dirt clumps, half hiding the unkempt white beard. The minute he saw me he started screaming to have me thrown out.

Fortunately, Jeffery had assured me that he had a good relationship with the guards and when they came rushing in, he just waved them away. When the guards left, my father kept his weary eyes down, occasionally looking up shooting daggers at me, his dark eyes peeking through his greasy hair. When I tried to talk to him, he turned away.

I had assumed he would react that way, so I tried another tactic. I stood up, started pacing the room, and began interrogating Jeffery Jacobs about his legal practice.

"Jeffery, I understand that most of your practice is... what most folks refer to as an ambulance chaser?"

Jeffery jerked back in his chair at my attack. "I am a Personal Injury attorney, I don't chase ambulances."

I smiled. "Sorry, didn't mean to insult you. So... how many of your," I held up my hands and made air quotes, "*personal injury*" cases have actually made it to a full jury trial in the last five years?"

Jeffery cleared his throat, looked down and began shuffling the three stacks of papers in front of him. "I've been fortunate to settle those cases without a trial."

"So... zero." I said. "Ok... how many criminal cases have you handled in your entire career?"

His forehead was glistening with beads of sweat. Shifting in his chair he said. "Ten."

"How many of those made it to trial?" The answer was two.

I looked over at my father, but he just looked away. "All the rest were settled with a plea agreement?"

"Yes," he said dejectedly.

"Ok then... of the two that made it to trial, what were the results?"

He shifted in his chair again and ran a nervous hand through his thinning hair. "One got the death penalty and the other got life without parole."

I glanced at my father again, but this time he didn't turn away and locked eyes with me.

"One last question." I sat back down in the chair next to him. "In the last five years, how many cases have you won?"

"Zero." He looked at my father and tried to explain. "I'm not that experienced as a criminal attorney, although I take a few cases each year. Joe's right. My specialty is personal injury, but I have to take court appointed cases to keep my bar license with the state."

I stared at my father for what seemed like five minutes. Finally, he gave me the nod. Jeffery had my father sign a dismissal form and there it was—I was now my father's attorney.

After wishing my father and me good luck, Jeffery left. We just sat there in silence for a while. I wasn't really sure what to do or say next. When I started to say something, he held up his hand and stopped me.

"Hold on a second. Let me talk first." He rubbed his wrist where the shackles had left dark red marks as he gathered his thoughts. "I'm sorry for being such a dick. I know you didn't want this to happen, but when you told us how I became a suspect in all of this, and that it was you who started it... and then they came and arrested me... well, you know me and my damn temper. I've had some time to think and I know this is not really your fault. Joe... you're a good person... and I didn't have much to do with that. I sucked as a father, and I was never there for you."

I tried to respond, but again he held up his hand. "Let me finish. I know this may be hard to hear and probably sounds wrong to you, but... when your mother got pregnant with you, I was just a kid myself. It was a different time back in those days. I was young, and fit, and handsome... and there were so many girls and so little time." He laughed softly, and gave me a sheepish smile. "You know what I'm talking about... you've heard all our stories about those days. We never tried to hide that from you. So... I was just not really ready to settle down and grow up, I guess. And when you were born, I just wasn't emotionally equipped to be a father. I wasn't ready to stop partying yet, so I didn't. And I did my best to ignore you. I left the raising to your mother."

I don't think I'd ever seen my father cry before, but he had tears in his eyes. "I know I've done you wrong, Joe, and I guess if it hadn't been for that judge... well, I'm pretty sure you wouldn't have turned out this good. I don't know if I've ever told you this before, but I'm real proud of you and what you have become."

Now, *I was crying*. He was right, he had never told me that before.

He wiped his eyes with the sleeve of the orange jumpsuit, trying to get control of his emotions. "I wish there was some way I could make up for all of that, but it's too late now... I know I can't. Joe... I have no idea what you think of me, but I promise you one thing... I'm not a murderer. I didn't kill that girl. You've got to believe that. I don't care what they think they've got on me, but it ain't right. I did not do this!" He looked me directly in the eyes. "Please help me, son."

I couldn't answer him for a few minutes. My emotions were wrecked and very close to spilling out, but the little voice inside my head held them back. For my entire life, I'd wanted my father to open up to me. Every son wanted to hear that their father was proud of them. It had taken 44 years, but he finally told me. I wanted to grab him, to hug him, to believe him desperately, but the bridge between us that had been built over so many years was long, and the water was deep. Something was holding me back... and then it hit me, along with the memory in vivid detail. I was wrong, I had seen my father cry once before... when I was 13... at the trial. In a flash, I relived that day watching him standing before Judge Daily shaking, trembling, and crying real tears... But that time it was just an act. And although I desperately wanted to believe him now, I just couldn't. Were his words and tears real... or just another "stellar" performance? I needed more...

I called for the guards to see if we could get something to drink. When my father was distracted talking to a guard, I reached into my briefcase and carefully opened the small bottle of patchouli oil I had bought that morning. I poured a few drops into his drink and smeared some on my neck.

While sipping our waters, I explained to my father what to expect next and did my best to assure him that I believed him. When it was time to leave, I stood up, walked around the table and gave him a hug. He immediately began gagging and coughing.

"Is that fucking patchouli you're wearing," he yelled. "I hate that shit!" He started retching like he was about to throw up. His face turned red, and his breathing seemed to be labored. Then he began to vomit all over the floor. The guards jumped back trying to get out of the way. He eventually stopped, but was breathing hard trying to catch his breath. The room reeked with the smell of his vomit, but within minutes the guards had taken him away to clean him up and had two inmates in the room with buckets mopping the floor.

"You finished with him?" the guard asked. "Or do you want us to bring him back?"

"No," I said. "I have what I need. Tell him I'll be back in a few days."

It wasn't much and wouldn't hold up in a court of law, but it was all I needed. The "more" I was looking for. I was convinced... my father may have been a horrible dad, but he couldn't have committed these murders. He was innocent!

As I walked to my car, I was torn with conflicting emotions— happy to have proof of my father's innocence, glad Jeffery Jacobs was no longer his lawyer, and scared to death that I might not be equipped to do the job. Before I could drive away, my cell phone vibrated in my pocket. I pulled it out and saw that it was Elizabeth.

Oh no, must be bad news about the judge.

"SOMETHING ABOUT YOUR PAST."

I was opening the door of my car when I answered my cell, but stopped dead in my tracks and almost dropped the phone when I heard the voice. "Joe, I need to see you." It was Judge Daily. "There's something I have to tell you. It's something about your past. Please, Joe, it's very important. When can you come?" His voice was hoarse and weak.

Elizabeth took the phone. "Joe, sorry to shock you, but he's been asking for you and insisted on calling. He's conscious and alert, but very weak. I don't know what this is about, but Please hurry." I ran to my car, sped to my hotel, checked out, and caught the next plane to Little Rock.

It wasn't until I was halfway through my second scotch that the knot in my stomach began to untangle and the stiffness in my neck and shoulders relaxed a little. Had it only been ten days since this all started? The judge's heart attack, Elizabeth, my father's arrest? It was too much, too quick to process. As I sat there, sipping on my scotch, I stared out the plane's small window and tried to assimilate all the data.

Judge Daily's image flashed in my head and I could hear his voice. "There's something I have to tell you, about your past."

Something about my past? I thought. What part? I couldn't imagine what it could be—Lowell Whiteman—my parents —Dr. Heart?

It could be anything, because my "past" was... well, unusual to say the least. Sipping my scotch, I drifted back, recalling my life...

I WAS at Lowell Whiteman for four years. I had just turned fifteen when Elizabeth mysteriously disappeared and the results of that painful experience made me withdraw further into my shell and deeper into my books. I was without a doubt the geekiest kid on campus. So, I can't say that my years at Lowell Whiteman were easy— they were not. Along with my social awkwardness, I was way behind the other kids in my knowledge. Although, I had scored high on my aptitude tests, the reality of going to an actual school, studying multiple subjects for the first time in my life was difficult for me. My years in the library had helped me in English and history, but I was weak in math and science and had to study really hard to keep up.

The first year I barely maintained that B average that was required to keep my tuition paid. The next year, in the 10th grade it was a little easier. I slowly began to catch up and improve in my math and science.

In my third year, the year Elizabeth didn't return, my science and biology teacher, Mr. Henry announced to the class that he would be willing to stay after school and tutor any students interested in getting some extra help. I was the only student that showed up.

For the rest of the year, two days a week, Mr. Henry met with me and helped me with my science and math studies. By the time I finished the 11th grade, I was making all A's, and maintaining a B average was no longer a problem. The next year, I graduated in the top 5% of my senior class with a 96% average.

Although that was good, it wasn't good enough to earn me the scholastic scholarships I'd hoped and prayed for to attend college. But again Judge Daily and my three benefactors came to the rescue with an offer to pay my college tuition, room and board, and books at the University of Arkansas in Fayetteville as long as I worked 20 hours a week at a part time job. Judge Daily wanted me to learn the value of a dollar and having to work for the extra things like my clothes, going to a movie or buying a pizza should make me appreciate what it took to get them.

Once I was settled into my new dorm room and got my class schedules sorted out, I went on a hunt to find a job, which wasn't easy to find, but I got lucky and landed one working for a small bookstore, cleaning, stocking, and eventually selling books. It only paid minimum wage, but that covered what I needed, which wasn't much.

You would think that the transition from attending a tiny school with a graduating senior class of only 16, to attending a University with over twenty thousand students would have been overwhelming to me, but it wasn't. Actually, I loved the anonymity of it. At Whiteman, every student and every teacher knew me and knew everything about me. At the University of Arkansas, I was invisible. No one knew me or cared what I did or who I was. It fit me perfectly. I was lucky to get into one of the single dorms, so I didn't have to deal with a roommate.

For the four years I attended the University of Arkansas, I went to classes in the morning, hung out and studied in the library in the afternoon, worked at the bookstore Monday through Friday in the evening, and honestly not much else. I made a few good friends, dated a few times, but nothing serious. I have to say, I loved it. It was a great time in my life and it just seemed to fly by. Before I knew it, I was graduating.

Unfortunately, during the four years at Lowell Whiteman and the four at College, my estranged relationship with my parents had not improved much. It began to fall apart the first year I was at Lowell Whiteman. The original plan was for me to attend school nine months and spend the summer months traveling with them. That never really worked out. I did get to visit them a few weeks the first summer, but I had to return to Lowell Whiteman, because my parents had landed a 6-month contract in a rock bar, in Singapore of all places. When they got back to the states, they drove up to see me in Colorado for the few days they had off before their next gig in Chicago. I saw them for a week that Christmas, but they were back in Singapore when Spring Break came around and they were away all the next summer. That became the eventual pattern of our lives. I would see them a few days here and a few days there, but not much over the four years I was in Colorado.

I got a letter from my mother every single week for the entire four years. Actually, they weren't letters, they were post cards with pictures of the cities and towns they were playing in. They were short and sweet, and lacked any real details of what was going on in their lives. All I knew was that they seemed to be working a lot and getting by. My father never wrote me and talked very little when we were together in person. We just didn't seem to have anything to say to each other, so we didn't try.

When we did, it always seemed to turn bad with him still blaming me, after all those years, for being so stupid to bring the cops back to their van that day. Or he would start accusing me of thinking I was better than him or smarter than him, looking down my nose at both of them sitting up there in Colorado in my fancy prep school. This usually was the result of him getting too drunk, too high, or way too stoned.

When I told Judge Daily about my visits with my parents, he immediately arranged for me to have bi-weekly meetings with a child psychologist. He said it would keep me focused and help get me through the major changes in my life.

The psychologist's name was Dr. Heart and I really didn't want to go at first, but when I saw her the first time, I never missed a session again. She was beautiful, young, and just out of college, with short brown hair and long tanned legs. I was 14 with raging hormones and could not take my eyes off her legs during the session.

In our second session, I finally forced myself to lift my gaze from her amazing legs to her face and she just smiled back at me.

"You like my legs, Joe?" she asked.

I was embarrassed and instantly looked away.

"It's ok," she said. "It's nothing to be embarrassed about. And just so you know, I don't mind, in fact, I'm flattered."

I slowly turned my head back toward her. "Really?"

"Really." She smiled. "Joe, you are fourteen and turning into a man. It's very natural. So look all you want."

I tried not to grin, but I couldn't stop. "Cool!" I said a little too enthusiastically.

"Joe, if our sessions are going to be effective, it's very important that we have no secrets between us. I want you to feel comfortable telling me everything that's on your mind. If I'm going to help you, then I need to know about anything that is troubling you... even if it's about sex. Are you going to be ok with that?"

I'm not sure how I would have survived without Dr. Heart's guidance over the next three years. She had a way of cutting through the emotional walls I had constructed around me in my youth and helped me see things clearly. I even told her about Elizabeth, but even Dr. Heart couldn't figure that one out.

The tools she used to get me to open up and reveal my deepest secrets, I realize now were not the standard, accepted practices of most psychologists, but they really worked on me. Strange as it may sound, she used her legs. Depending on how difficult and deep the subject was, determined how high her skirt rose during the session. It might sound a bit perverted, but it worked and she got me to talk about things that needed to come to the surface.

She uncovered and helped me understand so many things I had buried deep down inside of me. With her help, I was able to leave all that negative baggage behind me and focus on the positive future that she kept assuring me I had ahead of me. She especially helped me accept and understand the truth about my mother and father.

Before my sessions with Dr. Heart, I truly believed that my mother was a victim of my father's rock star desires. She was a saint in my eyes and couldn't have possibly been a willing participant in all the drugs and sex parties I had witnessed. But when Dr. Heart forced me to open my eyes and talk about what I had actually seen so many times in the past, it became clear that she was no victim.

When we talked about my father's anger and hostility toward me, she showed me numerous case studies that mirrored our relationship. My father's anger toward me was just his way of disguising his true feelings of failure.

"It is not unusual for a parent to be jealous of their children's success," she told me. "You got the break he never received. Your future is bright, his is not."

Knowing this about my parents gave me an entirely new window to look at them through. I had much more understanding and empathy for them and the lives they led.

My father's anger reached its pinnacle when I was in the 11th grade. It was the first test of my new empathy and understanding of him—a test I failed miserably.

My parents had shown up unexpectedly a week before my Christmas break. My father, stoned as usual, made a complete ass out of himself in front of all the students and teachers when he demanded that I drop everything, and skip my mid semester finals so I could play guitar with them in a gig they had landed in Denver. Apparently, Mooch had a family emergency and couldn't do the gig. They were broke as usual, and my father kept yelling at the top of his lungs that he was going to lose the gig and the money they needed desperately if they didn't show up with a full band.

I was only 16 years old at the time, but I was an inch taller than him and outweighed him by 15 pounds. We were standing nose to nose when I asked him what had happened to all the money he'd supposedly made from the Singapore gig they'd just finished.

"What did you do with all the money, Dad," I asked him, looking directly into his eyes. "Did you snort it all up your nose?"

He exploded and actually took a swing at me. He had no idea that I had been taking boxing classes in the gym for the past two years. I ducked his punch and instinctively landed a right cross on his exposed and very surprised chin. He dropped like a sack of rocks, out cold.

My mother screamed, but I could barely hear her through the applause and cheers from my classmates. They loved it, but my teachers, the principal, and the security guards did not.

Security quickly cleared the lobby and after a few minutes my father began to come to. My mother helped him to his feet and began trying to walk him out of the building on his still unsteady legs. When they reached the door, he stopped, turned around, and glared at me. "I guess you think you're a big man now."

I was sick to my stomach, ashamed of what I'd done. I was trying my best to still the quiver in my voice. "No sir, I don't."

He rubbed his chin and *smiled*. "Well, you sure throw a punch like one."

The next letter I received was from my father. It was short, and the only letter I've ever received from him. It simply said, *I was wrong. You were right. You make me proud.*

My mother continued to send me her weekly post cards, but they were different somehow, shorter and colder, more to the point.

Not surprising to me, they couldn't make my graduation from Lowell Whiteman. This time they were performing in a bar in Alaska.

I was hoping that moving from Colorado to the University of Arkansas would get me closer to my parents and allow us to repair some of the damage we had done to each other over the years, but that proved to be wishful thinking.

Actually, I saw less of them. I would get a call once every few months or so, but I rarely saw them over the four years. I didn't blame them. It was as much my fault as theirs. I had much more freedom in college and could have easily tried to contact them more often. I could have found more time to spend with them on the road, but I didn't.

I only heard from them once or twice a year and when I graduated from the University of Arkansas, again they didn't make it to the ceremony. The only familiar face I saw in the crowd was Judge Daily. He actually stood, cheered, and whistled when I walked across the stage to receive my diploma.

I was hurt and disappointed that my parents didn't consider my graduation from college important enough to make some kind of special arrangements to be there. Their nonchalance about missing it was crushing and demoralizing. I had worked so hard to get there, but they either didn't understand or they didn't care, and I wasn't sure which one it was.

THE MONEY

"Another scotch?" The voice came from a flight attendant hovering over me in the aisle. I had been so lost in thought I hadn't seen her walk up. I glanced at my watch. We'd be landing soon. I knew that whatever the judge had to tell me was important, so I shook my head no. "I think I've had enough. How about a cup of black coffee." I said. A few minutes later, trying to kill my buzz sipping my coffee, I drifted back to thoughts of my past... What was so important to the judge? Was it law school? Something about the money?

WHEN I WAS 20-YEARS OLD, I had my first college degree in my hand, but was not sure how to answer the question repeating over and over in my head... now what? I had played it safe in college and gone with my strengths, majoring in English with a minor in History. I had graduated with a 4.0 G.P.A., so I knew getting into a graduate school wouldn't be a problem, but what graduate school and what subject? I was even considering skipping graduate school altogether, enrolling in the police academy and finally becoming that cop I'd always wanted to be. I was pretty sure the reason Judge Daily had insisted on taking me to dinner after the ceremony was to discuss this and to once again try to convince me to go to law school.

He took me to one of those five-star restaurants that were obviously out of my price range. I must admit, it was the best steak I'd ever eaten. After dinner, we moved to a cigar bar where the judge ordered a cognac and fired up a long, fat cigar. He offered me one, but I refused. I had refrained from smoking for 20 years and planned on continuing that practice. I was still not of legal drinking age, but the judge ordered me a glass of wine anyway.

I sipped my wine, trying to gather my thoughts. Finally, I spoke up. "You know, judge... you're a great man, but a terrible liar."

The judge wrinkled his brow. "What are you talking about? I've never lied to you."

I took a sip of my wine and smiled. "Oh yeah? So after all these years, you're going to sit there looking me in the eyes and continue telling me that I have three mysterious benefactors that have paid for all this education? Really?"

The judge stared off into the distance and took a long draw of his cigar. "How long have you known?"

"I have suspected it was you all along, but didn't really know for sure until now. What I don't get is why? Why didn't you just tell me it was you eight years ago? Why the mysterious benefactor's story?"

His eyes sparkled with his grin. "I was wondering how long it was going to take you to figure this out. And to answer your question... let's just say it was less complicated that way. It's a lot easier for people, like your parents and Child Services, to accept the idea of three mysterious benefactors than explaining why, and more importantly, how I was paying for it myself."

I looked over the table at him. "I've done some research on you, and you don't appear to be a wealthy man. I can imagine explaining where all this money came from just might be a little hard to do. Some folks might even think that you're on the take, but I know without a doubt, that's not possible. Not Judge Royce Daily."

He roared, his belly shaking. "Ha, no... don't worry, I'm not on the take. Ha." He continued to chuckle as he drew on his cigar.

His laughing made me smile back. "I was never worried about that. I would like to know where the money came from, but honestly, my biggest question is, why? Why just me? They took us all away to foster care, all five of us, but you only helped me. Did you meet the other kids in your chambers like you did me?"

He nodded. "Yes, I did. I spent over an hour with the ones old enough."

I held out my hands. "They were in the same situation as me; traveling like Gypsies, living out of beat up vans, not going to school... They were just like me."

"That's where you're wrong, Joe. They were nothing like you. I know it may be hard for you to understand, but you were... very special. Smart as a whip, wise way beyond your age. But the biggest difference was your drive to get an education. Joe, you were walking miles to public libraries every day because you knew it was the only way you had to learn. That's remarkable! Joe, you were remarkable! The other kids were, well to be kind... simply not."

"I understand. I knew them well and that's what I've always assumed, but that doesn't take away the guilty feeling I had, and still have, about leaving them behind."

"You should not feel guilty about that. You can't honestly believe any one of those kids would have survived what you've lived through. Do you really think they had the desire and drive you had? That they would have worked this hard to get where you are? Come on, Joe, really? You can only help someone who wants to be helped."

"Ok, you're right, but there had to be a lot of kids that came through your court who did want to be helped. Why not one of them? Why did you pick me over all of those other kids?"

The judge tapped his cigar against the large black ashtray, knocking off the smoking gray ash. "Because I thought you deserved it, and you've proven me right."

I sat quietly for a moment, thinking about what he'd said. "Please don't take this wrong. There's no way I could ever accurately explain how much I appreciate what you've done for me. You've changed my life and put me on a path I would have never even considered taking. I know you want me to go to law school, but I just can't do it. You've done too much for me and I can't take another penny from you. And I promise you, somehow, someday I will pay you back every cent you've spent so far."

Judge Daily raised his eyebrows and set his snifter of cognac on the table. Then he leaned forward. "Wait. Back up, Joe. You don't owe me a cent. This was not a student loan. It was a gift and you've earned every penny. I don't want to hear another word about you paying me anything back!"

He lifted the snifter, took a slow sip, and leaned back. "And what makes you so sure you are the only one. Did you ever consider that maybe I helped some of those other kids as well?"

"Come on!" I said. "I know how much money a judge makes. Maybe a hundred grand a year and I'm costing you thirty... How many more kids could you possibly help?"

He grinned, took a long draw from his cigar, and blew it out slowly. "As of today, you made twenty-two."

I almost dropped my wine. "What? Really, you've helped twenty-two kids graduate from college? But how?"

Judge Daily set his cigar in the ashtray. "Actually, twenty-one. Number twenty-two is my granddaughter. She graduated from Cornell last week."

I opened my mouth, but couldn't seem to find any words.

"Believe it or not," the judge said, "this subject was on the agenda for tonight. I'd always planned on telling you, but I wanted to wait until you were old enough to comprehend it. However, I need you to give me your word that you'll never reveal to anyone, and I mean anyone, what we're going to talk about here tonight. You give me your word?"

I nodded. "Of course. You have my word, I promise."

The judge leaned forward, resting his elbows on the table. He sat silent for a moment gathering his thoughts, then he began. "Have you ever heard of Antonio Deluca?"

I thought for a moment. "The mafia guy? Yeah, I've heard of him."

"What do you know about him?" he asked.

"Not that much. In one of my classes we covered the rise and fall of the mafia in the United States. If I remember correctly, he was a crime boss in Boston and was killed in some kind of an accident, an explosion. Right?"

His face grew somber. "Yes, that's what most people think, even though it was called an accident. That was in 1949. He was my uncle."

I wasn't expecting that. "Antonio DeLuca was your uncle?"

"Yes, he was." The judge took a sip of water and cleared his throat. "I was born in Sicily in 1930. My father's name was Giovanni Deluca. He was Antonio's younger brother. When I was ten years old, Antonio sent for us, so we packed up and moved to Boston to be near him. By that time, Antonio had become a major player in the mafia and would soon be selected as head of the Boston family.

"My uncle didn't want my father to follow in his footsteps. He wanted him to go to school and become a doctor or a lawyer... anything but a mobster, but the money, the cars, and all the allure was something my father could not resist. So, against my uncle's wishes, he allowed him to become part of the family. My uncle did the best he could to keep my father small time, so he would never be arrested or in any real danger. And for a while everything went well.

"We lived in a beautiful apartment that overlooked the Boston skyline. We were very happy there. My father and I used to love to go to the movies. It was our thing and how we spent our time together. He was a real movie buff and was always quoting lines from famous movies. It would drive my mother crazy when he would do his impression of movie stars, but I thought it was great. In one of the movies we saw together, there was a house that had a unique hidden room. It was built behind a bookshelf and was an important part of the movie plot.

It was where the hero hid from the villain. For whatever reason, my father loved the idea of that secret room and had one built behind our fireplace. It was completely concealed behind a folding bookshelf. Unless you knew it was there, you'd never find it. I loved it and soon it became my playhouse. When my parents would have guests over for dinner or a party, I would sneak into the room and listen. Although it was totally hidden, it was not sound proof and I could hear every word being said in the living and dining room.

"I was thirteen when my uncle, Antonio, was selected to head up the Boston Family. It was not a popular decision among the other crime bosses, but he was chosen by 'The Commission' in New York, a new organization masterminded by Lucky Luciano himself, so even if they didn't like it, no one who wanted to live would question it. However, one crime boss just couldn't accept it. He ignored the Commission's warnings and decided to send a private message to my uncle.

I was in the secret room when I heard the crashing sounds of someone kicking in our front door. Then I heard gunshots, my mother scream, and two more gunshots. They killed my mother and father and would have killed me if they could have found me. I could hear them searching for me through the walls. They knew I was supposed to be there and were angry that they couldn't find me. I was terrified.

"I stayed in that room for twenty-four hours. I was afraid to come out, even when the cops came and took my parents' bodies away. I was scared to death, but somehow made my way across town to Uncle Antonio's house. When one of his men took me inside, he grabbed me into his arms, squeezed me tight, and cried and cried. That night, I was put into the trunk of a car and driven out of the city. From there I was put into another car and taken to New York. Two days later I was given a new name and new background identity and flown to the Thatcher School in Ojai, California."

I was mesmerized with his story, listening carefully and sipping my wine. Judge Daily stopped talking for a moment, picked up his cognac, and took a small sip. Then he lifted his glass to me. "You see, Joe, we have something in common. I too attended a boarding school... at about the same age."

I wasn't sure if the judge wanted me to respond or just sit there quietly listening, but I spoke up anyway. "So they hid you away from your parents' killers."

"Yes," the judge said. "I guess you could say it was the mafia's version of witness protection."

"Did they find out who killed your parents?"

"Yes, it was pretty obvious who had ordered the hit and that was dealt with swiftly and, as you can imagine, brutally."

"So, your uncle had him killed?" I asked.

"No, actually he didn't have to. This was 1943 and it was a violent time in our country. It was the beginning of what became known as 'Organized Crime.' The Commission that Luciano had put together ten years earlier was made up of one representative from each of the five major crime families in New York City. The Commission took it upon themselves to control every aspect of mafia activity in the United States. It was their decision which family would be in charge of what city and what area of crime they could be involved in. Gambling, bootlegging, prostitution, whatever... it was their decision, and that decision was not to be questioned or disputed. The mob boss that ordered the hit on my family became a violent and brutal example of their power.

"In one afternoon, that boss, all of his henchmen, his entire family, including his wife, children, and his parents, were murdered."

"Wow!" It was a lot to take in. I sat there thinking about what he'd said. "So, then you could come out of hiding, right?"

Judge Daily shook his head, "No. My uncle kept me under wraps and hidden away. No one, including his wife, knew my new identity or where I was."

I looked at him lifting my eyebrows. "If everybody was dead, what was he worried about?"

Judge Daily flipped his lighter and re-lit his cigar. He took in a long draw and blew it out slowly. "I don't really know why he did that, but I suspect it was his way of making sure I had no connection to him and never got involved with the family business. I never saw him or even talked to him again before he died. He was on vacation with my aunt and two cousins. They had chartered a yacht and were anchored off a small island in the Bahamas when it mysteriously exploded. They all died instantly. The authorities claimed that it was a simple gas leak, an accident. But I think it was pretty obvious what went down."

I didn't know how to respond, so I just looked at him. "I'm sorry."

He responded with a small head-shake and then sat there quietly for a long time sipping on his cognac and puffing on his cigar. Finally, he took a deep breath and continued his story. "I was a freshman in college when that happened and believe it or not, I was right here in Fayetteville attending the University of Arkansas. Why I was here in Arkansas was again an unanswered question to me. It was just where I was told to go by the counselors when I graduated from the Thatcher school in California. They handed me a package that contained a plane ticket to Fayetteville, my college enrollment papers, and a checkbook with a hefty balance.

"There was no letter of explanation, but I knew what to do. I just assumed that attending college in Arkansas was my uncle's way of keeping my identity a secret. Arkansas of all places would be the last place his enemies would look. I wasn't sure about it at first, but as it turned out, I loved it here. I met my wife here, went to law school here, raised my family here, and never left."

"That is quite a story, judge." I shook my head. "I don't... I don't really know what to say or how to respond. I'm sort of blown away. But I do think it's obvious that, although your uncle was..." I paused searching for the right word, "...a mobster, he really loved you and would be very proud of all you have accomplished."

Tears welled up in his eyes. "Thank you for saying that." He pulled out his handkerchief and wiped his face. "I've had many years to think about my uncle. I know he was not a good man. He was a murderer, a thief and a lot of other things I try not to think about, but I honestly believe he did what he did with great remorse. He hated who he was, and what he did. And I believe he knew how it would all end for him. That's why he didn't want his little brother, my father, following in his footsteps and when he couldn't prevent that, it's why he did everything in his power to assure that I had a different path to go down for my life. I thank God every day for what he did for me."

We sat in silence, me sipping my wine and the judge puffing on his cigar. "After you graduated law school and before you became a judge, you must have had a very successful law practice to earn enough money to do all of the great things you've done." I asked.

He smiled. "No, not really. After law school, I was an intern at the Little Rock District Attorney's office for two years. After I passed the bar exam, I went to work as a prosecutor and served as an assistant D.A. until a seat on the bench opened up and I was encouraged by the governor, the district attorney, and a few other judges to enter the race. I won the election and have been here ever since. So no, I've never really made much money as a lawyer."

I held up my hands and shook my head. "Then where did all the money come from?"

"About a week after my uncle died, I received a visit from a very strange little man I'd never seen before. 'Are you Royce Daily?' he asked.

"I wasn't sure if I should answer or run for my life, but before I could stop myself I said yes.

"He told me that he was an attorney and said, 'I received an anonymous letter this morning with a very generous fee I might add, and was instructed to deliver this to you.' He handed me a sealed, large brown envelope. I signed my name acknowledging I'd received it and he turned and walked away. I never saw him again.

"I hurried back to my dorm room and ripped open the brown envelope. Inside was a handwritten note that I assumed was from my uncle. It was not signed. It contained a Bible verse and three numbered Swiss bank accounts. The verse said, *Dearly beloved, avenge not yourselves, but rather give place unto wrath: for it is written, Vengeance is mine; I will repay, saith the Lord. Romans 12:19.*

"Underneath the three Swiss bank account numbers, he had written... *Do something good with this...* It took me a while to figure out how to check on the bank accounts and when I did, I was stunned... there was over thirty million dollars in the accounts. Suddenly I was very,

very rich, but I knew where that money came from. It was dirty money, blood money, and I didn't want anything to do with it. Truthfully, I was afraid it could be a link that could connect me to my uncle. So, I just let it sit earning interest for the next three years until I graduated college, trying my best not to think about it.

"My uncle had seen to it that the tuition had been prepaid for my four years at the University of Arkansas and I had been very frugal with the money that had somehow mysteriously been deposited into my checking account every month. I had more than enough to get by and graduate.

"But law school was a different story. I didn't have enough; even working a part-time job it was not going to be enough. It took almost every cent I had in the bank to pay the first year's tuition. I knew before that first year was over, as much as I hated the thought of it, I'd have to use some of the dirty money to make it. But by that time I was hooked, and no matter what it took, I was staying in law school."

"Joe, there's no way to explain to you how much I loved law school. It was difficult, challenging, and the workload was impossible, but I thrived on it. I loved every minute of every day I was there.

"I guess my enthusiasm was obvious because I soon became a favorite of one of my law professors. His name was Abraham Fischer. He took an instant liking to me and soon became my mentor who I went to with any problems, and trust me, there were a lot of them.

"Abraham knew the law better than anyone I've ever known. He was in his 70's, but he was like a walking law library. Not once did he not have an instant case study to refer to when I came to him with a hard legal question."

Judge Daily motioned for the waitress and ordered another cognac for him and another wine for me. We'd been sitting for over an hour. My legs were falling asleep. I needed to stand and walk to stop the dull pain in my back and get the blood flowing through my numb ass, but before I could, the judge started talking again. I had no idea where he was going with this story, but it appeared to be important for him to talk about it, so I just stretched out my legs under the table and readjusted my sitting position.

"Abraham was also a sports nut," he began again, "and loved to talk about football, baseball, and especially basketball. God that man loved basketball. We used to meet at this little coffee shop and talk for hours. He was the only person I trusted enough to talk to about my background and I eventually told him everything.

"As well as my law mentor, he soon became sort of like my surrogate grandfather. We were that close. So, when the money ran out, I went to him and told him the last secret of my life. I told him about the money. I had no choice at that point and needed to use some of it for law school. I also let him read the letter."

Judge Daily looked at me with a big grin. "I'll never forget the look on his face when I told him how much money was in those accounts. 'Thirty-four million dollars? You have thirty-four million dollars?' He almost fainted." The judge burst into laughter. "But after he regained his composure, you know what he said to me?"

"No sir, I have no idea."

"He said something very profound. Something that changed everything and gave me the solution I was searching for."

"What did he say?"

"He said, 'Royce, there are some things in our lives we can control and some things we cannot. Who our parents and relatives are is one of those things we have no control over. It is not our choice if they are rich or poor, good or bad. All we can do is either follow in their footsteps, or blaze a new path for ourselves. And although we may not want it, sometimes we need some help from our relatives, be they good or bad, to be able to keep going down that new unknown path we have chosen to follow. Royce, I think you need to use this money to help you stay on that path and maybe, just maybe, find someone else to help as well, someone like you whose parents or relatives have taken the wrong path. Now wouldn't that be 'doing something good'?

"With Abraham's help, I transferred all the money from the Swiss bank accounts into a non-profit entity that he set up. It was in the form of a public trust with the specific purpose of funding education costs to whomever I deemed worthy. That also included my education. That was forty-five years ago. Since then, I've helped lots of kids find their own path. Does that sound familiar, Joe?"

I nodded and smiled. "Yes sir, it does. So, that's what the U. A. D. E. Trust is. I've seen that name several times over the years on my transcripts."

"Any ideas what U. A. D. E. stands for?" He grinned at me with a mischievous look in his eyes, taking a long pull on his cigar.

I shook my head. "No sir, I have no idea."

"It stands for the Uncle Antonio DeLuca Educational Trust."

I had been so mesmerized listening to the judge's story, I hadn't realized how much time had passed. I glanced at my watch; we had been sitting there for almost three hours. Looking up, I noticed that the bartender and waiter were glaring at us. Apparently, it was past closing time and they were waiting for us to leave, so the judge paid the check and we headed out.

When we stepped outside the cool, crisp evening air hit us in the face. The dark threatening clouds that were looming earlier had moved on, leaving a crystal-clear sky sparkling with stars.

A green cab pulled to the front door of the restaurant and stopped in front of us. Judge Daily looked at me. "I feel like walking, how about you?"

"That sounds like a great idea. I need to stretch my legs. The campus is only a few blocks away."

As we slowly made our way along the five blocks back to the campus, Judge Daily stopped occasionally and pointed out a landmark or reminisced about the ones that had closed since his days at the university. He waited until the campus was in view before he finally brought up the subject I'd been expecting all night.

"Joe, do you remember much about that first day when we met? What were you, twelve or thirteen?"

"Yes, I remember it well. I was thirteen and scared to death.

The judge chuckled, "Yeah I remember you were shaking like a leaf, but you calmed down once I got a few M&M's in you."

"Are you still hiding candy in your top desk drawer?"

"Of course, but don't tell my wife." We both laughed at that.

The judge took a seat on one of the wooden benches that encircled the rose garden at the entrance of the university. "Take a seat," he said, "there's something else I would like to talk to you about."

"Finally," I thought to myself. "Here it comes."

The judge hesitated a moment, then asked, "Do you remember what you told me that day in my chambers when I asked you what you wanted to be when you grew up?"

"Yes sir, I told you I wanted to be a cop."

He nodded. "That's right. Do you still want to be a cop?"

"Yes, sir. I can't really explain it, but I know that's what I'm supposed to be. Deep down somewhere inside of me I've always known that being some kind of a cop was my destiny."

Judge Daily just sat there silently. I knew him well by now and I could tell his mind was whirling. There was no doubt that he was concocting some kind of plan. "Through all these years, have I ever asked you for anything in return for my help?"

"No, sir. You've never asked for anything."

"Well then, I think it's time that I do. First, let me be clear. If you want to be a cop, I will not stand in your way, in fact I want to help you, but if you're going to be a cop, then at least be the kind of cop that will take advantage of your education and your amazing intellect." He looked over at me. "Do you know why I told you every year exactly what your education cost?"

I thought about his question for a moment. "Actually, I thought it was to keep a tally of it so I could pay you back some day, but after what you told me tonight, I'm not sure."

The judge shook his head. "No, it was never about paying me back. I wanted you to know the value of your education, to realize that it was very expensive so it would give you inspiration to work hard and not waste one cent of it. And, I wanted you to know that there were people out there that believed in you enough to pay for it, at any cost. Joe, you did not disappoint me. Look what you've accomplished and you're only twenty years old.

"If you seriously want to repay me, then please do this one thing for me... go to law school. Even if you have no interest in practicing law, do it for me. You'll only be twenty-three when you finish; lots of time left to be a cop.

"I know it's really none of my business, but I believe that I've earned the right to express my opinion. I just can't imagine someone with your drive and intellect being satisfied working as a simple beat cop or even a detective with a gold shield. But if that's really what you want, I promise I'll do everything in my power to help you, if you'll just do this one favor for me and go to law school."

What could I say? "Judge, after all you've done for me... Sir, I would walk through fire if you asked me to. Of course I'll do it. I'd do anything for you."

Judge Daily grabbed me and gave me a hug. "Joe, I promise you will never regret it. In fact, I have one last suggestion." He grinned. "I promise I'll shut up after this. Have you ever considered the FBI? With a degree in law, and your intelligence, they would snap you up in a heartbeat. FBI, that's sort of a cop, right?"

He had surprised me with that. The FBI was something I'd never considered. But he was right... That was definitely a cop!

As my tribute to Judge Daily, I applied to the University of Arkansas School of Law, his old alma mater. You'd think he would have jumped up and down at the idea, but that was not his initial reaction. He did tell me that he was pleased at my decision to go to law school, but I knew deep down he was disappointed that I had not applied to Yale or Harvard. The judge had dropped those hints to me more than once, but it just made no sense to me. Practicing law was not going to be my final career choice and even if I could have gotten in to Yale or Harvard, which was questionable, the cost of a law degree from either one of those ivy-league schools was astronomical. It would have been a total waste of money. For my purposes, The University of Arkansas School of Law would do just fine.

My three years of law school were much different than Judge Daily's. I *did not* love every minute of every day I was there. He did not lie about the difficulty and enormous, almost impossible workload.

The first year was the hardest, having to study so many different fields of law required by the core curriculum—contracts, torts, constitutional law, criminal procedure, property law, civil procedure, legal writing, on and on. There were so many and so much reading! I didn't get a full nights sleep for that entire first year; just small catnaps between my reading sessions and my classes. It was a constant daily fight for me not to fall asleep, especially in classes studying areas of law that held absolutely no interest for me.

When I complained to Judge Daily, he just laughed and told me that he remembered how hard it was, but reminded me that I was learning the basic fundamentals of law, laying the necessary groundwork.

"Joe, these are the hardest courses you'll have to take in law school," he told me. "but they are critical. I can't stress enough how important it is for you to absorb as much as you possibly can in this first year because everything else will flow from this knowledge base. Everything!"

Somehow, I lived through the first year and discovered that Judge Daily was right. The second year, although still difficult, was at least manageable. I actually had enough time to sleep and get all my reading in. I finally found my footing in my third year, when I began to concentrate my studies in the areas of law that I was truly inter-ested in. I loved criminal law. I especially liked studying and researching murder cases, specifically, serial murders. It became evident very quickly that this was my thing. There was little doubt to me, or my professors, that criminal law would become my area of expertise.

After I graduated from law school, I took Judge Daily's advice once again. While I studied for the bar exam in the evenings, I spent my days working as an intern in the Little Rock District Attorney's office. After I passed the bar, I became a prosecutor and then worked as an assistant district attorney for two years.

I filled out and handed in my application to the FBI on my 27th birthday. Three months later, I was sent to the FBI training Center in Quantico, Virginia. Ironically, my first field assignment was Denver, Colorado. Exactly 14 years after Judge Daily had put me on that first plane. I had come a long way, baby!

I was assigned to the CID (Criminal Investigation Division.) It's the largest division in the FBI. In Denver, there were 24 special agents in this division, broken into 4 groups. Each group specialized and investigated different areas of criminal activity. My group was assigned to investigate the growing violent gang activity in Colorado. We also investigated organized crime, as well as white-collar crime.

When I told Judge Daily about my new assignment, he burst into laughter, which confused me at first.

"Don't you see the irony, Joe?"

I had to think about it for a moment and then it finally hit me. It was now my job to investigate and prevent organized crime. Organized crime money had paid for the education it took for me to get the job.

"Got it!" I said laughing. "I bet Uncle Antonio is turning over in his grave."

"No, I don't think so," he said. "Remember what he wrote in his letter to me? 'Do something good with it.' I think I did."

When I got settled in Denver, the first weekend I had off, I drove over to Steamboat Springs to visit some of my old teachers at Lowell Whiteman. I also gave Dr. Heart a call and took her to dinner.

Although I had kept in contact with her, it had been over 10 years since I'd seen her. She hadn't aged a day. She was 37, single, and as beautiful as ever. When she took off her coat in the restaurant, she gave me a big smile. "I wore this just for you." It was the shortest mini skirt I'd ever seen, exposing the objects of my childhood fantasies— those amazing legs.

After dinner and a few drinks, she took me back to her house and finally my childhood fantasies were fulfilled. That night, I did a whole lot more than just look at those legs.

THE SUDDEN DROP and whine of the engines adding power, shook me back to reality and out of my memories. The seatbelt pulled tight against my waist, as a plane dropped and twisted from the turbulence.

I caught my sliding cup of coffee the last second before it fell off the tray-table. The familiar fasten your seatbelt chime echoed through the plane and the light was illuminated. The guy sitting next to me gripped the arms of his seat and closed his eyes. Turbulence on an airplane never has scared me, so I just took another sip from my cold coffee, leaned back and tried to relax. I didn't like it, but it always seemed to happen and was all part of flying that you had to get used to.

Eventually the turbulence stopped and once again everything was calm. Sipping my coffee, I decided to stop trying to figure out what part of *"my past"* Judge Daily wanted to talk to me about. Too many twists and turns to know. I would know soon enough. How important could it actually be? What impact could it really have on my crazy life? According to the judge everything was pre-planned anyway.

"Joe, your life is not in your hands," he had preached for years, "it's in God's. It's predestined before you're born. All a man can do is pray for the wisdom to recognize the path he's planned for you to go down, so you don't wind up going down the wrong one." It was the one thing I'd always questioned and scoffed at. Had I gone down one of those wrong paths?

The view from a window seat in an airplane at thirty thousand feet had always thrilled me. The white fluffy clouds against the clear blue sky were truly a majestic sight. It always made me feel small in the grand scope of things. It had been a while since I'd prayed and talked to God... If ever there was a time, it was now.

"God, is this really your plan? You wanted me to live through that kind of a crazy childhood and everything else I've fought my way through... just to get to here? Is this why Judge Daily insisted I become a lawyer when all I really wanted to be was a cop? Did you really plan all of this, so one day I could save my father? Really?"

I lifted my cup of coffee and held it up to the window. "Well, here's to you, God. If this is your plan, I have to tell you... you've got one hell of a sense of humor!"

THE LETTERS

W hen I landed in Little Rock, I called Elizabeth and told her I had arrived, and then rushed to the rental car desk and rented the only car they had left, which was a big silver monster; one of those giant SUV's. Although it was full of gas, I pulled into the first gas station I could find so I could get directions to the Arkansas Heart Hospital. Apparently, the small hospital in Jacksonville wasn't equipped to take care of the judge and Elizabeth had had him transferred there a few days earlier.

The traffic was backed up and it took me almost thirty minutes to get there, but when I walked into the lobby, Elizabeth was there waiting. When she saw me, she ran toward me and threw herself into my arms. We hugged for a long time.

"He's dying, Joe," she whispered tearfully in my ear. "His doctor said it won't be long; a few days, maybe a week." Her lips parted again trying to talk, but she was crying too hard to form the words. She stopped trying, wailing in my ear as I held her in my arms.

She released her grip on me and stepped back, sucking back her tears, wiping her cheeks with her sleeve. A beautiful woman standing next to her handed Elizabeth a Kleenex and she wiped her swollen, red eyes.

"You must be, Joe," she said holding out her hand. "I'm River. Nice to finally meet you. I've heard a lot about you from Elizabeth and the judge."

She had a surprisingly firm handshake and an amazing smile. I tried my best not to be obvious checking her out, but it was difficult not to stare. She was stunning, tall, with long auburn hair.

"I'm sorry," Elizabeth said, "where are my manners? River works with me. She's a private investigator."

"Nice to meet you, River." I forced myself to look into her eyes and not stare at her body.

I followed them down the long hall of the ICU to the judge's room. Although, I was trying my best, it was impossible not to notice River's firm ass dancing with every step she made. When we stopped at the closed door of the judge's room, I looked up. River was smiling at me with a twinkle in her eye. Apparently, I hadn't been as discreet with my glances as I thought I had.

The judge sat in a large, brown leather recliner, but he was sound asleep. Elizabeth gently nudged his shoulder to wake him. "Grandpa, wake up. Joe's here."

He slowly lifted his head and when he saw me standing in the doorway his face lit up. "Joe... I'm so glad you're here." I walked to him and shook his hand. Then the judge looked past me and saw River.

"Do you remember me?" she asked, walking up to him and taking his hand.

He chuckled, his eyes dancing watching her walk toward him. "River, any man who doesn't remember you needs to be taken out to the woods and shot!"

River leaned down and kissed him on the cheek. "You've always been such a dirty old man."

The judge grinned and gave her a wink. "Yes I am, and hope to be 'til the day I die."

We all laughed, trying not to think about that day coming soon.

"River, I'm so glad you came to see me, but I need to talk privately with Joe and Elizabeth about something. Would you mind coming back later? I need to talk to you too."

"Anything for you, judge," she said. "I'll drop back by in a few hours."

When she left the room, Judge Daily asked us to pull up chairs next to him. When we were close, he held out his hands and we both took one. He looked back and forth at each of us for a few minutes without saying anything. Then he cleared his throat. "I've wanted to tell you two something for years, but I just didn't have the courage, but they tell me I don't have much longer and I have to tell you what I've done and why I did what I did to you."

"What are you talking about?" Elizabeth asked.

"Please honey, let me say this. I did it because I just wasn't sure about Joe and how he was going to turn out. He was so young and had been exposed to so much... I just wasn't sure..."

I thought I knew what he was going to say. It was the only thing that made any sense, but I didn't want to interrupt him, so I remained silent.

Elizabeth's eyes darted toward me. "What are you trying to say, Grandpa?"

"Your letters. I hid the letters that you wrote to Joe. I never mailed them."

"What about my letters?" I said, finally breaking my silence.

"Do you remember Mr. Henry at Lowell Whiteman? The professor that gave you all that extra time?" he asked.

"Of course, without him I would've never caught up to the rest of the class."

His lips curled and smiled. "George Henry came into my court-room when he was only twelve years old. He's one of my success stories. I helped him, just like you, to get into Lowell Whiteman and when he graduated from college, all he wanted was to go back there and see if he could help other kids like him—like you, Joe. That's why he was so willing to stay after classes and help you."

His hand felt cool to my touch. I squeezed it gently and smiled back. "And he did. He made a huge impact on my life. But how does he figure into my letters?"

"He was also in charge of all the mail that went into and out of

Lowell Whiteman. He took all your letters and sent them to me." The judge pointed toward a cardboard box on the floor next to his bed. "They're all in that box—every one of them. I wanted you to have them back before I die."

Elizabeth looked at me with tears welling up in her eyes. She wet her lips with her tongue, opened her mouth slightly, trying to speak, but no words came out.

"Judge Daily," I said, " I'm not going to lie and tell you that losing Elizabeth didn't hurt me. It did. It took me years to get over it, but none of that matters now. There's nothing you could ever do that could take away what you've done for me, and there's nothing anyone could ever do or say to change the way I feel about you. You saved me, changed my life, and made me who I am today."

"I love you too, Joe, but I have to tell you why I did it."

I looked at Elizabeth. Our eyes locked. I could hear her short, quick breaths. Her face was flushed and her eyes were filled with tears. She pursed her lips, slowly shook her head and raised her shoulders. I understood, I felt it too; disbelief, anger, betrayal, disappointment, but we couldn't show those emotions to the judge. Not now.

"No, you don't." Elizabeth said, leaning down, hugging him tightly. "Whatever you did, we both know you did it because you thought it was the right thing to do."

"At the time, I did think it was the right thing, but now I'm sure I've made a terrible mistake...and before I die... I have to make this right. I had John dig this old box out from my basement a few days ago. I hope you two will forgive me, but I've spent the last few days reading your letters—all of them."

"Grandpa, Joe and I were just kids when we wrote those letters," Elizabeth said. "I'm engaged to be married... Joe knows that. Everything has worked out fine for the both of us."

I squeezed his hand. "You need to let this go, judge. Right or wrong, we forgive you."

The judge's energy was fading, his face was gray, his eyes began to droop, his breathing labored, so we helped him back to the bed and tucked him in. When he was settled, again he held out his hands for us to hold. "I know that my time is coming to an end soon," he said in almost a whisper. "I've had an amazing life. I had a good and honorable career. I married the perfect woman, had a wonderful, loving child and have a brilliant and beautiful granddaughter. I think I've done something *good* with Uncle Antonio's money. All I have to do is look at you, Joe, and I have my proof. You've made me so proud. Just promise me you'll read those letters. It may be too late for you two, but once upon a time you were the center of each other's universe. Promise me that you'll read your letters?"

"I promise," I said.

"Today... I promise I'll read them today." Elizabeth wiped tears away from her cheek.

"Good, because if he lets me through those pearly gates, I want to be able to look him in the eye and tell him I did my best." With those words, he dropped off to sleep.

We stood there on each side of his bed holding his hands, watching his labored breathing for a few minutes. Then as quietly as I could, I picked up the box with our letters and started walking toward the door.

"Joe, don't go yet," the judge whispered. "We haven't talked about your father."

"Why don't you just rest now," I said. "We can talk about that later."

"I'm really not that tired. It's just the medicine." He rose up on the bed. "I keep dozing off. I'd like to talk about it now. How's your father?"

I put the box down and walked back to his bedside. "He's... not doing so well."

Elizabeth walked up and stood beside me.

The judge looked up. "I had a long talk with John Kelly and he filled me in. Have you fired his idiot lawyer yet?"

I was at a loss for words. I had no idea he knew John Kelly. "I don't suppose you had anything to do with John's insistence that I take on my father's case?"

Judge Daily gave me a sly look and shrugged his shoulders.

I smiled. "I was wondering how John knew that I was, how did he put it, 'a damn good ADA."

"So, are you? Taking your father's case?" He offered no apologies for his meddling.

I sighed and nodded. "Yes, sir. But I'm not sure it's the best thing for my father. I've never tried a case on that side. I have no experience as a defense attorney, but as of yesterday, I'm his attorney of record. Honestly, I'm scared to death for my father. I'm not sure I can give him what he needs."

The judge took my hand and squeezed it. "You never could see it, because your eyes were always filled with your desires to be a cop, but Joe... you are a great lawyer with a real understanding of a jury trial. Prosecution or defense, it's still a trial. I know you can do it."

"I pray you're right," I said.

"What you need is an experienced criminal defense co-counsel," he said.

"I know, but where am I going to find an experienced second chair that will work for free? Dad's dead broke, and I just can't come up with that kind of money to hire one.

"What about me?" Elizabeth said.

I turned to look at her. She was smiling. "Are you serious? I... I can't let you do that."

Her smile disappeared. "Yes, you can. It's your father... Let's save him together."

My mind spun. Too much to process too quickly. So I just stood there.

"It's the right thing to do, Joe." Judge Daily whispered below me. "She has a brilliant legal mind. You need her... and your *father* needs her."

I finally found my voice. "Elizabeth, are you sure? This could be a long trial. Do you really have that much time to dedicate to this?"

"Yes, I've already cleared it with my partners."

I looked down at the judge. "I don't suppose you had anything to do with this?"

He grinned. "I might have had a little to do with it. That's why I had to tell you both about the letters. If you're going to work together, there has to be complete trust between you. And now, you both know."

He held out his hands to us again and we both took one. "Elizabeth, Joe has never lied to you and Joe, Elizabeth didn't lie to you either. That was my doing. The trust you two once had for each other is still there. You can do this... You'll make a great team."

IT WAS ALMOST 1 p.m. when we walked to the hospital parking lot and found my giant rental car. I loaded the box of letters in the rear area while Elizabeth tried to climb up into the passenger seat in her tight skirt. We were both starving. Following her directions, I drove to one of her favorite places to grab lunch. On the way, Elizabeth called her office to let them know where she'd be in case something came up.

"Bring the box," she said when we parked.

"Are you sure you want to do that now?"

"Not really, but we promised we would."

Inside, she asked for a large booth. We settled in, sitting opposite each other with the box between us. I opened it, pulled out the letters, and laid them on the table. There were eight bundles, held together with rubber bands. Four bundles were my letters to her, and four were her letters to me.

They were neatly arranged in chronological order, from our first to our last. After placing our lunch order with the waitress, we both began to read from the first ones.

Dear Joe,

I don't know why, but my parents have put me into an all girls' school in New Hampshire. I begged them not to, but they did it anyway. So, I won't be coming back to Lowell Whiteman this semester and I'm going to miss you so much, but I promise to write you every week! My parents tell me that I'm too young to say this, but I don't care what they think. I know that I love you and I always will. We were meant to be together, so please don't forget me. Maybe we can see each other on the holidays. I miss you so much! Please write me back soon!

Forever yours,

Elizabeth

When I finished reading her letter, I looked up at Elizabeth. Her head was still down reading mine. Tears rolled down her cheeks. When she finally finished, she looked up at me and tried to speak, but all she could say was, "Oh, Joe..."

We both heard a familiar voice shout, "There they are!"

As Rob made his way to our table, I quickly gathered up the bundles of letters, put them back into the box, and stuffed it under the table.

"Joe!" He said, smiling widely as he held out his hand. "Great to see you again!"

I got out from behind the booth table and shook his hand. "Rob, good to see you too. How have you been?"

"Great!" He slid into the booth next to Elizabeth and kissed her. "You're crying? Has the judge had a turn for the worse?"

She wiped her eyes with her napkin. "No, not really. I've just been filling Joe in on his condition."

Rob's expression fell. "His doctors tell us that he's only got about twenty percent of his heart functioning and his oxygen levels are slowly decreasing. Outside of a heart transplant, and due to his age and frail condition they don't think he'd survive the surgery, there's nothing more they can do."

Our food arrived and mercifully the conversation ended. I wasn't in much of a mood to talk and apparently, neither was Elizabeth. Fortunately, Rob picked up on the vibe and stopped as well.

My heart was full, and my emotions teetered on the edge. I didn't want to hear one more thing about Judge Daily because all I could think about was Elizabeth and the letters.

Other than Rob explaining how he'd called her office to find out where we were having lunch, nobody talked much during our meal, but when we'd finished, Rob asked, "What's in the box?"

I panicked, but before I could come up with an answer, Elizabeth said. "Evidence on one of my cases. And no, Mr. Assistant District Attorney, you can't look inside."

I drove Elizabeth back to the hospital to get her car. We divided up the letters and set a time for me to meet her at her office the next morning to start planning our strategy for my father's case. I checked into a nearby hotel and took a quick shower. Then I settled on the couch and started reading the letters. After reading a few, I desperately wanted to call and talk to Elizabeth, but I forced myself not to. But I couldn't stop myself from praying long into the night that my phone would ring.

RIVER

W hen River made it back to the hospital, she was disappointed that Elizabeth wasn't there. River had hoped she could give her a heads up about what Judge Daily wanted to talk to her about.

It had been almost 6 months since she'd had a conversation with him, but she knew that whatever he wanted, no matter what, she would do it. She owed Judge Daily big time. He had used the power of his bench and his influence more than a few times to pull her out of a fire she'd gotten herself into when she'd crossed the wrong lines with her work. Crossing those lines came with the job and were why a private investigator was sometimes more fruitful than an official police investigation. The police had barriers they couldn't cross, she didn't, but if she got caught crossing them, there could be serious consequences. She could lose her PI license or worse—go to jail. That's why most cops hated PI's and loved it when they screwed up, but Judge Daily had always had her back and come to her rescue.

She had loved the judge from the first moment she heard him speak in a trial she was called to testify in. The jury was all male and the defense attorney had suggested that she wear something appropriate with that in mind. After her testimony and her purposefully slow walk back to her seat, Judge Daily took out his handkerchief and wiped his forehead. Then he said something that was still considered (in the legal community) to be one of his most legendary and hilarious lines.

"Ladies and especially the gentlemen," Judge Daily began. "I think it would be advisable to take a short ten-minute recess at this time. John, see if you can find some air freshener to spray in here to help get rid of this pungent aroma of testosterone that's hanging in the air." With that, he slammed down his gavel and walked out. The entire courtroom exploded in laughter.

Some women may have been offended by his remarks, claiming inappropriate sexual harassment, but not her. She has never considered it sexual harassment when a man was attracted to her, even when they said something about it. Of course, some militant women's libbers would disagree with that attitude and believed she set back the women's movement about 20 years, but she truly believed that some men just couldn't help themselves when they saw a pretty girl. They had to look, it's all part of their male DNA. She knew this, and used it to her advantage. She was laughing as loud as anyone in the room and took it as a funny and brilliant way to complement her.

Of course, hearing that sort of thing was not new to her. Her effect on men was something she had discovered at only 13-years-old. She developed early, growing full breasts at 12, round hips at 13, and other than growing a few more inches taller, her dimensions hadn't changed since her 14th birthday.

All through high school, her mother never knew that she would leave the house wearing one of her homemade dresses, but would change into something a little more revealing once she got to school. Right or wrong, she soon realized that the tighter and shorter her skirts were, the higher her grades rose and the easier high school became. She graduated at the top of her class and because of her outstanding grades, she received several scholastic scholarships that paid for her to go to college.

In her second semester at the University of Arkansas, she took a class called, "Basic Sexual Human Nature and Psychology." That's when all the pieces for her fell into place and helped her realize the full potential and power of her looks. From that moment on, she began to take full advantage of what she referred to as 'The Power of 46XX.' Not referring to her breast size, but to the unique scientific chromosome structure of a woman.

Of course, when she visited her parents she always dressed appropriately conservative, but in her real life she used her 46XX powers to get her all the way through law school.

"YOU WANTED TO SEE ME, JUDGE?" She walked up to his hospital bed.

With his remote control, he raised up the top section of his bed so he could look her in the eyes. "Yes, I did. River, you are always a sight to behold, but today you are especially radiant."

River stepped back and did a slow model turn. "Do you like my outfit? I wore it just for you."

"Yes ma'am, I do, but you may need to keep a close watch on my heart monitor. I'm not sure my old ticker can take it." He chuckled.

She moved closer and took one of his hands. "So, what do you want to talk about?"

"We'll get to that in a moment," he said. "River, I guess you know that I've always been fond of you, and it's not just because you're so damned good looking, but because you are smart and so good at what you do. Can I ask you a personal question I've always wondered about?"

"Sure. Ask me anything."

"Why haven't you ever taken the bar exam? I think you'd make a damn fine attorney."

Her body stiffened. She let go of his hand and stepped back from his bed.

"I didn't mean to hit some kind of a nerve or offend you," he said. "I apologize if I did."

She had a serious look on her face, but it was soon replaced by a warm smile. "No... I'm not offended. It's just a very long story."

He returned her smile. "I've always been curious about it, ever since I found out that you and I had graduated from the same law school. And from the first day I heard you testify in my court... well, there was just something about your testimony... I knew you weren't the typical private investigator. There was a lot more. That's when I did a little digging and found out about your law degree. And why I insisted that Elizabeth hire you immediately when she decided to go into criminal defense."

River moved close and leaned over his bed. "Is that why you've always looked after me all these years?"

Judge Daily chuckled. "I guess I have pulled a few strings for you over the years. I don't mean to be pushy, but why haven't you ever taken the bar exam?"

River stood silently for a few minutes to gather her thoughts. "Well...it's not as a result of some tragedy I had. Nothing really dramatic. And honestly, I've fought with myself about it for years. Three times I've filled out my application for the Board of Examiners to do their background check, paid the money and studied for it, but I always backed out at the last minute. It stems from my last year of law school. That's when I discovered what being an attorney really was, and... it's not who I am."

She took a bottle of water out of her purse, unscrewed the top, and took a sip.

"I love the law, its process, and what it stands for. And when those brilliant legal scholars wrote all those books, I believe they loved it as well. Our justice system, in theory, is without a doubt, the best in the world. No country has even come close to matching it, but in reality, it's become broken. Most attorneys, and forgive me for saying this, most judges, are more concerned with clearing their calendar than assuring that justice has been served in their court. I know it's because of the amazing backlog of cases, but running them through as quickly as they can just to save on time and the court costs is not justice.

"Our system is so overcrowded it's lost the true meaning of what it's supposed to stand for. I just can't be a part of that. But as a PI, I have the opportunity to possibly discover something to help someone who might normally be swept under the rug and convinced by a too busy lawyer and crowded court system to take a bad plea."

She took another sip of her water. " I know that as an attorney I might be able to do that as well, but as you know, cases are expensive and even the most dedicated lawyers all fall into the money trap, and are forced by their firm or partners to either settle, or end it quickly. Justice is never the main concern and that is simply wrong! I love my job and I'm very good at it. I might change my mind someday, but for now I'm content to do what I do best."

The judge took her hand and kissed it. "I've always known that you were special, and now I know why. You are a very impressive young woman. Thanks for telling me that, it makes me love you even more." He relaxed his smile, pulled her close and whispered in her ear, "Especially your ass."

River giggled, slapped his arm and stepped back. "Ok, you old horn dog, enough about my ass. What did you want to talk to me about?"

The judge asked her to help him out of his bed and into the recliner. Once he was settled, he said, "I know you just met Joe Jensen today, but he's very special to me. I've known him for most of his life. He has truly come from ashes to what he is today, and I am very proud that I've had something to do with that. I think it's important for you to know that when Joe and Elizabeth were very young, they fell desperately and completely in love with each other."

Elizabeth had told River that she'd known Joe since he was a kid, but she'd never mentioned that she was once in love with him.

"River, I've done two things today that had to be done. One, I should have taken care of years ago, but just didn't have the courage. I only did it now because I had a long talk with my doctors yesterday and they tell me that my time is coming to an end soon."

River's eyes filled with tears. "Yes... Elizabeth told me."

"Listen to me, young lady, don't you be crying over me," he said. "I've always wanted to go to heaven, it's just coming a little sooner than I'd planned. Come on now, no more tears."

River wiped her eyes and sat down in a chair next to him. "Ok, I promise, no more tears. So, what two things did you do today?"

Judge Daily took a deep breath and shook his head. "I finally told them the truth." This time *he* had the tears in his eyes. "When they were kids, I split them up. And the worst part... I made them believe each of them just moved on. They had written some letters to each other that I intercepted and kept secret. I gave them those letters today."

River stood up and began pacing the room. "Judge Daily, that doesn't sound like you. You just let them believe they moved on without any explanation? That's a horrible thing to do. Why would you do such a thing?"

"I don't know... It's hard to explain now, but they were so young and Elizabeth was so gifted... Brilliant. I wanted her to have everything and just wasn't sure Joe was good for her."

"But you said that you loved Joe?" River said confused.

"I did... I still do, but his background..." Judge Daily let his words trail off.

"You mentioned something about ashes?"

He wiped his eyes with the sleeve of his pajamas and sighed. "That's a bit of an exaggeration, but not by much. His parents were hippies. You're probably too young to understand. Do you know what a hippie was?"

River grinned. "I'm not *that* young, of course I know what a hippie was."

"I'm sure you think you do, but the reality is, it was much worse than the history books say. In those days, it wasn't just the drugs, sex, and flower power, it was a dangerous time for the children. Free love as they called it, created an unprecedented culture of neglect and abuse for thousands of those children. They were dropping babies in record numbers and half of them didn't even know who their fathers were."

"Is that what happened to Joe?" River asked.

"No, Joe knew his parents, but they were..." he paused to find the right words, "worse than most. I'm pretty certain that Joe's father was stoned when he came to my court with a child neglect charge against him. Although his parents denied that they had taken drugs in front of

Joe, I knew they were lying. Eventually, I did get Joe out of that damaging environment and got him into a good boarding school where he excelled, but I just wasn't sure how much he had been effected. The things he'd been exposed to at such a young age could have severely damaged him. I made arrangements for him to see a child psychiatrist where he eventually opened up. The stories he told her about what he'd seen were frightening. How he has become what he is today is nothing shy of a miracle."

River sat back down in the chair next to the judge. "I guess I've missed something. Why are you telling me all of this?"

"I know this may sound a bit confusing to you, I apologize for my rambling, but it will all be clear to you in a moment. The second thing I did today was to convince Elizabeth to work with Joe on his father's murder trial. And I know that once they read those letters..."

"But what about Rob?" River asked. "Have you forgotten about him?"

"Rob is a wonderful man, but he's not Joe. Joe is... well... I believe still holding Elizabeth's heart. I know in my heart that soon they'll be back together. It's inevitable. If you had read those letters you'd know it too."

"I still don't understand. If you didn't want this to happen, then why have you gone so far to put them back together?"

Judge Daily started to say something, then stopped, apparently rethinking his response. After a few seconds, he asked, "Do you believe in God?"

She wasn't expecting the question. Trying to hide her shock, she took a long sip of her water to gather her thoughts. It took her a moment to recover and think through an answer. "My parents were devout Christians, and I was raised as a believer, but honestly, they were so... how can I say this... convinced that everything in this world that I wanted was the devil's work, that it turned me away from any kind of religion for years. So, to answer your question, yes, I believe in God and his son, Jesus Christ. I'm just not so sure that he's a Jehovah's Witness."

Judge Daily burst into laughter. When he stopped, he took her hand and squeezed it. "I'm glad to hear you are a believer and I'm with you, I'm not sure God is even a Baptist. But I do believe that he has a plan for all of us, and I just want to make sure that with all my meddling, I didn't mess up his plans for Joe and Elizabeth. That's why I've done what I've done. I had to get out of their way and let God take it from there."

River nodded. "I think I understand, but I'm still not sure what you need me to do."

The judge rocked back and forth two times before he was able to stand. "I'm getting a little tired. Could you help me back to my bed?"

River took his arm and helped him to the edge of the bed. Once he laid back, she covered him with the sheets and blanket. "If you need to rest, I can come back later."

Winded and wheezing from the short walk, it took him a moment to get his breath and speak. "No... please... stay just a little longer."

"Sure, but are you ok? You look pretty pale. Want me to call a nurse to check on you?"

Still out of breath and taking in deep gasping breaths, he whispered, "There's not much they can do for me. Give me a second, I'll be ok."

River waited patiently until his breathing slowed and he could talk again. Then she said, "So, you believe that Elizabeth is still in love with Joe? What about Joe? Is he still in love with her?"

"That's my problem, I just don't know enough about who Joe is now, as an adult. I made a deal with God to tell them the truth and get out of the way, and I know I should have more faith... Maybe I'm just an old stubborn fool, but that doesn't stop me from worrying."

River took his hand. "I don't think you have to worry about Elizabeth; she's a pretty smart cookie."

"Yes, she's brilliant and I've done everything in my power to make her life easier. And just so you know, her practice is very well funded and I've done that so she doesn't fall into that money trap you talked about earlier. She can do what she needs to do on any case. She's a good person with a big heart and I know she'll be ok with her law practice, but it's that big heart I'm so worried about. Please understand, I love Joe, but I love Elizabeth more. I can't go to my grave not knowing for sure that she's going to be all right."

"What do you need me to do to help convince you that she will?"

Judge Daily sighed, dropped his head, then slowly looked up at River. "This may be nothing, but I just have to know for sure. It's in that green file over there." He pointed at the dresser.

River walked over, picked up the file, and opened it. "This is almost twenty-five years old. Who is Doctor Heart?"

"She was Joe's child psychologist," he said. "And from what I hear, for almost ten years...she's also been his lover."

"Oh really? That's very interesting. Is that what's got you so worried?"

"No, not that," he said. Then he grinned at her. "But I bet it's making old Sigmund Freud turn over in his grave."

River laughed. "Did Joe tell you that?"

"No, but I have my sources."

"I bet you do. So, what's in this file that has you so worried?"

"Do you know anything about dissociative identity disorder?"

"Multiple personalities?" she said a little shocked. "Was that her diagnosis of Joe?"

"No, but she mentions several times in her notes that it was a possibility she needed to explore more. It's all in that file."

"And you need me to find out if those explorations came up with anything?" River thought for a moment. "I don't understand, if you hired her, why don't you just ask her?"

"I did, last week, but I was too late. When Joe turned eighteen he was no longer under my guardianship and she couldn't legally tell me anything. She's bound by the HIPPA privacy laws. But she did tell me I shouldn't worry about that."

"But you don't believe her, right?"

"I don't know what to believe. When I first met Joe, we had a long talk about his life. I knew that although he was only thirteen, he was playing every night in his parent's rock band. But when I asked him about it, he just shook his head and said, 'That's not me, that's Jake.'

"Who's Jake?"

Judge Daily raised his eyebrows. "That's exactly what I asked him, but he seemed to get agitated and didn't want to talk about it, so I let it go. We'd made a good connection and I didn't want to lose it, so I moved on to other things. And honestly, he was such an extraordinary young boy and impressed me in so many other areas, I didn't give it a second thought until I read that file."

"When did you get this?" River held up the file.

He sighed and looked away, "I've had that file for years. She sent it to me when Joe ended their sessions and entered college. He had done so well, I... I just didn't see any need to read it."

"So what made you read it now?"

"Has Elizabeth filled you in on Joe's father's arrest?" he asked.

"No, we're supposed to go over that in the morning. What about it?"

"His father was charged with the murder of a US Congressman's granddaughter. The evidence links to six other murders, across six states over the past twenty-six years. Because it was multiple states and possibly a serial killer, the FBI was brought in and Joe was assigned the case. Unfortunately, he uncovered a strange coincidence... each murder took place in small towns that his parent's band were playing in at the time. He also discovered that the murder weapon left behind a unique imprint that matched a handmade macramé guitar strap made by," he took a deep breath, "his mother."

"His mother made the strap?" River asked. "Who did she make it for?"

"It was his father's. Apparently, his mother was very good at macramé and used to make all the bands' guitar straps. Each one was her own unique design. That's how Joe caught it and ironically, he would have been the only agent that would have."

"He arrested his own father?" She gasped.

"No, but it was his discovery of the evidence and his identification of that strap that caused it to happen."

"How could he have done that?" River said.

"He had no choice and it was the right thing to do. Please don't lose focus here. He had no idea that the case he was working would lead to his father, but the evidence was just too compelling for him to ignore. So, he turned it over and is now trying to find a way to prove his own evidence is wrong."

River sat down in the recliner and raised her hands. "I'm lost. In one breath you tell me you suspect that Joe could have a split personality called Jake, and in the other, you tell me that he's some kind of hero!"

"See my problem? I need you to find out which one he is. Not just for me... for Elizabeth," he said. "And one more thing."

"What's that?" She stood up and walked back to his bed.

"I need you to hurry. I'm not sure how much longer I've got."

ON HER DRIVE BACK to her apartment, River made four calls on her cell; the first to Elizabeth, explaining why she wouldn't be able to make their planned meeting in the morning to go over Joe's father's case. She made up a bogus excuse about having to work on another one of her pressing cases, but it wasn't very convincing. She could hear Elizabeth's skepticism in her not happy reply.

The second was to Sam. She was another PI River dealt with on occasion. Actually Sam (Samantha,) was more of a computer hacker than a private investigator, but she had an amazing ability to dig out information on someone that may be hidden from normal searches.

The third call was to Wes London. He had been very persistent in his quest to take her out to dinner. She'd always turned him down before, but he was an FBI agent working out of the Little Rock field office and if he could give her what she wanted, Wes just might get lucky and get that date.

The last call was to Southwest Airlines to book a flight to Jackson, Mississippi. She'd learned a long time ago that the fastest way to learn about someone was to talk to the person who raised them. Joe's mother, Hannah, knew Joe better than anyone and if Jake was real, she would know.

In less than two hours, she had acquired Joe's official FBI record and Sam had given her everything she could find about Doctor Heart and H. Joe Jensen, but there was nothing in any of the reports that threw up a red flag. And Sam had completely struck out finding anything even remotely connected to someone called Jake.

Joe's bank records did reveal something that caught her eye. Two years earlier, Joe had closed on a new house in Virginia, but only a few months ago had stopped paying for a storage room he'd paid on monthly for years in Colorado. It wasn't the new house that held her interest, it was what he may have moved in from that storage room. If he had any secrets, that would've been a good place to hide them.

She knew what she had to do, but it would be risky. After meeting with Joe's mother, she would have to fly to Virginia and break into Joe's house. She didn't have time for her usual careful process of taking a few days or in some cases a few weeks to stake out a building she needed to get inside. She had to get into Joe's house as soon as possible.

Sitting on the tarmac on the plane to Jackson, she tried to call the judge to tell him what she was going to do, but when she reached the nurses' station they told her that he had taken a turn for the worse and couldn't take a phone call. Because she wasn't immediate family, they wouldn't tell her any more. She was running out of time.

RIVER AND HANNAH

W hen Hannah answered the door, River wasn't sure she was at the right house. She didn't know this woman's exact age, but Hannah had to be well into her sixties; this woman looked more like she was in her forties.

"Hello, are you Hannah Jensen?"

Hannah frowned, scanning River from head to toe. "Yes, but if you're with the press, I have nothing to say."

River smiled and handed her a card. "I'm not with the press. My name is River Rivers. I'm a private investigator working with the law firm representing your husband, Luke. I would like to ask you some questions. Do you have a few minutes?"

Hannah studied the card. "You work with Jeffery Jacobs? Why would he hire a private investigator from Little Rock, Arkansas?"

"No, I work with Elizabeth Weller's firm. She has agreed to be your son Joe's second chair on Luke's case."

Hannah squinted her eyes, exposing wrinkles in her forehead. "Elizabeth who? Jeffery Jacobs is Luke's attorney. I think you've made some kind of mistake."

"Please, Hannah." River moved a step closer to the door. "Let me come in and I'll explain everything. I don't have much time, I have to catch a plane to Virginia in a few hours. I promise this is not a mistake. Please, may I come in?"

River sat across from Hannah at a small table in the kitchen and explained the situation. Not knowing the actual details of how Joe became Luke's attorney, she did her best to improvise a few of the facts. After a few minutes, Hannah seemed to relax and reluctantly accept the news. "I can't say that I'm happy about this, but it's Luke's decision." Hannah stood. "I need some tea, would you like some? Or maybe some coffee?'

River smiled. "I know we just met, and I hope you don't think this is too forward, but do you have anything stronger? It's been a long day."

Hannah grinned. "From the first moment I saw you standing in the doorway, I knew I was going to like you." She opened the refrigerator and pulled out a bottle of white wine.

River sat quietly watching Hannah move around the small kitchen, opening up drawers, searching. "Luke doesn't drink anymore and I try not to drink alone, so it's been a while, but I know I have a corkscrew in here somewhere." She eventually found it and opened the bottle.

River was mesmerized watching Hannah glide around the kitchen. She did not move or have any resemblance of a woman in her sixties. She was dressed in light gray knee-high form-fitting Yoga pants with a matching sleeveless tank top. There wasn't one ounce of visible fat on her body. Her blonde waist-length hair flowed down her back in soft ringlet curls. Her face was youthful and virtually wrinkle free. She was barefoot and even her feet looked young, with bright red manicured nails.

Hannah set two empty wine goblets on the table and filled both half way. "We can start with this, but I've got more if needed." She settled in her chair.

"Can I ask you a personal question?" River lifted her glass and took a sip of the wine.

"That's what you're here for, isn't it? Ask me anything you want."

River took another sip. "I know Joe is in his mid-forties. You look incredible, how old are you?"

Hannah laughed. "Am I under oath? I usually lie about that."

"Whatever you tell me I'll believe, because you look, maybe, 39?"

Hannah laughed out loud. "I wasn't going to lie that bad. I hate to admit it, but the truth is I turned sixty-four in May."

"That's impossible! How do you do it? What's your secret?"

Hannah lifted her glass. "Good genes, good wine, and years of Yoga!" Her eyes twinkled as she laughed. "I was about to ask you the same thing. River, you're stunning. What's your secret?"

River flushed. "Thank you, but it's all genetics, definitely not Yoga, but after meeting you, I'm signing up as soon as I can."

For the next few minutes, the conversation was easy and flowed between them as if they were old friends. It was exactly what River had hoped for. Hannah seemed to trust her and that was what she needed.

"What about Joe's job in Virginia? Is he leaving the FBI? I can't imagine that."

It was a question River couldn't really answer, so she improvised. "I don't think so. It's just a temporary leave of absence, so he can work the case."

"Work the case? I don't understand."

River set her wine down and leaned forward, resting her elbows on the table. "I don't know the exact details, but I do know that an FBI agent can't work a case that involves a relative. It's a conflict of interest, but as Luke's lawyer, it's not. I believe it's just Joe's way of trying to help his father. Why, does that bother you?"

Hannah stared into her glass expressionless. "I'm still very angry at Joe. He did this. He's the reason Luke's in jail."

River reached across the table and took Hannah's hand. "Hannah, look at me. I know you don't believe that. You know Joe had no choice. He had to turn over the evidence he'd uncovered. If there's anyone that knows Joe, the real Joe, it's you. Do you really think he wanted this to happen? Really"

Hannah sat silent, staring forward. She wiped a tear from her cheek with her hand. "No, not really. Joe told me the same thing, but..." Hannah blinked as tears rolled down her face. "I was so angry at him, I didn't want to listen."

River kept quiet, allowing Hannah time to think and calm down.

"I know I need to forgive him for what he did and I'm trying, but..." After a few moments of awkward silence, Hannah turned toward River and faked a small smile. "So, why are you here? What did you want to talk to me about?"

It wasn't the time to reveal her first reason for being there, so River began with her second, Luke's case. "The evidence against Luke is very compelling. My job is to try to uncover something, anything that we can use in his defense to explain that evidence, and hopefully, reveal the identity of the real murderer."

Hannah's eyes widened. "You think I know who the murderer is? I have no idea. I'd love to help you, but I don't think I can."

River nodded with understanding. "I'm not sure you can either, but if Luke is innocent, someone in the band is not. There's too much evidence. It has to be someone in the band, someone connected, or something that happened because of the band. I had to start somewhere and that's why I'm here. I just got this case and I know nothing about the band, nothing about you or Luke or the other band members. You may think you don't know anything, but Hannah, something caused this. Please, tell me about the band."

Hannah stood, walked to the refrigerator, and pulled out another bottle of wine. "I think I'm gonna need some more of this." She sighed. "I'm not ashamed of my life, but there are things I've done that I'm not proud of and have tried to forget. I know I wasn't the best mother." She looked at River, her face full of gloom. "How far back do you want me to go?"

"It's your call. How about from the beginning?"

Hannah, opened the bottle, filled their glasses and began. "Joe's always told me that I was not a typical mom and I guess he's right. For better or worse, I've had a unique life that has molded and created the person I've become. My life started out very normal. I was like most little girls, into frilly things, playing with dolls, and dreaming of getting married in a big church, wearing a beautiful white wedding dress with a long veil trailing behind me as I walked down the aisle on my father's arm. But all those dreams and my childhood ended suddenly when my mother and father were killed in a car wreck."

River gasped. "Oh my God! I'm so sorry."

Hannah twirled her wine glass staring somberly down at the table. "They were driving from Denver to Vail, Colorado in the snow and somehow my father lost control and drove off a mountain. It took almost four days to find and retrieve their bodies. When that happened, every thought I'd ever had about who I was, who I was going to be, and how I would live my life changed."

"Oh, Hannah. I'm so sorry. How old were you?"

"I'd just had my fourteenth birthday. Ironically, my mother had lost her parents when she was only fourteen as well."

"That's so tragic. Were you raised in an orphanage or did you have family?"

"I had aunts and uncles, but no one seemed to want me, so my father's parents took me in, but I was miserable there."

Hannah paused and took a sip of her wine. "I loved them and they were wonderful people, but they were very British, devout Catholics and in their late seventies. They tried their best, but they were from a different world and never understood or related to me."

River gently patted Hannah's hand. "That must have been so hard for you."

"There were so many things wrong. My grandfather was a retired tailor, working over fifty years in the same garment factory in the Bronx in New York City. My grandmother had never worked and had always been a housewife. She was an amazing cook, but when she wasn't in the kitchen cooking or cleaning, she was at Saint Jerome's for mass.

"My parents had been Catholic as well, but weren't nearly as devout; only going to mass on Sundays, but that changed for me quickly. When I wasn't in Catholic school, walking with my grandmother to Saint Jerome's for early mass was the daily ritual. She was there every morning from 7:30 to 9:30, Monday through Friday; then, the Saturday vigil from 4:00 to 5:30 and every Sunday morning at 7:30."

River shook her head. "My parents were very religious too. I know exactly how you felt."

Hannah shrugged and sipped her wine. "I hope you responded better than I did. I was young and still grieving over my parents and did some stupid things. My grandparents were so strict. The only music allowed in the house was classical or religious, but I was a teenager and that was not my music. To hear the music I loved, I had to stop at the record store on my walks home from school, and I did it almost every day. There, I would listen to Jimi Hendrix, the Rolling Stones, the Beatles, or Led Zeppelin.

"When I was fifteen, I met a boy at that record store that I really liked. His name was Rudy and he was older, I think about nineteen. He was really cute, had long sideburns and wore his hair slicked-back like Elvis, always had on a black motorcycle jacket and smoked. One day Rudy took me for a ride on his motorcycle and we wound up at his house. His parents were at work, so we had the place to ourselves. He took me to his bedroom to show me his record collection and then gave me my very first kiss. I liked it, so I kissed him back and, well... things progressed from there.

"I realize now that it was Rudy's influence, but pretty soon after that, I became a rebellious teenager. I started taking drugs, drinking, and smoking, and having a lot of sex with Rudy and even some of his friends. My grandparents tried, but they couldn't control me. So, at seventeen, I stole some money out of my grandmother's purse, packed a bag, and hitchhiked to California.

"All of Rudy's friends used to tell me that I looked like a movie star or a model. Not trying to sound conceited, but I knew that I was pretty. I was tall and had long blonde hair, so like a lot of other foolish girls, I thought I would make it big in Hollywood, but when I got there, there were about a million other pretty girls trying to do exactly the same thing.

"In Los Angeles, I met some people that were going to San Francisco. It was 1968 and when they told me about the revolution happening there in the Haight Ashbury district, with all the hippies, love, and flower children, I knew that was where I belonged, so I went with them."

River leaned toward her. "I've read a lot of stories about that. 1968, didn't they call that the Summer of Love?"

"Yes it was, and it was a magical time. There were thousands of us there, living on the streets and in the parks. The rest of the world was full of hate. It was the middle of the Vietnam war and the newspapers were full of death and violence, but there at that time in San Francisco, it was the definition of peace, love, and happiness. Everybody was young, free, and beautiful, dancing in the streets, stoned on weed, rushing on cocaine, tripping on acid, playing music and loving life. It was like being in the middle of a dream, a non-stop party that never ended. No one wanted for anything. Everybody was happy to share whatever they had—their food, their drugs, their clothes. It was absolute euphoria and I loved every second of it."

"It almost sounds like you're talking about a fairytale. It doesn't sound real. Is that where you met the other band members?" River asked.

"Not all of them, only two, the rest came later." Hannah gazed off into space, lost in her memories. "One day I saw this very tall, dark, and handsome guy walking around carrying a suitcase, with a guitar on his back. He looked lost, so I went up to him and introduced myself."

"That's how you met Luke?"

Hannah shook her head. "No, it wasn't Luke. When I walked up to him, he told me his name was Bummer and it made me laugh. 'That's a silly name,' I said.

"He was so handsome, but when he began to tell me where he got his nickname, I quickly realized that Bummer was not normal. It was like listening to a little kid. He was completely lost, alone, and so innocent it broke my heart, so I told him to come with me."

River jerked her head up and her eyes opened wide. "Bummer was mentally challenged?"

Hannah's expression softened. "Yes he was, he still is. He has the mental capacity of a child. I guess it was the mothering instinct inside of me, but I somehow knew I needed to take him under my wing and protect him. I introduced him to everyone I knew and they all loved him and they didn't seem to care or notice he was different. He was so sweet and full of love, he fit right in."

Hannah paused and took a long sip of her wine. Her expression was blank, emotionless. "I'm not sure how detailed you want me to be. I don't want to bore you or worse shock you with some of the things I did back then. Do you want me to skip to the parts when we were traveling in the band?"

"I doubt you could shock me," River said. "I've been a private investigator for nine years, there's not much that I haven't seen or heard. Of course, I'd love to hear every detail of your life, but if there are parts you're uncomfortable talking about I understand. Tell me whatever you want, I'm not here to judge you."

"Ok," Hannah sighed and took a deep breath. "You are way too young to understand what it was like back then and I make no apologies about my life in those years, but there is one thing I did that I will always regret.

"I took Bummer to a party one afternoon and we all dropped acid. When I woke the next morning, Bummer was in my bed and we were naked. When he woke up, he told me that he loved me and couldn't stop talking about how much he loved what we did. It was his first time and that was all it had taken. He immediately started talking about getting married and even asked me if we could have children.

I wasn't sure what to do. I loved Bummer too, but not in that way. The problem was that Bummer didn't have the emotional mental ability to truly understand what had happened between us. I hope you don't think bad of me, but back then, sex was very different. You didn't have sex with someone only because you were in love with them, you had sex with them because you wanted to give them love. It was the greatest expression of love you could share. And in those days, everyone loved everyone and that's what we did.

"I did my best to explain to Bummer the difference between true love; the kind of love for someone you wanted to marry and spend the rest of your life with and the kind of love that we had for each other... and that it was different. Even though he said he understood, I knew he really didn't."

"Of course, I don't think bad of you," River said softly. "I've done things I regret too, everybody has. So, was that the end for you and Bummer?"

Hannah dropped her head, staring down at the table. "It probably should have been, but no, I couldn't hurt him anymore. I didn't stop having sex with him, but from that day forward, I never let it become emotional. There was no more kissing and we began experimenting with different things that were not emotional, like using vibrators, sex toys, light bondage, and choking. I had met a couple in Los Angeles who were into autoerotic asphyxiation and had done it to me a few times and it was amazing."

River lifted her glass to her lips, trying to hide her reaction. The real reason she was there, was to learn as much as she could about Joe and maybe something about this Jake character, but unknowingly, Hannah had just raised a red flag. River had only glanced at the FBI report and didn't know all of the details, but she did know that all seven girls were tied to beds, bondage style, and strangled. She wasn't sure what it meant or if it had anything to do with the murders, but it was very coincidental.

"I've never experienced it myself, but I've read about autoerotic asphyxiation," River said. "It's very dangerous. Weren't you worried?"

Hannah shrugged. "I was eighteen and on so many drugs dying never crossed my mind. I know now how lucky I was, but back then I was immortal."

"Did you do this to Bummer or did he do this to you?"

"Bummer didn't like it when I did it to him, but he loved doing it to me, staring into my eyes watching me orgasm. He was careful and very good at it, so most of the time that was what we did." Hannah shrugged and looked at River. "Sorry for being so graphic, but you wanted to know the truth. It was stupid, I know."

"You were lucky," River said. "So, how did you meet Luke?"

Hannah's face lit up. "I was dancing in the street handing out flowers to strangers when I first saw him. I can't really explain it, but there was just something different about him and I knew immediately we were meant to be together. At that time of my life, I certainly wasn't looking for a soul mate, but suddenly there he was and there was no way to deny it."

"Love at first sight. Romantic."

"Oh yes." Hannah glowed. "He was so handsome and very romantic back then."

"So, that's when you guys got married and put the band together." River wrote a few notes in her pad. "When did Joe come along?"

"The band and Joe came a few years later, but not in San Francisco. About a month after Luke and I met, he started talking about a commune he had heard about in the farm country. When he talked about it he would get very excited, so along with most of my friends, we packed up and drove there.

"It probably would've been the best thing for Bummer if I would have just left him there in San Francisco, but I just couldn't do it. It would've been like abandoning a lost child, so we took Bummer with us, even though our relationship had changed. Bummer still was completely and totally in love with me and I knew it, but I also knew that it was not a good thing for him, so when I met Luke I did my best to explain to him that Luke was that special kind of love that we had talked about before and because of Luke, we couldn't have sex any more. It broke my heart to hurt him that way, but I knew he needed to move on. I could never give him the kind of love that he deserved."

"So, you moved to a commune? What was that like?

Hannah's eyes opened wide as she smiled. "I don't know what you've heard or read about communes, but unless you were there there's no words that can truly define it. All I can say is it was a wonderful experience and a very special place to live, full of families with kindred spirits. There was no violence or petty jealousies like in today's societies. We were all just happy to be alive and in love. Of course, we were young and very naïve to the real world, I know that now.

"Luke bought two tents from the Salvation Army—one for Bummer and one for us. For the first time in a long time we had a permanent place to cook and lay our heads.

"There was a beautiful huge garden that everyone tended to, with every kind of vegetable you could imagine. Wild fruit trees with apricots and oranges grew all over the property and there were several lakes and large streams full of fish. It was truly like living in paradise. I had my nineteenth birthday there and had grown tired of all of the drugs and wild parties. For the first time since I'd lost my parents, I felt truly happy and content. I loved working in the garden and cooking, and that's how I spent most of my days. I also loved visiting with our friends, singing and dancing around the nightly campfires. It was a wonderful, magical time in my life."

"Is that where you and Luke got married?"

Hannah shook her head. "No, but that's were Little Joe was born. We had been there for almost a year when I missed my first period. When the second one didn't come, I knew I was pregnant. I was ecstatic about having a child, but Luke was not that happy about it. I guess he wasn't ready to settle down and grow up, but he eventually accepted the idea that he was going to be a father whether he liked it or not." Hannah stood and walked to a cabinet in the living room. When she returned, she laid a photo album on the table.

"There he is. He was a beautiful baby." She pointed at the first photo. "I gave birth to little Joe two days after my twentieth birthday. It was a difficult birth, but he was healthy, had all his fingers and toes, and that's all that mattered to me."

River set down her wine. "Forgive me for asking this, but what about the drugs. Did you worry about that? Is that why your pregnancy was so difficult?"

Hannah smiled. "It was probably one of the only smart things I ever did in those days, but when I found out I was pregnant, I stopped drinking, smoking pot, and taking any kind of drugs."

While River flipped through the photo album, Hannah sipped her wine and studied River's business card. "River Rivers? Really? I thought I was the only one who branded children with silly names."

River laughed. "Yes. River Rivers. My parents... well, what can I say, they thought it was creative. They named my brother Lake." River furrowed her brow. "I must be missing something. Joe seems like a pretty normal name to me."

Hannah shook her head and chuckled. "You must not know his full name."

River shrugged. "All he told me was that his name was Joe Jensen."

"That doesn't surprise me," Hannah said laughing. "A few days after the birth when I felt better, Luke and I smoked some pot and got really stoned. There were about twenty of us sitting around the fire trying to think of a great name for him. Everyone started yelling out names, 'How about Garcia? After Jerry Garcia and the Grateful Dead, that would be so cool!'

"'Garcia Jensen,' Luke yelled back. 'No way! Too Mexican.' Everybody laughed. 'How about Ringo?' Someone else yelled out. Again, Luke said, 'No way!'

"This went on for hours and everyone seemed to have a name for him. Eventually, we decided on Joe. Actually, on his birth certificate we named him Hey Joe in honor of my favorite song and musician, Jimi Hendrix. I know, it was a horrible thing to do to a child, but we were very young, very stoned, and it sounded perfect at the time."

"Poor Joe," River said laughing. She glanced at her watch. There was no way she'd make it to the airport in time, but she didn't want to stop Hannah's story, she'd just gotten to Joe and she wasn't sure she'd ever get an opportunity like this again.

"Hannah, it looks like I'm going to miss my plane. Could you hold on a few minutes? I need to call and change to a later flight."

While River was on the phone, Hannah puttered around the kitchen, straightening up. When River finished, Hannah suggested they move to the living room.

"It's more comfortable in here."

They settled on the couch next to each other. "I think you'd just named Joe when we stopped." River said. "Tell me about Joe."

Hannah smiled, her face almost glowing. "The months seemed to fly by and little Joe grew like a weed. Soon he was walking and talking. Bummer was there holding my hand when he was born and had barely left his side ever since. He was our full-time babysitter and was constantly playing games with Joe. I think he loved him as much as I did."

"How did Luke handle being a father?"

Hannah shrugged. "I can't say that Luke was the greatest father. He tried one time to change his diaper, but started gagging and ran outside and threw up." They both laughed.

"Honestly, Luke was a little standoffish with Joe. He didn't like to hold him and would get angry if he cried too much. I knew that he loved him, but also realized that he didn't really know how to be a father yet. And until he figured out what that was, he wasn't going to play much of a part in raising him. It was all going to be up to me.

"Please don't get me wrong, Luke wasn't a bad guy, just a little immature in those days. We hadn't planned to get pregnant, so suddenly being a father had overwhelmed him. It wasn't part of his plan, so it took him a while to grasp the reality of it. I never worried; I knew that eventually he would become a good father because he had a good heart and also by the way he had sort of adopted Bummer."

River shifted in her seat, folding her legs under her. "Luke didn't mind that you and Bummer had been together?"

"No, not at all. He loved Bummer as much as I did. He had been protective from the first day he'd met him and was always very sweet to him. At the commune, he looked after Bummer, making sure he had enough food and clothes and helped him with anything he needed. He also spent a lot of time with him, teaching him how to play the bass guitar. Sadly, Bummer knew he was not smart and had low self-esteem because of it. Luke caught on to that immediately, and always let him know when he was doing something good.

"He was always saying things to him like, 'Wow, Bummer, that's a great idea' or 'Bummer, you did that really well!' When he said those kind of things, Bummer would just beam!

"It was about that time that Luke began to get serious about his guitar playing and would practice for hours and hours. Somehow, he found us a gig about an hour and a half away from the commune and almost every weekend we would drive there to perform. It was just the three of us, Bummer on bass, Luke on guitar, and I would sing. It was my first time actually performing on stage for an audience and I really liked it."

"So, that's when you guys formed the band?" River asked.

"Yes, not too long after that. One night when we were driving back from the gig, Luke told me that he was worried because no one actually owned the commune land and he had heard a rumor that the owner was trying to evict everyone. He was right. A few days after Joe's second birthday, the owner, with several uniformed sheriffs, showed up and told us we had to leave. So we packed up, drove to Los Angeles, and put together the band."

"That's when you started traveling and playing in bars?"

"Yes, we traveled for years. All of the driving and traveling was difficult, especially with a two-year-old in the beginning, but little Joe seemed happy and adapted well. Bummer and the rest of the band played games with him and kept him occupied, and I did my best to teach him how to do arithmetic, and how to read and write."

"Sounds like Joe liked being on the road. So, you homeschooled him?"

Hannah shook her head. "Not really. That was before anyone had ever heard of that, and legally he was supposed to be enrolled in a public school, but we were never anywhere long enough for that, so I did what I could. When he was about five I started taking him to public libraries and we'd pick out books and read them together. By the time he was six, he learned to read well, and loved it. Every time he finished a new book I would make him write a book report about it, so I could tell if he was really reading it or just scanning through the pages. It didn't take me long to realize that he was a very smart little boy. At only six years old, he had good handwriting and his book reports were very detailed.

"At seven, Luke started teaching him how to play the guitar and how to read music. For some reason, Joe didn't seem to like that much, but after their lessons Luke would always go on and on, telling me about how amazing he was and how quickly he was learning. At eight, Joe began finding the local public libraries himself and would walk to them almost every day. Each week he would give me a book report on the new books he'd been reading."

"Are you telling me that Joe is all self-taught?" River's eyes were wide, shocked. "He's never had any formal education?"

Hannah's expression suddenly grew grim. Her forehead wrinkled, her eyes filled with tears and her lips tightened. "No, I'm just telling you that he didn't go to school back when we were traveling on the road." She looked away and wiped her eyes. "Eventually, he did get a good education, but that's another very long story."

With Hannah upset and emotional, it wouldn't be long before she stopped talking. It was time to bring up Jake. "Hannah, I don't mean to interrupt your train of thought, but could I ask you about something I've come across and would like to know more about?"

"Of course." Hannah wiped away another tear on her cheek. "What do you want to know?"

Still unsure if it was the right thing to do, or how she would react, River asked, "Can you tell me something about Jake. Who is Jake?"

Hannah laughed out loud. "How do you know about Jake? I haven't thought about him in years."

"It's a name I came across in one of my reports. So, who is he? Was he in the band?"

Hannah took a long sip of her wine and laughed again. "Joe developed very early and grew to almost six feet tall by the time he was nine years old. He looked more like a skinny teenager than a child. He was only about eight when Luke first started bringing him on stage to play his guitar with the band for a set or two, and honestly that was the only time he acted his age. He would cry and beg me not to make him do it, but Luke insisted. At first, his knees would literally shake and he would just stand there staring at the floor, barely stroking his guitar. 'He's just got a little stage fright,' Luke would tell me, 'He'll get over it.' But he never did. I used to beg Luke not to make him do it, but he thought it was good for him to learn some social skills, so I stayed out of it. Until Joe was about ten years old, it was always a battle to get him up on that stage, but that all changed one night when he introduced us to 'Jake.'"

River sat up in her chair. *Finally.* "So, he is real?"

Hannah shrugged. "I guess you could say that he was real, sort of. When you're with someone every day you just don't notice the subtle changes in their appearance. So when Joe walked in one night with his hair slicked-back, wearing leather pants, a leather vest and a red macramé headband, I had no idea who he was. I had never seen those clothes before, so I didn't recognize him. I don't think Luke did either, but the band all seemed to know it was Joe.

"So Jake is really Joe? I'm confused."

Hannah grinned. "It *was* a little strange and I was confused too, but when he smiled at me I realized it was him. 'Call me Jake,' he said and then started playing a lead on his guitar, jumping around the stage and sliding on his knees. The band joined in and started rocking with Jake's guitar. After that, it was never Joe on the stage, it was always Jake.

River wanted to know more details, but didn't want to push her too far. "How could he change to another person so convincingly? That doesn't sound like a normal thing a child would do."

Hannah was quiet for a few seconds. "I'm not sure how he did it, but he did it every night. I wasn't sure it was a healthy thing for him to be able to change into two completely different people; Joe, the weird little bookworm that hung out at the library in the daytime, and Jake, the rock star maniac jumping all over the stage at night. As it turned out, I didn't have to worry about that very long, because when he turned thirteen, I lost my little Joe forever."

River turned toward Hannah. "Lost him? I don't understand. How did you lose him?"

Hannah sighed and stood. "River, I'm sorry, but I'm getting really tired. That's a very long story I just don't want to relive. I'm not emotionally ready for that now." She turned her head and stared into River's eyes. "Simply, the courts took Joe away from us and my life has never been the same since. I think it would be best for you to talk to Joe about that part of his life."

Her face was flushed red, her long lashes blinking away her tears. "He was thirteen when they took him away and honestly River, I don't know much more about Joe after that. I can count on my fingers the number of times I've seen him since. I know it's a horrible thing to say, but in my mind, when they took him away, it was almost as if he'd died."

THE BREAK IN

River was glad she had taken a cab to Hannah's house, because after drinking almost a full bottle of wine listening to Hannah's story, she was in no condition to drive. In the cab on the 40-minute ride back to the airport, she scribbled a few notes on her yellow pad. Unfortunately, other than Bummer, Hannah never talked about the other band members and stopped when she finally got to Jake. And although she tried a few more times to get Hannah to talk about why the court took Joe away and what happened to him after that, she wouldn't talk.

If Joe's own mother didn't know much about him from the age of thirteen on, then who would?

Even though she had learned a lot about Hannah, Luke, Bummer, and Joe's early childhood and now understood who Jake was, it wasn't enough. Risky or not, there was no other way. She had to break into Joe's house and see if she could find the truth about Joe and maybe discover something about Jake.

River got the last flight out of Jackson, and her plane landed in Virginia at almost midnight. By the time she'd rented a car it was after 1:00 in the morning—too late and too risky to break in tonight. She had to at least find out if he had an alarm, but so far, Sam hadn't been able to get her that information. In the daylight, she would be able to see the obvious signs of an alarm and depending on what kind it was, she could figure out how to bypass it. There was nothing left to do but check in a hotel and try to catch a few hours of sleep.

Six hours later, she made her first pass by Joe's house. She made her second pass fifteen minutes later. At 8, she parked at a strip mall about half a mile away, walked back to his house, and slipped into his back yard. She scanned the windows, but saw no security in place, so she took out her lock picks and went to work.

Once inside, she waited and listened in silence for an alarm, but thank God there wasn't one. It was stupid being there with no previous surveillance, but she had no choice.

The dining room was empty–no table or chairs, but the kitchen was well equipped with copper pots and pans hanging over a granite island stove. Black stainless steel appliances complimented the black granite countertops and rich walnut cabinets. She was impressed.

It was an open, high ceiling layout with the kitchen, dining, and living room all under a vaulted ceiling. The living room had a large dark brown leather couch and one dark brown leather recliner sitting next to a tall brass standing lamp and a beautiful glass covered coffee table made from a cross cut section of a Redwood tree.

Over the fireplace was what looked like an original Thomas Kinkade. The smallest of the two guest bedrooms was empty, except for a large box from IKEA containing a computer desk that Joe apparently hadn't taken the time to assemble yet. The other guest bedroom was sparsely furnished with only a bed and a small dresser. No lamps or end tables and the walls were blank. The closet was full of boxes.

The master bedroom had a king size bed with no headboard and an old scarred up dresser with a cracked mirror. The master bath was all white marble with top of the line fixtures. The large glass shower was floor to ceiling tile that opened up to reveal a very large whirlpool bathtub. It was very nice, but there were no towels or washcloths in sight.

What do you dry off with, Joe?

The walk-in closet was the first thing she'd seen that gave her any clues of who he was. It was lined with his clothes, but they were all obviously carefully positioned exactly three inches apart.

Agent H. Joe Jensen, your OCD is showing.

The shelves above the clothes were carefully stacked with plastic see-through storage bins. His shoes lined the opposite wall in perfect order: running shoes, dress shoes, snow boots, work boots. Even his flip-flops were in exact alignment.

Elizabeth honey, there's something you need to know about Joe, she said, laughing to herself.

She walked back to the center of the house and turned around, slowly taking everything in. The house was spotless: not one thing out of place, but something felt wrong. It made sense to be this neat and clean, especially after her visit to Joe's over-the-top OCD closet. That really didn't bother her, it reminded her of her own closet. She could relate to that obsession, but something still tugged at her.

What am I missing here? What is the problem?

She retraced her steps, spending more time in each of the rooms. When she made it back to the living room she sat down on the leather recliner, trying to assimilate the data. Finally, she saw it, or rather the lack of it.

In the entire house, there wasn't one picture of his mother or father; no photos of his friends; no framed diplomas, no yearbooks in the bookshelves. Not even a photo of himself. It was totally devoid of anything to remind him of his life. The only word she could think of to describe it was sterile. It wasn't a home, just a facsimile of one.

For the next two hours, she unpacked and carefully repacked the boxes in the guest bedroom, looking for clues that might shine a light on who Joe Jensen really was, but nothing seemed out of the ordinary. Most were filled with books—old law books and FBI training manuals. The others were full of old clothes—work out sweats and white athletic socks and t-shirts.

She did find it interesting that the clothes were stuffed into the boxes, not neatly folded and packed precisely in some obsessive order.

Joe, I'm shocked. Where's that OCD you're so famous for?

When she finished with the boxes, she moved to the walk-in closet.

Before she began, she snapped a few pictures with her phone, so she could remember how to put everything back in its precise order. Carefully, she took down the clear plastic storage containers one by one. When she opened the first one she began to laugh.

There you are. She laughed. *Hello, Mr. Obsessive Compulsive.*

The containers were meticulously organized with each item of clothing folded like they were about to go on display at Macy's. None of the containers were filled to the top. Most were half full and some only covered the bottom, in one layer. In total, there were 22 containers, but all of the contents could have been placed in only 5 or 6. Most were filled, like the other boxes, with old clothes, but these contained his old dress shirts and ties. All of the shirts were white and folded perfectly, even the ones with frayed collars and cuffs. Several contained meticulously folded underwear and socks.

Carefully, she unfolded one pair of black socks and one pair of dingy white BVD briefs. She laughed. There were holes in the toe of each sock and the underwear had two large holes in the back and the elastic was stretched out.

Joe, why would you keep these?

Once the plastic containers were back in their place, she stood in the middle of the closet and looked again at his perfectly organized clothes. Most of the dark suits were well worn, but on the right side there were two plastic garment bags labeled "Brook's Brothers." When she peeked inside, they appeared to be brand new suits. She knew a Brook's Brothers suit was at least a grand a piece.

Damn, Joe! That's at least two grand!

Then she realized that every one of the hanging white dress shirts looked brand new, with no signs of wear and again were all labeled Brook's Brothers. Back in his bedroom, she pulled open the drawers of his old beat up dresser and found the expected neat order of precisely folded and meticulously arranged socks, ties, and underwear. Again, they were brand new, some still pinned with the original labels.

Walking out of the master bedroom, she stopped to study a beautiful, very colorful painting hanging on the wall. It reminded her of a

Matisse or Pollock. It was signed by Marc Freeman. She didn't recognize the name, so she pulled out her cell and did a Google search. According to the article about him, his paintings sold for $25,000 to $100,000. She did another quick search of the Kinkade she recognized over the fireplace, and was shocked when she learned the value to be well over $30,000.

How does an FBI agent earning less than a hundred grand a year afford this kind of art, and what's up with the new clothes? Who are you, Joe?

She still had no idea. There was only one place left to search, the garage. In there she found the washer and dryer. She looked inside the dryer, it was full of towels and washcloths.

There they are, but how could you just leave them here, not folded and in their place in the bathroom? What's up with you Joe? It's like there's two people living here.

Whispering to her self during surveillance was just part of her process. It kept her thoughts organized. Usually her whispers were just her random thoughts, but when she thought about what she'd just said... maybe there were two people living in this house.

Is Jake Mr. OCD or is it you, Joe?

The garage had an older, faded Toyota Corolla parked on one side. The other parking area was empty, but she saw several more cardboard boxes stacked in the back corner. She un-stacked them one by one and laid them in a row in the empty parking space. They were packed more like the boxes in the guest room with no particular order of the contents. She found scattered tools and three wooden handled hammers in one box. In the others were more old t-shirts and sports equipment, but in two were stacks of framed pictures of Joe's parents and what looked like his friends.

Why aren't these inside, on your walls? Why would you just leave them out here?

She re-stacked the boxes like she had found them and continued looking around the garage. She opened a door to what appeared to be a small storage room. It was empty except for one small box and two black garbage bags.

The first bag was filled with brown paper, the kind used to protect glasses and dishes in a move. In the second one she found more clothes, but not like the old t-shirts and socks she'd found in the other boxes. In this bag, she found a pair of leather pants. They were adorned with black rhinestones running down each leg; a red macramé headband, a macramé belt; a leather vest and a bright red sleeveless t-shirt with AC-DC printed on the front. In the bottom was a pair of high-top black boots that laced up the front with bright red laces.

What the hell was this? She whispered. *Why are you saving socks with holes in them, but throwing expensive leather clothes away?*

She was pretty sure she had found her first sign of Jake.

She laid everything out on the floor and took a few pictures of each item of clothing, then stuffed it all back into the garbage bag.

She checked her watch. It was almost 2 p.m., she'd been inside for six hours. She needed to wrap it up and get out of there soon.

She picked up the last box and set it on top of the washer. It was taped closed. In the kitchen, she found a knife and carefully cut the tape and opened the small box. Inside, there were two silver frames. One was his framed Bachelor of Arts degree from the University of Arkansas and the other was his Arkansas State Bar Certificate. Underneath the frames was a shoe-box, also taped closed.

When she got it opened, it was almost full of handwritten picture post cards. They were all addressed to Joe and written and signed by Hannah. Each one had a different picture and post mark from all over the United States. There had to be at least a hundred of them, maybe more. She knew she didn't have time to read them all, but something in her gut told her they were important. She took the box into the kitchen, laid it on the island and one by one, front and back, took pictures of the cards with her phone.

When she had finally finished, she re-taped the shoe-box with a roll of clear packing tape she'd discovered in the garage and put it back on the bottom of the small cardboard box she had found them in. Carefully placing back the frames, she closed the box, re-taped it and put it back in the storeroom and closed the door.

Once more she checked her watch.

Damn!

It was almost 6, it had taken over 3 hours to take the pictures and it would be getting dark soon. She had to get out of there.

Rather than being seen coming out of Joe's backyard gate, she decided that she would leave through the front door, acting like she belonged there.

She was exhausted and hadn't realized how far of a walk it was back to her rental car. It was almost 6:30 when she drove out of the strip center's parking lot on her way to the airport.

ELIZABETH

After her lunch with Joe and Rob, Elizabeth walked into her office and the first thing she did was lock the four bundles of Joe's letters away in the bottom file drawer of her desk. When she whirled her chair around she saw Judy, her paralegal, standing in the doorway.

"How is Judge Daily?" Judy asked.

"He's very weak, but awake and talking."

"I've been praying for him."

Elizabeth smiled. "Thanks, Judy. That's about all we can do now." Not wanting to talk anymore about the judge, she changed the subject. "Did we get anything from the Jackson D.A. yet?"

Judy shook her head. "No, and they're not being very cooperative. I've called them twice and all they're saying is that it's on the way. I'm assuming they're overnighting them. Hopefully, we'll have everything in the morning."

Elizabeth pulled a yellow legal-sized notepad out of her briefcase and laid it on her desk. "We need to start putting together a 'To Do' list on this case. How's your schedule this afternoon? Could we start on that in maybe thirty minutes?"

Judy looked at her watch. "I've got a few things to finish, could we make it in an hour?"

"Ok. Let's do it in the small conference room at three fifteen. Could you check with Will and see if he's available too? I'd like his input on this."

"You got it." Judy spun around to leave.

"Hey Judy," Elizabeth said before she walked off.

"Need something else?"

"Yeah... could you spread the word to the others that I'd like to be alone until our meeting. I can't take anymore sad faces today."

When Judy left, Elizabeth closed her office door, pulled the privacy drapes, stepped out of her heels, and plopped down on her sofa.

She sat in the dark watching the tiny particles of dust dancing in a beam of sunshine that was streaming through the slits of the window blinds. It reminded her of the times she used to walk to her grandfather's courthouse and wait for him in his chambers after school. He had a window by his desk in almost the same place, and on sunny days sitting on his couch doing her homework, she remembered seeing the same light show.

Closing her eyes, she let her mind wander. What would life be like without her grandfather in it. He'd always been there. More like a father than a grandfather. Although she loved her real father, he'd never been a big part of her life. Her parents divorced when she was only five and he just seemed to disappear from her life. Even now, after all these years, she didn't know all of the circumstances that caused the split between her parents. Whatever caused it must have been bad because her mother had always refused to talk about it.

Through the years, she'd seen her father often, but their relationship had never been close. She'd tried to reconnect with him once she'd become an adult, but he just didn't respond, so she let it go.

Truthfully, not having her father in her life left no real scars because she'd always had the judge. Realizing now what a busy schedule he'd had made her love him even more for everything he must have sacrificed to somehow always be there for her. He was there at every soccer game, school play, or graduation she'd ever had. He went out of his way to spoil her, buying her first car, and insisting on buying her a new wardrobe for every season of every year she could remember. He paid for her college and law school, and absolutely wouldn't take no for an answer about funding her law practice.

And somehow through all of his spoiling, he had taught her not to become arrogant, entitled, or develop any kind of superior attitude about who she was. He did this by making her constantly work, volunteering for numerous charities and serving food at homeless shelters.

When she was a teenager, she had rebelled and refused, but his reaction changed that quickly. He didn't yell or even raise his voice. Actually, it wasn't anything he said. It was the disappointment in his eyes that broke her heart. So, reluctantly she agreed to go with him to a homeless shelter one Saturday. When he walked in the door, everyone rushed up to him and gave him hugs. They all seemed to know him. There was a young family living there who had two kids. He introduced her to them and suggested that she stay with them while he got the food ready, so she did.

Both of the kids were younger than her and very shy. The boy was only about eight or nine, and the little girl was five. She could still remember that sweet, tiny child holding up her hand and counting her fingers when she had asked her how old she was. The parents were shy and meek as well, but couldn't stop talking about what a special person her grandfather was.

"He's been so good to us," the mother said. "He got Billy a new job. We're going to have a real home again soon."

Elizabeth couldn't help but notice the frayed and worn clothes they were wearing. They were clean, but very shabby.

"I like your bracelet," the little girl said. "It's so pretty. Daddy told me he'd get me a bracelet too someday. I've always wanted one."

Elizabeth could still remember how she felt hearing those words. Until that day, she'd just assumed that everyone was like her. She thought every little girl had a closet full of new dresses and had a jewelry chest full of bracelets.

The judge rang a bell. "Come on everyone, come and get it while it's hot."

The two kids jumped up and ran to the front of the line. The parents said, "Please excuse us," and followed their children.

Although the food smelled good, she had no appetite. The judge waved at her, so she walked behind the long service tables and helped dish out the dessert. Her grandfather knew everyone's name and asked each person he served how they were getting along. For over an hour, she watched him smiling and laughing at everyone who passed him. That night, she realized who he really was and it made her proud to be his granddaughter.

On their way out, she stopped to say goodbye to the family she'd met. "I want you to have this." She slipped off her bracelet and handed it to the little girl.

"Really!" The little girl screamed with excitement.

"Yes, really. It's all yours now," she said.

"Will you help me put it on?" the little girl asked, staring up at her with big blue eyes as she held out her arm.

Elizabeth had never forgotten that day, because it changed her. That was all it had taken to make her realize just how fortunate she was. And seeing her grandfather's generosity and true heart that night made her sincerely appreciate everything he did for his family, for everyone else, and the life he'd given her. And every time Judy pulled out that bracelet and wore it to work, it made her smile and feel good about herself and the life she was trying to live.

The clock above her desk said 2:30. She had 45 minutes left until the meeting. Although she knew it probably wasn't a good idea, she walked in her bare feet to her desk and pulled out a bundle of Joe's letters and started to read.

ELIZABETH HEARD a knock on her door and looked up.

"It's 3:20, you still want to meet today?" Judy asked.

Elizabeth glanced at her watch. "Yes, I'm sorry. I lost track of time. I'll meet you there in a few minutes."

Judy stood in the door and watched Elizabeth reach for a tissue and wipe her eyes. "Honey, we don't have to do this today. You don't look like you're in any mood to talk business. Why don't you call it a day and go home?"

"No," she said. "Work is exactly what I need. Anything to get my mind off this."

Elizabeth knew that Judy thought she was talking about the judge and he *was* part of her problem, but in reality, it was Joe's letters that kept playing and replaying over in her head.

Somehow, she managed to block the letters and pull herself together to make it through the meeting with Judy and her older brother Will.

Will had grown up to be a fine man and a very talented attorney. He, like his sister Judy (with some help from the judge) had come a long way from that homeless shelter where Elizabeth had first met them so many years ago.

They had become an important and integral part of her law firm, as well as being her two most trusted friends. They both arrived on her doorstep the first day she opened her firm. Of course, she recognized the judge's large hands in all of it, but they seemed very sincere. They had been with her since that first day and they made a great team. And although she had three other very capable associate attorneys working in her firm, Judy and Will were the only ones with whom she could confide her darkest secrets and problems.

They ended the meeting at 5:15. When she walked out she saw Rob standing in the lobby.

He kissed her. "How about seafood tonight? There's a new place that just opened up out by the reservoir and I hear it's yummy! Kate and Dave are gonna meet us there at 6:30."

Elizabeth shook her head. "I'm sorry, but I'm not up for that tonight. I just want to go home and soak in the tub with a nice Chardonnay. Would you mind going without me?"

"Are you sure? Want me to bring you a doggie bag full of fish to go with your Chardonnay?"

"No thanks. I'll fix something at home. You go on and have fun. I'll see you tomorrow."

It was actually a nice Pinot Grigio and soaking in the hot tub of soapy water helped relax her. When she picked up the bottle to pour herself a second glass, the label reminded her of the Biltmore mansion and winery where she had bought the bottle. The trip to Asheville had been a surprise gift from Rob and she had loved it. On their last night staying in the historic Biltmore hotel, sitting on the long veranda with its amazing view of the Smokey Mountains, Rob had popped the question.

They had been dating for almost two years and it was, as he put it that night, "the next logical step."

It was typical Rob. Trying to be romantic, but blowing the moment because he couldn't help himself and his analytical mind from stating the obvious. He was right, it was the next logical step. So, without any hesitation, she said yes.

After her long soak, she turned on the shower, washed her hair, dried off, and threw on a t-shirt and a pair of sweatpants. In the kitchen, she found some leftover rotisserie chicken, made a small spinach salad, and settled on the couch in the living room. She had made it through three of the four bundles of Joe's letters at the office, so she removed the rubber bands from the fourth bundle and began to read while she picked at her dinner and drank her wine.

As she read, she wondered if Joe was reading hers at the same time. She tried to recall what she'd said in her letters, but it had been too long to visualize the words. She did remember the hurt she felt inside and how angry and disappointed she was.

Suddenly, the words she had written in one of her last letters to Joe flashed in her mind. "Why won't you at least write me back to say goodbye?"

She remembered it only because she had just read those exact words in one of Joe's letters.

She wasn't sure why, maybe it was the wine, but she wasn't crying anymore. So when she got to Joe's last letter, his words didn't make her sad. Instead, his words made her open her eyes and admit something was missing in her life.

For the third time, she opened his last letter and slowly, read his words again.

Elizabeth,

This will be my last letter. I don't know what I've done wrong or why you've decided to do this, but I have to accept your decision and move on with my life. I just hope that someday I will find someone who I love as much as I love you now. Someone who makes my heart pound with just a touch of her hand. Someone with eyes I can get lost in. Someone who can make me feel weak from just a kiss. Someone who I can't imagine not spending the rest of my life with. Someone I truly love with all of my heart, someone... like you.

I miss you desperately!

Love,

Joe

She refolded the letter, slipped it back into the envelope and leaned back on the sofa. Her cell phone rang behind her on the kitchen cabinet. Her watch showed 10:16. She didn't have the energy to walk to it, so she just let it ring. She knew who it was... and the last person she wanted to talk to now was Rob.

A familiar chime sounded on her phone. "Good, he left a voice-mail. I'll listen to it tomorrow." Then, her house phone rang.

"God, why is he being so persistent?" When she stood, she could feel the buzz from the three glasses of wine, but made it to the phone on the fourth ring. "Hello?"

"Is this Elizabeth Weller?" An unfamiliar female voice asked.

"Yes," she said,

"Elizabeth, I'm Doctor Molly Stern, I'm the resident on call tonight at the Arkansas Heart Hospital and you were on the emergency call list for Royce Daily."

"Oh God! What's wrong?

"Mr. Daily's heart went into an irregular arrhythmia about twenty minutes ago. His heart rate began beating erratically, but we were able to get it back under control. He's stable now, but still under close observation and in a guarded condition. His heart rate is at fifty-five now and slowly climbing, but his oxygen levels are very low. I'd like to intubate him to try to get them up."

Suddenly completely sober, she took several deep breaths forcing herself to calm down and think. "Intubate... that means a breathing tube, right? Are you aware of his DNR? I'm his medical power of attorney and he's given me very specific instructions about this."

"That's why I'm calling. I can't do it without your permission because of that DNR, but in my opinion, this procedure shouldn't be considered as life support. It would only be a temporary fix to help him get his oxygen level up."

Elizabeth's mind filled with her grandfather's face. The memory was of the day he told her that he wanted her to be his medical power of attorney.

"I don't think your mother could make the correct decision," he had said. "Please don't let them put me on a machine just to keep my body alive. When that time comes, promise me you will not let that happen. Unplug me and leave it to God to decide if it's my time. Don't get in his way. Promise me."

"Dr. Stern, in your opinion, what will happen if you don't install the breathing tube? Will he die?" Elizabeth asked softly.

"Probably not. Not immediately anyway. His oxygen level is very low, but not falling. If we do nothing, it's possible they will rise or just remain where they are. However, at their current levels, eventually his internal organs will stop functioning and shut down. I realize this puts you in a difficult position, but honestly Elizabeth, in his current condition, with his heart only working at about twenty percent... he's not going to live much longer anyway, a few weeks at most. A temporary breathing tube for a few hours isn't, in my opinion, going against his wishes of not being resuscitated. He is conscious and alert. This is not a resuscitation, it is a simple medical procedure to improve his condition. That's all."

She didn't immediately respond, lost in thought. "Elizabeth, are you still there?"

"Yes," she said. "This is a difficult decision. If we do this, you have to promise me that it will only be for a few hours and if I tell you to remove it, you're not going to fight me."

"You have my word on that. Twenty-four hours at the most,"

she said.

"Dr. Stern, I know my grandfather pretty well. If he's awake and alert like you say, he's probably going to fight you on this."

"No, I've already explained to him why I wanted to do it and he seemed ok with it."

"Ok then, that makes this easier. You have my permission. How long will it take?"

"We need to sedate him first, it should be over in thirty minutes or so."

Elizabeth hung up, ran up the stairs, threw on some running shoes, and flew out the door. They let her in to see him at 11:15. The sight of the large breathing apparatus connected to him shocked her so much she had to sit down. He appeared to still be asleep from the sedation. He was propped up with several pillows behind him, in almost a sitting position.

Regaining her composure, she stood up from the chair, walked to his bedside, and took his hand in hers. "I hope you're not mad at me for letting them do this to you," she whispered.

He squeezed her hand. Then he slowly opened his eyes, looked up at her, and nodded.

"Yes, you're mad at me?" she asked.

He furrowed his brow, squinted his eyes, and shook his head side to side.

"No? You're not mad at me? I know you told me not to let them ever do something like this, but..."

He squeezed her hand harder and made a writing motion with his other hand.

"You want a pen and paper?"

He nodded.

She walked to the nurses' station and asked for a notepad and pen. Back by his bedside, she put the pen in his hand and laid the yellow lined notepad on his lap. He began to write. When he finished, he held up the pad.

It's ok. It's not my time yet.

She smiled at him. "I agree, Grandpa, not for a long time yet."

He began writing again and held up the pad. **What's wrong?**

"Are you kidding?" she yelled. "You almost died!"

He began writing again. **I'll be ok, but you can't fool me. What's wrong?**

He had always been able to see right through her. "It's not important. We can talk about it when you're better."

He wrote something and held up the pad again. **You read the letters?**

She dropped her head. "Yes, but let's talk about it tomorrow."

He wrote on the pad and looked into her eyes as he showed her the pad. **There may not be a tomorrow.**

Elizabeth's eyes filled with tears. "Please don't say that!"

He wrote for a long time, then turned the pad around for her to read. **I'm counting on you to be brave and help your mother get through this. Remember, I'll be in heaven and very happy. No need for sadness and tears. Please tell me what's wrong.**

Elizabeth sighed, and shook her head. "Ok... but I don't really know what to tell you other than, yes, I've read all of Joe's letters and you were right to make me promise to read them. It was important for me to know what he went through and how he felt about me then." She stopped to wipe her eyes. "It was such a long time ago when he wrote those letters... I have no idea if he still feels that way."

Judge Daily wrote again on the pad. **How do you feel about him?**

She couldn't hold back any longer. She burst into tears, fell across his bed, and cried. "I guess I've never stopped loving him," she said through her tears. "I don't know what to do now."

When she raised back up, the judge took the pen and began to write. **Promise me. You will follow wherever your heart takes you.**

"I promise, but what if Joe doesn't feel the same?"

The judge only had to write one more note. **It's out of your control, but you will know soon. What's important is, what will you do if he does? Read Joe's last letter once more, then ask yourself... Is that how you feel about Rob?**

When she got home, the last thing she did before crying herself to sleep, was read Joe's letter.

THE POST CARDS

Waiting for takeoff sitting on the Tarmac, River pulled her cell out of her purse and punched in her password. There were two voice messages from when she was in Joe's house. The first one was from Samantha telling her that Joe had actually canceled the existing security contract on his new house that was installed by the previous owners.

"I assume he thought that nobody in their right mind would break into an FBI agent's house." Sam snickered in the message. "But I guess he doesn't know you very well! Call me back when you can, and be careful."

The second message was from Elizabeth. "River, they put the judge on a respirator. His heart went into v-fib and we almost lost him, but he's stable now. The respirator is only temporary to help get his oxygen levels up. Are you going to make the nine o'clock meeting? I've called you three times. Where the hell are you? I need you at this meeting." She didn't say goodbye.

River dialed Elizabeth's number, but before she could hit send, the flight attendant said, "You need to turn that off and put it away." River turned off the phone.

As soon as the plane reached altitude and leveled and River heard the chimes, she hit the button on her arm rest, reclined her seat, and closed her eyes. She was exhausted and wished she could fall asleep, but her mind was racing, flashing pictures in her head as her brain began sorting through everything she'd seen and done that day. She tried to concentrate on some of the flashing images, but all she could think about was the judge and Elizabeth's message.

The flight attendant set the white wine she'd ordered on her tray table and she took a long-needed sip. It was not very good; so dry it made her wince and shake her head, but at least it contained something she needed... alcohol. The second sip went down a little easier. The crisp desert dryness made her think about the judge again and the last time she'd had dinner with him.

Even with complete strangers, the judge couldn't help himself. If he saw someone making a mistake or doing something wrong, in his own unique way he would help them figure it out.

The dinner was River's attempt at compensation to the judge. He had just saved her once again, helping her get out of some real trouble. A good steak was the only thing he'd accept as payment for what he'd done. She'd taken him to what she'd heard was one of the finest restaurants in Little Rock. He insisted on buying the wine and had reluctantly agreed to let her buy the food. When the bottle of Cabernet Sauvignon arrived, the very young waiter, trying to use a French accent, went through a very impressive routine presenting the bottle. Then he removed the cork and poured just a sip in the judge's glass for him to taste.

"For you, monsieur," he said badly. His presentation was a bit over the top, exaggerating his every move.

The judge lifted his glass, holding it by the base of the stem, swirled it around and sniffed it like a wine Sommelier. Then he took a sip, swished it around in his mouth and, to the horror of their young, pompous wine steward, spit it into his water glass.

"Très bon!" the judge said smiling.

Not knowing what to do next, the waiter asked, "Is there a problem with the wine, sir?"

The judge, still smiling said, "Vous êtes plein de merde!"

Forgetting his phony French accent, the waiter said, "What?"

The judge gave him a sympathetic look. "Son, I know you're trying hard, but you're not fooling anyone with that accent. Take some advice from an old, wise man. Nobody likes a phony."

The waiter dropped his head. "I'm sorry, I just started here and I thought that maybe—"

"That's a common problem with being young," the judge interrupted. "Just be yourself. I'd bet you're a pretty good guy. Be proud of who you are, just be yourself and you'll do just fine in this world."

The waiter smiled. "I'll do that, thanks." He started to leave, but turned back around. "Was that French?" he asked. "What does it mean?"

The judge laughed. "Yes, it was French and the first time I said, Très bon! That means very good! So, you can pour the wine."

"I don't get it? If it was good, then why did you spit it out?"

"Well, young man, with all your French-ness and pomp and circumstance I thought I was at a wine tasting, and spitting out your wine after you taste it is proper etiquette."

"Really?" He controted his face and curled up his lip. "That's gross! What was that last thing you said?"

The judge grinned. "You mean, 'vous, êtes, plein, de merde'? Look it up. It's something you don't want to be."

When the waiter walked away, River said, "Vous êtes plein de merde? I'm not looking it up. What does it mean?"

Breaking into a loud belly laugh, he said, "You're full of shit."

"Would you like another glass of wine?" The voice startled River out of her memory,. She looked up to see the flight attendant standing over her.

"Another wine?" the attendant asked.

"I'd like to switch to a red. Do you have a nice Cabernet Sauvignon?"

"Let me check in first class. If they have it, I'll sneak it out for you." She did, and it was wonderful, both glasses.

The plane landed hard, waking River up. She looked at her watch and couldn't believe that she'd actually fallen asleep for almost an hour. On her drive home, she forced her worries about the judge out of her head and let her mind flash the same pictures it had started on the plane: her conversation with Hannah, what she'd found in Joe's house, the new suits, the shirts perfectly positioned three inches apart, the shoes lined up in exact order, the expensive paintings. Not one personal item in the entire house, only in the garage. What did it all mean?

And the trash bag of leather clothes, just thrown away. Was Joe trying to remove evidence of Jake? What about the shoe box of post cards from Joe's mother? Why were they so important to her—so important that she spent three hours taking pictures of them? Why did she do that? What could they actually tell her? She had no idea, but she'd learned to always go with her hunches. It's usually those unexplained intuitive feelings she got, that opened a door or shined a brilliant light on something she would have otherwise missed.

On her way home, she stopped at a 24-hour Walmart and bought a box of postcard size photo paper. When she got to her apartment, she loaded the paper in her printer and began printing the postcard photos. She stapled the front and backs of each postcard together and organized them by dates. Her hands were throbbing from squeezing the stapler and her back was killing her from leaning over, but after two hours, they were all stacked neatly on her dining room table.

She counted them carefully. There were three hundred and five of them, dating from 1983 to 1989. *Wow! Hannah sent Joe a postcard every week for six years*, she said out loud. *Wait, that doesn't add up.*

She grabbed her phone, opened the calculator app, and punched in fifty-two times six. The screen showed three hundred and twelve. So, once again, slower this time she recounted the postcards. There were only three hundred and five, not three hundred twelve. She was sure she had taken pictures of each postcard in that box. She wouldn't have been that careless to miss seven of them. She thought about taking the pictures. She had been meticulous. Laying ten out at a time and then carefully moving and stacking them to the other countertop. No, she was confident she'd taken them all. Why did Hannah not send one on those weeks?

She glanced at the clock on the microwave. It was 2 a.m. and she could barely hold her eyes open. She was supposed to meet with Elizabeth and Joe at 9 a.m., but she had more to do for the judge before that meeting. She still had nothing solid to tell him, but considering his current decline, she knew she had to hurry. There had to be something here, and her gut was telling her that the answer was somewhere buried in those missing postcards.

She was having trouble concentrating and knew she was too tired to go on, so she decided to go to bed and start again in the morning.

JOHN KELLY

John Kelly's rise to Special Agent in Charge of the State of Mississippi was historic. He was the youngest agent to rise to that position in the history of the FBI. And although he enjoyed the prestige and power that came with the job, deep inside he missed being in the field. His job included more paperwork and administrative decisions than he'd counted on, but it was his job and he'd accepted his fate.

Until now he had been able to ignore his desires to be out pounding the street, digging up leads to solve a case, but this case was personal. Joe Jensen was his long-time friend, probably his best friend, and he just couldn't follow his normal path this time. So he put the word out in the Bureau, giving instructions to be personally contacted immediately on each and every development in Joe's father's case, no matter how insignificant.

His cell phone rang by his bed at 11 p.m. He wasn't asleep so he answered on the second ring.

"John Kelly," he said into the phone.

"John, I apologize for calling this late. My name is Bob Barret. I'm a special agent working out of Quantico, Virginia and I've come across something I think you might be interested in."

"What do you do at Quantico?" John asked.

"I'm an instructor. My background is in IT and they recruited me to help in the Cyber Crime division. So really, I'm just another computer geek on the government's payroll," he said with a chuckle.

"Ha! I doubt that. Cyber Crime is out of control and we need experts like you in the Bureau just to try and keep up. So, what's up?"

"I'm not sure if it's anything, but when I ran it, I came across a red flag to contact you."

"A red flag?" John said confused.

"Yeah, there's a pin on special agent Joe Jensen's file to contact you with any information concerning him or his family. His father, Luke Jensen has been arrested, right?" he asked. "Is that why it's flagged?"

"Yes. So is this about his father, Luke?"

"No, it's concerning Joe. Like I said, it may not be anything, but because of the flag I thought I should at least report it to you. Joe and I live in the same neighborhood. When I first heard about it, I didn't think much of it and was just going to let it go, but when I saw your flag and read about Joe's father's arrest, I reconsidered."

John walked downstairs and made some coffee while he listened to Bob's recount of what his neighborhood watch guy had told him. "He actually saw her coming out of Joe's house?" John asked.

"Yes, but when he realized that she was walking, he got suspicious."

"Did he get a good look at her?"

Bob started laughing, "Oh yes. He said that she was without a doubt the hottest woman he'd ever seen. He couldn't stop talking about her ass."

"Any more accurate description, other than an amazing ass? So far, I'm thinking Jennifer Lopez did it."

"Long legs, big boobs, very short and very tight dress, and of course, a world class ass!"

"And you were just going to let this one go by?" John said. "What's wrong with you, man?"

He laughed again. "Well, I guess it was my wife and five kids that slowed me down."

"Did he check out Joe's house? Any signs of a break in?"

"After he told me, we rode over to Joe's house, but saw nothing suspicious," Bob said. "He did get her plate."

"I thought you said she was walking."

"She was, but he followed her to a strip center where she got into a rental car. I ran the plates. It was rented to a River Rivers from Little Rock, Arkansas. Apparently, she's a PI. It made me wonder, why would a PI from Arkansas be breaking into an FBI agent's house in Virginia? That's why I ran Joe's ticket and found your flag!"

"Seriously, River Rivers? Her parents must have a warped sense of humor. Anything else?"

"Not that I can think of. Would you like to talk to the neighborhood watch guy? I can get you his contact info if you want it," he said. "Oh yeah, he did say that when she saw him, she just smiled real big and waved like she knew him. Brass balls. I bet she's a damn good PI."

"If she's that good, how did she get caught by the neighborhood watch? Send me the watch guy's info and tell him to keep a close watch on Joe's house. Thanks for calling, Bob. Hope to get to meet you in person someday. I'll look you up the next time I'm in Quantico." John hung up the phone and immediately made a call to two of his agents.

BUSTED

River's alarm buzzed at 6 a.m. She felt like hell, with a slight headache, but three Tylenols and a hot shower revived her. There wasn't time to dry her hair, so she just pulled it back, towel dried, into a pony tail. She slipped on some shorts, a tank top and settled in her bare feet, sipping her coffee at the dining room table behind the stack of postcards.

The first thing she did was locate the missing weeks in the stack and mark the spot with an over-sized blank sheet of paper. Then she went back and wrote down the date of each missing week, hoping to find an obvious pattern. There wasn't one. Then, she pulled each post-card Joe's mother had sent the week before, and laid them down in front of her. After reading the first one, she figured it out.

Dear Joe,

Looking forward to seeing you next week in Tyler. It will be good to see Jake again too. Please drive safe.

Love,

Mom

She felt stupid. It was so obvious. How could she not have thought of that before? Hannah didn't send Joe a postcard because he was there with her.

Realizing why the cards were missing, she then saw a pattern on four of the dates. They were all in the Summer, when Joe was on break from school. But two were not. One was in October and the other in February. She located the cards for the week before, and slowly read them.

Dear Joe,

I know this is terrible timing, but your father has to have gallbladder surgery next week and we really need you to help out. Is there any way you could get away and come play next week? We can't afford to lose the money from this gig. Please, Joe. Can you come?

You can reach me at this number. 901-775-3321 room 232.

We need you.

Love,

Mom

The second card was a similar emergency about his father's appendix. "Well...that explains it," she said, leaning back in her chair.

She walked back to the kitchen, poured herself another cup of coffee, and sat back down behind the postcards. Sitting in silence sipping her coffee, she tried to force herself to move on and concentrate on something else; something constructive to tell the judge, but her mind kept returning to the postcards.

Ok brain... I give up. What am I missing?

She scanned the dates again, but nothing seemed obvious. Still, her persistent nagging intuition was normally right and what she was looking for was usually staring her in the face.

What is it?

She just couldn't see anything, so she climbed the stairs and began putting on her makeup and worked on her hair. Then she changed into a tight gray skirt, and navy silk blouse, and strapped on a pair of matching navy heels. After a few checks in the mirror, she walked back down the stairs, but didn't sit at the table.

She had to force herself to think of something else to break this deadlock, so she settled on the couch and started reading Sam and Wes's reports again, hoping something would jump out at her, but nothing did. Sam had also included Joe's father's arrest report and she'd scanned it, but if she was going to keep her appointment with Elizabeth and Joe at 9 a.m., it wouldn't hurt to read it more carefully.

The dates of six cold case murders caught her attention. They stretched back over twenty years from 1983 to 1989.

That's interesting.

The old murders took place during the same years Hannah had sent Joe all those post cards. It was a very interesting coincidence, but her training as a private investigator told her to never believe in coincidences.

To double check, she picked up the file and walked back to the table and sat down. She flipped through the pages to find the date of the first old murder case and wrote it down. Then the second, third, fourth, fifth, and finally the sixth.

When she laid the murder dates next to the dates of the missing postcards, except for one, they matched exactly. Her heart thundered.

What is this saying? What could this mean?

She re-read the seven postcards of the week before the missing ones. Only two mentioned where Joe was meeting the band. The first mentioned Tyler. She flipped back through the police report and checked the location of the first murder and her heart sank; it was Tyler, Texas.

The only other mention of a city where Joe was meeting the band was when his father was having his appendectomy surgery. The hospital was in Memphis, but the club was in Collierville, according to Hannah's card. She flipped back through the pages... Her heart raced when she saw that the fourth murder was in Collierville, Tennessee.

There was no other mention of the cities where Joe met the band, so she had no way of knowing if they matched too. Then suddenly, she had one last and startling epiphany: Joe's father couldn't have committed at least two of the murders, because he was flat on his back in a hospital.

She finally understood what her intuition was trying to show her. This evidence could easily free Joe's father, but at the same time put

Joe—or was it Jake?—in his place. The problem was, of course, this evidence was inadmissible because she had stolen it.

What in the hell do I do now? And what am I going to tell the judge?

River packed the postcards and the police report into her briefcase, locked her front door, and began walking toward her car.

———

"Is that her? It has to be!" The agent asked Wes London.

Wes sighed, "Yes, that's her. She's never going to forgive me for this."

"I don't mean to be rude dude, but how in the hell did you ever get her to agree to a date in the first place?" The female agent asked, grinning.

"It took me two years..."

"Sorry, Wes, but she's not just way out of your league, she's in a completely different stratosphere."

When River reached her car, out of the corner of her eye she saw Wes and two strangers, a man and a woman walking toward her. "Oh God," she whispered, "what does he want now?"

"Hi, River," he said.

Smiling at the three of them, she said, "Oh, hi Wes. I'm sorry I can't talk now, I'm late for a meeting."

He just shrugged his shoulders and gave her a weird look.

"Are you River Rivers?" the woman asked.

She stopped smiling. "That depends. Why are you asking?" She shot Wes daggers from her eyes.

This time the man spoke, "Were you in Virginia yesterday?"

A rush of blood raced through her body. "What business is that of yours?"

"River, I'm Special Agent Miles and this is my partner Special Agent Fletcher. We're with the FBI out of the Jackson, Mississippi field office. We've been assigned to bring you to Jackson for a meeting with our boss."

"Am I under arrest?" she asked calmly.

"No ma'am, but if you don't cooperate and come with us peace-fully, we do have that authority," the woman agent said.

"On what charge?"

The man smiled. "Well, let me think. How about suspicion of burglary?"

"Burglary is a local police matter, the FBI has no jurisdiction," River said, facing them, folding her arms in front of her.

"How about we just handcuff you right here and drag your ass to to the Little Rock jail as a person of interest on seven serial murders! Would that pass your jurisdiction test?" the female agent shouted.

"River, please," Wes said. "Cooperate and go with them. They're good people. Please, just relax and go. They don't want it to go down like this."

"Ok... Let's go," she said holding out her hands to be cuffed.

"That's not going to be necessary," the male agent said, "you're not under arrest."

In the black SUV, on their way to the airport, River said, "Wes, when this is over and I get back to Little Rock, you can forget about that date!"

When they landed in Jackson, there was another black SUV wait-ing. On the ride to the FBI office, the female agent turned and looked at her. "Wes had nothing to do with this. I've known him for years. He's really a sweet guy. Why don't you give him another chance?"

River rolled her eyes, turned her head and looked away.

FROM HIS LATE-NIGHT PHONE CALL, John Kelly knew River was going to be a looker, but when the agents brought her into his office it took him a moment to gather his professional demeanor. His first reaction was to whistle and pound his chest. The neighborhood watch guy wasn't exaggerating. She was stunning.

Forcing himself to look into her eyes, he said, "Miss Rivers, I'm John Kelly and I'm the agent in charge of the state of Mississippi. I have a few questions to ask you."

She crossed her legs, and smiled at him, exposing her perfect gleaming white teeth. "What happened to," she held up her hands making air quotes, "special?"

It took him a moment to catch her remark. "I've never liked that part of my title, just call me John."

"Ok John, what's this all about?"

"May I call you River?"

"Please," she said crossing her legs to the other side.

"River, this is all about a very good friend of mine I think you might know. His name is Joe Jensen. Ever heard of him?"

Trying to remain calm, River smiled again. "Yes, I met him a few days ago."

"Where did you meet him?" John asked.

"At the Arkansas Heart Hospital, he was there visiting a friend of mine."

"What's this mutual friend's name?"

River frowned and looked down. "Judge Royce Daily."

John blinked in surprise. "You know Judge Daily? How's he doing?"

"I'm not sure. I got a voice mail from his granddaughter last night, he's taken a turn for the worst and they had to put him on a respirator. You know him too?" she asked.

"I've never met him in person, but we've had a few long chats about Joe. He seems like a great man. How do you know him?"

"I've known him for years. I met him through my work."

"Your work as a private investigator?"

"Yes. I testified in a few trials he oversaw and now I also work with his granddaughter, Elizabeth."

John stood, walked around his desk, and sat on the edge in front of her. "I understand that he's terminal. I sure hate to hear that. So... if you know Joe, the judge, and work for his granddaughter, you must have had a key to Joe's house, right?"

River tried, but couldn't hold her expression and her face dropped. "I'm not exactly sure what you're talking about, but if it has to do with my trip to Virginia, then I can't tell you that."

John shook his head. "Ok, I understand, so you were working a case in Virginia?"

"Yes," she said.

"Who is the client?"

"I don't have to tell you that."

John raised his eyebrows and tilted his head. "I understand that normally you wouldn't have to reveal your client, but in this case I think you need to."

He walked back behind his desk and picked up a file. "Says here that you're only licensed in the states of Arkansas, Louisiana, Texas, and Tennessee. I don't see anything here about Virginia." John looked directly into River's eyes. "We have an eye witness that will testify that he saw you coming out of Joe's house yesterday and we have a rental car receipt in your name that was parked near his house. And, we have three other men who would be more than willing to pick you out of a line up, just to get another look at you, as the woman who drove off in that car. And let's not forget the copy of Joe's FBI file my agents found in your apartment." He paused. "Do I need to go on?"

River shrugged and shook her head. "The old guy in the golf cart?"

"Yes," John grinned. "He was the neighborhood watch. And there are three other older guys who watched you walk to his house at exactly 8 a.m. To quote them, 'You don't see something like her walking down the sidewalk every day.'"

"So what now? Are you going to turn me over to the Virginia police?"

John rolled his eyes and shook his head. "There's been no police report filed and you can thank a *Special Agent* for that." He lifted his hands and made air quotes like she had earlier. "He's one of Joe's neighbors and the one the watch guy reported your break-in to. He called me first and that's why you're here."

"Why did he call you?" she asked.

John sat down next to her. "Look, River, I'm not sure why, but you broke into an FBI agent's house." He frowned. "And that agent just happens to be my best friend. If that wasn't enough, that agent's father has been arrested in a serial murder case that includes the granddaughter of a United States Congressman. How long do you think it would take me to have your license pulled over this? I'm under huge pressure to resolve this case by the congressman, so I don't have time for games. I want to know why you were in Joe's house, who sent you there and what you found. And I want to know now!"

River sat silent, contemplating her options, but this time there weren't any.

"Talk to me, River," John said. "You don't want to lose your license over this do you, or worse, go to jail?"

She shook her head, "No, but—"

"There are no buts here, tell me who sent you there," John said interrupting her. "No client is worth your career."

River looked at the floor. "It wasn't really a client. I was just trying to find out something for Judge Daily. About Joe."

"Judge Daily sent you there?" John straightened up in his chair.

"Not specifically, he just wanted me to figure out if Joe is who he thinks he is. I came up with nothing with my normal process, so I thought that if he had something to hide, his house would be the obvious place to look."

John stood and paced the room. "I've talked to the judge three times. He's never once had anything but praise for Joe. This makes no sense. What is he so worried about?"

River didn't answer.

He stopped pacing and looked at her. "Ok, I understand you not wanting to break the judge's confidence. So, you broke into Joe's house searching for information for the judge. And then you got caught by a seventy-seven-year-old neighborhood watch guy in a golf cart. I have a full report on my desk about you. It says that you are a very good and professional PI. How could you have been so careless?"

"I promised the judge I would find out about Joe before he died. I didn't have time not to be careless. It was stupid, but..."

"But what?" John asked. "Did you find something?"

"I'm not sure, but I think so," she said.

"Something about Joe?"

She nodded and opened her briefcase. "And about his father."

JOE AND ELIZABETH

J oe heard the loud ringing, but couldn't figure out what it was. Eventually he realized it was a telephone, but where was it coming from and where in the hell was he? Gradually, his sleepy brain awakened and he realized he was in a hotel room and the ringing phone was his wake-up call.

Forcing himself to get up, he stumbled to the bathroom and turned on the shower. The memories of the day before came rushing back the moment he stepped under the hot water. Images of the judge, Elizabeth, and her letters filled his head. He couldn't remember when he'd fallen asleep, but he knew it had to have been after 4 a.m. because that's what it was the last time he'd looked.

There had been 35 letters in all, and he'd read them several times. Her words had begun as incredulous, but gradually changed to feelings of abandonment and finally anger—from love to hate. He couldn't stop thinking of what she'd said in her last one.

Mr. Joe Jensen,

If we ever pass on the street someday, just walk on by like we've never known each other because truthfully, I don't think we ever did.

I hope that someday, someone will hurt you, like you've hurt me.

Elizabeth

He tried to remember what he'd said in his last letter to her, but couldn't bring it back. The one thing he did remember was that he had never stopped loving her and had always hoped he'd see her again someday. Although he couldn't recall the exact words he'd written, he was sure that even in his last letter he'd told her how much he missed her and that he still loved her.

Lost in thoughts of Elizabeth, almost subconsciously, he stepped out of the shower, toweled his hair, and put on the white terry cloth bathrobe hanging on the door. Then he walked to the bed and carefully folded the letters, put them back into the envelopes and then arranged them in four stacks and bound them together with the rubber bands.

Back in the bathroom shaving, he looked into his own eyes in the mirror wondering what he should do next. There was no denying what he was feeling for Elizabeth, and although he now knew it wasn't her fault, along with those feelings he had growing in his heart for her came the memories of the pain he had lived through; pain he wasn't sure he could survive a second time. It was because of that pain he'd never allowed himself to fall in love again, the reason he couldn't let anyone even get close.

Was she feeling the same way? Did she even read his letters? Could someone hate you for 20 years and somehow change? Even if they found out it wasn't your fault, was it possible for them to love you again? He had no answers.

"I bet Dr. Heart would love to hear about this," he said.

He thought about calling her for some advice, but the more he thought about it, he realized that it might put her in an awkward position. Trained psychologist or not, she was still a woman—the woman who had been sleeping with him for years and he wasn't sure how she would react. He knew she cared about him and always claimed that their relationship was just a friends with benefits thing, but he had always wondered if she was hiding her true feelings because she knew he would just run away if she told him.

He probably needed her advice and he would have to tell her about

Elizabeth eventually, but the last thing he wanted was to hurt her, so he decided to wait.

Not having a clue what to say to Elizabeth or how to act when he saw her, he got in his car and drove to her office.

On the way, he rehearsed a few lines, but they all seemed wrong, so he decided to say nothing and let her lead the way.

"You must be Joe. I'm Judy," a tiny, but beautiful blonde said when he walked in. "Sorry, but Elizabeth is running a little late. Would you like some coffee?"

"Sure, but can you actually reach the coffee pot?"

Judy spun around and smiled. "Am I going to have trouble with you? Read the sign." She pointed at her office door. It said, "No Short Joke Zone"

"You got it, Grumpy," Joe said with a grin.

"Just couldn't help yourself, could you!" She led him into the conference room and introduced him to Will.

He held out his hand and shook Joe's. "Don't let Dopey bother you, she's not good with strangers."

Judy whacked him on his arm with her yellow pad. "Enough with the dwarf references or I'll tell Mom."

"You guys are brother and sister?" Joe asked.

"Yes," Judy said, sitting in the chair across from him. "I'm Elizabeth's paralegal and Will is an associate attorney. We've known Elizabeth and Judge Daily since we were kids."

"Really, that's great," Joe said. "I've known them a long time too. How's the judge doing today?"

"That's why Elizabeth is running late, she wanted to check on him this morning," Will said. "He had a turn last night and they had to intubate him."

"They put him on a respirator?" Joe instantly regretted not visiting him earlier this morning. "What kind of turn?"

Before Will could answer, Elizabeth rushed into the conference room. "Sorry I'm so late, but I wanted to check on the judge and I'm so glad I did!" A big smile spread over her face. "He's doing so much better this morning. His oxygen levels are climbing!"

"Thank God! Judy shouted.

"Is he still on the respirator?" Joe asked.

"Yes, but they said they think they can take it out tonight!" Elizabeth looked across the table at Joe.

The second their eyes met, his heart skipped a beat. "That's great news!" Lost in her eyes, Joe's heart began to race.

Breaking the obvious spell between them, Judy said, "Elizabeth, could I talk to you privately for a second?"

Very slowly, Elizabeth broke the eye lock with Joe and looked at Judy. "Sure, but can't it wait until after our meeting?"

"I don't think so, this is..." Judy paused, searching for words, "Important."

Elizabeth followed Judy out the door and into her office, but before she closed her door completely, he heard Judy exclaim, "Where is your ring?"

Trying to hear their muffled conversation through the door and not be obvious at the same time, Joe turned toward Will, raised his eyebrows, and shrugged. Will returned his shrug, lifted his arms, and silently communicated, "I have no idea either."

Sitting in awkward silence in the conference room trying to do the impossible and not listen, Will and Joe heard the obviously very heated and animated, but indistinguishable sounds coming from Elizabeth's office.

Finally, the door opened and Elizabeth and Judy walked back into the conference room. Judy's face was flushed, but held a slight smile. Elizabeth's revealed nothing obvious.

The only thing Joe had overheard was something about a ring, so instinctively he looked at Elizabeth's hands. It only took him a second to catch it; the large two carat diamond solitaire engagement ring he had noticed on her left hand the day before was missing.

Without any further explanation, Elizabeth took a file from the center of the conference table and opened it. "We received these files this morning from the Jackson, Mississippi district attorney's office," she began. "Supposedly, it contains all of the evidence as well as an explanation of the charges that have been filed against Joe's father, Luke Jensen."

"Where is River?" Will asked. "Wasn't she supposed to be here this morning?"

Elizabeth sighed and took a deep breath. "That's a very good question. I have called her three times, left her two emails, and texted her three times this morning, but she hasn't responded."

"That doesn't sound like River. Think she's ok?" Judy asked.

Elizabeth shook her head. "She told me she had to do a few things to wrap up another case, but promised me she would be here this morning. I'm not really worried about River, she can certainly take care of herself, but I can't imagine why she couldn't at least call or text even if she is working undercover somewhere."

"Does she do that a lot? I mean work undercover?" Joe asked.

"Yeah, a few times and she's very good at it; that's what makes her so effective, but she's never not communicated with me."

"Do we really need her now, at this stage?" Will asked.

Elizabeth nodded. "I think River and what she can dig up is going to be the key to solving this case. We know that Luke didn't commit these murders, but the evidence is pretty compelling. Our job will be to find someone else to shine a light on to create reasonable doubt, that's our only chance. Joe believes, and I agree with him, that the real murderer has to be someone in the band, or someone connected in some way. We all know how River works and how good she is. If there is anyone who can figure this out, it's her. That's why we need her here and we need her here NOW! WHERE IN THE HELL IS SHE?"

"Look, I don't know River at all, " Joe said, "but from what I'm hearing this is not her normal style. Rather than jumping to any conclusions, why don't we give her one more day to surface. Wherever she is, and whatever she's doing must have her in an unusual situation. How many copies of that file do we have?"

"Only one, we just got it this morning, but I can make more," Judy said.

"Ok then, why don't we each take a copy and go through it carefully today to see if anything jumps out. We can meet here again in the morning. Hopefully with River."

Judy jumped up to make the copies and Will stood and shook my hand. "I've got a few calls to make. It's nice to meet you, Joe. See you in the morning."

Finally alone, Joe stood, walked around the conference table, and took Elizabeth's left hand in his. Looking down at the empty ring finger, he said, "Does this mean anything?"

Elizabeth whispered, "I sure hope so."

As Joe walked to his car on his way to the hospital to check on Judge Daily, for the first time in his life he realized what people meant when they said they were floating on air.

Somehow, all of the troubles that lay head, his father's murder trial, Judge Daily's imminent death, even his future with the FBI didn't seem so overwhelming. He knew he could survive anything now, no matter how difficult it may be. Finally, he had his Elizabeth back.

RIVER

"That's everything I've come up with so far. I promise that's it." River sat back in her chair, took a deep breath and sighed.

John Kelly paced the room for a few more minutes, then dropped into the chair next to River. "All that in twenty-four hours? Ever thought about joining the Bureau? I could use someone like you."

River smiled. "It's crossed my mind a few times, but I look terrible in dark suits."

"I doubt that." John chuckled. "When this is all over I think we should talk about it."

"Ok," River said, "but what do we do now?"

John's mind spun, overwhelmed with everything River had told him. His heart hurt even thinking about the possibility that Joe, his best friend, could be involved in this. He stood again and paced his office, trying to decide the best way to go next.

"The problem is, we really don't have any useable evidence. What we have is inadmissible, because you stole it," he chided. "We have to get the box of postcards legally. Once we have them, Joe and Elizabeth can make a case to the D.A. to arrange for an emergency hearing to, at the very least, get Joe's father out on bail. I know the district attorney well, he hates to lose. He's getting the same pressure I'm getting from the congressman and if he lost a high-profile case like this, his career would be over. If we can put our hands on actual evidence that Luke was in a hospital at the time of two of the murders, that blows a big hole in the serial murder theory. Although he does have the murder weapon, he knows it could be argued that it was planted. I thnk this might be enough to get the DA to rethink his case."

"Is that what you want me to do? Find that evidence?" River asked.

"No, let me work on that. I need those postcards," John said. "That's what I want you to do."

"How do I do that without betraying the judge's confidence?"

John stopped pacing and sat behind his desk. "I don't think you can. You're going to have to tell Joe what you did and why. He's the only one that can allow us to get those postcards. No judge would give us a search warrant on his house. He's not even a person of interest in this case."

"Not yet," River said quietly.

They sat in silence without talking for several minutes. Finally breaking the silence, River asked, "Do I tell Joe everything I discovered?"

"If we were only talking about the Joe I know, I would say yes, but this Jake thing has got to be investigated no matter how unfathomable it may sound. I think I need to take a trip to Colorado and spend some time with this Dr. Heart. I've got to find out if it was just a passing thought she wrote in her notes or if it's a real possibility."

"What about the paintings in his house, and the new clothes?"

John frowned. "I don't want to think about that now. Let's take this one step at a time. For now, you need to get back to Little Rock and talk to Joe."

"What do I tell Elizabeth? I know she's angry. She's been calling and texting me, but I didn't know what to say."

"That's your call, River. But think about it hard before you let her in the loop. If the judge thinks she's still in love with Joe, be careful about how much you tell her. Just make sure you can trust her not to warn Joe. As crazy as it sounds, if this Jake character is real, he might just bolt if he knows we're closing in."

It was 9 p.m. when the FBI plane landed at the Little Rock airport. River was met by Wes, and another field agent she had never met before. Wes tried to start up a conversation with her, but she didn't respond and remained silent all the way back to her apartment.

Inside, she stepped out of her clothes and walked to the bathroom. Soaking in the hot soapy water in her tub, she contemplated what to do next. Elizabeth had been her friend for almost 10 years, and the judge for almost 14. She knew she had no other choice, she had to betray the judge's confidence, but she couldn't betray Elizabeth too. She deserved to know the truth. The whole truth about Joe...

ELIZABETH AND RIVER

The judge's oxygen had climbed to a safe enough level to remove the breathing tube, but the ordeal had exhausted him. When he tried to talk, his voice was barely above a whisper, so they told him to get some rest and left him alone.

During dinner, Joe and Elizabeth didn't talk much. Neither one of them knew what to say or even how to start. So, they just looked in each other's eyes and smiled.

When they got back to Elizabeth's apartment, she asked, "Want to come inside? Maybe for a little while?"

Joe smiled, "I've dreamed about you asking me that for twenty years and I can't think of anything I'd rather do, but... for now... I think we should take this slow." He bent down, kissed her gently and backed away. She grabbed his shirt and pulled him back into her arms. They kissed for a long, long time.

"I'll see you in the morning," she whispered in his ear.

She watched him walk away and slowly closed her door. Stepping out of her heels, she shuffled in her bare feet to the kitchen counter, found the remains of the Cabernet Sauvignon she had opened the night before, pulled the cork, and emptied it into a glass.

On her way to the living room, her doorbell rang. "Joe! You

changed your mind!" She ran to the door and jerked it open, but it wasn't Joe. It was River.

Disappointed it wasn't Joe and shocked to see River, she just stood there.

"Well," River said smiling. "Are you just going to stand there, or are you going to invite me in?"

"Oh... I'm, I'm sorry," Elizabeth sputtered. "Yes, please come in."

"Have any more of that?" River pointed at her glass of wine.

"No more red, but I think I have some Chardonnay in the fridge. Want some?"

"Absolutely." River flopped on her couch. "Bring the whole bottle."

Elizabeth removed the cork, poured some in a glass and then carried the glass and the bottle to the living room. "Where the hell have you been? And why haven't you returned my calls?"

River looked up at Elizabeth. Her eyes were red and tearing up. "Elizabeth, I've got to tell you something that," she took a deep breath and wiped her eyes, "that you're not going to want to hear."

For the next two hours, River sipped her wine, and told Elizabeth everything. When she finished, they just stared at each other for a long time in silence.

Elizabeth walked back into the kitchen and returned with another bottle of wine.

As she was filling their glasses, River noticed her naked ring finger. "Where's your ring?"

Elizabeth sat down, tucked her bare feet under her body and leaned back into the couch. "There's something... I need to tell you too."

THE CONFRONTATION

J oe slept like a baby and woke up feeling rested for the first time in months. Skipping breakfast, he stopped by the hospital to visit with the judge a few minutes before he drove to Elizabeth's office for the meeting. Although he'd tried to looked through his copy of the Jackson district attorney's file before he'd gone to sleep, he couldn't concentrate on it. All he could think about was Elizabeth and that kiss. He couldn't wait to see her again this morning.

He was the last one to arrive and took a seat directly across from Elizabeth and River.

"Good morning, Joe" Elizabeth said, not looking at him as he settled in.

"Morning everyone," he said.

Still not looking at him, Elizabeth opened her file. "Now that we're all here, let's begin."

For the next hour, she averted his eyes and completely ignored him, only asking questions from River, Will, and Judy.

Why was she acting like this? He wondered. What could have changed overnight? Maybe Rob had dropped by after he'd left. Was she having second thoughts? It wasn't only Elizabeth. River wouldn't look at him either. The longer the meeting went on, the more frustrated he got. Finally, it was over.

"Joe, could I talk to you in private?" Elizabeth said, making eye contact for the first time.

He instantly saw that there was something different in her eyes. "Of course."

"Meet me in my office in ten minutes." She picked up her file and walked away.

"Do you know what's going on with her?" He asked River, but she didn't respond.

"Where can I find Smooth, Mooch, and this Bummer guy?" She asked, looking down at her phone.

Irritated at her lack of response to his question, he just shrugged his shoulders.

"Ok... thanks for the help, I'll track them down myself," she said angrily.

"You're welcome," he shot back.

He sat alone in the conference room, checking his watch every few seconds. It was a long ten minutes. Finally, he walked to Elizabeth's office and opened the door. She was crying.

His heart sank. "What's wrong?"

She pointed to the chair facing her desk, and wiped her eyes. "Please sit down, we need to talk."

"If it's Rob, just tell me." Joe said. "I won't like it, but if that's what you want..."

"What?" Elizabeth said confused.

"Rob, you're going back to Rob. It's ok, I understand. Please don't cry."

"No... it's not Rob, it's you."

"Me? What did I do since last night? Was it because I didn't come in? I was trying to be a gentleman, just trying—"

"Stop!" Elizabeth held up her hand. "It's not about that!"

Totally confused, Joe sat down in the chair facing her.

"I don't know the best way to say this, so I'm just going to say it."

"Say what?"

"Please Joe, let me do this." Elizabeth wiped her tears away with her fingers. "River found something in your house that's important."

"River was in my house? Why in the hell was she in my house?"

"Please Joe, let me finish. I'll explain that later, it's not important. What is important is what she found."

Shocked and angry, Joe shouted, "She had no right to break into my house!"

"I know that! Please let me finish. Do you want to know why I'm crying?"

Joe pulled in his anger and calmed down. "Yes, of course I do."

"Then please just let me talk. I promise to tell you everything."

Joe sighed. "Ok, I'll shut up. What did she find?"

"She found a shoe box with postcards your mother had written to you."

"Yeah, they were in the storeroom in my garage. She wrote me one every week when I was a kid. What's wrong with that? They are just postcards."

"You promised to listen, not talk."

"Ok, ok, I'll shut up, but I don't get it."

"It's not the postcards, it's what they told her. It's where your mother mailed them from and the dates she mailed them. And especially what your mother had written on two of them." Elizabeth wasn't crying anymore. She was thinking clearly, pushing back her emotions. "Do you remember your mother writing about two operations your father had?"

"Yeah, he had an emergency appendectomy, and I think the other was his gallbladder, am I right?"

"Yes, that's right. She wrote you asking for your help; to come and take his place in the band, so they wouldn't lose the job. Did you do that?"

"Yes, I did," Joe said. "I remember on one of those gigs I had to miss my mid-term exams, but they let me take them when I got back. I'm trying Elizabeth, but I don't understand why that has upset you so much."

"That's not what's bothering me. Actually, this may be a critical discovery in your father's case."

"How could that be so important?"

Elizabeth thought a moment, took a deep breath and said, "I was going to explain that later, but maybe we should talk about that now. The reason you were assigned this case was because of your expertise in profiling and connecting linking evidence to serial killers, right?"

"Yes, it was a US Congressman's granddaughter, very high profile. That's why the director picked me."

"Is it your opinion that the evidence of the congressman's grand-daughter's murder matches the evidence of all of the past murders?"

Joe nodded. "Yes, whoever killed his granddaughter killed all those other women."

"Are you absolutely positive that it's the same person? Only one person could have murdered all seven? It's not multiple killers or maybe a copycat?"

Joe considered the questions a few moments. Elizabeth sat silently watching him. "I guess it's possible the last one could have been a copycat," he began, "but he would have had to use the same murder weapon, which was a handmade unique designed macramé strap made by my mother. And honestly, that is highly unlikely. He would also have to have access to the same antique Polaroid camera, because it's been positively matched to the other negatives. Why are you asking me all this?"

"Hold on." She held up her hand again. "So, you're convinced that it has to be one and only one person who committed all seven of these murders?"

"Yes, there's just too much exact linking evidence. It has to be the same guy."

"You keep saying, guy, or him. Couldn't it be a woman?"

"No, I don't think so. There's only been a handful of female serials ever reported. If our killer is female, because all the crimes were sexual, she'd have to be lesbian and a very strong one. The brute force and violence some of the victims received was from someone extremely powerful. I just can't see it being a woman.

"Joe, if we could prove that your father couldn't have committed two of the seven murders, in your opinion would that be enough to exonerate him?"

"Yes, absolutely I think it would. At the very least it would create enough reasonable doubt the district attorney couldn't possibly overcome it. How can we prove it?"

"When your father had those surgeries, he was in a hospital bed at the time of two of the murders. He couldn't possibly have done them."

Joe jumped to his feet and began waving his arms. "Those postcards can prove that? That's fantastic!"

"Please Joe, sit down. That's the good news."

He sighed and lowered himself back in the chair and stared at Elizabeth. "So what's the bad news?"

She looked away and lowered her head. "The bad news... is that you weren't in a hospital. You were there, Joe; in the same cities the murders were committed... both of them... at the same time."

Joe jerked his head around and stared at Elizabeth. "What? You think I'm the killer? Just because I happened to be in the same towns of two of the murders at the same time? Why on earth would you think that?"

Her eyes filled with tears again. "Because it wasn't just two, you were there at all of them."

"I was? How do you know that?"

She lifted her head "She wrote you every week, Joe... except for seven weeks. Why didn't she write you on those weeks?"

Like running into a brick wall, the obvious hit him hard. "My mother didn't write me those weeks, because I was there..."

"Why didn't you tell that to the FBI director when you were incriminating your father? Why didn't you tell me?"

Joe jumped to his feet, "Because I didn't know. It's been over twenty years! And to be honest, I've tried to put all those memories out of my head because those memories included you. I swear I didn't know this." He lowered himself back down in the chair. "I swear this is just a coincidence. Why would you think this? You know me, Elizabeth... how could you possibly believe I could do such a horrible thing?"

"Joe... who's Jake?"

Still reeling inside from everything she had said, he was completely stunned at the question. "What? Jake? What's he got to do with this?"

"Is he real? Please tell me. Is he real?"

Completely losing control of his anger, he slammed his fist down hard on the arm of the chair and exploded. "FUCK NO, HE'S NOT REAL!"

The office door jerked opened and River rushed in. "Are you ok?"

Elizabeth was trembling, standing behind her desk, frightened by Joes violent reaction.

"Are you ok, Elizabeth?" River repeated louder.

Elizabeth looked at Joe. "I don't know. Am I ok, Joe?"

Glaring at Elizabeth, he growled, "I think I should leave now."

Joe turned to walk away, but River blocked his path. "Before you leave, you need to sign this." She held out a type written paper. "It's for your father—giving your permission to retrieve the shoebox of post-cards from your house."

Joe grabbed the pen, signed the paper, and walked out the door.

25

JOHN KELLY AND DR. HEART

R isking his job and entire career, John had kept Joe's name out of any official investigation documents and to the surprise of everyone in his office, had suddenly decided to take two vacation days.

Since it wasn't an official FBI investigation, he couldn't use the normal Bureau travel arrangements, but all it had taken was one call to the congressman and two hours later he was taking off in his private plane.

Through the small window, John watched the snow-capped Rocky Mountains in all their majesty, growing closer as the Gulfstream V made its final approach. They were landing at the Yampa Valley airport about 25 miles west of Steamboat Springs. It was the closest airport with a runway long enough to land. As promised, the black, unmarked Cadillac Escalade was waiting in the parking lot as well as a marked map directing him to Steamboat Springs.

The drive was breathtaking. It was his first trip to Colorado in years and every turn revealed another magnificent aspen covered, golden glistening mountain valley. The memory of his last trip there flashed through his mind.

It was four years ago at about the same time of the year, early

October, when he and his wife had driven to Colorado and spent their last vacation together. It was on her bucket list. She had always wanted to drive through the beautiful Rocky Mountains of Colorado and stay at different unique and quaint B&B's all along the way.

It was a wonderful two weeks and the last time he had taken any vacation days. Three weeks after their Colorado trip, his wife had succumbed to her cancer and died peacefully in his arms.

He had met his wife Beverly, in the seventh grade and married her two days after he'd graduated college. She had been his one and only girl. They had dated all through high school and college and had been married 24 years when she passed. She had been his lover, his best friend, his rock, his sounding board, and his psychologist.

She was one of those unique people who woke up smiling and was always in a good mood. He was just the opposite, always grumpy in the mornings.

She only saw the positive, no matter how dire the situation may have been, her glass was always half full. He again was the opposite, always looking at the dark side of things, but she kept him balanced. Even in her final days, she was always smiling and her only fears were for his future. The last words she said to him, before she slipped into a coma were, "John, promise me, you'll find someone."

In the four years since her death, he hadn't dated one time. He just couldn't imagine being with someone else, so he hadn't tried.

He lost his parents when he was in his 30's and his only sister when she was 41, so he had no family to lean on through Beverly's illness, but somehow Joe Jensen found out about it, and showed up on his doorstep during her last days. Joe had taken a leave of absence from his job at Quantico and didn't leave his side for the next three weeks.

He drove him to the hospital every day and sat by his side until visiting hours were over. He made him eat, sleep, bathe, brush his teeth, shave, and put on clean clothes each day. After visiting hours were over at the hospital, he drove John home each night and stayed up with him talking until he fell asleep. When Beverly finally died, Joe was there with him. The next day Joe made all of the arrangements for her funeral and through it all, never left his side.

Joe stayed with him for two more weeks and wouldn't leave until he assured him he was going to be all right. For almost a year after that, he called him a few times every week to check up and see how he was doing.

During those dark days, John got to know the real Joe Jensen. Joe was the most unselfish, loving, and caring person he'd ever known. Without him John wasn't sure he would have survived the loss of Beverly.

Joe Jensen was much more than just a friend to him, more like his brother. That's why none of this made any sense to him and why he was willing to risk his career or anything else he had in his life, to find out what was going on.

It only took about 30 minutes for John to drive from the Yampa Valley airport to Steamboat Springs. When he pulled into the city, driving down Lincoln Avenue, he pulled over to take in the incredible view. He had forgotten how beautiful Steamboat Springs was with its old historic buildings framed by the majestic Rocky Mountains in the background. It was like looking at a live post card.

After checking into The Victorian, a historic mansion built in 1880 that had been restored and converted to an upscale bed and breakfast, the same one he'd stayed in with Beverly four years earlier, he drove back downtown to find Dr. Heart's office. It was in an old, restored historic building as well, just one street off of Lincoln Avenue.

There was no available parking, so he drove around the block, parked on Lincoln and walked three blocks back to her office and rang the doorbell.

John didn't know what to expect. All he knew about the doctor was what he had read in her file on his flight there. Most of the information came from an interview one of his agents had conducted with her nanny who had raised her until she was 10 years old. Apparently, her very rich parents divorced when she was five years old. They had basically abandoned her as they traveled the world on their private jets and yachts, leaving her in the care of her nanny until she was old enough to be enrolled in Lowell Whiteman.

When she was only sixteen, her father died and left her twenty-five million dollars. She was devastated by her father's death and as a result, became a rebellious teenager. That got her kicked out of Lowell Whiteman and sent to a school for troubled kids in Wyoming. At that school she met her mentor—a child psychologist who apparently straightened her out. She went from there to Smith College in Massachusetts graduating summa cum laude, then went on to graduate at the top of her class in medical school at Princeton. She did her residency at Boston Children's Hospital and at twenty-seven years old, she moved back to Steamboat springs and hung out her shingle. She had just started her practice when she met Joe.

When Dr. Heart opened the door, he assumed he was talking to her assistant. "Hello, I would like to talk to Dr. Heart, if she's available."

"That's me." She said with a grin.

John stood there frozen, speechless. His report said that Dr. Leah Heart was his age—52. This woman looked much younger—late 30s or early 40s. She was absolutely gorgeous, with long, glistening brown hair to her waist, amazing emerald green eyes, and large pouting lips. She was dressed in a short form-fitting gray skirt that clung to her hips, revealing tanned, athletic legs, and her red stiletto heels just enhanced her sexy image. Her snug silk navy blouse accentuated her breasts, making it hard for him not to stare.

"May I help you?" She asked, breaking the spell.

"I hope so. Are you Dr. Leah Heart?"

"Yes, and you are?" Her eyes sparkled as she smiled revealing her perfect white teeth.

The radiance of her beauty was so unexpected, he had to think for a second to remember what his name was. "I'm, ahhh...

"It's really not that hard of a question," she said laughing. "What's your name?"

He could feel the blood rushing through his body, flushing his face, "I'm, ahhh... ahhh... I'm sorry, my name is John, John Kelly."

"Well hello there, John, John Kelly," she repeated back. "What can I do for you?"

He opened his ID wallet and held it up for her to see. "I'm with the FBI out of the Jackson, Mississippi office and I was hoping to talk to you about one of your former patients."

Dr. Heart read his credentials carefully then stepped back. "I'm not sure what I can tell you about one of my patients, but please come in."

He followed her through a waiting area to her office. He couldn't help but notice that it was furnished in what appeared to be real and very expensive antiques. The walls were covered with several original Thomas Kincaid paintings and the wood floors had numerous beautiful Persian rugs.

"You a collector?" he asked. "The antiques." He pointed at an antique hall chest. "My wife loved going antiquing. She dragged me all over the country searching for them."

"It's one of my worst vices." She pointed to a large, antique red sofa. "Have a seat. Would you like some coffee or tea?"

"No thanks," John said. "I've been drinking it all morning on my drive here."

"You must be tired. It's a long drive from Denver to Steamboat."

"No, I didn't come from Denver, we landed at Yampa Valley and I drove over from there. Only took about thirty minutes."

Dr. Heart sat in an armchair next to him. "Your credentials said that you are the special agent in charge of the state of Mississippi, is that right? You're in charge of the whole state?"

John nodded. "Yes, I've been there for nine years."

Dr. Heart raised her eyebrows. "This must be very important for the big boss to come all this way. You couldn't have just sent an agent over from Denver to talk to me?"

"Well, to be honest with you, I'm not here on an official FBI investigation, it's actually something I'm doing on my own."

"Ok..." Dr. Heart said. "Special Agent Kelly, I assume you realize that the HIPPA laws prevent me from divulging any private information about my clients. You would need a warrant or court order for that and since this isn't an official FBI matter, I don't know how I can help you."

John looked directly at her. "Dr. Heart, do you have a first name? It feels a little awkward to keep calling you Dr. Heart. Please call me John."

She smiled, flashing those beautiful teeth at him again. "It's Leah."

""Leah? That's a pretty name. Ok Leah, let me put my cards on the table. I'm here about a mutual friend of ours, and I'm trying my best to keep him out of a current serial murder investigation I'm involved in, but something came up that ties him to it. I'm hoping that you can help me clear it up."

"Who is this mutual friend?" she asked.

"Joe Jensen."

"Joe?" she said, obviously surprised. "He's a suspect in serial murders?"

"No, not now," John said. "That's why I'm here. I'm trying to keep him from being a suspect."

Dr. Heart eyes widened. "Joe? There has to be some mistake. It... it can't be Joe. How well do you know him?"

"Leah, I know him well. To be honest, I've probably never had a better friend in my life. If I wasn't so close to him, I wouldn't be here. And if what I know gets back to my superiors, I may lose my job over this."

Dr. Heart stood and walked to a small antique serving cart. "Are you sure you don't want any coffee? I think I need some."

"If you're going to have some, sure," he said. "I take it black." John watched her hands shake as she poured the coffee. "Leah, can you tell me anything about Jake?"

"Oh God! Is that what this is about?" She handed him his cup.

"I'm praying not," he said grimly, "but I need to know if Jake is a real possibility. Leah, did Joe have dissociative identity disorder?"

Dr. Heart sat down next to him and with trembling hands lifted her cup and took a slow sip of her coffee. "John, I've worked very hard to build my practice and I think I do a lot of good here. I specialize in helping messed up kids who need me. I can't risk losing my license revealing private information about my patients, even if it's Joe. I can't tell you anything without a court order, you know that."

John shrugged his shoulders and dropped his head. "I know. I just thought that maybe because you and Joe were..." He stopped himself.

Dr. Heart's eyes narrowed and she stood. "Lovers. Is that what you were about to say? Special Agent Kelly, my relationship with Joe is none of yours or the FBI's business, but apparently, you've already done a thorough investigation on me. I think you should leave now!"

Knowing he'd crossed a line, he left without saying anything else, and possibly making things worse. But he didn't get what he needed, so he decided to wait and try again tomorrow after she cooled down. The only thing he did get was very troubling, her reaction when he mentioned Jake was not what he wanted to see.

Back at the Victorian, he unpacked his overnight case and pulled out his tooth brush and razor. After a shower, he called the Cafe Diva and made a reservation for 8 pm.

He wasn't sure if what he was doing was healthy, but he couldn't stop himself. Staying at the Victorian in the same suite he'd spent his last real night with Beverly and eating at the Cafe Diva again was probably the wrong thing to do, but for some reason he couldn't explain, he knew he had to.

"Will you be dining alone, sir?" The hostess asked when he walked in to Cafe Diva.

"Yes, I have a reservation for 8 p.m. Would it be possible to sit over there, by the window?" Again, he was compelled to sit at the same table he'd shared with Beverly four years earlier.

"Of course," the hostess said. "Follow me, sir." .

He even ordered the same bottle of wine. He sipped it slowly, staring out the window at the mountains.

"I didn't realize that stalking was part of an FBI investigation," a familiar voice said behind him.

When he turned around he saw Dr. Heart standing there. "Leah, what a pleasant surprise."

She smiled. "Surprise? Are you sure this is just a coincidence? You didn't have your team track me down?"

"Scouts honor," he said, holding up two fingers. "Are you meeting someone?"

Still smiling at him, she said, "No, I'm alone."

John stood and pulled out the chair next to his. "Please join me, I hate eating alone."

Dr. Heart thought for a second. "Are you sure your wife won't mind?"

His expression fell. "No, actually, I lost my wife four years ago."

Dr. Heart sat down. "I'm so sorry, I didn't realize. It was your ring. I noticed it today in the office and just assumed..."

John held up his hand and looked at the gold band on his ring finger. "It's ok. I know I probably should, but I just can't take it off. I guess it's my way of always having her with me."

She shook her head. "I understand. Were you together long?"

John smiled. "I met her when I was eleven years old."

"You married your childhood sweetheart," she said. "Sounds like a true love story."

"Yes, it was..." he said softly.

The waiter walked up and after a few minutes studying the menus, they placed their orders.

After the wine steward filled Dr. Heart's glass and finally left them alone, she said, "I'm glad this happened, running into you like this. I felt bad after you left today. I want to apologize. I overreacted."

"There's no need to apologize. I shouldn't have brought that up, it was out of line. And you're right, it's none of my business or the FBI's. I'm just grasping at straws. I'm not sure what to do next to protect Joe."

Dr. Heart sipped her wine and gazed out the window at the sunset on the snow-capped mountains. "I love this view. How did you find this restaurant?"

John smiled again. "I didn't, my wife found it. We sat right here at this very table four years ago, looking at that same view. She loved it too."

"John, I hope you understand that when you came to my office today to talk to me about all of this I didn't know you from Adam. I wasn't sure that you weren't there undercover or something. I just didn't know," she said. "Is Joe really your friend?"

John thought for a few minutes. "I guess it says a lot about who I am, but I've never had a lot of friends in my life, other than Beverly. She was always my best friend and all I needed. And honestly, it wasn't any of my doings—this friendship with Joe. We've known each other for years off and on through the Bureau, but when Beverly got sick, Joe was suddenly there and probably saved my life. He's much more than a friend."

The food arrived and the conversation lulled while they ate.

"If I talk to you about Joe," Dr. Heart said, breaking the silence, "could what I tell you become part of an official investigation or will it just be between us?"

"I guess that would depend on what you tell me," John said.

Dr. Heart picked at her food. "Ok then, if we talked in hypotheticals, would that be of any help?"

"I'm not sure," John said, "but I'd like to give it a try. Could you start by explaining dissociative identity disorder?"

"Sure, what would you like to know about it?"

John thought for a moment. "I guess I need to be convinced that it's apodictic. In my business when a multiple personality defense is used, it's normally considered... well to be blunt, BS. Is it a real approved medical diagnosis?"

"Yes, it is, but let me make it clear that I am not a psychiatrist, I am a psychologist and this is a little out of my area. I did study it in college and I have done some rather extensive research on it after that." She gave John a knowing look.

"Because of Joe?" he asked.

She smiled. "Let's just say I did this research because of one of my patients."

John got the hint. "Ok, so why did you think you needed to research this for this hypothetical patient? Did he have symptoms of dissociative identity disorder?"

"Not really, not any classic symptoms, but due to his background he was a prime candidate."

"Dissociative identity disorder is caused by someone's background?"

Dr. Heart nodded. "Oh yes. It's usually caused from child abuse. It is present in all races, but is more common in American children. And because females experience more childhood abuse than males by 10 to 1, more females suffer from D.I.D., however, males that have been abused may experience pathological dissociation. Dissociative identity disorder is typically caused by trauma occurring when they are very young. Normally at less than nine years of age. The earlier the age of abuse predicts a greater degree of dissociation.

"The problem I had with this hypothetical patient was that he showed no sociopathic tendencies and only showed signs of one other possible personality and that's not the norm. The average number of alternate personalities a person with D.I.D. has is between eight and thirteen, but there have been cases reported of more than a hundred personalities within one individual. And in most cases, the patient or one or more of their personalities is a sociopath."

John sipped his wine, considering what she had said. "So, because your patient was not sociopathic and only had one other personality... are you saying that he didn't have D.I.D.?"

"No, I'm not saying that. Having only one other personality doesn't rule someone out necessarily. I'm just saying that it would be unusual and a very rare case. And this particular patient was certainly not a sociopath." She took another sip of her wine and sat back in her chair. "Let me put this another way. Kids that have D.I.D. have suffered serious traumatic abuse and are very broken. These multiple personalities evolve to help them deal with the trauma. And it's never just one that can help them."

"Leah, in my business I deal with sociopaths on a daily basis and if there's one thing I know about Joe Jensen, he's no sociopath. If anything he's just the opposite."

"I agree."

"So back to this hypothetical patient. Did you rule him out of possibly having D.I.D.?"

She sighed and nodded her head. "I wish I could say an absolute yes, but I can't. This patient never opened up about it. In fact, he would regress every time I brought it up. He did admit to at times taking on a different persona, but he claimed it was just an act to help him with his stage fright. When I pressed him to explain it in more detail he wouldn't talk about it. That's when I began my research on D.I.D.

"My main concern was his childhood. His abuse wasn't physical or mental, it was sexual. And although he was always a more than willing participant, it was still child abuse. He had sex for the first time when he was only ten years old. It wasn't parental abuse, it was a complete stranger he met in a bar. Can you imagine a ten-year-old boy getting picked up in a bar?"

John just shook his head in disgust.

"Can you now understand my concerns? He suffered real sexual abuse that started at ten. Also, when he was even younger, he experienced several other things that children should never even see."

John turned to look at her. "I think I understand why you were so concerned. How could he have lived through all of that and not have been effected in some way."

"Somehow, he did," she said smiling. "I have had the pleasure of getting to know this hypothetical patient as an adult, and it's my professional and personal opinion, that as miraculous as it may sound, he has developed into a well-rounded and wonderful person and hasn't shown any signs of D.I.D." She flashed her beautiful white teeth at John. "Did our hypothetical discussion help to ease your mind any?"

He nodded. "For me personally, absolutely, but unless you can definitively tell me that this Jake character is not a possible split personality of Joe, it doesn't clear him in my investigation."

Instinctively, Dr. Heart reached over and took one of John's hands. "I think you know how much I care for Joe and I know how much you care about him, but I can't tell you that. I wish I could. The possibility, although highly unlikely, just can't definitively be ruled out."

Although, they had stopped talking, Dr. Heart held his hand a few beats longer than he had expected.

She finally let go and sat back in her seat. "John, I can't help but feel like I'm imposing here."

Confused, John raised his eyebrows. "Imposing? Imposing on what?"

"On your memories. Your time here, this restaurant, at this very table... on your wife."

John grinned. "I wouldn't worry about that, in fact, I have a strange feeling that Beverly may have had a hand in all of this."

Dr. Heart lowered her eyebrows and tilted her head, "What? What are you talking about?"

"In her last few months, Beverly became more and more concerned about my future. She constantly made me promise I would date again, but I haven't been able to do it."

Dr. Heart smiled wide. "Is this a date?"

John smiled back. "Well, I did take you out to dinner, didn't I?"

"As long as you're paying for it, I guess you could call it a date."

John laughed. "It's my treat, but if I remember correctly, this place is very proud of its food. You might have to loan me a little money to pay the tab."

FOR MOST OF John's adult life he had been a sound sleeper, one of those people that the second their head hit the pillow they were out like a light. But that changed the day he found out about Beverly's cancer and his adventure with insomnia and catnaps began.

It wasn't that he couldn't go to sleep, it just never lasted. His normal pattern was about 30 to 45 minutes of sleep and then an hour of trying to shut off his brain long enough to get another 30. But when the phone rang, startling him awake, and he looked at the clock, he was amazed. For the first time in six years, he had slept through the night. And, for the first time in six years, he felt completely rested.

On his drive back to the Yampa Valley Airport, John's thoughts constantly switched back-and-forth between what Dr. Heart had told him about Joe... and Dr. Heart herself.

He had hoped that she could have given him something more, something absolute to clear Joe and remove him from any possible suspicion, but that hadn't happened. And as much as he hated the idea, he knew he had no choice but to put Joe or Jake, whoever he was, on the list of possible suspects.

He was trying hard to concentrate on what he was going to do about Joe, but images of his dinner with Dr. Heart kept popping up in his head.

"Ok Beverly, that's enough. I can't think about that now!" He shook his head. "What are you doing, John?"

Ever since Beverly's death, almost every day he had talked to her, always saying the words out loud. He knew it was crazy, but he couldn't seem to stop doing it and as strange as it seemed, on several occasions he truly believed that she had answered him.

The first time was when he was running late for an appointment with the governor. He was actually receiving an award and it was sort of a big deal with a lot of big brass attending, even the director of the FBI was supposed to be there. He'd had another sleepless night and slept through his alarm. When he took the exit off the freeway, he glanced at the dashboard clock and knew he was never going to make it in time. He'd driven that street a thousand times before and knew that the red lights were timed to slow the traffic. No matter what speed he drove, he always caught every single red light. It was a busy road with a ton of traffic and each light took what seemed to be forever.

After he caught the second light, he yelled, "Beverly, can you help me out here? I'm never gonna make it!"

The light turned green, miraculously, and the next 7 were green as well, all the way to the governor's mansion. He was actually a few minutes early. The second time was even weirder.

He hadn't been himself since Beverly died, becoming more and more absentminded and doing stupid things. Before her death, multitasking was one of his best attributes. Being able to switch his focus between multiple cases was what he did every day and keeping track of the separate details was never a problem, but after her death he'd been constantly doing really stupid things like losing his keys and forgetting important meetings. Without a doubt, the worst thing he had ever done was when he misplaced his FBI credentials. When he did that, he began to wonder if he was losing his mind.

He'd searched everywhere for it, but the black ID wallet was nowhere to be found. Losing your FBI identification was a serious thing—if it got into the wrong hands there was no telling where it could lead. It was one thing for a rookie agent to do it, but the special agent in charge of an entire state, well that was another thing all together.

As a last resort, he asked Beverly. "Babe, I've really screwed up this time. Have any idea what I've done with it?"

Just seconds after he'd said those words out loud his doorbell rang.

It was his next-door neighbor standing there smiling, holding up his FBI badge. "Hello sir, I'm Special Agent John Kelly from the FBI and you're under arrest!" Somehow it had slipped out of John's suit jacket. His neighbor found it on the ground under his car.

Driving along the winding mountain road to the airport, John switched on the car radio. It was something he never did—listening to music when he drove—but he thought it might help get his mind off Dr. Heart.

It took him a minute to find a clear station and he had to punch the search button several times. Finally, he found one and heard the DJ say, "I haven't played this song in years. It doesn't really fit our programming, but I felt compelled to play it. I guess there must be someone out there listening who needs to hear it."

John normally paid no attention to the lyrics, but after hearing what the DJ had said he was curious, so he listened carefully.

"I hope you never lose your sense of wonder.
You get your fill to eat but always keep that hunger
May you never take one single breath for granted.
God forbid love ever leave you empty handed.
I hope you still feel small when you stand beside the ocean.
Whenever one door closes I hope one more opens
Promise me that you'll give faith a fighting chance.

And when you get the choice to sit it out or dance,
I hope you dance."

His eyes filled with tears and his heart began to pound in his chest. Losing control of his emotion, he switched off the radio, and pulled over to the side of the road. "Ok Beverly, you win. Yes, I liked her."

He sat there crying for a long time, then wiped his face and pulled back onto the road. Once he reached full speed, he flipped the radio back on.

"Here's another one I haven't played in years," the DJ said, but this one didn't make him sad, it made him bust out laughing. He knew the lyrics to this one. It was a song by Rick Springfield called "Jessie's Girl."

"I get it Beverly. I promise I'll clear it with Joe before I see her again."

26

RIVER

F ollowing John Kelly's orders, River contacted his team in Jackson and let them know she had the signed authorization from Joe to retrieve the postcards from his house. They told her they would send a team from the Virginia field office and pick them up.

With nothing left to do for John, River started her investigation of the other members of the band. She needed to talk to all of them and decided Smooth would be the first.

On the small commuter flight to Pensacola, she studied her notes about Smooth. All she really knew was his real name, Gordon Martin, that he was married, he lived in Gulf Breeze, Florida, was currently a field representative for Pearl Drums USA, and he'd been the drummer in the band during the time of the murders.

At the Pensacola Regional Airport, she picked up her rental car and drove the 30 miles south to Gulf Breeze. She had never heard of the place before, but when she arrived, she could see why Smooth would want to live there. It was located on a small peninsula that jutted out into the Gulf with sugar white beaches and beautiful turquoise blue waves crashing on the shores.

She called Smooth when she landed so he'd be expecting her. It took her almost 40 minutes to drive there and locate his house. When she pulled up, he opened the front door and waved.

He didn't look anything at all like the old band pictures. There was no resemblance at all to the long-haired, bearded hippy she'd seen smiling in those old photos. He looked like any typical retired, gray-haired old man you might see at the mall.

"Are you River?" he yelled from the front door.

"Yes, that's me." She walked toward the door. "I want to thank you again for seeing me on such short notice."

"You're welcome. I was off today and had no real plans anyway. My wife, Linda, is at work, I hope you don't mind being alone here with me."

River smiled. "Oh I think I'll be all right, Mr. Martin, you look pretty safe to me."

He smiled back. "Call me Smooth. You think I'm safe, huh? Well, I guess I am pretty safe these days, but I've got to tell you if this was back in my younger days and someone looking like you walked up to my door, well... you just might be in trouble."

She laughed and followed him inside. "This is a beautiful town. I had no idea Florida had beaches this white."

"We love it here. My wife and I discovered it about twenty-five years ago when we took a vacation in Destin. It's not far from here, but it's way too expensive to live there, so we drove down the beach a few miles and found this place. Want something to drink? A coke or coffee? That's about all we have around here."

"Sure, a coke sounds good."

They settled around a glass table beside his pool and after a few sips of her coke, she asked, "Why do you go by Smooth?"

He grinned and shook his head. "When I was sixteen, the track coach made me run the anchor leg of the four-forty relay. I absolutely hated track, but could actually run pretty fast. It was a big district track meet and the stands were packed. Just as I was about to finish the race the drawstring of my track shorts came untied and my pants fell to the ground, tripping me at the finish line flat on my face with my jock strapped, naked bare ass mooning everyone. I could hear everybody laughing, including my coach. I wasn't sure what to do next, so I just stood up, pulled up my shorts, re-tied the string securely, smiled, bowed to the crowd and jogged to the dressing room just like nothing had happened. The next day all my friends kept telling me that that was a pretty smooth move. Before long, everybody would just wave and say 'smooth' to me when they passed me in the hallway. It stuck and that's what all my friends have called me ever since."

River laughed out loud. "That *was* a pretty smooth move."

Smooth shrugged his shoulders. "Yeah, I guess it was."

River took another sip and set her glass on the table. "I guess you've heard about Luke's arrest?"

Smooth frowned. "Yeah, Joe called and told me about it. What are they saying he did?"

"Luke's accused of murdering seven women. The last one was a few weeks ago, right after your reunion concert, but the others happened when you guys were out on the road in the seventies and eighties."

Smooth raised his eyebrows and shook his head. "They think Luke's a murderer? That's bullshit! He loved women. No way he's a killer, not Luke."

"We don't think so either, that's why I'm here. If it's not Luke, do you have any ideas who it could be? The evidence points to someone in the band or at least connected in some way. Anyone come to mind?"

Smooth sat silent for several minutes, sipping his coke. "I guess I need to ask if I'm a suspect too?"

River smiled. "No you're not a suspect, but technically every member of the band has to be considered. That's another reason I'm here, so I can find something solid to rule you out."

Smooth's expression grew grim. "What kind of something?"

"I'm not sure. It would be very difficult to rule you out of the old ones, because it's been so many years, so let's concentrate on the last one. We're pretty sure all the murders were committed by the same person, so if we can find hard evidence to rule you out of that one, that should be enough."

"When did the last one happen?" he asked.

River opened her briefcase and pulled out her notepad. She flipped through a few pages. "It happened on Sunday morning, a few hours after your reunion concert. The coroner set the time of her death at about three thirty a.m."

Smooth smiled and got up from his chair. "I'll be right back."

He returned in a few minutes and handed her a plane ticket. "Will that work?"

River looked at it and smiled. "Yes I think so. This is all we need. You keep your tickets?"

"Oh yeah. I've had a little trouble with the IRS in the past. I keep everything I can to prove what I write off." He said with a chuckle. "You can count Mooch out too, because he was on the same plane. We barely made it that night. The concert ran later than we'd planned. I guess it's a damn good thing we made that plane!"

River pulled out her phone and took a few pictures of the ticket. "Keep this in a safe place."

"It's going in my safe right now." He picked up the ticket, and walked back into his house.

When Smooth returned and sat back down, River said, "I had a long visit with Hannah a few days ago, and learned a lot about Joe, Bummer, Hannah, and Luke, but I don't know anything about you. Could you tell me a little about you and how you came to join the band?"

"Sure, do you want the real truth or do you want me to filter out some of the rough stuff?"

River smiled. "I need to hear the truth."

"Ok, but I'm not sure where to start."

"How about when you joined the band?" River said.

Smooth sipped his coke and gathered his thoughts. "I was the third drummer in the band. What I heard was that the first one couldn't keep his eyes and eventually his hands off Hannah. The second one had a slight problem with heroin or at least that's what Luke told me when he offered me the gig. Now understand, it wasn't like we didn't smoke a little weed and maybe snort a line or two on occasion in those days, but we all drew the line when it came to shooting up black-tar. That shit will kill you."

River nodded in agreement. "Was Luke a good band leader? Did you like him?"

Smooth grinned. "When I met Luke, he seemed like a pretty cool guy, and I figured his band had to be better than the giant asshole I was currently working for. His name was Walt Wilson and he had an ego so big he could barely walk into a room. He was the worst musician in the group and could barely carry a tune, but somehow got booked in some of the best rooms in town and he paid really well. But after putting up with Walt's bullshit for six long months, I was ready for a change."

"What about Hannah?" River asked. "Did you like her too?"

Smooth raised his eyebrows and shook his head. "You've seen her, right? Well, just imagine how she looked forty years ago!" He whistled and grinned. "When I first saw her, I had instant sympathy for drummer number one. She was truly unbelievable, a real stunner. She looked like a model with long blonde hair to her waist and was real tall and thin, but with big boobs and legs that reached all the way up to heaven. And then there were her eyes." He laughed. "Well, let's just say I did my best to avoid looking directly into those because it wouldn't take very long for a man to get lost in there. She was something else!

"She could sing too, but I couldn't watch her. She had this natural slow hip moving thing that would make you lose your mind. And that's what she did to every guy and a surprising number of women in every bar we played. So, I just averted my eyes and kept a low profile. On the occasions when our eyes did meet and she would give me that smile of hers, I would either drop a beat or lose one of my sticks. It was like being hit with a volt of electricity. I know that this may sound like I'm exaggerating, but I'm not."

"Oh, I can believe it. She is a beautiful woman. Seems impossible she's sixty-four."

Smooth shook his head. "She's never looked her age. She's still beautiful today, but if you could have only seen her in her twenties..."

"Were there any problems between her and Luke?" River asked. "Were they a happy married couple or did they fight a lot? Living on the road like that had to be hard, for all of you."

"Remember you wanted the ugly truth." He sipped his coke. "River, you need to keep in mind that it was a very different time. We were all very young and in those days, all we really cared about was getting high and getting laid. Married or not, Luke and Hannah were the same.

"Luke was pretty much exactly what I had expected, with the exception of how he played that guitar. He was a hell of a lot better than he'd led me to believe. He wasn't just a guitar player who could sing, he was one of the best rock guitar players I've ever heard. But like most band leaders, he had the ego that always came with the job. It also became evident pretty quick that he didn't really appreciate or realize what he had with Hannah. He was a real horn dog, chasing pussy like he was unattached. And he was very successful at it." Smooth's face turned red. "Sorry, that sort of slipped out, I didn't mean to offend you with my language."

River rolled her eyes. "Come on, Smooth, you'll have to do better than that to offend me."

"Ok then, I won't pull any punches. Now, remember this was the 1970's and trust me when I tell you that groupies were not a myth. I called them road whores or barflies, but I guess *groupies* was the technical term. They swarmed around us like honeybees trying to get a taste. Now don't get me wrong, I'm certainly not complaining. It was after all the age of Aquarius, free love and all that jazz and I'll admit that I did my fair share, but Luke was the world champion. I've always wanted to go to the Rock 'n' Roll Hall of Fame to see if by chance there was a statue of Luke as the man who has scored more pussy than any other man on the planet." They both laughed.

When River finally stopped laughing she took another drink. "Hannah explained to me that Bummer was... slow. If he was mentally challenged, how could he play music?"

Smooth's expression changed to a small smile. "How do I explain Bummer? When I first met him, I didn't know what to think. I had no complaints about the way he played, actually he was a damn good bass player, but the more I talked to him and got to know him, the more I realized that his elevator didn't go all the way up to the top floor. He was one of the sweetest guys I'd ever met, always willing to pitch in with a helping hand loading and unloading my drums, always had a smile on his face and worked extra hard to make sure he knew all the songs. The sad part was that Bummer was aware that he wasn't normal."

River frowned. "That's so sad. So, he knew he was slow?"

"Oh yeah. He was always saying things like, 'If I was smarter, maybe I could do better.' And that would just break my heart." Smooth paused and wiped his eyes. "Luke was always very protective of Bummer, but at the same time didn't cut him any slack when it came to the band. I guess that was a good thing, because it made Bummer a better musician. He had to practice a lot harder than the rest of us to keep up with the new music we were learning. Actually, musically he was as solid as the rest of the band, but off stage he could be a problem. He was constantly getting short changed and ripped off because he couldn't count very well."

"I haven't met Bummer yet," River said, "but from Hannah's description, he must be very handsome."

"Actually, Bummer was a real good-looking guy and all the girls would go crazy over him when he was performing on stage, but off stage he wasn't that successful. Once they talked to him a few minutes, they quickly made their way to Luke, but that never seemed to bother Bummer. He would just walk away smiling. I always figured that it was because he was utterly and totally in love with Hannah and didn't have room in his heart for anyone else."

River shook her head. "Hannah told me that he's always been in love with her. Poor guy."

"Yeah." Smooth stared down at the table. "It was a little pathetic. He worshiped the ground she walked on. Still does."

River flipped a page on her yellow pad. "What about Beaux Williams? I'm meeting him tomorrow. What's he like?"

Smooth chuckled. "You're meeting Mooch and Hellen tomorrow? Oh my. They're going to love you."

"Oh really," River said. "Why do say that?"

"You'll see!" He chuckled. "Mooch is a real piece of work."

"In what way?" River asked.

"He has to be the kinkiest guy I have ever known in my entire life. I'm not sure what he is into now, but in those days he loved porn. Every time we landed in a new town, he was always trying to get me to go with him to find the dirty bookstore, so he could buy some more of those damn nasty magazines. You know the kind I'm talking about: Beaver, Screw, Hustler. He was into the up close, real graphic stuff. He wasn't shy about it either. The inside of his van was plastered with pictures from those books—pictures of naked women taped up everywhere. He spent half his paycheck on 1-900 sex calls. That's where he met his wife, Hellen.

"One night we walked into one of those sex stores and she was working behind the counter. Mooch smiled at me and said, 'Look at her. She's cute as hell and working in a porn store. I think I'm in love!'

"Apparently, he was, because the next thing I knew, she was out there on the road with us and about a year later they got married and had their son, Alexander. But that didn't slow 'em down much. They were still wild as hell."

River smiled. "Are they still that way?"

"Oh yeah. Mooch was a little older than me, so he's got to be crowding seventy, but don't let that fool you. Don't worry, I'll give him a call and tell him to pull it back a notch. Otherwise, the way you look, you may not make it out of their house with your clothes on."

River laughed. "I'll be on guard. I can't wait to meet them; they sound like an interesting couple. Did Luke and Hannah know Mooch was that way?"

"Oh yeah," he said, smiling. "Unlike me, Mooch made no effort whatsoever to withhold his admiration of Hannah's sex appeal. When

Hannah was on stage he never took his eyes off her and was always saying something lewd about how big her boobs looked in that blouse or how sexy her legs looked in her mini skirt. The funny part was that Luke just laughed it off, it didn't seem to bother him at all. And Hannah appeared to actually like all the compliments. It made me wonder about drummer number one. How could he have been worse than Mooch? We all just over-looked Mooch's sexual craziness back then because he was one hell of a keyboard player. He traveled with a B3 Hammond organ and two Leslie speakers. When we all got cooking with Bummer on his bass, Mooch on that B3, Luke on his guitar, and Hannah moving those hips and singing we were hard to beat."

The conversation lulled a few minutes as they sipped their cokes and River flipped through her notes. Finally, she looked up. "Can you tell me what happened to Joe? Hannah wouldn't tell me anything except that she somehow lost him when he was thirteen."

Smooth shook his head with understanding. "That doesn't surprise me at all. That was a tough time for all of us. I really don't want to get into the gory details, but suffice it to say that we all screwed up pretty bad one day and the authorities came and took away our kids. Linda and I had to fight like hell to get them back, so did Mooch and Helen, but eventually we did. Unfortunately, Bummer's son wasn't actually his, so they kept him and put him into a foster home. I'm not sure exactly why, but Joe wasn't placed into foster care, he was sent away to this fancy boarding school in Colorado."

River wrote a few notes on her pad. "I guess I don't understand. Why would Hannah say she lost him? If he was in a boarding school, wouldn't they have seen him in the summers and on the Christmas breaks? "

Smooth raised his eyebrows. "I don't really have an answer for that. We did see him off and on, but not that often. For whatever reason, their relationship with Joe seemed to just grow apart once he went to that school. But between me and you, I think it was a great thing for Joe. Just look how he's turned out."

River shook her head, wanting to ask him about Jake, but waited for a better time. "You said Bummer had a son?"

Smooth frowned. "Yeah, the dumbass got married to this skank junkie and she took off and left her kid behind with Bummer. He did his best, but Austin was a rotten kid—especially after he came back from that foster home."

"The court let him leave the foster home and come back to Bummer?"

"No," Smooth shook his head. "He ran away after about six months. Bummer hid him in his van for a while, but back then they had more foster kids to worry about than they could handle, so no one ever came looking for him. He was always trouble, but Bummer loved him. He wound up going to prison—he's only been out a few years."

River wrote on her pad. "I think I need to find out a little more about Austin."

"He's always been trouble, but not that kind—more of a junkie like his mother."

"You're probably right. He would have been just a kid when this started." River said putting down her pen. "What about your children? How did they turn out?"

Smooth frowned and wrinkled his forehead. "Well to be honest with you, Linda was pretty upset when they took away our kids like that, so we started looking for a place she could settle in and put our kids into a real school. Then when Austin showed back up, that was the final straw for her. He was a bad influence. That's when we found this place and she got off the road and raised our kids here. They're both married now, got good jobs, and have their own kids. They're doing really good."

River smiled and widened her eyes. "So you're a grandfather!"

Grinning, he leaned over in his chair, pulled out his wallet and showed her some pictures. "Got two, a boy and a girl. I do my best to spoil them rotten every chance I get," he chuckled.

River flipped through the pictures. "Smooth, if it's not you, Mooch, Bummer or Luke... that only leaves Hannah. What about her?"

He thought a long time before he answered. "How exactly were these girls killed?"

River filled him in on the crime scenes and how they all fit together. "That's why we're certain we're dealing with only one killer. Do you think Hannah could have done this?"

He looked down and shifted in his chair.

"Smooth, if there's anything you can tell me about this..." she said softly, her words trailing off. "Do you think it could be Hannah?"

"I just can't imagine it, but I guess you're gonna find out anyway. Hannah was a real freak when it came to sex in those days. She was into choking. Autoerotic asphyxiation, you know, the same thing that killed that Kung Fu guy last year, David Carradine."

River shook her head. "I remember reading about that. Hannah was into that?"

"Not with me, but Mooch used to tell me about it all the time. He said that was the only way she could get off. Excuse me for being so blunt, but you asked. And what you're describing sounds a lot like what Mooch used to talk about when they fooled around. Maybe these murders were just accidents. Ever think about that? "

"No, there was too much violence, these were well planned and purposeful. Can I ask you one more question?"

"Sure, ask anything you want."

"Can you tell me about Jake?"

He smiled and shrugged his shoulders. "Sure, what about him?"

"Was he real?" she asked. "Do you think it's possible that Joe had a split personality?"

He looked concerned. "Is Joe a suspect too? I can tell you right now, that's an impossibility. Joe is the kindest and most generous person I've ever had the pleasure of knowing. And no! Jake wasn't real, he was just a stage persona Joe used to overcome his stage fright. And to tell you the truth, he wasn't very good at it. He tried to pretend to be this tough bad ass called Jake, but the second any one of us or anyone else had a problem on or off stage, there was Joe, doing what he always did, helping out."

"Helping out in what way?" she asked.

"It was Joe's nature to run toward trouble rather than run away like most people do. I guess that's why he's such a good FBI agent.

"One night, a rather large and very drunk woman got real sick and started throwing up on the dance floor. Then she fainted and fell right on her face. The dance floor cleared instantly. Everybody ran away and just left her laying there. Tough guy 'Jake' was right in the middle of one of his leaping Rock Star moves when she fell. Instantly, he threw off his guitar and ran to her, lifting her head out of the vomit and gently stroking her face. He was covered in her vomit, but he stayed there with her until the ambulance came.

"Here's another one. One night Mooch had the flu and was sick as a dog. But you know the old saying, 'the show must go on', so he played anyway. Between every song, Mr. Bad Ass, Rock Star Jake would check on him, making sure he was all right. He kept bringing him water or anything else he needed all night long. When the gig was over, he walked him to his van and forgetting he was still in his famous leather Jake outfit, packed up all Mooch's equipment and loaded it into his van. Does that sound like a split personality to you? I have about a thousand other stories like that. So, no. Jake was not real."

THE NEXT DAY, River flew to Houston Texas and spent the afternoon with Mooch and his wife. She discovered quickly that Smooth wasn't exaggerating—the second they opened the door and got a look at her, both of them started flirting with her. Because Smooth had warned her, and she knew what to expect, it didn't bother her at all—actually she thought it was flattering and kind of cute. They were both in their late sixties, but apparently still had a very active sex life.

When the conversation turned toward Hannah and the autoerotic asphyxiation, it *was* a little uncomfortable to hear Mooch describe his sexual encounters with her, especially with his wife sitting next to him, listening to every word he said.

"When she had an orgasm, it was like a volcano," Mooch shouted. "She always wanted me to stare into her eyes when she was coming. It was like riding a bucking bronco!" Both of them laughed.

"If you'd like to find out what it feels like, we'd be glad to show you," he said scanning her body. "What I'd give to see you naked and tied to a bed. Wouldn't that be something, mama?" He turned toward Hellen.

Actually licking her lips, she said, "Yes, that would really be something."

River blushed. "I'm not sure what to think about you guys. Smooth warned me about you two. But I think I'm gonna pass on that."

Trying to find a non-sexual subject and get her interview back under control, she asked them about Jake. Once again, she heard story after story of Joe forgetting his act and breaking out of the Jake character. They also went on and on about Joe's kindness and generosity.

"I'm not exactly sure how he did it," Mooch's wife said, "but somehow Joe arranged for Alexander to go to college."

"Neither one of us can figure out where Alexander got the brains from," Mooch added. " He sure didn't get it from me, but he was real smart and always made good grades. When he graduated from high school, he got accepted at the University of Texas, but his tuition, room and board were gonna cost over $36,000 a year. We just didn't have it, but when Joe found out about it, he showed up one day with a check. He said it was from a judge friend of his and if Alexander maintained a B average and worked twenty hours each week at a part time job, the judge would pay every year after that."

They looked at each other with pride. "Alexander is a doctor now, a cardiologist," Mooch's wife said. "We owe everything to Joe. You've got to believe us, there is no way he could be involved in something like this. He's a wonderful man."

When River asked them about Bummer, again she heard the same story. It couldn't possibly be Bummer, but to be thorough she knew she had to find out for herself.

It wasn't easy, but she eventually got out of Mooch and Hellen's door with all her clothes in place.

She took the next flight she could book to Oklahoma City.

JOHN KELLY

W aiting for the cloud cover to clear enough for the Gulfstream V to take off, John sat in a plush leather seat in the small cabin, sipping his coffee, trying to decide what he should do next.

It was time to put everything out on the table with Joe. He had to let him know what he had on him and what he was thinking. Of course, if he did that, he would be breaking every rule in the FBI training manual on how to handle an investigation, but he didn't care. This was Joe Jensen he was talking about. Joe was his best friend and he was worth the risk.

Checking the reception bars on his cell, he was surprised to see two. He called Joe's cell, but it instantly went to voicemail. Then he opened his briefcase and found the yellow pad he'd written Elizabeth's law firm number on. The receptionist answered and put him through.

"Hello Elizabeth, I'm John Kelly with the FBI. We haven't met, but I know your grandfather and I'm a good friend of Joe Jensen."

Elizabeth sighed and took a breath. She was still distraught over her fight with Joe and the last thing she wanted right now was to have a long discussion with the FBI about it. "Hello John, I know who you are. River told me about you and your meeting in Jackson."

"I was hoping you'd talked to her," he said. "I heard a lot of good things about you from River. How is Judge Daily?"

Elizabeth took a deep breath and slowly let it out, trying to get her nerves and courage under control. It took a second. Finally, she said, "Thanks for asking. He's stable, but that's the only good thing I can say. Unfortunately, there's nothing medically they can do for him. It's just a matter of time, but he was in good spirits this morning. So, what can I do for you?"

John nervously cleared his throat. "Actually, I need to talk to Joe. Is he there? I tried his cell, but it went to voicemail."

"No, I'm sorry he's not here."

"Really? I understood from River you'd agreed to be his co-counsel on his father's case. I just assumed he'd be there with you working on it."

Elizabeth sighed. "He was here, but to be honest with you John, we had an argument and he left."

"An argument? What about?"

"I think you know. Please don't be angry at River, I know you asked her not to tell me everything, but she's my friend and couldn't help herself. And I'm sorry, but I had to talk to Joe about it."

John sat there trying to gather his thoughts. "I understand. River told me how you feel about Joe. I hope she told you how I feel about him as well. I think we want the same thing. So, I gather he didn't take the news well."

"No. He exploded and drove off. He couldn't believe I could even consider the possibility. I feel terrible, but I... I just had to know why he didn't tell me he was there at the times of those murders... and I had to ask him about Jake."

John paused for a moment, then asked her. "Do you have any idea where he went or possibly what hotel he's checked into?"

"No, but I don't think he's still in Little Rock. He called and told one of my associates that he was going back to Jackson to find the documentation of his father's surgeries at his mother's house. He said if he found it, he would let me know. So far we haven't heard back. He's either on his way or there now."

"Ok, let me see if I can track him down. And Elizabeth, I may need your help with this. Not to arrest him, but to get him some help."

"Oh my God! Is it that bad? You think he needs professional help?"

John could hear her crying. He'd said too much. "I'm sorry, that didn't come out right. Listen to me. I know you love Joe, but I want you to understand that I love him too. He's very important to me and I'm doing everything I can to protect him. I just want to get him in front of an FBI psychiatrist for an evaluation, so we can put an end to this. I didn't mean to suggest I thought this Jake character is real or that he was involved in these murders, but we have to find Joe so we can rule him out once and for all. I'll call you later when I find him."

THREE HOURS LATER, John landed at the Little Rock Airport and was met by two FBI field agents. They drove him straight to Elizabeth's office.

When Judy told her he was there, her heart sunk. "He's here?" Although she'd never seen him before, the moment she saw the expression on his face, she knew something was terribly wrong.

John looked at her grimly. "I think he's in the wind."

Elizabeth stood behind her desk and clutched the back of her chair, trying to steady her trembling hands, "Why do you think that?"

"My team can't find any sign of him. He paid for the night at the Hampton Inn, but checked out at 8:15 last night. There's no record of him on any flights, and there are no car rentals in his name either. He's just vanished. That was my biggest fear." John stood in her doorway. "I hope you don't mind me coming here, but I wanted to tell you in person. His mother is also missing."

Elizabeth fell into her chair, crying. "John, do you think he could have done something like this? Killed those girls?"

John sat down in the chair facing her, but was silent for a long time, lost in thought. Then he looked up at Elizabeth and whispered, "Not the Joe I know... but why else would he run?"

For the next 15 minutes, they both sat quietly not talking, trying to come up with that answer. Finally, John stood up. "Elizabeth, I hope you understand that it's out of my control now. I have no choice but to put out an All Points Bulletin on Joe, and name him at the very least, a person of interest on this case. "

Elizabeth wiped her eyes and nodded her head with understanding.

"If you hear from him, try your best to convince him to come in. And please Elizabeth, if he contacts you, call me immediately. I can bring him in safely. It's for his own good."

An hour after John left her office, Judy opened her door and laid a FAX on her desk in front of her. The cover page said:

Facsimile

To: Elizabeth Weller

From: Joe Jensen

Note: I've attached my father's old hospital records. This should be enough for a new bail hearing. File it ASAP.

I'm in a little trouble here, but will be back in touch when I figure a way out of it.

Joe

She handed the fax back to Judy. "Get a copy of this to John Kelly immediately." She picked up her cell and punched in Joe's number. It immediately went to his voicemail. She tried again, but got the same results. "Why is your phone turned off, Joe? Where are you?"

Her cell phone rang on her desk. She jerked it up and without looking at the screen she yelled, "Joe, where are you?"

"Sorry, it's not Joe," she heard on the other end. "It's River. Were you expecting him to call?"

No longer able to hold back her emotions, she burst out crying.

"What's happened?" River asked. "Is it the judge?"

Through her tears, almost inaudible, she sputtered, "No... it's... it's Joe. He's gone."

"Elizabeth, please calm down and talk to me. What do you mean he's gone?"

She slowly regained her composure. "He's real. Jake is real. He killed all those girls!"

River didn't respond. She sat down on the edge of her hotel bed and lit a cigarette considering what she'd just heard..

"Are you smoking again?" Elizabeth said, sniffling in the phone.

River rolled her eyes. "You could hear that? Ok, yes I am, but I promise to quit when this is over. We'll talk about that later. How do you know that Jake is real? Who told you that?"

"John Kelly, he was here. Joe has disappeared. John thinks he's running. He put a warrant out to arrest him."

"He's wrong," River said. "It's not Joe. I know it's not him. I'm certain of it!"

Elizabeth wiped her eyes, "How do you know?"

"You've known me a long time," River said. "Do you trust me and my judgement?"

"Yes, of course I do."

"Ok then, believe me when I say this. Joe is a great guy, and this Jake character is absolutely not a real person. My intuition is never wrong. I don't know where Joe is, but I know he's not the murderer and he's not running."

Elizabeth stopped crying. "Are you sure, River? This is quite a change of heart. What has caused you to change your mind about Joe?"

"It's too long of a story to tell you now. Just trust me on this, but I really need to find him. I've stumbled onto something I think is important. He's really missing? You don't have any idea where he is?"

"No idea, but we did just receive a fax from him. He found his father's hospital records."

"That's great!" River said. "Ok, what's the origin phone number? It should be on the cover page somewhere."

When River traced down the number she was more confused than ever. Joe had sent the fax from a truck stop in Vicksburg, Mississippi. "What the hell, Joe?" River said to herself, "Where in the world are you?"

Every time she called his cell it immediately went to his voicemail, but she didn't give up trying. She hit her redial button every 15 minutes and left a message every time until she'd filled up his mailbox. She left the same message every time.

"Joe, call me. It's very important. Do not call John Kelly or Elizabeth. Be careful, there's an APB out on you. Don't get arrested, I need your help. It's about Bummer. Call me, now!"

28

JOE

When I left Elizabeth's office I was so furious I drove to the first bar I could find, ordered a double scotch, and slammed it down. Then, sipping on the next one I began to calm down and replay the traumatic scene I'd just lived through in my head. I tried to remember Elizabeth's exact words and what I'd said back to her.

As the effects of the scotch numbed me, I began to see Elizabeth's side of it and how much my reaction must have shocked and hurt her. We hadn't seen each other in over 20 years and people can change, and after seeing my violent, angry reflex, I was sure she was totally complexed about who I was now.

When I put myself in her place, and thought about what I would've done if I had learned she had conveniently left out some serious self-incriminating evidence in a murder case, I would've had the exact same reaction and would have wanted to ask her about it privately. That's exactly what she was trying to do. Add my bad reaction to all of the old feelings she had for me coming back to the surface... she had to be devastated.

The more I thought about it, the more I realized that I had been a fool. Elizabeth deserved to hear the truth without the anger and my overreaction. Truthfully, it was her question about Jake that threw me.

Jake was hard to explain, an embarrassing part of my past. When someone asked me about him, I don't know why, but just the mention of his name dredged up uncontrollable negative feelings and anger. He's a part of my past I couldn't deny, but would've liked to forget.

Sipping my Scotch and reliving Elizabeth's words, I started thinking about my father's old surgeries. Both times I had to drop everything and drive to those cities. When I visited my father in the hospital, he never once thanked me for covering the gig. He showed no real appreciation at everything I had to sacrifice to do it. Neither did my mother. They both acted like it was my duty.

I tried to remember how old I had been, but couldn't recall exactly. The first one, I believed was when I was at Lowell Whiteman and the last one was my freshman year of college. I did remember having to talk one of my professors into letting me do a make-up test to keep my grade. But that was all water under the bridge. What was important now was that those surgeries may prove my father's innocence.

The problem was that all we really had was the mention of the surgeries in some old postcards. We needed real evidence; documentation somehow. The odds of those hospitals keeping records for thirty years was slim, if the hospitals were even still there, but I knew my mother well, she never threw anything away. If there was any documentation of Dad's old surgeries, I'd bet my house that my mother would still have them in some old file box somewhere.

I pulled out my phone and dialed my parents' number, but my mother didn't answer. I scrolled down my contacts and found her Macramé Studio number, but she didn't answer there either. On a whim, I flipped through my contacts on my phone and dialed their next-door neighbors.

"Hi Bill, this is Joe Jensen, Hannah and Luke's son. I'm trying to get in touch with my mother, but she hasn't answered her phone in several days. Have you seen her?"

"Oh hi, Joe. We're so sorry to hear about Luke. Actually, we haven't seen hide nor hair of her in several days. We thought she may have left town or something... you know... because of Luke's arrest."

"Is her van there?" I asked.

"Hang on a second, I'll go look." He was gone a few minutes. "Joe, yeah the van is in the driveway, but I don't see any lights on in the house. Want me to knock on her door and see if she's all right?"

"Yes, that would be great, but don't tell her I'm checking on her. You know how headstrong she can be."

"Boy do I," he said laughing. "Hang on, I'll be right back."

It was almost 15 minutes before he came back. "She's there all right, but she doesn't look so good. Betty and I will take her over some food later."

"Thanks, Bill, I'd really appreciate that. Thanks for checking on her for me. I'll be there to check on her myself soon."

When I hung up, my stomach was in a knot. I had been so wrapped up with worries about my father's arrest, the judge's heart attack, and everything with Elizabeth, I hadn't even considered how distraught and upset my mother must be. I needed to get back to Jackson and fast.

I paid my bar tab, drove to my hotel, and checked out. On my way to the airport, I called Elizabeth's office, but Will told me that she didn't want to talk to me. I didn't blame her.

"Please tell her that I'm sorry for acting like such an ass and that I understand what she was trying to do. Tell her I'm going to Jackson to see if my mother has the old hospital files documenting my father's surgeries. If I find them, I will let her know so we can file for an emergency bail hearing for my father based on this new evidence."

When I hung up, I drove to the airport rental car area, parked my car, and dropped off my keys. Unfortunately, when I got to the ticket area of the airport, there wasn't a flight available until the next day. I checked my map on my phone and saw that it was only a four-and-a-half-hour drive, so I walked back to the rental car desk, but struck out there as well. There weren't any cars available, from any of the rental car places. Even the car I'd just turned in was gone. I was stuck.

I walked to the food area, bought a hamburger, some coffee, and found a seat. While I ate my food and sipped my coffee, I considered my dilemma.

The only person I could think to call for help was John Simon, Judge Daily's old bailiff.

"Hello John, this is Joe Jensen. Got a second?"

"Hi, Joe!" he said excited. "You bet, what's up?"

I explained my problem to John and he offered to come pick me up and let me borrow his second car. It was an old MG he had been restoring. It looked a little rough, but it had good tires, and cranked right up.

"I know she ain't pretty yet," John told me. "I'm planning on getting her painted fire-engine red someday, but she's a damn fine vehicle. She runs like a top."

The old sports car didn't have AC, so I pulled back the convertible roof, threw my bags in the trunk, jumped in, and headed to Jackson.

Five hours later, I pulled into my mother's driveway. I knocked on her door several times, but she didn't answer. I tried a few more times and finally gave up and drove to the Jackson County Jail to visit my father. It took me a while to convince them that it was an emergency visit, but eventually they let me in and led me back to the same dreary, gloomy room I'd seen him in a few days earlier.

About twenty minutes later the guards showed up with my father. His wet hair dripped onto the orange jumpsuit clinging to his still damp body. They must have thrown him in the shower to wash away his stench before our meeting.

"Are you ok?" I asked him.

He looked up, rubbing his wrists where the shackles had been. "Yeah, I'm all right. You're not wearing that patchouli crap, are you? Why'd you do that to me last time? You know I can't be around that shit!"

"No, I didn't know that. I knew you didn't like it, but I didn't know it made you sick."

"I'm allergic to it. Kind of like some people are to peanuts. My throat closes up and it makes me puke."

"Have you always been allergic to it or is this something new?"

"Always." He continued rubbing his wrists. "I found out when I first met your mother. She told me it was some kind of an aphrodisiac and poured it all over me one night. We were kissing and fooling around I got sick as a dog and told her I had to leave. When I made it to my van, I started puking. I couldn't seem to stop and was having trouble breathing, so I drove to a hospital. They told me later that if I hadn't done that, I probably would have died. They said it was pretty rare and started telling me all about how it mixes with the proteins in my skin. I had no idea what they were talking about, but I was smart enough to know not to get around it anymore if I could help it"

"Dad, I had no idea. Does mother know about this?"

"No. She really liked it. I was a little embarrassed and never told her about having to go to the hospital. The smell didn't really affect me that much, so when she had it on I just made sure I didn't get it on my skin. I eventually told her I didn't like the smell, so after a while she stopped using it."

I tried to think back. "I can remember hearing you tell the band how much you hated the smell."

He smiled. "Yeah, they all were into it back then. I guess they thought it would make their dicks harder or something. The whole stage used to reek from that damn smell, so I told them they couldn't wear it when they were on stage."

"But the real reason was that you were afraid of getting it on your skin, right?"

"Yeah. Fucking Bummer was always hugging me and he used to take baths with that shit. At least that's how he smelled most of the time."

"I'm sorry, Dad. I wouldn't have done that if I'd known, but it's good I found out."

He raised his eyebrows. "What are you talking about? You did that on purpose?"

"Yeah, it was sort of a test. It has something to do with the evidence they have against you."

"What? Patchouli oil is part of all this? Well, if that's all they got, they're barking up the wrong tree."

"I think they just might be, but there's more. Are you up to talk about this? I mean the case and the evidence?" I asked.

"Damn right I am," he said. "I could sure use a cigarette, think you could talk them guards into letting me smoke in here?"

I talked to the guards, but they said we'd have to go outside into the yard. They shackled my father again and led us back through a few secured doors into a small exercise area. It was surrounded by a twelve-foot high, chain-link fence topped with razor wire.

One of the guards pulled a pack out of his pocket and handed it to my father. Then he handed me the lighter. "He can't have this, so hold on to it. I'll want it back when you're done here."

For years, I'd been trying to get my father to stop smoking, but watching him light that cigarette and seeing the pleasure he got from it made me glad he still smoked. If there was ever a time to smoke a cigarette, it would be now.

He took several long drags. "What the hell does patchouli oil have to do with these murders?"

I looked him in the eyes, watching for a reaction. "Six of the girls were drenched in it. Specifically, their private parts were covered with it."

His face wrinkled up like he was smelling a skunk. "Well, that sure as hell wasn't me! Why would anybody do that? That's weird."

"We don't know," I said.

He dropped the cigarette butt on the ground and stamped it out with his shoe. Then he pulled another one out of the pack and waved at me to light it.

After a long pull, he blew smoke out. "You said they have more? What else do they have?"

I smiled. "They don't know this yet, but I think I can prove that you couldn't have done at least two of the murders."

He took another long drag, and blew it out. "How can you prove that?"

"Remember your emergency appendectomy and that gallbladder surgery you had? If Mom kept the hospital records, that will prove you were flat on your back at the time. Think she still has those records?"

He laughed. "Oh yeah. That woman keeps everything. Probably in the garage. Will that get me out of here?"

I shook my head. "I'm not sure, but if I can find those records and get you a blood test that's shows your allergic to patchouli, that should be enough to at least get you out on bail."

He frowned. "Only bail? What the hell else do they have?"

"The strap, Dad. They've got the strap."

"Yeah, I remember. They seemed to get all excited when they found it. What's so important about that strap?"

I tried not to show the concern on my face, but I was sure it did anyway. "It's... the murder weapon, Dad. Whoever killed those girls used your strap to do it."

"My strap?" he shouted. "That's fucking impossible! I didn't do it!"

I put my hand on his shoulder. "Calm down and stop yelling. We don't want the guards to come back. We've got a lot more to talk about. I know you didn't do it. All I said was that whoever this is somehow had access to your strap and used it to do it."

It took him a few minutes to settle back down and one more cigarette. Finally, in a calm voice he asked, "How do you know for sure it was my strap?"

"It's the pattern, the circle with the double cross, it's unique. You know Mom never repeated her patterns, they're one of a kind. The pattern on your strap was imbedded around the necks of the victims."

He grimaced. "They were strangled? What a horrible way to die."

Then his eyes widened. "Wait! Were they tied up too? I mean to the bed? Like maybe they were having some kind of kinky sex?"

"Actually, yes. They had ligature marks on their hands and ankles and apparently had been tied to the bed while they were murdered, but I'd never considered that it might be from some kind of bondage sex game."

The color drained from his face. "What's wrong, Dad? Is this something you've seen before?"

He just stood there puffing on his cigarette, not talking.

"At least tell me why you and mother were so shocked when they found your strap in the bedroom"

"Cause I didn't put it there. Last time I saw it, it was on my Les Paul."

"Dad, they didn't find the Les Paul either. Do you know where it is?"

He thought for a moment, then a small smile showed on his face. "The cops didn't find it?" He laughed. "I guess I did better than I thought."

"What's so funny? You did *what* better than you thought?"

"My secret room. If the cops didn't find it, then those fucking thieves won't either."

"I'm confused, Dad. What secret room? What thieves?"

"It's in the garage, behind my workbench. When we moved in that house twenty years ago, it was a good place to live, but now it's turned into a pretty rough neighborhood. Most of my neighbors have had their houses broken into, so when you called me and told me that those records were so valuable, I built a secret room to hide 'em in. I even ran an AC duct in there, so it's a good place to put them. I practice in there sometimes too. I put a bunch of insulation in the walls so I could go in there and turn up my amp and play. It's got all my guitars and the old albums in there. That strap was in my guitar case in that room. I damn sure didn't put it in a drawer in my bedroom. Why the hell would I do that?"

"When was the last time you saw it before the cops found it in the bedroom?"

He started pacing around the yard thinking. "I put it in my case after the reunion concert. Then I put that case in my secret room with the rest of my equipment. I know I did." He stopped pacing suddenly, raised his head and looked at me. "What else do they have?" He asked in a raspy voice.

"Pictures," I said. "Of the murdered girls. Actually, just the negatives."

He stared into my eyes. "Let me guess, from an old Polaroid camera, right?"

"Yes, but how—"

"I don't want to talk about this anymore. Guards!" He yelled, waving his arms.

He turned his back to me and walked toward the gate where the guards were standing.

"Damn it, Dad! Don't just walk away. Do you know who moved the strap? Dad, tell me who it was!"

He didn't answer. He just held out his arms so they could put on his shackles and shuffled away with the guards.

On my way out, I handed the lighter back to the guard and made my way through the loud, clanking metal doors to the lobby and out the front door. As I walked to the car, there was no question in my mind that my father was innocent. He couldn't be the killer, but I was also convinced that he knew more than he was telling me. The evidence of the victims' bondage had struck a nerve, but his instant knowledge of the Polaroid camera and his refusal to talk anymore after that was the capper. He was protecting someone. Was it someone in the band? Smooth or Mooch? Bummer? Could it be my mother? Or was it someone I hadn't even considered?

I drove to my parent's house and rang the doorbell, but my mother didn't answer. Their old Ford van was parked in the driveway, so I knew she was home. I rang the bell a few more times with no response. Frustrated, I stepped off the front porch and walked around the house to the detached garage in the back. I knew where they hid the key, so I retrieved it from the phony stone in the flower bed, unlocked the garage and raised up the door.

I scanned the room for obvious signs of the hidden room Dad had talked about, but didn't see anything. He said it was behind his work bench, so I made my way around the lawn mower and his motorcycle to the bench on the back wall. I still couldn't see any obvious signs, but as I was searching, I noticed a line of small white boxes stacked neatly on shelves covering the entire left wall of the garage, all marked with my mother's handwriting. They were her old tax records stacked in perfect chronological order from 1976 to 2016. Four shelves with 10 boxes on each row.

I pulled out my cell phone and opened my notes. I found the dates of the six old murders and pulled down the box from each year. I didn't remember the years my father had the surgeries, so starting with the first box I began searching for hospital documents.

I found the first one, his appendectomy, in the box labeled 1985 and the second, his gallbladder surgery, in 1987. I carefully folded the documents and slipped them into my coat pocket, then put the boxes back in their place.

Those hospital documents and a blood test proving his allergic reaction to patchouli would be enough to get my father out on bail, but to get him off completely I had to figure out who was trying to frame him.

I walked back to the work-bench and started searching again for any signs of a hidden opening. There was nothing there, but when I ran my hand along the wood trim on the left side, I felt an indentation that my fingers fit in. When I pulled on the wood, the entire wall moved and revealed the hidden room. It was about five feet deep and ran the entire width of the garage. The back wall was stacked with the boxes containing the old Blackfish albums and the right wall was covered with hanging guitars. In front of the wall of guitars was my father's Fender Twin amplifier and a brown guitar case leaning against it. I opened it and peaked inside. It contained the 1952 Les Paul Custom I had tracked down and bought for his last birthday. Lying next to the guitar case, was a black duffel bag. It was open, so I looked inside and my heart jumped.

Laying in plain sight, on top of an old Polaroid camera, were black-and-white pictures of women tied to beds with the macramé guitar strap looped around their necks. With a pen I took from my pocket, I carefully moved them around to look at each one. There were 14 pictures. Underneath the pictures, lying next to the old camera, was a pint-sized bottle of patchouli oil.

"What are you doing in here?"

Startled, I jerked around to see my mother standing there, pointing a gun at me.

"God, Joe you scared me to death. I thought you were a burglar!" she yelled.

"Calm down, Mom. " I held up my hands. "I'm not a burglar, you can put down the gun. Dad told me about the secret room."

"When did you talk to your father? When did he tell you about this room?"

"Put down the gun, Mom. I just left him at the jail. I'm his lawyer now."

"Yeah, I know that. I found out from River. Why didn't you tell me?" She was still pointing the gun.

"Because you wouldn't answer the door or my phone calls!" I yelled. "Are you going to shoot me or what? Put down the fucking gun, Mom. NOW!"

Without a word, she lowered the gun, turned, and walked away toward the house.

I carefully closed the wall, trying not to disturb any possible trace evidence, and followed her to the house.

I found her sitting in the dark in her bedroom. I flipped on the light and sat on the edge of the bed. "Mother, we need to talk."

She didn't respond, just looked up at me, her eyes filled with tears. "I know you're angry at me and don't really understand why I did what I did, but I had no choice. I had to tell them what I discovered. Things have changed now. I know Dad is innocent and I think I can prove it."

She lifted her head. "How can you do that?"

I grinned. "It's a long story. Are you willing to hear it?"

"Yes, but not in here. I need some tea." She wiped her eyes with her sleeve, stood, walked into the kitchen, and turned on the fire under the teapot.

In silence, she brewed her tea and I made myself a cup of coffee. We settled, facing each other in two of the yellow ladder-back chairs around the small glass-top breakfast table in the corner of the kitchen.

"How can you prove it?" She sipped her tea.

"Like I said, this is a long story that goes all the way back to when you and Dad first met. All the way through the 1980's."

She lowered her brow. "What could that have to do with anything now?"

"It proves that Dad couldn't have committed these murders. Maybe not completely, but it blows a huge hole in the case against him."

She set down her tea and stared at me. "What does?"

"I've discovered two very interesting things." I reached into my pocket and pulled out the hospital documents. "These will prove that Dad was having surgery at the exact time two of the seven murders were being committed."

She looked at the documents. "They can tell the exact time of the murders, even way back then?"

"Absolutely, down to the hour they died."

She took the papers and scanned them carefully.

"Mom, I'm absolutely convinced that Dad didn't do this. I think whoever did is trying to frame him, but they've made a critical mistake."

"Mistake? What mistake?"

"It's the patchouli oil. That's the mistake. The real killer didn't know that Dad is violently allergic to it."

"He's not allergic, he just doesn't like the smell much," she said confidently. "It's a natural essential oil, no one can be allergic to it."

I smiled. "You just made my point. Even *you* didn't know he was allergic and you're wrong. It's just a myth that essential oils are non-allergenic. Some can be. It's rare, but it has to do with how it interacts with the proteins in the body. Dad is one of those rare people and all it will take to prove it is a simple blood test."

She sat silent, staring down at her teacup. I picked up my cup and took a sip of coffee watching her reactions carefully. "Do you remember pouring it all over him one night when you guys first met?"

She shook her head. "No, not really. That was a long time ago."

"Well Dad remembers it well because it almost killed him. He had to go to the emergency room that night. That's when he found out, but because you liked it so much, he never told you."

Her mouth opened slightly. After a moment, she looked over at me. "Do you know who it is?" she shifted in her chair.

I smiled. "I'm pretty good, but not that good. No, I don't have any idea. All I've got so far only helps to convince me that it couldn't be Dad, but what I just found in that hidden room just might."

She sat up and stared at me. "What did you find?"

"I found the evidence, the pictures of the murdered women, the old camera that took them, and a bottle of patchouli oil."

"I don't understand," she said shaking her head. "If you found that in his secret room, wouldn't that just incriminate Luke more?"

"That's what you'd think. And, I believe it was planted there with that exact thought in mind. Whoever planted it is the real killer."

She shifted in her seat again. "And you can tell who that was? How, from fingerprints?"

"No, not fingerprints. I don't think he's that stupid. I assume he wore gloves or was very careful and wiped down every surface he touched. Honestly, I'm not certain I can prove anything, because who every this is, is good, but even the best make mistakes."

I took another sip of my coffee and paused, studying her face. Her brow was furrowed, lost in thought.

"That's why I was being so careful not to touch anything. We have amazing technology these days. If the murderer touched anything he planted in that duffel bag with his bare hand, we've got him. I'm betting he couldn't have loaded the film pack in that camera wearing gloves, he would have left behind epithelia. It's what we call trace evidence. From that we can get his DNA and identify him."

"So, whoever loaded that film—"

"Is the murderer," I answered for her. "If he left behind his DNA, it will be indisputable evidence–game over."

I pulled out my phone and tried to call John Kelly's office, but he was still not back from his vacation. I didn't want the local police involved in collecting the evidence, it had to be either a Crime Scene Investigation Unit (CSI) or the FBI Forensic Team to preserve the trace evidence and it was going to take someone with some heat to keep the local police away and make that happen. John Kelly was the only one who had that much power.

"Mother, I need to go back to the jail and talk to Dad about what I've found. I shouldn't leave this evidence until it is processed, so you're going to have to guard it for me. I'm hoping dad can help me figure out who might be trying to frame him. I'm going to call my friend John Kelly with the FBI on the way, but this is very important. Don't let anyone in the garage unless they are CSI or FBI. I'm going to lock the door and put the key back in the fake rock. Don't let the local police in that room. Only FBI or CSI, understand?"

She nodded, but seemed to be in a daze. "Mom," I said louder, "Did you hear me? This is very important."

"Yes, I heard you," she said softly.

After locking the door, I jumped into John Simon's old car and drove back to the jail. On the way, I tried John again on his private cell, but it just went to voice mail.

When I made it inside the jail, my stubborn father wouldn't see me again, so I asked the guard if he would at least take him a note. I tore off a sheet from my yellow notepad and wrote, **Dad, I found evidence in the secret room. Someone is framing you. At least tell me who else knew about this room**.

A few minutes later the guard handed me back my note. On the other side, my dad had written, **Your mother and the band**.

"Great," I said out loud. "Back to square one."

Sitting in John's old car, I contemplated what to do next. The only thing I knew for sure was that I had to protect the crime scene and keep the possible trace evidence from being contaminated. I had to drive back and stay with my mother until I could make contact with John Kelly.

When I pulled into the driveway my heart sank. The old Ford van was gone, the garage door was up and the door to the secret room was standing wide open. When I looked inside, the black duffel bag with the evidence was gone. I retrieved the keys again from the fake rock, opened the back door and searched the house.

It was dark, silent, and empty.

29

THE BREAKDOWN

The chaos started about 40 miles west of Jackson. I was headed back to Little Rock driving John Simon's old MG when I first heard the knock. Going back to Arkansas was the only thing I could think of to do. I knew I'd probably lose my job, but I just couldn't do it this time.

My mother had committed a serious crime. At the very least, it was obstruction of justice when she removed the evidence, but in my heart I knew there had to be more to it. I was racking my brain to come up with any other possible reason she would remove the evidence and run away, but there just wasn't one. The thought of it was killing me inside, but when I forced myself to open my eyes, unfortunately all the pieces began to fit.

Since my childhood, I'd heard things about my mother from many different sources. I'd even overheard Mooch and Smooth talking about her a few times. And what I heard were things no kid should hear about his mother. Although I'd tried to block it out, Dr. Heart forced me to bring it back to the surface.

The facts were, my mother was into some bizarre sex games, like light bondage and choking. When I was only about 9 years old, I actually looked up autoerotic asphyxiation in a World Book Encyclopedia to learn what it meant. I was too young to completely understand what I was reading, but the part that bothered me the most was the danger of it. I couldn't imagine why anyone would be willing to do it, if it could possibly kill them.

It took years, but eventually Dr. Heart got me to talk about the things I'd heard about my mother. Once it was all out in the open, she helped me to understand that some people were more sexually driven and more open to experimentation. The fact that I'd seen my mother with other women didn't necessarily mean she was lesbian or even bi-sexual. It was Dr. Heart's opinion that my mother had just gotten caught up in the sexual revolution that started in the late sixties and ended when the world discovered HIV. She didn't expect me to simply accept all the things she had done, but to have a better understanding of why she did them. Although it was hard, I came to accept those facts and learned how to deal with them when I was fifteen. Again with Dr. Heart's help, it didn't change my true feelings for my mother. I loved her then and I still did, but knowing what I knew about her, although I didn't want to admit it, forced me to accept the possibility that she could be the one. The first piece of the puzzle fit.

I had to consider that she also had access to my father's guitar and his strap. And although I had tried my best not to see them, I had vivid memories of her taking pictures with that old polaroid camera. Two more of the pieces.

The patchouli oil was another part that fit. When I first saw the evidence, I assumed the use of the patchouli oil at the crime scenes was to help cover the smell. It wasn't unusual for someone to lose their bowels when they died. The horrific odor at a death crime scene wasn't only the smell of decay. Patchouli had a very distinct overpowering scent. The power of that scent was why I thought the victim's private parts were drenched in it. When I'd told my mother about the killer's mistake and about Dad's severe allergic reaction to patchouli, I could tell she was stunned and obviously surprised. She had no idea. At the time, I didn't think much of it, but now it made sense.

The last piece was my father's reaction when I told him about the murder scenes, and the bondage. He stopped talking because he was protecting her.

I guess subconsciously I had suspected her all along, because when I pulled into her driveway and discovered that she had run away... I wasn't surprised. Deep down I knew telling her everything I had discovered about the case was my way of warning her.

I had no idea where she might have gone and knew I should call and tell John Kelly about it, but I just couldn't. Honestly, all that was important to me now was to get my father out of that damn jail. I'd worry about my mother after that.

It was the wrong thing to do, but I pulled out of her driveway and headed back to Little Rock anyway.

When I made it to Vicksburg, the knocking was getting really bad, so I pulled into a truck stop and checked the oil, but it was full. There wasn't a mechanic on duty to check it out, so I decided to take a chance and try to make it back to Little Rock. Realizing it was possible that I could break down on the way, I faxed my father's hospital records to Elizabeth's office from the truck stop, so she could start the process of arranging for a new bail hearing for my father right away.

Trying to take it easy on the old car, I limped along at about 50 miles an hour, but about halfway there, at a place called Lake Village, the old girl gave up and stopped running. I had to push her for over a mile to get her to a gas station, that was fortunately a large truck stop. I was exhausted when I finally made it to a parking spot at the edge of the property.

There was a mechanic on duty, but the second he laid eyes on the old MG, he backed up. "I'm sorry, sir, that's a little out of my league. You're gonna have to haul it back to Little Rock."

Frustrated, I sat down in the driver's seat and pulled out my cell to call John Simon to tell him the bad news. My phone was dead. I got out, opened the trunk, and started rummaging through my luggage to find the charger, but it wasn't there. I tried to remember the last time I'd used it and a vivid image of it sitting on the hotel computer desk flashed in my head. I'd been in such a rush to leave, I'd left it there still plugged into the socket. I assumed they probably sold cell phone chargers inside the truck stop, so I headed toward the entrance.

A giant 18-wheeler pulled in front of me, blocking my path, so I waited for it to go by. Printed on the side in large letters was B. H. Driscoll Trucking. When it pulled by me, I saw printed in a handwriting font on the back, "Don't let life be a bummer."

It made me laugh. The name printed on the side of that truck flashed in my head again. B. H. Driscoll Trucking. Bummer's real name was Billy Horatio Driscoll. It was too much of a coincidence. It had to be his truck. I ran to the driver's door, but it wasn't Bummer who stepped out. I followed the driver inside, but he went into the 'Driver's Only' shower area.

In the truck stop store, I bought a charger that fit my phone, located a seat near an outlet in the cafe and plugged it in. It took about five minutes for it to come back alive and when it did, it started beeping like crazy. I had 46 voice messages. Three were from John Kelly, four from Elizabeth, but all of the rest were from River. She had left me 39 voicemails.

"What the hell, River?" I said out loud.

Since she'd left so many, I listened to hers first. When I listened to her first message and heard about the APB that was out on me, I shouted, "What the fuck?" Disturbing two burly-looking truck drivers sitting in the next booth.

The next two messages were exactly the same, so I hit redial and after two rings she answered. "Where in the hell have you been?"

"It's a long story." I sighed. "What's all this crap about an APB? Are you and Elizabeth that convinced I'm a killer?"

"No, we didn't have anything to do with it. It was John Kelly."

"What? John did this? Why on earth would he—"

"Shut up a minute and let me talk!" she interrupted. "That's a long story too, but that's not what's important, I'll fill you in later. What *is* important, is that there is a nationwide manhunt for you going on right now. You need to be very careful."

Trying not to be overheard by the drivers in the booth behind me,

I cupped the phone in my palm. "River, I didn't kill those girls. I swear!"

"Look, Joe, I know we didn't exactly hit it off when we first met, but I think I was wrong about you. If I am, I hope you will forgive me for being such a bitch, but for now, you need to trust me. I don't believe you are the murderer, but I think I may know who it is."

"You know it's my mother?" I said surprised.

"What? No, it's not Hannah, it's Bummer."

"What the hell are you talking about? It can't be Bummer. He's not smart enough to pull off something like this."

"That's where your wrong, Joe. He's been fooling you and everyone else for years. He's a lot smarter than you think."

"River, I don't know you very well and everybody tells me that you are great at what you do, but I'm telling you, you are going down the wrong road this time. I've known Bummer all my life. He's... well to be blunt, he's retarded. He'd have to be the greatest actor ever born to fool all of us all these years. It can't possibly be him."

"Oh really? Have you ever heard of B. H. Driscoll Trucking Industries?"

My mouth flew open in shock. "Well, actually yes, but not before a few minutes ago. I just saw one of their trucks. What about it?"

"The president and CEO of that company is Billy Horatio Driscoll. That company grossed over three million dollars last year."

"That can't be right." I exclaimed. "Are you sure it's not another Billy Driscoll?"

"I'm absolutely sure of it. Billy Horatio Driscoll's picture is on their web page. It's Bummer."

I lowered the phone away from my ear, and sat there in a daze. My head spun with new possibilities. Could it be true? Had Bummer been faking dumb all these years? Could he be the one? Did my mother take the evidence and run to protect Bummer? Is that who my father didn't want to talk about?

My cell phone vibrated in my hand, shocking me back to reality.

"Where the fuck did you go?" River yelled in my ear.

"I'm sorry, I didn't realize I'd hung up. Bummer? I just can't believe it's him."

"Believe it, Joe. It has to be him. Think about it. If he fooled all of you all these years, what else is he capable of? It fits. He's the one, I just know it," she said. "Why did you say it was Hannah?"

I took a deep breath and sighed. "It's a long story too, but simply, I found some of the evidence of the murders in the garage. I told her to guard it, but instead she took it and disappeared. If it's not her, why would she do that?"

River was silent on the other end.

"Did you hear me?"

"Yes, I heard you," she finally said. "I don't know, Joe. I can't answer that. I had a long talk with her a few days ago, and... " River took a breath. "I thought I had this figured out, but you've got my head spinning. I will tell you, she did say something that might be incriminating."

"What was that?"

"I don't want to get into that now, it was something about auto-erotic asphyxiation. Where are you?"

I grimaced hearing those words again. My brain was fogged and for a moment I couldn't remember where I was, but when I looked around the room the reality of my situation came back. "I'm at a truck stop somewhere in Arkansas. I think it's called Lake Village."

"What the hell are you doing there?"

"I borrowed a car from John Simon and it broke down about a mile from here. I need to call a wrecker to haul it back to Little Rock. I'm gonna try to catch a ride with the tow truck."

"What are you wearing?"

"What?" I looked down at my suit. "What I always wear. Why?"

"Let me guess, dark suit, white shirt, dark tie, black shoes. Why don't you just get FBI tattooed on your forehead? For God's sake, Joe, there's an APB out on you. Look around you. Think you might be sticking out a little?"

I laughed. "Yeah, I guess I'm not exactly blending in."

"You need to take off the monkey suit and change your appearance somehow. I'm in Oklahoma City and I need your help."

I thought about my situation for a moment. "River, I can't just hide. I have three voice messages from John Kelly on my phone. If I don't call him back and turn myself in, it's just going to make matters worse."

"You're right and you can do that in a few days. At this point, a day or two won't make a difference, but now I need your help to figure this out. We need to get something solid before we call John. I really need your help here, especially with Bummer. You know him, I don't. I'm not sure what to think about Hannah and why she did that, but my guts are telling me it's still Bummer. Together we may be able to come up with a way to trap him. If we can do that, all this will be over."

I turned off the power of my phone when I hung up. That way it would continue to go to voicemail like it did with my dead battery and give me some sort of explanation why I hadn't called John back. In the truck stop store, I bought a pair of reading glasses, some baby oil, a t-shirt, a baseball cap and a quilted, puffy looking vest.

In the bathroom, I put the baby oil on my hair and slicked it back. I put the cap, t-shirt, and vest on and then stuffed my suit jacket, shirt, and tie in the trash.

Taking one last look in the mirror, I slipped on my new glasses. " Hello Jake, good to see you again."

When I walked out, I saw the driver I had followed from Bummer's truck walking into the cafe. I took a seat at a table next to him.

When we made eye contact, I smiled. "Are you driving that B.H. Driscoll truck?"

He looked out the window, admiring his rig. "Yeah, that's me."

"Mind if I join you?"

"Sure," he said. "Move on over. It'd be nice to have a conversation with a real person for a change. I get tired of only talking to folks on that damn CB."

I moved over and sat across from him in the booth. "Where are you headed?"

The waitress brought a pot of coffee to the table and poured us both a cup. "I'm dropping off a load in Vicksburg," he said. "Then I'm heading back to Oklahoma City. I'm not sure where I'll be going next, but they'll have me loaded up and headed somewhere in a few days."

I smiled. "Sounds like they're keeping you busy. Is it a good company to work for?"

The driver picked up his coffee and took a sip. "To be honest, they're all about the same, but at least this one doesn't make me sneak around, dodging scales because I'm overloaded."

I shook my head like I knew what he was talking about, but I had no idea. "I hope you don't mind me being nosy, but I used to know a driver named Billy Driscoll. I was just wondering if that B painted on the side of your truck stood for Billy?"

The driver shook his head. "No, I don't think it does. I think it stands for Bummer."

Trying not to show my excitement, I said, "Are you kidding? That's what the driver I was talking about went by. We all called him Bummer. It's got to be the same guy. What does he look like?"

The driver thought for a second. "I've only been driving for 'em a few months and just seen him a few times. He's usually back in his office when I check in, but I'd guess he's in his sixties, pretty tall, with grayish hair. Kind of a dark complexion. I figured he's Italian or something. Like I said, I've only seen him a few times, I normally just talk to Mr. Matthews."

I sat back and took a few sips from my coffee. The driver's food came, so I shut up and let him enjoy his meal.

In between bites, he asked, "You think it's the same guy?"

I shook my head. "Yeah, I think so. I'd bet my house on it if I had one. The last time I saw him he'd just started driving, hauling furniture coast to coast. That's been almost ten years. Sure sounds like he's done pretty good for himself since then."

"Yeah, he must be. They've got about twenty or thirty rigs out here. You gotta have some serious money to do that. They cost about a quarter million each."

That number boggled my mind. I couldn't believe what I was hearing. Sitting in front of Bummer with one of my math books, trying to teach him how to multiply flashed in my head. It was impossible. If Bummer was faking it all those years, he deserved to win an Oscar.

The driver finished his meal and ordered another cup of coffee. "So, you've known him a long time?"

I grinned. "Since I was born. He played bass guitar in my parent's rock band. He used to babysit me and play games with me when I was a little kid. I'd love to see him again."

"So, where are you headed?" the driver asked.

I held up my hands. "Well, I was trying to get to Oklahoma City, but my piece of shit car broke down about a mile from here. That's her parked over there." I pointed at the old MG.

"Why were you going to Oklahoma City?"

Putting on my best frown, I said, "I have a job interview there in the morning, but I guess I can forget about that now."

The driver sat silent, sipping his coffee for a few minutes, then looked up at me, and smiled. "What time is that interview tomorrow?"

Still frowning, I said, "No set time. They just told me to show up when I could, but there's no way I can make it there now."

He smiled at me again, "We have a rule against picking up hitch-hikers, but since you know my boss, I figure they won't give a shit. If you don't mind riding shotgun in my tractor, I figure I can get you to Oklahoma City around noon.

JOE AND RIVER

I t was almost 2:00 am by the time I loaded my suitcase into the huge 18-wheeler and we slowly pulled out on our way to Vicksburg. The truck, or tractor as the driver called it, was a brand new Peterbilt. It was my first time to ride in a big rig and I was surprised at how nice it was inside. The plush electric powered leather passenger seat was as nice as a new Cadillac and the sleeper cabin located behind the seats was amazing. It had a full-sized bed, microwave, built in stereo, and a 30-inch flat screen TV.

The driver's name was Travis Alvarez, although he showed no signs of being Hispanic. He explained that his father was born in Mexico City, but he took after his mother who was raised on a farm in Tennessee. He was half Mexican, but you'd never know it.

It didn't take long to see that Travis knew what he was doing. The truck had 12 gears, 10 forward and 2 for reverse, and he moved through them all like the expert he was.

I called River before we pulled out to let her know I was on my way and made arrangements for her to pick me up when we made it to Oklahoma City. It only took us two hours to make the 96 miles to Vicksburg, but when we got to the warehouse to unload, it was closed. Travis was pretty pissed off about it and when the manager finally showed 45 minutes later, he let him have it. I was impressed at his use of expletives. I wasn't sure I'd ever heard that many in one sentence before.

An hour later, we pulled onto I-10 on our way to Dallas. It didn't take me long to figure out what he'd been talking about earlier when he mentioned dodging the scales. At every state line, we had to pull into a weight station to check our load, but since we were empty, they just waived us through. Six hours later, we made the turn to I-35 and four hours after that we pulled into a rest area a few miles south of Oklahoma City.

I thanked Travis for the ride and introduced him to River who was leaning against the hood of her rental car, waiting for us. I wasn't sure Travis was going to be able to actually form words when he first saw River. She was wearing a skin-tight mini skirt that had ridden up a bit too far as she leaned back on her car, exposing every inch of her legs.

"River, I'd like you to meet my friend, Travis."

She raised up from the car, and held out her hand. "Hi Travis."

Travis didn't respond. He was lost in a trance, staring at her cleavage peeking out behind her tight, low cut blouse. I had to bump him twice to get his attention. He shook her hand, but never raised his eyes away from her boobs while he did.

River was still laughing about it as she pulled out of the rest area, leaving poor Travis standing there beside his truck in a trance.

Once we pulled onto the highway, she looked over at me. "Love the outfit, especially the greasy hair."

"Thanks," I said, "I paid top dollar for it, glad you approve."

The oncoming headlights illuminated River's face in the darkness. "Tell me about your mother. Why do you think it's her?"

I filled her in on the details about Mother, the black duffel bag, the evidence I found inside, and her disappearance. She had no responses. She was as baffled as I was about it. "There has to be some explanation," she finally said. "But it doesn't feel right to me. I just can't see Hannah as a cold-blooded murderer."

I shook my head in agreement. "I don't want to believe it either.

I've gone over it a million times in my head, but the pieces fit. I can't just ignore it... it could be her."

"Do you have any idea where she may have gone?" River asked.

"Not a clue."

River drove in silence for a few miles. "Joe, my gut told me I was wrong about you and it's telling me it's not Hannah either. I still like Bummer for it. Are you ready to hear what I've dug up on him?"

"I still say it can't be him, but sure, let's hear it."

"He formed the trucking company in 2004 when he financed his first truck. He was hauling for North American Van Lines at that time and apparently had a five-year contract with them. Believe it or not, the papers showed that Smooth and Mooch both co-signed on that first truck, but apparently he didn't need them for his next one in 2009. But things begin to get very interesting in 2011. Somehow, he was able to arrange financing for three more trucks that year and he has added at least that many every year since. He has a total of 17 trucks and 34 trailers financed at this time. His total debt is something around 4 million. He operates out of a large office warehouse complex a few miles north of the city line."

"From what I can tell, his company is in good financial shape, they grossed a little over three million last year and made a profit of about four hundred thousand. But his personal expenses are way out of line."

Nothing she was saying made any sense. The thought of Bummer making 400 grand last year was unfathomable. A guy who couldn't make change for a five made almost half of a million last year? I felt like pinching myself to make sure this wasn't some kind of never ending nightmare.

All I could say was, "This just can't be. Are you absolutely positive we're talking about the same Billy Driscoll? I'm telling you, River, I don't care what you think you've found, this can't be Bummer."

When we arrived at her hotel, she checked me in with her credit card and I used an alias, making sure I didn't leave a paper trail. After a quick shower, I changed out of my trucker clothes and met River in the hotel bar. We settled in a booth and when I sat down, she handed me a piece of paper.

"Is that him?" she asked.

It was dark in the bar, so I hit the flashlight app on my phone, shined it down on the paper, and took a look. Smiling up at me right above the large printed words, *President and CEO* was my old babysitter and hide and seek playmate. There was no question about it... it was Bummer.

Suddenly, I was full of rage. "You piece of shit, rotten bastard!"

"Keep it down, Joe," River whispered touching my arm. "People are staring."

I shook my head. "Ok, Ok, sorry." I leaned into her and whispered, "All these years this sorry prick has been fucking with me, but never again. If he did this, I'm gonna take him down and make him pay for those girls and what he tried to do to my father."

The waiter brought our wine and filled our glasses. River lifted hers and clanked it against mine. "To Lawrence Olivier."

"What? To who?" I clinked her glass and took my first sip.

She smiled. "Laurence Olivier. I used to think he was the world's greatest actor, but now, I'm beginning to think he's been replaced."

Neither one of us talked for the next few minutes. We just sat there people watching, sipping our wine.

"You said something about his personal expenses being out of line," I said. "What do you mean?"

She put down her wine and scrolled through her phone. "He owns two houses, three cars, a new Harley, and a $75,000 ski boat. At least the bank does. Everything is financed to the hilt with very high interest rates. His credit score is not good. He's obviously overextended, so I'm not sure how he's pulled all of this off. It looks like it's built up over the years, but it's a house of cards and soon, it's gonna all come crashing down.

"Pretty stupid. Now that sounds like Bummer. What kind of houses?"

She raised her eyebrows. "The houses are very strange choices. One is located in a pretty rough area and is only worth about sixty-five grand. The other one is in Automobile Alley. A very upscale area and that house is worth about $900,000." She shook her head. "Why he would have those completely different houses has me baffled."

"Which one does he live in?"

She held up her hands. "You got me. According to the utility records, he lives in both. Yeah, weird I know."

I sipped my wine and thought about it for a few moments. How could Bummer be smart enough to fool us all these years, smart enough to build a successful business, but dumb enough to get so personally overextended? Finally, I asked, "What kind of cars?"

River grinned. "Again, very strange choices. A new Bentley, a new Jag convertible, and... a 2008 Ford pickup."

I had no response. None of it, not one part made any sense. I finished my wine, and set my glass on the table. "Are you up for a little surveillance?"

About an hour later, we slowly cruised by the first house. She was right, it was a seedy neighborhood, multiracial, but seriously lacking one race—Caucasian. Primarily Hispanic and black. In almost every yard, or on the street was a broken-down car. All of the houses were in some form of disarray, with missing shingles or taped up windows.

We were driving in Oklahoma City's version of the hood. But right in the center of this ghetto was Bummer's house, clean and neat. In the darkness it was hard to tell, but it looked like the grass had just been mowed. It was the only trimmed, mowed yard on the entire street and the only one that didn't need a paint job.

The Ford pickup was parked in the drive and the flickering rainbow light of the television glowed through the front window. Someone was living there.

Next, we drove north and located the B. H. Driscoll Industries office complex. The only activity we saw was from the guardhouse at the entrance. Apparently, the guard was watching TV too. We didn't stop, just cruised by slowly. Then we continued on to Automobile Alley to find the other house.

The elaborate brick entrance was also guarded, so we drove past,

turned around and slowly passed by once more before heading back
to the hotel.

As we pulled into the hotel drive, River's phone rang. She looked at
the screen. "It's Elizabeth."

I held up my hands. "You can't tell her I'm here. She's an officer of
the court and would have to turn me in. If she didn't, she could get
disbarred. Please don't put her in that kind of position."

River nodded. "Hey, what's up?"

I could hear Elizabeth's voice and tell she was crying, but I couldn't
make out what she was saying.

"Elizabeth, listen to me... stop that. I don't care what he said, he's
wrong. I know he cares about him too, but he's... Elizabeth... please
stop... remember what you told me? That you trusted my judgment.
You've got to keep believing me when I say Joe is innocent. It doesn't
matter that he's still missing. You've got to trust me."

River turned to look at me and whispered, "I've got to give her
something, she's losing it."

"Ok," I whispered back, "just don't tell her I'm here with you."

"Elizabeth, calm down. Listen to me. I know where Joe is. I've
talked to him and he's not running. He's undercover working the case.
He thinks he knows who the real murderer is." She was silent for what
seemed like a long time. "Elizabeth, are you still there?"

I could hear Elizabeth's voice on the other end saying something
softly. "Yes, I have," River said in the phone. "Yes... I promise. Yes... he's
safe ... yes... I will. He wanted me to tell you that he loves you desperately. I will... I promise. This will be over soon and I'm sure he'll want
to tell you that too. Ok, I need to go now. I'll call you tomorrow.
Good night."

Although I hadn't actually heard her words, I knew what she
had said.

I had tears in my eyes when River hung up. She turned in her seat,
looked at me and smiled. "I sure hope your kids look like her."

JOHN KELLY

I n his business there wasn't much to smile about, but when John Kelly hung up the phone he was grinning from ear to ear. The call was from the wanna-be governor Jackson District Attorney letting him know that he was dropping the charges against Luke Jensen.

Of course, he was trying to save face and lay the blame on the Bureau, and John personally for putting him in this cluster fuck in the first place. That was a quote from the DA, but when John reminded him about their earlier conversation when he'd warned him that he was jumping the gun making the arrest in the first place, and told him that he had documentation of that conversation, the esteemed district attorney suddenly changed his tune.

John knew him well. All he really cared about were his political aspirations. He'd made the arrest hoping to impress the congressman with his brilliance. Now his fuck up was biting him in the butt and he needed the cooperation of the FBI to help save his sorry ass. John had him by the balls and was loving it.

John used his newfound influence on the district attorney to get Luke immediately moved from general lockup to a secure area in the infirmary. It would take at least 24 hours to get all the paperwork in place to get him released, but for his safety, John wanted him out of that jail now. That was the least he could do for Joe.

After he hung up with Elizabeth, telling her the good news about Luke, he was perplexed. Her response wasn't what he'd expected. She was happy to hear that Luke was being released, but she didn't ask him about Joe. Not one thing. He had planned on giving her a complete update, although there wasn't much he could tell her, but before he could bring it up, she rushed him off the phone. All her tears and devastation were mysteriously gone and he thought he knew why. She knew something about Joe that he didn't—something she didn't want to tell him and he knew what it had to be. She knew where he was, or at the very least... why he ran.

When John walked out of the Jackson County Jail he was more puzzled than ever. Unfortunately, he'd left Joe's father frantic and shattered. He went there to tell him he was being released in the morning, but it didn't seem to matter to him or even register. All he wanted to know was where Hannah was.

"I've been calling her every time the guards let me, but she's not there!" he said concerned. "Where is she? What's happened to her?"

When John told him that she was missing, he went ballistic. He started screaming, "If he hurts her, I swear I'll kill him." He kept repeating it over and over, screaming it into the air.

John knew it wasn't pointed at him, but couldn't get him to say who it was. He was out of control, like a mad man. Fortunately, he was in the infirmary and not in lockup, so the guards were able to subdue him while the medical team injected him with a sedative.

"Don't hurt him," John said to the guards. "He's getting out tomorrow, but just found out his wife is missing, he's just upset."

When the sedative took effect, Luke calmed down and sat in a chair across from John. "You swear you don't have her?"

"Luke, you've got to trust me. I have no idea where she is, but we'll find her, I promise. Who were you shouting about. Tell me who you are afraid of and think might hurt her? Are you talking about Jake? Do you think he has taken her somewhere?"

Luke slowly raised up in his chair. "What the fuck are you talking about? Jake? Who the fuck is Jake?"

John sat back and lifted his head. "You've never heard of Jake?"

Luke frowned. "Who is Jake? I don't have a friggin' clue who you're talking about."

"It's Joe," he said softly. "Don't you remember when he used to turn into Jake?"

Luke glared at John. "When he was a kid? Are you serious? Is that what you're talking about?"

"Yes, that was Jake," John said.

"What have you been smoking, don't you understand he was just a little kid pretending, playing a game? Jake was just some stupid name he made up. What the hell does that have to do with Hannah?"

As gently as he could, John told him about Dr. Heart and her suspicions and tried his best to explain what dissociative identity disorder was. "If this is true, Luke, and Joe does have another personality living inside him, it's probable that Joe doesn't even know it, and it could be Jake who has killed all these girls.

The sedative was taking hold. Luke's head was bobbing and his eyelids were half open. Slurring his words, he said, "That doc is wrong. Joe's a good boy. Jake wasn't real, just ask Smooth, he'll tell you. Joe was just pretending. I know my boy. It's not him...he's no killer."

John leaned across the table. Luke's eyes were closed. "Luke, wake up!"

His eyelids fluttered. The sedative was in full force. John shook him. "Luke, don't go to sleep yet. You know who did this. Tell me so I can find Hannah. Tell me where to look. Where do you think she is?"

"Bummer," he whispered. "Find Bummer." That was all he could get out.

John waved at the guards. They picked Luke up and carried him to the bed.

"If anything happens to this man tonight, I'll have your asses in jail tomorrow. Understand me?"

He was surprised to see the dark sky when he walked out the door. He'd been in with Luke a lot longer than he realized.

Driving back to his office, he pulled out his cell and tried to call River, but she didn't answer. In his office, sitting behind his desk, he opened his file on the band and flipped through the pages until he found the report on Billy Driscoll, a.k.a. Bummer.

After he read the file, he tried River again, but got no answer. He didn't leave a message, he'd already done that two times earlier and was a little pissed she hadn't called back.

"What are you doing here so late?" a voice said at his door.

John looked up to see Ward Rogers, one of his agents, standing in the doorway. "Hey Ward, I could ask you the same thing. I'm trying to catch up on a case, what's your excuse?"

Ward smiled. "Same deal, working on some reports."

"Hey, while you're here, do you know how to track a cell phone?" John asked.

Ward shook his head. "Not really, that's Philip's thing, but give me the number and I'll get him on it."

John wrote River's number on a sticky note and handed it to him. "I need to know where this phone is now and who she's been talking to."

Thirty minutes later his desk phone rang. "John Kelly," he answered.

"John, this is Philip. I've got that information on the cell phone you wanted. It's currently in Oklahoma City and it's only connected to two numbers in the last twenty-four hours."

When John wrote down the numbers he recognized them instantly. She had talked to Joe and Elizabeth. "Is the phone working now? I've tried to call it several times, but it just goes to voicemail."

Philip laughed. "Hate to tell you, but it sounds like you're being avoided. The phone is working fine. The last call that came in was only a few minutes ago."

John looked down at the file and highlighted Billy Driscoll's address.

Something was going down in Oklahoma City.

CONFUSION

R iver met me for breakfast at 6:30 a.m. When she walked in the door, every head in the place followed her all the way to my table. She was wearing red Stiletto heels, with a pair of white skin-tight leggings that began just below her calves and advertised every curve she had all the way up to her hips. Her top was an oversized long-sleeve red sweater that hid her skinny waist, but cut just low enough to expose her ample upper body assets.

I shook my head and smiled when she sat down. "You ever get tired of that?"

"Of what?" she asked, grinning.

"Of people dropping their forks and running into walls when you walk in."

"Oh, I'm sorry, did you bump your head?" she said slyly.

I laughed. "No, not me, but that guy over there may need stitches."

There was no doubt that she liked the attention as she put on quite a show every time she went back to the buffet line.

"You ought to be ashamed, you're not playing fair," I said every time she got back, but she just smiled innocently and ate her breakfast.

River was quite for a few minutes then she looked over at me. "Joe,

I know you don't like talking about this and I'm pretty sure I already know the answer, but I have to know the truth. I spent some time with Mooch and Smooth and heard what they had to say about it, but I need to hear this out of your mouth." She took a deep breath, staring down at her food. " Who the hell is Jake?"

I shook my head. "Shit, you too?"

"I'm sorry, Joe, but I've got to know for sure."

I sat silent, sipping my coffee for a few beats. "Ok, ok, I'll try to explain it, but it's not easy." I leaned back in my seat and sighed. "When I was about 7 years old, my father started teaching me music. It was something I had no passion for, but my father insisted. He made me study and learn how to read music and how to play the guitar. I didn't really have a choice. Then, when I was only eight years old, he started bringing me on stage to perform with the band. I was way too young to even be in the joint, but no one seemed to give it a second thought. Before long, when I was about 9, I was performing with the band every night.

"I didn't really mind learning how to read music or play the guitar, that came pretty easy to me, but having to perform on stage with everybody staring at me was a terrifying experience. Every night I would get sick and would literally have to throw up before I walked on stage. I realized now that that is not an uncommon thing about performers. I'd read stories about Barbra Streisand, who even to this day continues to have severe stage fright. What I'd read about other performers that experienced this, was usually the moment the music started and the lights came up, that devastating stage fright disappeared and the performer took over. I guessed it was because I was so young when my father first began forcing me to go on stage, that stomach churning, devastating fear never went away. My parents and the rest of the band knew how much I hated being on stage, but in those days we got paid by the number of musicians and my father told me that we needed the money, so I did it.

"One night after a gig, the guys in the band took me aside and told me that when I was on stage I should pretend that I was someone else; pretend I was an actor playing a part in a movie or a play. They told me to act like I was Jimi Hendrix or maybe even Eric Clapton; anybody else but me.

"Just think of it like you're playing a game," I remember Smooth saying. "I bet Jimi Hendrix doesn't get stage fright!"

As strange as that might sound, it worked, and it was the only way I could've lived through that time of my life. From that day on, when I was forced to perform by my father, it wasn't me, I always transformed into Jake. He was the polar opposite of me. He even looked different. He slicked his hair back like Elvis and jumped all over the stage like Mick Jagger with a guitar. Looking back, it probably wasn't the best thing for me to do. Possibly not sane or healthy, but it was the only way I could think of to overcome my fears and live through those days."

River didn't respond for a few minutes, staring at me across the table. "I think I understand, but if Jake was just an act, then why was Dr. Heart so concerned with Jake and the possibility of dissociative identity disorder?"

I jerked my head up and stared at her. "Damn, River! You *are* good. How the hell do you know about Dr. Heart and what she was concerned with when I was a kid?"

"Thanks, but I can't take credit for that," she said, "the judge let me read Dr. Heart's reports on you."

The blood rushed through my temples fueling my anger. "IS THAT WHERE ALL OF THIS SHIT IS COMING FROM? JUDGE DAILY AND SOME 20 YEAR OLD REPORT FROM DR. HEART?"

River glared at me. "Stop yelling, people are staring." River smiled, nodded and shrugged to people sitting in the tables around us. After a few moments of silence to let things calm down, she turned toward me. "You know the judge. He loves you, Joe, but he loves Elizabeth more. Look, he knows you two are destined to be together. He's dying, Joe. Dr. Heart's report scared him. He just wants to make sure you're not some kind of wacko. That's why he asked me to check up on you–why I broke into your house. So I'm going to ask you again, if Jake was just an act why was she so concerned about it?

I forced myself to take a few deep breaths to calm down. "I was pretty screwed up back then. I guess she was just trying to be thorough, but if she thought I was a psycho or some kind a split personality I'm pretty sure she would have told me. We are... well..."

"You don't have to say it, Joe. River said grinning. "I think I figured it out. Unless that red and black thong I found in your dryer is yours?"

I grinned back. "Does the Judge know about her too?"

"What do you think?" She said.

I didn't respond. Of course he did. The judge knew everything.

The conversation lulled for a few minutes as we sipped our coffee. "After the reunion concert," she asked, "on that last night, where did you go?"

"What difference does that make? "I asked.

River shook her head. "Are you sure you're really a cop? Think about it, Joe, it might mean a lot. Where were you that night at 2:00 am?"

I thought about it a few seconds. "On a plane to Denver."

"What?" River yelled, slamming her cup down, spilling coffee across the table. Again everyone in the room was staring at us. "You were on a plane?"

I wiped the spilled coffee with my napkin and I held my finger to my lips and shushed her.

She rolled her eyes. "Answer the damn question. You're sure you were on a plane at that time?"

"Yes, I'm sure. Dr. Heart met me at the airport."

River threw up her hands. "Why in the hell didn't you say that before? Why didn't you tell that to Elizabeth or John Kelly days ago? That clears you on the last murder."

"You want to say that again with a bit more volume? I don't think the couple in the back corner heard you."

She glared at me. "This is not funny! Why didn't you tell anyone this before?"

I lifted my hands and shrugged. "I don't know. Maybe it was because I didn't know I was a friggin' suspect until Elizabeth blindsided me that day. I got so pissed off I wasn't thinking."

River took her cell phone out of her purse and punched in a

number. "Sam, I need you to confirm a passenger on a flight from Jackson, Mississippi to Denver, Colorado..."

I waited for River to finish her call and hang up. "I guess we need to let John Kelly know about this."

"Duhh. Yeah, that's probably a good idea before you get your ass locked up or shot."

"I'll talk to him later, but I don't want to tell him about my mother yet and I want to know a lot more about Bummer before I make the call."

"Ok. So, what's the plan?" River asked.

"I'm not sure. I've been thinking about that all night. I want to just go bang on Bummer's door and confront him, but that's probably not the best idea."

River frowned. "Probably not. I say let's just take it slow and see where it takes us. Bummer doesn't know we're on to him, so I think we just watch him for a while."

I agreed with her. "So, where do we start?"

She finished her last bite of banana nut muffin. "First, we need to know where he's living. My money is on the big house, but I'd sure like to know who's living in that small one in the hood. I say we start there."

At 7:30 a.m. we made our first pass by the house in the ghetto. I was right, the yard looked like it had just been mowed. In the daylight, we could see that whoever lived in that house took good care of it. It stuck out in the neighborhood like a bright beautiful flower in a field of weeds.

On our third pass, we pulled to the curb a few houses down and just watched. At 7:45 the front door opened and Bummer walked out. He was wearing work boots, an old pair of faded jeans, a white T-shirt and a frayed baseball cap. He walked to the mailbox and deposited two letters, raised up the flag, picked up his newspaper, and jumped into the Ford pickup and backed out the drive.

"Was that Bummer?" River asked.

"Yep, that's him."

"He sure didn't look like a CEO to me," River said. "More like one of his drivers."

I cranked the car and fell in behind him. He made one stop to get gas and a huge drink. We followed him all the way to the entrance of B. H. Driscoll Trucking Industries office complex.

When he drove up, the security guard opened the gate and yelled, "Hey, good morning Bummer." Bummer waved and drove through the gate.

River raised her shoulders. "I don't get it. You'd think the guard would have called the big boss Mr. Driscoll, instead of Bummer!"

We drove to the entrance of the other house and pulled to the gate. I got out of the car and held up my ID. "I need to get inside the gates and I don't want to be announced to anyone. Do you understand?"

When the guard saw what my ID said, his eyes widened. "FBI? What's going on?"

I frowned at him. "Just open the gate, sir, and tell no one we're here. Got it?"

He snapped to attention and hit the button. "Yes sir, you can count on me."

River was grinning when I got back in the car. "Poor guy almost shit his pants when he realized you were FBI. I'm so impressed, I had no idea you were such a bad ass cop."

I rolled my eyes. "Very funny. Just drive on through, Ms. Rivers."

We parked two houses down, then got out and walked. This wasn't your typical neighborhood. All the houses were built on huge wooded lots—at least an acre for each resident. The ostentatious mansions were all set back on their property, allowing for impressive winding circular driveways leading to massive grandiose entrances.

Bummer's was one of the largest awe-inspiring mansions on the block. It was obviously inspired by Tara, the huge plantation mansion in Gone With the Wind, giant white columns and all.

We walked back to the car, but when we got there, a marked security car pulled up next to us. "Can I be of any help?" the driver asked, gawking at River.

I held up my ID. "Yeah, who lives in that house?" I said, pointing at Bummer's mansion.

Obviously impressed by my badge, he jumped out of his car and held out his hand. "I've never met an FBI agent before! I'm Lieutenant Wilts, but call me Burt."

I shook his hand. "Nice to meet you, Burt, I'm Joe and that's River. So, who lives there?"

"That's Mr. Matthews's place," he said.

"Does he live there alone?"

"Yes, sir. He's single, but he's always got a lot of women coming and going there. One of those rich playboys, I figure."

"What does he look like?" River asked.

Burt stared down at her cleavage. "He's average height, sort of thin, with real short gray hair. I saw him one time without his shirt and he's covered in tattoos. And I mean covered."

I looked at River and she was as confused as I was. "Burt, we need to hang out here for a while and we'd like to keep it under the radar, so would you mind getting out of here with that marked car?"

"Doing some surveillance, huh. Sure, I'll leave you alone. It was a pleasure to meet you, and to meet you too ma'am," he said.

We sat there for over two hours watching the house with no signs of life inside. We were about to give up and leave when suddenly one of the garage doors opened and a black Bentley backed out. The car pulled under the large canopy jutting out from the front entry and stopped. The drivers' door opened and a man with short gray hair, dressed in a dark pinstriped suit stepped out and walked in the front door.

"Mr. Matthews I presume?" River smirked.

A few minutes later the man returned, got back into the Bentley and drove off. We followed him a few cars back all the way to the entrance of the B. H. Driscoll Offices

When he pulled up, the guard snapped to attention, opened the gate and said, "Good morning, Mr. Matthews."

River looked at me. "What the hell? It's Mr. Matthews to this guy, but 'Hey, Bummer' to the CEO? That makes no sense."

We pulled into a parking spot at the building across the street. We were facing the entrance with a good view of the guard shack.

"What now Special Agent Jensen?" River said.

I shook my head. "I haven't a friggin' clue. This just keeps getting weirder and weirder. Do you have any idea who Mr. Matthews may be? Did you run across his name anywhere?"

River frowned. "No, he didn't show up anywhere. And that's what bothers me. It's obvious he's a big part of this company, but his name is on none of the paperwork. He lives in that palace while Bummer lives in a piece of shit in a ghetto. He drives the Bentley and the CEO of the company drives an old pickup. This is nuts!"

"I've seen that guy before," I said. "I'm sure of it, but can't remember where. I know I've seen that face."

I checked my watch, it was almost 11:00 a.m. "How about an early lunch?"

When I started the car and backed out, I saw an old van pull up and stop at the guard shack. It was an old Ford 150. My heart pounded. The van was familiar. When I saw the bumper sticker, I knew for sure. "That's my father's van!" I yelled.

I pulled back into the parking space and watched the guard walk up to the passenger window, motioning for the driver to roll it down. Instead of rolling down the window, the door opened and my mother stepped out.

"Isn't that Hannah?" River asked.

I couldn't answer. I tried, but nothing came out.

"Joe," she said again. "That's Hannah!"

"Yes, it is," I finally said. "What the hell is she doing here?" I slammed the car into reverse and backed out of the space.

Skidding to a stop behind the van, I jumped out, ran up to the guard, held up my FBI identification, and yelled, "Don't open that gate!"

My mother slumped, fell back against the van, and began to cry. "I'm sorry, Joe. I had to do it."

"Not here, Mother! Don't say another word." I wasn't sure what she was about to tell me, but if it was a confession, I didn't want the guard to witness it.

River walked to her and put her arm around her shoulder. "Hannah, come with me."

River walked her back to the rental car and opened the passenger door. I jumped into the van, backed out, and followed them, leaving the guard standing there with his mouth wide open in stunned shock at what had just gone down.

———

EVERYTHING HAD HAPPENED SO FAST, the guard wasn't sure what to do. He didn't actually have time to read what the man had flashed in front of his eyes. He wasn't sure, but he thought it said FBI. Watching the van back out and drive away, he memorized the license plate. Still unsure exactly what to do, he picked up the phone and dialed 911.

———

I FOLLOWED them back to the hotel. When I parked the van and pulled out the key, I saw the black duffel bag sitting on the passenger seat floorboard. When I opened it, the pictures, camera, and patchouli oil were there, but laying on top was a gun—the same gun my mother had pointed at me two days earlier.

In River's room, she ordered coffee and tea from room service and we all settled in, sitting in silence in the living area—Mother and River on the couch and me in the chair.

My mother wasn't crying any longer. She just sat there silently, staring down at the floor.

I let her take a few sips of her tea before I said anything.

"Mother," I said, as gently as I could. "Look at me." Slowly, she raised her head and looked in my eyes. "No more games, Mom. It's time for you to tell me the truth. Did you do this? Did you kill those girls?"

She gasped. "What?" Her eyes flew open wide and her hands trembled, spilling her tea. "You think I killed those girls? Oh my God!" She burst out crying. "No, God no!"

River put her arm around her shoulder and hugged her as she cried. "Hannah," she said softly. "Calm down. I've never believed it was you, but we do need to know why you took the evidence and ran away."

She mumbled something, but I couldn't understand what she was saying. "Please, Mom. You've got to get control of yourself. You've got to stop crying and talk to us. Why did you take the bag and run away?"

She took several deep breaths, clinching and un-clinching her jaw, trying to regain her composure. River handed her a Kleenex and she wiped her eyes. "It's the epithelia," she whispered, "on the camera. You said it would be indisputable evidence."

River looked at me confused. "Epithelia? What are you talking about, Hannah?"

"Joe said that whoever loaded that camera would have left behind his epithelia and with that they could get his DNA. That would be indisputable evidence. Isn't that what you said, Joe?"

I nodded. "Yes, I did. DNA is indisputable."

"That's why I took it. It would be Luke's DNA. He was the one who loaded that camera."

"What are you saying? Dad did this? He actually killed those girls?"

"NO!" she yelled. "You were right, someone is framing him and I know who it is! It's Austin!"

River looked at me. "Austin? Who's Austin?"

"Bummer's stepson," I said.

River's eyes widened with understanding. "Yes, I remember. Smooth said something about him being a bad influence on his kids. Hannah, why do you think it's him?"

"Wait, back up," I interrupted. "Mother, I haven't heard anything about Austin for years. I thought he was in prison?"

My mother looked back at me squinting her eyes, wrinkling her brow. "He got out of prison four years ago. Joe, you saw him last month, at the concert. I saw you talking to him."

"Austin was at the concert? I talked to him?" I had no idea what she was talking about. "He wasn't there."

"Yes, he was. He was there both nights, helping Bummer set up his gear. Don't you remember?"

"The trucker guy with all the tattoos? That was Austin?" The second the words came out of my mouth, it hit me. I looked over at River. "It's Matthews. The gray headed guy in the Bentley!"

My mind raced, images of the mansion and Austin driving that Bentley flashing through my thoughts. "I remember talking to him now, but I had no idea it was Austin. He's changed a lot since he was a kid. I thought he was one of Bummer's trucker friends."

"Hannah," River said. "Why are you so sure it's him?"

My mother turned and stared out the window. "On Sunday, the day after the reunion concert, he and Bummer came by our house before they left town. He had that camera with him." She turned and looked over at me. Her face was drawn, her eyes filling with tears. "I gave him that camera when he was sixteen... and that black duffle bag."

Trying to lighten the mood, I smiled at her. "I remember when Dad bought that camera. He was so amazed how the pictures would just magically appear on the film. He used to drive us crazy taking pictures all the time. I didn't know you'd given it to Austin."

She lowered her eyes, staring at the floor. "I didn't want it anymore, so I gave it to him. When they dropped by, he told us he had just found it again and had searched for months for the old film on the internet." She sighed, shaking her head. "He said he couldn't remember how to load the film and asked Luke to do it. It took Luke a long time to figure it out, but he finally got it in. Austin had him snap a few pictures of us with it." She wiped her eyes and looked up at me. "Luke's epithelia would have been all over it."

"You're right, it would have." I paused and took a sip of my coffee. "Did Dad show Austin the secret room?"

"Some secret," she scoffed. "Your dad showed that room to everyone that came to the house."

"So Austin put the bag in there that day?"

She shook her head. "No, your father would have seen it. I'm not sure when he did it. It had to have been after they arrested Luke, but somehow he got into that room and put that bag there." Her eyes filled with tears again. "When you left, I went to the secret room. When I saw that black duffle and those pictures, I knew."

I shook my head. "That's why you took it. I think I understand, but why did you come here?"

She looked away.

"Mother, look at me. Why did you come to Oklahoma City?" I looked into her eyes. "And why did you bring the gun? What were you planning to do with it?"

River raised her eyebrows. "What gun?"

I frowned. "The black duffle and the evidence is in the van. Sitting on top of the pictures is my dad's old '38 Smith and Wesson." I turned back and looked into my mother's eyes. "Why did you bring the gun? Were you going to shoot him?"

She turned away again. "Not just him."

River touched her hand. "I don't understand, Hannah. Who else was the gun for?"

Tears rolled down her cheeks, falling from her long eyelashes as she blinked. "For me... This is all my fault. I did this to him. I turned him into a monster and I have to end it."

"For you!" I yelled, jumping to my feet. "You were going to shoot Austin and then shoot yourself? It's all your fault? What the hell are you talking about?"

River scowled at me. "Calm down, Joe. You're not helping. Sit down and let her talk."

I stood there trying to pull in my rage. After a few moments, I sat back down and picked up my coffee.

River took my mother's hand and in almost a whisper said, "Hannah, why do you think this is all your fault?"

She shook her head. "I can't."

"Hannah, please tell me," River said softly. "Why is this your fault?"

She shook her head again. "Not with Joe here. I can't talk about this in front of him. It's horrible."

River looked over at me and gave me a look. "I'm not going anywhere," I said. "I don't care what you've done. Just say it."

My mother pulled her knees up to her chest and rocked back and forth. "No, no, no." She mumbled. "I can't tell you. I can't."

River's eyes narrowed as she scowled at me. "Go downstairs and get some coffee. Give us a few minutes, Joe. Please."

Reluctantly, I stood up and walked out, leaving them alone.

RIVER AND HANNAH

"He's gone, Hannah," River said softly. "You can tell me. Why is this your fault?"

Hannah didn't respond. She was crying, mumbling to herself, staring down at the floor, rocking back and forth with her arms wrapped around her knees, pulling them tight against her chest.

"Please Hannah, talk to me. It can't be that bad."

She stopped rocking and looked at River. "I didn't mean for it to happen. I was just so lonely."

"Why were you lonely?"

She sighed. "When they took Joe away, we both just lost it. Luke blamed himself and started drinking pretty bad. For years he was drunk or stoned most of the time. It got so bad I couldn't live with him, so we would stay in separate hotel rooms and only see each other on stage."

"That must have been hard for you, traveling to strange places and being alone like that."

Hannah frowned and shook her head. "It was a dark time in my life. I was devastated over losing Joe and so angry at Luke. I started doing more and more drugs and... other things."

River poured her more tea and handed her the cup. "Like what?"

Hannah looked in her eyes. "Sex," she whispered. "A lot of sex. With just about anyone."

River took the cup and set it on the table before taking both of Hannah's hands in hers. "I think I understand. You had sex with Austin."

"Yes," Hannah whispered. "He was only... sixteen." River held onto her hands tightly as she cried. "I knew it was wrong. I didn't mean for it to happen, but... one night he came to my room and... "

River reached for a Kleenex and wiped Hannah's face. "How long did it last?"

"Only a few months. I had to end it. It was so wrong."

"Did Austin understand?"

Hannah stared down at the table. "No. He got very angry and threatened to show Luke the pictures."

"What pictures?"

"I was so stupid back then, but that's why I know it's him. When I saw the pictures in the bag of those girls... I taught him that. I showed him how to tie me up and about autoerotic asphyxiation. He loved it. After we finished, he would take pictures of me tied to the bed."

"Did he ever show Luke the pictures?" River asked.

"He said he did, but Luke never said anything about it. That's why I gave him that camera. I couldn't look at it anymore."

River thought for a moment. "Hannah, you said you saw the pictures of the murdered girls. Were they tied up the same way?"

Hannah wiped her eyes. "Yes, they are exactly the same. He even used the same macramé straps. It's all my fault."

"Hannah, you're wrong. It's not your fault. Look at me."

Hannah slowly turned her eyes toward River. "Yes, it is."

"He didn't just tie these girls up. He killed them. You didn't teach him that."

Hannah didn't respond or turn away. "Why did he kill them?"

"I don't know, but I do know it wasn't because of you. If it is Austin, and honestly, I'm not convinced it is, there's something much deeper involved here than just teenage sex."

Hannah wrinkled her forehead. "You don't believe it's Austin? Who else could it be?"

River stood and walked to the window. She could see the van in the parking lot below. "Hannah, when you were with Bummer, did you do the same things with him, the bondage and choking?"

Hannah looked up at River. "Yes, but it can't be Bummer."

River turned her back to the window. "Bummer's not who you think he is. He's fooled all of you for years. If Austin is involved, I think it's only to help Bummer."

"What? How has he fooled us?"

"He's rich, Hannah. He owns a big company and I believe these murders are the results of his life-long obsession over you. You said he's always been in love with you, right?"

"Bummer is rich?" Hannah said stunned.

The sounds of loud police sirens filled the room. River turned back to the window to see Joe surrounded by cops, on his knees in the parking lot, with his hands behind his head. "Oh shit!"

"What's wrong?" Hannah jumped to her feet and ran to the window beside River. "Why are they arresting Joe?"

The police loaded Joe into the back and drove away.

"Shit, shit, shit!" River yelled. "Because the FBI thinks Joe's the murderer. It's a long story." River ran to the table, picked up the van keys and handed them to Hannah. "This is very serious. I've got to help Joe, but please, please promise me you will drive back to Jackson, put the evidence back where you found it, and stay out of this. They didn't take the van, but they may come back for it. You need to hurry. Please Hannah, do this for me and Joe!"

The moment Hannah left, River pulled out her cell and dialed John Kelly's number.

UNDERCOVER

R iver was careful not to lose sight of the Bentley, staying only a few cars back. She was wearing her shortest skirt, her tightest blouse, and her tallest boots.

She smiled when the Bentley pulled to a stop at the valet stand in front of the night club. "This may be easier than I thought." She pulled to a stop behind the Bentley.

Austin was talking to the valet when she stepped out of her car. They both fell silent and stared as she threw her keys to the valet, slowly walked past them, and opened the door to the club.

She took a seat at the bar and waited for Austin to make his entrance. Everyone seemed to know him, yelling out his name as he walked through the room to a large booth in the back. He was instantly surrounded by three very young and very pretty girls.

Damn! She mumbled under her breath. Her shortest skirt and tightest blouse just got some stiff competition. Not giving up, she moved to a small table only a few feet from Austin's booth and ordered a drink.

When the music started, the three girls jumped up and pulled Austin to the dance floor. She was impressed by his moves. He could dance.

After the DJ mixed the second song in seamlessly, Austin took off his jacket, threw it to a waitress and continued dancing. The waitress laid it carefully in his booth.

His collarless and sleeveless tight shirt revealed two things: his tattoos and his very muscular body. Both of his arms were completely covered from his shoulders to his wrist with tats, full sleeves. Although his neck wasn't completely covered, two ran up each side of his neck to his chin. The large, well-developed muscles in his arms and chest flexed as he danced.

After four songs he was still on the floor, and River decided to accept her next offer to dance. Twirling and spinning, she worked her way across the floor. When she got next to him, he immediately started staring, watching her dance.

When she turned to leave after the song ended, Austin grabbed her hand. "Where you going, beautiful?" He yelled over the music.

"Over there." She yelled back, pointing to her table. Austin followed her, ogling her as she walked.

"I'm over here." He pointed at his booth. "Why don't you join me?"

River smiled. "Sure, but what about the other girls that you were with earlier?"

He laughed. "You've been watching me, huh? I like that. Don't worry baby, I'm all yours. I'll tell 'em to get lost."

"What's your name?" River asked, sliding into the booth next to him, and letting her mini skirt ride up.

Not taking his eyes off her exposed thighs, he said. "Austin Matthews. What's yours?"

RIVER IS MISSING

A t the police station, they read me my rights, took my picture, fingerprinted me, and locked me up for the night. I asked for my phone call, but they just laughed.

Surprisingly, I guess from pure exhaustion, I slept through the night like a log. The next morning, they led me back to an interrogation room and brought me some coffee. It was my first time being on the wrong side of the table, and I didn't like it much. I sat there for almost 45 minutes wondering who was staring at me through the one-way mirror. The door finally opened, and in walked a smiling John Kelly.

"What's up with the hair, Joe?" he said laughing as he pulled out a chair. "Is that how all you jailbirds are wearing it these days?"

I looked at my image in the mirror. My hair was standing straight up. I used my hands to smooth it down, with little luck. "Glad you're in such a good mood this morning. You gonna get me out of here or what?"

"Yeah, I had a long talk with River yesterday. They're working on the paperwork now. I probably could have gotten you out last night, but I thought it served you right for putting me through all this hell. Sleep good?"

"Actually, pretty good." I said. "So, River filled you in? Where do we go from here?"

John sat back in his chair and ran his fingers through his hair. "I'm not sure. Once we get you out of here, I'd like for you and River to meet with me and a few other agents to come up with a plan."

I called River's cell as we were pulling away from the jail, but she didn't answer. I tried her hotel room, but she wasn't there either. "Didn't she know I was getting out this morning?"

"Yes, she did." John frowned. "I told her I wanted to meet as soon as I got you out." He pulled over and tried calling her on his cell. "Something's not right about this."

I punched in Elizabeth's cell and after a few rings she answered. "Joe!" she screamed in my ear. "Is this really you?"

It was the first time we'd talked since I'd stormed out of her office. "Yes, it's me. I'm so sorry for..."

"I love you, Joe," she said before I could finish my sentence. "River told me everything. I just hope you'll forgive me for..."

"I love you too!" I said. "I want to see you soon, so we can talk about everything, but I can't now. When did you talk to River? She's missing."

"What?" She gasped. "She called me last night. What do you mean she's missing?"

"She's not answering her cell. We're on our way to her hotel now. What did she tell you last night?"

Elizabeth was silent on the other end for a few seconds. "We talked a long time, about you, and the case. She said she believed that Austin was trying to help out his father for some reason and that's why he planted the evidence at your dad's house."

I relayed to John what Elizabeth was saying. "Ask her if River said anything about trying to talk or meet Austin?"

"Did you hear that?" I asked Elizabeth.

"Yes. Tell him she didn't say that exactly, but she did say she was going to try to find out more about Austin. It wouldn't surprise me if she tried something like that. Maybe working undercover."

We searched River's room at the hotel, but found no signs of her.

Her rental car wasn't there either. John and I both tried her cell again with no luck.

I looked at John. "I think it's time we confront Bummer and Austin."

John stared back. "Which house first?"

BUMMER

We flew to the house in the hood, weaving around the slower traffic. When we pulled onto his street, I immediately saw my mother's Ford van parked in Bummer's driveway, next to the old pickup.

We parked a few houses away. When I got to the van, I looked inside. The black duffle was still on the floorboard. John motioned for me.

He was at the front window looking through the blinds. "Hannah and Bummer are sitting on the couch, side by side. I can't tell if there's anyone else in the room. He's holding something in his hand," he whispered. "Can't make it out from here. Might be a gun."

"I'm going to try to enter from the back of the house." I said. You come in the front door, but wait until you hear me yell."

The fence gate was unlocked, so as quiet as I could, I opened it and slipped into the backyard. I tried to look in the windows, but they were all blocked with dark drapes. At the back door, I turned the knob and it clicked open. I walked through the door into a small kitchen. I heard what sounded like a muffled shot and ran around the corner with my gun drawn.

Bummer and my mother sat on a couch with their backs to me. In front of them, was a large flat screen TV mounted on the wall.

Slowly, I moved closer to them, but jumped back when Bummer jerked his body to the left, then back to the right and yelled, "Got ya!"

He was holding something in his hand. I moved closer to get a better look. When I saw it, I lowered my gun. Bummer was playing a video game.

"Got ya!" He yelled again, and laughed like a kid. My mother laughed with him. I smiled. We'd all been wrong. He was the same old Bummer I always thought he was. Just a big kid.

I touched him on his shoulder and he spun around. "Joe!"

He instantly jumped to his feet and started running around the couch to hug me, but his video controller plugged into the TV jerked him back, almost making him fall. He just laughed, dropped it, and ran to me. He actually lifted me off the ground with his bear hug. "It's so good to see you, I've missed you so much!"

When he sat down, the front door flew open and John Kelly ran in with his gun drawn.

"It's ok, John!" I yelled. "It's all clear."

RIVER OPENED HER EYES, but couldn't seem to focus. She was groggy and felt nauseous. When she tried to move her arms and legs she couldn't, something was binding her ankles and wrists.

After a few more minutes, her mind began to clear and her eyes finally began to work. When she looked down, she realized she was naked and tied to a bed. She struggled, but the bindings were too tight. She couldn't move.

"Looks like sleeping beauty is waking up." The voice came from her left. It was low, husky, just above a whisper.

She turned her head, but couldn't see anyone in the dark room. "Austin? Is that you?"

From the dark shadows, Austin's image appeared. Naked, leering at the foot of the bed, he unscrewed the top of a small bottle and began sprinkling the warm liquid on her thighs.

"You drugged me. Why are you doing this? Untie me." She said.

In silence, he moved to the side of the bed and with his right hand massaged the oil on her skin. River jerked hard against the macramé binding when he touched her vagina. "You're so smooth. I was hoping to see if you were a real redhead, but you've shaved and I can't tell. Now, why would a nice girl go to all that trouble?"

She pulled hard against her bindings, trying to move away from his touch. As she pulled, the macramé strap binding her right hand slipped. Pulling with all her strength once more, it slipped again. If she could at least get one hand loose, she might have a chance, but she needed time.

"I never said I was a nice girl," she purred.

Austin looked in her eyes. "You never said a lot of things, River. That *is* your real name, right?"

"Yes," she said hoping to get him to talk. "So I lied about my real name, what's wrong with that? You were a stranger, I didn't know you."

"There you go, lying again. You knew who I was, that's why you were there asking all those questions. You see, River," he whispered, squeezing her nipple. "The girls I meet at that club aren't interested in my job or who my father is. They're interested in my muscles and tattoos. All they want to do is fuck me." He laughed. "But all you wanted to talk about was my job and my father."

River pulled on the strap again. It slipped another inch. "Ok, you're right. I'll admit it. I'm more interested in your father than you. He's very rich, right?"

Enraged, Austin threw the bottle, shattering it against the wall behind her. "I'M THE RICH ONE! AND HE'S NOT MY FUCKING FATHER!"

Trying to take advantage of his rage and keep him talking, River yelled back. "Billy Driscoll is the CEO, not you!"

Throwing up his hands, pacing around the bed, he yelled, "YOU

STUPID GOLD DIGGING BITCH! YOU DON'T KNOW ANYTHING! I DID THIS! THIS IS MY COMPANY! HE DIDN'T DO A FUCKING THING BUT SIGN HIS NAME AND PLAY THOSE STUPID VIDEO GAMES!"

HANNAH AND BUMMER

J ohn Kelly and I each took a chair in Bummers living room. "What are you doing here, Mother? You were supposed to be driving back to Jackson."

She moved her head, motioning toward the kitchen. "Bummer, could you show John how to play your video game?" I grinned at John. "He's a real good shot."

In the kitchen with my mother, we heard Bummer explaining the controls to John. "Push here to go up and down, and there to go sideways. Push this to fire!"

I looked down at my mother. "Damn it, Mom, you promised to go home."

"I know," she said, "but when River told me that Bummer had been fooling us all these years, I just had to find out. You're all wrong about him." Her eyes twinkled, watching him jerking around on the couch, laughing when John missed his shot.

"I know and you were right. It has to be Austin."

John's cell rang. Handing the controller to Bummer, he answered, "John Kelly." He listened quietly for a few seconds. "Where was it?"

Leaving Bummer on the couch, John walked to us in the kitchen. "They found River's rental. It was left in the valet lot at a nightclub."

"Are they there now?" I asked.

"Yes, they're with the valet guy."

"Ask him if he remembers seeing a black Bentley last night."

John asked his agent, waited a few minutes, then looked up at me grimly and nodded.

I looked down at my mother. "We have to go. I think Austin has River. Stay here with Bummer."

I ran out the door, following John to his car.

———

BUMMER LOOKED AWAY from his video game. "Where are they going? They didn't say goodbye."

Hannah sat down next to him. "Don't worry, they'll be back. They're going to go see Austin." Hannah patted Bummer's hand. "Do you know where Austin lives?"

Bummer smiled wide. "Sure! He lives in this great big house. It's real fancy and it even has a swimming pool."

"Could you take me there? I'd love to see his house."

38

AUSTIN

Austin ranted, and yelled as he paced the room. "I could have done all of this without him, but when you're an ex-con, the fucking bankers won't even talk to you. Bummer, that fucking moron had perfect credit! He can't even count, but that idiot had perfect credit! Can you believe that?"

River pulled on the strap with everything she had. She felt a slight pop and it came loose. She looked up at Austin, but he didn't seem to notice the slip. She strained with her left arm, but it wouldn't budge. She couldn't fight him off with just one hand—he was too strong. Her only hope was more time to get her other hand free. She prayed Joe and John Kelly had discovered she was missing and would track her down.

"Why did you kill those girls?"

Austin froze, stopping his rant. "What did you say?"

Letting him know she knew about the murders was a risk, but it was all she could think of that might keep him talking. "Why did you murder those seven girls?"

He stood there with his mouth open. "How do you know about that?"

"Austin, it's over. I'm working undercover for the FBI, with Joe. Any minute, he's going to bust through your front door."

Austin rushed out of the room. River thrashed with all her might, yanking and straining against her bindings. Her right leg broke free, then her left, but the strap on her left wrist wouldn't budge.

She rolled off the bed and frantically tried to untie the strap from the head-board with her free hand.

"You lying bitch, there's no one outside." Austin growled in her ear from behind her as he slipped a macramé strap around her neck.

"I'm not lying!" she yelled. "Joe knows I'm here."

He cut her wrist loose from the headboard with a knife, yanked hard on the strap, pulling her to her feet and pressed a gun against the back of her head.

"I don't believe you bitch, but just in case, we're getting out of here. Try anything and I'll blow the top of your head off. Holding the pistol against her head, he walked her out of the room and down a long hallway toward the back of the house. River caught a glimpse of her naked image as they shuffled past a large mirror. Austin was barefoot, but wasn't naked. He had somehow slipped on pants and a shirt.

As soon as the security gate opened wide enough, John floored it and flew through them. Their tires screeched as they slid through the turn onto the mansion's street.

Joe pointed. "The white one, on the right with the big columns."

The black Bentley was parked under the front entrance overhang. Sliding to a stop, Joe yanked the door handle and jumped out.

"Joe, no!" John yelled. "Let's call for backup!"

"Make the call, I'm going in."

"No, damn it! Wait for backup!" John yelled again, but Joe was already at the door.

The massive, etched glass front door was locked. Joe pulled his gun and fired three shots, shattering the glass. Kicking away the metal framing and remaining shards, Joe cleared an opening and stepped through the door.

"Heeeee's here." A voice echoed down the large hall-way.

Raising his gun, Joe slowly walked toward the sound of the voice. He rushed through a door on his left, sweeping the room with his gun. It was empty. Back in the hall-way, he moved toward the next room. The double wooden doors were open. The room was lined with empty wooden bookshelves, but there was no sign of River or Austin.

"Just a little farther, Joe. You're almost in my sights." The acoustics from the high ceilings and hard paneled walls amplified the voice, echoing louder this time. He was getting closer.

"Let her go, Austin! I can help you out of this."

"Sorry, old buddy, but you can't get me out of this one."

Joe moved down the hall a few more feet.

AFTER JOHN KELLY called for backup, he jumped out of the car and ran toward the right side of the house. As he made his way, he carefully scanned through the windows of each empty room, slowly working his way to the pool deck at the rear of the house. The entire back wall was glass windows. He could see Austin standing with his back to him. He was in the kitchen behind a large granite island. River stood directly in front of him. She was completely naked, and standing very still. He moved a few feet closer trying to decide what to do, then he saw the gun pressed against the back of River's head.

39

THE STANDOFF

When Bummer and Hannah pulled to a stop at the guarded entrance, the security guard smiled. "Hey, Bummer. Long time no see. Going swimming at Mr. Matthews's house again today?"

Bummer smiled back. "Not today, didn't bring my stuff. Just showing Hannah Austin's house."

The gate opened and Bummer pulled through. When they drove up the circle drive, Hannah saw the shattered door and the black Escalade parked behind the Bentley.

"What's going on?" Bummer said. "Somebody broke his door."

Hannah turned toward him. "Will you do me a favor?"

Bummer shook his head. "Sure. What kind of favor?"

"Promise me you'll stay here in the truck and let me go find out what's going on. I want this to be a big surprise for Austin. Do you promise?"

Bummer grinned wide. "Ok, I promise, but boy is he gonna be surprised!"

"I'll come get you in a minute. Just stay here, ok?"

Joe turned a corner and found himself standing in the kitchen, twenty feet away from Austin and a nude, very frightened River.

"That's far enough." Austin said, taking the gun from behind River's head, and aiming it under her chin.

"Come on, Austin, let her go, put down the gun and I promise I can get you out of this alive."

Joe could see John Kelly pointing his gun at Austin's back through the glass window behind them, but with River so close there was no way he could take the shot.

"Sorry, I can't do that." Austin put the barrel of the pistol against River's temple. "I have a better idea. You drop your gun or watch me blow her brains out all over the floor. You've got five seconds. Five, four, three..."

"Wait!" Joe yelled. "How about a trade? My gun for River?" Joe dropped his gun to the floor by his feet. "You're in control now, that's a fair trade, right?"

Austin thought for a moment, smiled, dropped the gun to his side and pushed River toward him. Joe took off his jacket and wrapped it around her. She was shivering.

"My, my, aren't you the gentleman. Kick it away. Now!"

Joe kicked his gun behind him. It slid to a stop at the entrance of the hallway.

"Please, Austin. Put down the gun and let me walk you out of here."

Austin waved the gun in the air and laughed. "I don't think so."

Joe forced himself not to break eye contact, but in his peripheral vision he could see John Kelly behind him in a shooting posture.

"Austin, listen to me, I called for backup. They'll be here soon. Please, put down the gun and let me walk you out of here before they get here. There's no other way out."

Austin smirked. "Very good, Joe. Did you learn that in your FBI training: make it personal, always use the first name when engaging the suspect. Sorry, old buddy, that shit's not gonna work on me. You think I'm that stupid! Now, suddenly you're my old friend. You didn't even recognize me at the concert. You treated me like I was a fucking roadie, just like Luke, that arrogant sack of shit!"

"You're right, I didn't recognize you. I'm sorry. I've only seen you a few times since they took us away."

Austin started pacing behind the island, waving his gun in the air. "Yeah, it's been years all right, but that's where you're wrong. They didn't take *us* away. They took *me* away, they didn't take *you* anywhere. They sent *you* to a fancy boarding school. You know what they did to me? They put me in a fucking foster home with seven other whining, slobbering little bastards. And you know why they did that, Joe?"

"Austin, Judge Daily had no choice; Bummer wasn't your legal guardian and your mother had abandoned you. He did it so you could have a good place to live and go to school. It was the right thing to do, for your own good."

"FOR MY OWN GOOD!" Austin screamed. "Do you have any idea what it was like living in that place? Always reading the bible to us. Jesus this and Jesus that. All those sniveling, crying bastards. I fucking hated it!"

"They were just trying to help you and be good foster parents."

He stopped pacing and glared. "I didn't need foster parents. I had a mother!"

"But Austin, she abandoned you. Nobody knew where she was."

His eyes flared. "SHE DID NOT ABANDON ME! SHE LOVED ME!" He waved the gun.

Where the hell was the backup? A police siren, anything to prove he wasn't bluffing. Austin was losing control and if he aimed the gun at Joe, John would take him out.

"If she loved you," River said, surprising both of them, "then why did she leave?"

Austin turned his head toward her and glared. "Shut up, bitch! You don't know a damn thing about this."

"But it is a good question," Joe said. "Why did she leave you if she loved you so much?"

"Because of your fucking father. That's why."

Joe shook his head. "What are you talking about? What did he have to do with it?"

"She could sing, Joe. She was really good, but Luke wouldn't even let her try out. It broke her heart. That's why she did all those drugs. Luke, that sorry piece of shit wouldn't even let her try one song. Just like he never let me play either. I was as good as you, but that fuck never let me on the stage. But you... you got to play anytime you wanted. Do you know how ridiculous you looked in that stupid leather outfit jumping around all over the stage? I was better than you, but NO FUCKING WAY WOULD HE LET ME UP THERE!"

"Is that why you tried to frame him?" Joe asked calmly, trying to bring him back down from his rage. "Why you killed all those girls?"

Austin's head jerked up suddenly. His eyes widened, staring past Joe.

"It wasn't Luke who wouldn't let her sing. It was me. I didn't want her in the band."

Joe spun around. Hannah stood a few feet behind him. "What the hell are you doing here, Mother?"

THE TRUTH

Bummer sat patiently in the pickup waiting for Hannah to come and get him. He promised to stay in the truck, but the shattered front door was really bothering him. Maybe he could fix it. Just checking out the door wouldn't be breaking his promise not to come in, would it? He opened his door and slowly walked up the steps and began inspecting the damage.

HANNAH TRIED to walk past Joe, but he grabbed her arm and pulled her back.

"All these years you thought it was Luke? That's why you've done this?" Hannah said, just above a whisper. "Killed all these girls?"

Austin stood silent, his mouth open, his expression blank. "It was you? Why?"

"She..." Hannah paused, searching for words. "She was... I'm sorry, Austin, but she was shooting up heroin, she was a junky and I didn't want her around Joe. She was no good—for you or Bummer. I made her leave."

The sound of police sirens suddenly echoed through the house.

Austin turned his eyes toward Joe and shrugged. "I guess we're too late. There's no way out now."

Joe shook his head. "We still have time. Please, put down the gun, let me help you."

Joe could actually see fear in his eyes for the first time. He was getting through, but needed more time. John wouldn't make any moves unless he was forced. As long as he kept the gun down, nothing would happen.

"Do you know what I do at the FBI?" Joe asked, staring into Austin's eyes.

"Yeah, you're a fucking cop," Austin said, smiling. "Just like you always wanted to be."

His smile was a good sign, he was calming down. Joe smiled back. "Yeah, I guess I am, but my specialty is profiling—specifically, serial murderers. And that's what's got me so confused. You don't fit the profile of a serial killer."

Austin tilted his head and wrinkled his brow. "I killed seven girls. That's not enough?"

Joe nodded his head. "Anything over two works for me, but in all my cases and research, I found that there was always a catalyst, something started it and they liked it." Austin turned away, breaking eye contact. "Killing one girl to frame my father I could understand, but six more doesn't add up for me. Framing my father wasn't the real reason you did this. You've killed before... and you liked it. My father was just an excuse to do it again. Am I right?"

Austin lowered his gun. "Very good, Joe. I guess everybody's been right about you all these years. You're pretty damn smart. Yeah, I killed before and I loved it."

"Who was the first one? How did it happen?"

Austin leaned back against the counter and took a deep breath. "It was right after I ran away from the foster home and tracked Bummer down. He was so happy I was back he decided to celebrate and got real fucked up. He picked up this chick and she took him home with her. About an hour later he came rushing into the hotel room babbling something about accidentally killing her. Dumb bastard choked her too long. He was out of his mind, wanting to call the cops, but I wouldn't let him. I told him I would go back to her apartment and see if I could fix things."

"But when you got there, she wasn't dead, right?"

Austin stared in Joe's eyes. "You really are good at this. No, she was alive, but when she started screaming... I finished the job." Austin shook his head and laughed. "When she died... well, what can I say? I can't explain why, but I came in my pants. It was the most intense orgasm I'd ever had in my life."

Hannah gasped and began to cry. "Please, Austin," she said through her tears, "you're sick. Let us help you"

"She wasn't dead?" A voice said behind them. Bummer was standing in the hall.

"GET THE FUCK OUT OF HERE!" Austin screamed.

Bummer bent down and picked up Joe's gun from the floor. "You told me she was already dead, that I killed her. All these years you made me think that?"

"Put down the gun, dumb ass!" Austin yelled. "Go back home and play your stupid video games!"

Bummer walked further into the room. "You killed that nice girl. You're a bad person. It's all my fault. I was a bad father."

"YOU ARE NOT MY FUCKING FATHER!" Austin screamed. "YOU ARE JUST A STUPID RETARD!"

"I don't like those names. I'm warning you, don't call me bad names!" Bummer yelled, pointing the gun at Austin.

Austin started laughing. "What you gonna do, idiot, shoot me?"

Bummer took another step toward Austin. "Did you really kill those nice girls?"

"YES I DID, MORON! AND I LOVED KILLING EVERY SINGLE ONE! PUT DOWN THE FUCKING GUN OR I SWEAR, I'LL SHOOT JOE RIGHT IN THE HEAD!" Austin pointed his gun at Joe.

The gun in Bummer's hand fired, knocking Austin back against the counter. Blood trickled down freely from his left shoulder.

"YOU FUCK! YOU SHOT ME! JUST FOR THAT, I'M GOING TO

KILL YOUR BELOVED HANNAH!" He aimed the gun at Hannah and fired, but Bummer jumped in the way.

River dropped to the floor, jerked the gun out of Bummer's hand and fired at Austin, hitting him in the stomach. He fell forward, leaning against the island. Slowly, he raised his gun and aimed it once again at Joe.

He smiled. "Sorry, Joe."

There was no time for Joe to jump out of the way–nothing he could do, so he closed his eyes and waited for the impact of the bullet. In his mind, he saw Elizabeth's face, then he heard the loud explosion.

When he opened his eyes, only seconds later, Austin was gone. He was no longer leaning against the island, he was lying in a heap on the floor behind it.

"Are you hit?" Joe looked toward the voice. John Kelly stood on the pool deck with his gun still aimed. The explosion had been the large plate glass shattering from John's shot.

Joe shook his head and ran to Bummer who lay in Hannah's arms. River pushed him out of the way and began giving Bummer CPR.

Joe walked behind the island and bent down to Austin. He was gasping. When he saw Joe, he grabbed Joe's hand and stared up into his eyes, "I could play as good as you."

"I know, " Joe said. "That's why my dad wouldn't ever let you play. You were better than me."

Austin coughed, blood trickled down his chin, his teeth and gums covered, glistening red. He coughed more blood and tried to smile. "Really, you mean that Joe?"

With the piercing sounds of approaching police sirens echoing through the hallway, Austin squeezed Joe's hand, stared deep into his eyes, and took one last breath.

EPILOGUE

Austin's epithelia was found on my father's strap and the DNA linked him to all seven of the murders. In a safe in his master bedroom closet, they found more Polaroid pictures Austin had taken of each of the seven murdered girls, along with five others that were eventually linked to unsolved cold cases. Austin had murdered twelve, young beautiful girls over a twenty-six year span, five apparently, he had killed just for fun. The gap between the murders was explained by his 16 years locked up in the Texas Department of Corrections.

During his rants, Austin told River the truth about Driscoll Trucking. Using Bummer's identity and credit, he had been able to finance eighteen big rigs. Unfortunately, the company's bank accounts were almost empty. He had spent the profits.

Elizabeth had a very long talk with Rob and had tearfully explained to him that although she did love him, it wasn't the same kind of love she had for me for all those years. Being the nice guy and true gentlemen he was, he understood, accepted the news gracefully and moved on with his life.

Judge Daily amazed his doctors with his recovery and was allowed to go home and survived three more months. He got to go on one more fishing trip with John Simon and lived long enough to see the engagement ring I gave Elizabeth before dying peacefully in his sleep two days before his 86th birthday.

He was an ornery cuss and contrary to the very end, and finally convinced River to take the bar exam and was well enough to make a toast at her celebration party the day she signed the papers to apply.

He also accomplished something he'd wanted for years. The conversation went something like this:

"Joe, I'm a big believer in fate. I'm convinced God has our future all planned out. He put something in your heart when you were just a little boy. You were meant to be that cop you always wanted to be because you needed all that training to survive in that room. God put you there that day to save your mother, free your father, and stop Austin once and for all. Just think about what might have happened if you hadn't been there.

"It was your fate to be there at that moment, but that's behind you now and I believe God has a new plan for you. This will be the last thing I'll ever ask of you. I know you, Joe, and you can be a little stubborn, so I'm not going to play fair this time. Son, it's my dying wish to know that you're going to use that intellect of yours for something other than being an FBI agent. It's a waste of your talents. You were always meant to be a lawyer. I know this from the depths of my soul. Please do this one last thing for me. I know it's your new destiny."

After the events at Oklahoma City, I flew to Jackson and spent a few weeks with my parents trying to repair some of the damage we had done to each other through the years. It was a therapeutic, healing process for me. My father and I had some long talks about the future and for the first time in our lives we seemed to actually like each other. It was harder for me and my mother. And although some of the things she had done were hard for me to forgive, I did. The truth was, no matter what they've done or how crazy they were, I would always love them, warts and all.

The judge's funeral was held in the University of Arkansas auditorium. It was the only place Elizabeth and I thought would be appropriate and large enough to hold the 3,000 plus that attended. As it turned out, one of the kids the judge had helped through college was an anchor on CNN, and after his 30-minute tribute on Judge Daily aired, Elizabeth's phone lit up. She had to hire a temporary secretary just to keep up with all the calls. The judge had touched so many lives, literally around the world, and they all wanted to pay their respects.

Believe it or not, my parents actually made it to Judge Daily's funeral. When they walked in, I almost didn't recognize my father. He had cut his long hair and shaved his beard. He was wearing a new charcoal gray suit with a beautiful silk tie and, with his new hairdo, looked more like a lawyer than an old hippie.

My mother looked incredible. She wore a long flowing black dress and her long blonde hair rippled down her back in ringlets. She looked like a retired super model. She was beautiful.

John Kelly was there with Dr. Heart on his arm and of course she was wearing one of her famous short skirts. John had a long talk with me about Dr. Heart to make sure the path was clear and they had become very close, very quick. It was apparently important enough for John to request a transfer to the Denver field office. They seemed really happy together.

Even Mooch and Smooth, their wives and children were there to pay their respects.

When River walked in with Special Agent Wes London, Elizabeth asked her, "Who's the hunk?"

River rolled her eyes. "I know he's a little boring to look at, but he's so damn persistent."

I was actually shocked to see River in a very conservative navy blue two-piece suit. No cleavage, no stripper heels, nothing sexual at all.

We all sat down front together in the section reserved for the family. Because there were so many attending, the family section viewed the body first. One by one we each got up and spent a private moment alone with the judge, saying our last goodbyes.

When it was River's turn, she walked up and spent her time quietly looking down at the judge. She reached down and touched him a few times while she was there. Before she left, she bent over and gave him a kiss on his cheek. When she did, the split in the back of her dress opened up just enough to reveal her black thong, black garter belt, and thigh-high black hose. The entire auditorium let out a gasp. Elizabeth and I had to put our hands over our faces to suppress our laughter.

When River got back to her seat. She smiled at us. "The judge would have loved that."

After the funeral, we all went out to dinner. My parents, John and Dr. Heart, River and Wes, Elizabeth and I all sat around a big table telling stories about the judge. Everyone seemed to have one, even my parents. I had no idea that it was the judge who had helped my parents open up their studio in Jackson. He had arranged all of the financing and negotiated their lease.

River told her testosterone story, when the judge had asked his bailiff to find the air freshener and I thought my father was going to choke to death on that one. He couldn't stop laughing,

Finally, honoring the judge's last request, Elizabeth and I made the announcement about my resignation from the FBI and plans of moving to Little Rock to join her firm along with her newest associate attorney, River Rivers.

"Our first case will be representing Bummer," I said proudly.

"How's he doing?" John asked.

"Physically, he's doing great." I said. "He lost a kidney, but he's going to make a full recovery. We're trying to unravel the mess he's in because of all the fraudulent documents Austin had him sign, but it looks like after we liquidate everything, he should come out ok. He should be able to keep his house and pickup and hopefully, one tractor and trailer, so he can keep driving.

"He wants to keep that house in the hood?" River asked.

"Oh yeah, he loves it there and apparently, his neighbors love him too. I've talked to several of them when they visited him at the hospital. They've all been there. They're even cutting his grass for him. Go figure." I said laughing. "I guess everybody loves Bummer."

After dinner, in honor of the judge, we all went to a cigar bar and everyone, even my mother, Elizabeth, Dr. Heart, and River fired one up.

We stood around tall tables, puffing on our cigars, sipping our cognac, and swapping stories.

Between her puffs, River leaned across the table. "I need to ask you something, Joe?"

"Fire away," I said.

"Are you some kind of an investment wizard or an art collector?"

That made me laugh. "What? Me, an investment wizard? Are you kidding, I can barely balance my checkbook. An art collector? What are you talking about?"

River noticed that John and Leah were listening. "Ok, it's probably none of my business anyway."

"No," I said, "Go on, you've got me curious now."

"I don't want to get you in trouble, but I know what an FBI agent makes, so how in the world could you afford all that expensive original art hanging on your walls in your house?"

"What are you talking about? Art on my walls? Are you sure that's just a cigar you're smoking?"

"I'm serious, Joe, I was there. You have at least a hundred grand worth of paintings on your walls!"

I busted out laughing. "River, I think you broke into the wrong house. I haven't been there for a while, but the last time I was, there was a lawn chair in the den and the only art on my wall was a picture of five bulldogs playing poker."

"Are you talking about Joe's house?" Dr. Heart asked.

"I don't think so," I said. "You've seen my house, it's a junk pile."

"When was the last time you were there?" Dr. Heart asked.

I thought a moment. "A couple of months I guess. I've been a little busy."

"I meant to tell you. I had my interior decorator from New York do a little redecorating as a house warming gift."

"A little!" River yelled. "You've got to see it, Joe. It's amazing." River turned toward Dr. Heart. "You just gave him all that as a gift? Honey, we need to talk!"

"River, didn't you know that Dr. Heart is loaded." I said. "She's got more money than Oprah!"

River put her arm around Dr. Heart and said, "Is same sex marriage legal in Colorado?"

On our way out, Dr. Heart smiled at me. "You can keep the furniture and the suits, but those paintings are mine."

"You bought me new suits too?"

She shook her head. "God knows you needed some new clothes. You're welcome!"

River stopped us at the front door. "Can I ask you two more questions, Joe?"

"Sure. About what?"

"Why are your family pictures and your framed degree in boxes in the garage and not hung on your walls."

I shrugged. "I just got those boxes in the garage from my old storeroom in Denver. I haven't had time to go through them yet. What's your other question?"

"Why did you throw away the leather outfit and the boots? Have you finally retired Jake?"

I looked over at Dr. Heart. "You threw the leather outfit away too?"

She held up her hands grinning. "Joe, when was the last time you had that cleaned? Your entire closet reeked, so I stuffed it in a garbage bag and threw it in the garage."

"You don't clean leather!" I yelled. "I can't believe you did that."

Walking down the sidewalks toward our cars, I stopped, shook my head and wrinkled my brow. "Man, Jake is going to be pissed off when he finds out about this."

They all froze in their tracks and stared at me. River and John exchanged quick glances. Dr. Heart tilted her head, her eyes wide. "Joe, what did you just say?"

I let them stand there stewing a few minutes. "Chill out guys. Just kidding."

The End

A NOTE FROM BEN

Thanks for reading **Children Of The Band**. This was my second novel and it took me almost a year to finish. If you haven't read my first novel, **Sing Roses For Me** you can download it free on Amazon. Just search for **Ben Marney books**.

Sing Roses For Me is a suspense- thriller based on a true story that actually happened to me. I am very proud of this book. It's been downloaded to over 40,000 readers and has been ranked in Amazon's Kindle Free top 10 for Suspense, Thriller, Mystery and Romance categories since it's release in May of 2017. I am currently working on the sequel and it will be my third novel.

One more thing... Writing is a lonely job, so meeting and getting to know my readers is a thrill and one of the best perks of being an author. I would like to invite you to join my **private readers' group** and in return I'll give you a **FREE** copy of **Lyrics Of My Life**. This is a collection of autobiographical short stories about my amazing life so far.

I really would like to meet you! Please join the group here:

www.benmarneybooks.com

Made in the USA
Columbia, SC
19 February 2022

56477789R00183